Castalia Boys

NATHAN GARCIA

Dedicated to my Martha, my Isabella, my Benjamin, and
my Little Boy whom I am yet to meet.
I love you all.

CONTENTS

Chapter 1

Sarah was up earlier than usual. She was hovering over a rusted stovetop, jittery as ever. She was a woman of singular purpose in that moment, and that was to not burn breakfast. For most, this is a simple enough task. For Sarah, the remainder of her day depended on this outcome. Her frizzy auburn hair looked wild as ever as she fervently worked to ensure this meal was cooked to perfection. As she was nearing the end of her task, she heard footsteps pattering toward the kitchen. At first, this was cause for alarm for Sarah, until she recognized the speed and the tone of the footsteps. The pitter-pattering heard was that of her son, thankfully. Erik reached what would be considered the doorway of his parents' mobile home's kitchen.

"Hey hun, I'm surprised I didn't have to wake you," Sarah said, barely above a whisper, as every moment her husband, Jared, was not awake was a moment of peace for her.

"Yeah, mom, I have to go in early to make up the math test, no breakfast," Erik responded to his mother, in the same hushed tone.

"Well," before Sarah could properly object, her son was already slipping on his beat-to-hell, once-white Converse low cuts. He slung his pack, an absolute steal at two dollars from the GoodWill, over his shoulder and slipped out the trailer's dented up door and onto the cigarette butt-littered stoop. Before scampering down the cracked-up steps he threw a somewhat apologetic look to his mother, who returned the glance with her sweet smile that only ever truthfully crossed her lips when she was looking at her baby boy. She heard him make his way around the side of the house to the carport, which housed a '96 Chevrolet Cavalier, which now sported more rust than it did clear coat. Alongside the old Chevy stood

Erik's blue Huffy, which he had outgrown by a few Christmases now. Erik swung his leg up over his bike's seat, looked at the old Cavalier and muttered, "I hope to God you're not around by the time I can get my license next year." He scooted closer to the old family car on his bike and gave the front passenger-side tire a playful kick before chuckling to himself quietly and pedaling down the gravel driveway and onto Limerick Road. It now dawned on Sarah that breakfast would soon be cold. The fruits of her labor would be less than desirable before long. Jared was still asleep. This was the bridge that the young wife and mother now had to cross. I'll wait ten minutes, she told herself in her own mind. Ten minutes more sleep, and I can microwave the food quick. He'll never know. Two Lucky Strikes and ten minutes elapsed, and Sarah made her move. She zapped her husband's meal in the cancer cooker for a minute and was sure to hit the stop button before the alarm sounded, as this would have certainly damned her. She placed the plate of eggs, bacon and biscuits on the pop-up card table, which served as the family dining spot. Like a thief in the night, Sarah began to slink down the solitary hallway in her home and gently pressed her ear to the bedroom door. She knew Jared was on quite the binge last night, so a gentle approach here was absolutely crucial. Sarah gingerly pressed her open hand up to the door, which was left slightly ajar. She knew the hinges would squeak as they always have, ever since they moved into the place. She braced for the screech of the old brass, which certainly happened. Jared began to stir, and after the first two or three steps that Sarah had traversed into the dingy back bedroom of the most decrepit trailer in the entire park, Jared shot straight up. He seemed alarmed at first upon waking but quickly settled.

"Morning, hun," Sarah started, trying her best not to sound nervous. "Breakfast is out on the table." The artificial grin spread across her thin, chapped lips. Jared rubbed his eyes for a moment, rose from the bed, and uttered a less than sincere 'thank you'. He put his slippers on and shuffled to the bathroom, the whole while scratching his ass and yawning. He urinated, pretended to wash his hands, then splashed some cold water on his face. He emerged without so much as a passing glance to his wife, making his way out to the kitchen. He sat down on the flimsy folding chair and began to sip his coffee. He then proceeded to inspect his breakfast, with the scrutiny of an army general examining the shaves and uniform condition of his troops. He grabbed his fork and dug into his reheated eggs. He was none the wiser.

"Thanks, hun," he grumbled between bites and sips of Folgers. That was it. The weight of the world had been lifted from Sarah's scrawny, pale shoulders. Breakfast was good. It was going to be a good day.

Chapter 2

Erik cruised down Limerick, the wind tousling his, better yet, his mother's, shoulder-length auburn hair. He frequently checked over his left shoulder for cars coming up behind, as just last spring he had a close call with what he could only presume to be a drunk or texting driver. He hit the crest of the hill and knew it was a smooth coast of about sixty or so yards to the park. He began to huff slightly at the apex. He had only been smoking for a short while, but already began to consider the harm it may have done to his respiratory system. He saw the silver Chrysler 300 on his descent of Limerick Hill, and soon after, he heard the music blaring through its nearly shot speakers. From what Erik could tell, Bose, the driver of the car, was alone. Bose was simply known as "Bose". Nobody was ever able to decipher a full or proper name for the young man. All that was known was that he was short, pudgy, half-Mexican or Puerto Rican, or something of the like, and he sold high school kids shitty weed. He was almost always seen with a cigarette tucked behind his ear, and typically donned a black, plain beanie on his shaved head. From what Erik could gather, he was in his mid-twenties, and it was rumored that he used his status as a low-level pot dealer to get close to several high school girls, some being even younger than Erik. However, this was hearsay. Perhaps Erik was a little biased, or he just didn't care enough, but Bose never came across as that type to him. Erik mustered a few more lazy pedals of his undersized bike before reaching the muddy, dirt and gravel parking lot of Limerick Park. Bose lessened the volume of his garbled, trash rap music, and slowly pushed open his car door. He was sporting his typical black skull cap, along with a long-sleeved South Pole tee. Erik commended his confidence for that alone. He was puffing his trademark Newport as he shuffled around the front end of the car his grandfather was kind enough to buy him before passing only years prior. He was digging into the front pocket of his Dickies as Erik thought of something to say. Before he could conceive anything cool enough, he had a baggie in his hand, and was reaching into his pack for the ten dollars he was now indebted.

"Th-thanks, Bose," he sputtered out. "That last shit was great," he continued. 'Shit was great'. Am I Tony Fucking Tiger? Erik thought.

"Thanks, bud," Bose's hoarse voice cracked. "Hey, so I got some extra too if you want," he continued. His free hand plunged into his other front pocket, retrieving yet another Ziploc, this one containing four small, round white pills. "Perc fives, twenty bucks bud." Erik stood motionless, hand still extended with the crumpled up ten-dollar bill pinched between his index and middle finger.

"Ungh, nah, man, just the weed is cool. I only have five more dollars for lunch anyway," Erik stammered.

"Alright man, you're cool," Bose crushed out his cigarette.

"Next time, maybe." Erik smiled and nodded, passing his allowance to a twenty-something, basement-dwelling dog shit-level dealer. He accepted the bag of weed and immediately opened it up, taking a long, deep sniff for show. Erik actually hated the smell of reefer but loved the feeling of being high and the social aspect of smoking. He pretended to know what he was saying.

"Good, sticky shit, man. Stuff is Grade A." Bose cracked a slight smile which quickly vanished as he remembered he still had product to move.

"If any of your boys is interested in these you send 'em my way, okay," he waved the Percocet in Erik's face.

"Uh, yeah, for sure man, I'll let you know." Bose nodded and waddled back to his car. He threw Erik a parting glance and climbed back inside, and then instantly began blasting his music again. Erik pedaled out, and made haste, because he wasn't lying to his mother that morning. He did, in fact, have a math test to make up in Mr. Steinn's algebra class. Being a stoner is not nearly as bad as being a liar, he kept reassuring himself. *If Mom asks anything, I'll always answer honestly. I'll always tell her the truth. There's always honor in that.* The young toker hustled through the last half-mile stretch before reaching Castalia High School. Only the early buses were unloading, which meant plenty of time to pencil-whip a math quiz. Erik reached the bike racks on the south side of the large, horseshoe-shaped schoolhouse. This was the gap or U-shape of the building. There were doors on either end of the U and a door centered on the opposite side of the building. The courtyard in the middle served as a lunch spot for students, and a smoking area for faculty when the weather permitted it. Erik dismounted his bicycle and rummaged through his bag for his lock. Once this was secured, he trotted to the right-side door of the U, just as he always did. He swung the door open and jogged down the still vacant hallway and up the stairway to his right, this being in the far-right corner of the building, when looking at it from Erik's view upon arriving each morning. The young man reached the first landing, then proceeded to make an immediate one-eighty turn to climb the next half-flight of steps. He reached the second, and topmost floor of the edifice. Steinn's door was immediately on the left upon reaching the floor. Erik caught him just as he was coming down the hall with his coffee, keys jingling in his other hand.

"Erik, you beat me to it," he exclaimed, smiling, sauntering between the lockers with mug in hand like an awkward waitress her first day on the job. Steinn was a short, wiry man, roughly the same stature and height as Erik. He still had a full head of hair at near-retirement age, equal parts salt and pepper. He wore small, round spectacles which seemed to be constantly sliding down his pointed nose. Dwayne Steinn's father was an immigrant who reached America's shores soon after World War II, and although rumored to be a Nazi or at least a sympathizer, this was never proven. Mr. Steinn taught at Castalia High long enough to recall Erik's father, and all of his older siblings. Erik was a breath of fresh air in comparison. The apple can fall far from the tree, after all. The teacher and student convened at the classroom door simultaneously. Erik caught a whiff of Mr. Steinn's coffee breath, and, for a moment, questioned if Steinn could smell the dime bag in his backpack. If he did, he gave no indication that this was the case. The pair shuffled into the dark classroom. Steinn hit the lights and Erik made his way to his seat, which was located at the very front and center of the assembly of antiquated desks. Steinn paused en route to his desk and let out a small chuckle. Erik looked puzzled.

"Sorry, it's just always a funny little thing to me," the old teacher explained. "How students just arbitrarily migrate to what they know. I mean, you could have selected any desk in the room, yet you still gravitate to what you know, as if it would make any difference, seeing how it's just you and I in here now." The old man carefully placed his mug on his desk.

"Ha, yeah. We're just creatures of habit, I guess," Erik weakly responded. Steinn smiled in return and reached behind him without looking, snatching up the packet of papers to hand to his pupil.

"Take your time. Class doesn't start for a half hour yet. I know that's ample time for you, Erik." Mr. Steinn moseyed behind his desk, opening up the center drawer and retrieving his crossword puzzle, which was now a few days off the press. He began plugging away, while young Erik zipped through page one of five of the exam. He always had a strong penchant for mathematics, although he would never dare admit it to his friends or even to himself most of the time. He viewed it all as a puzzle or a game. Just as Mr. Steinn chipped away at his word puzzle six feet away, Erik tackled his own puzzle of numbers. He didn't mind it. He didn't loathe it, as many of his own peers seemed to. Completing each problem, each equation provided some sense of accomplishment, a sense of pride for the youth. It was fun. And it was actually something productive and positive in Erik Serling's life. Within five minutes of first picking up his mechanical pencil and starting the quiz, he was finished. There was plenty time to spare. He sat, motionless at first. He didn't want to disturb Steinn as he appeared to really be giving it to that New York Times crossword. Erik did a less than authentic cough, which briefly caught the eye of Steinn, who raised his eyebrows in a slightly surprised manner.

"Geez, you know it's not a race, right," the old teacher laughed. Erik rose from his seat, smiling himself. He passed the packet to his favorite teacher, just as he had passed a ten dollar note to his favorite dealer, the only dealer he knew, only twenty minutes before. This really resonated with Erik for the briefest of moments, then he collected his things and made his exit from room 201, but not before a quick but heartfelt farewell to Mr. Dwayne Steinn. He made quick strides down the math hallway and rounded the corner to face the English hall. It was here that Erik began a typical day at school, in room 212, with two of his closest friends, Damien and Shiloh. Damien earned the affectionate nickname "Guido", as he ethnically was Italian. His parents owned and operated Mazetti's Grocery & Delicatessen, which Damien Sr. inherited from his own father when he passed. The small store served the village of Castalia since 1960, when it was founded by the original Damien Mazetti, shortly after moving to the village after immigrating from Sicily. Damien was short, wiry and only helped perpetuate his nickname by always looking at least slightly greasy. His face was pockmarked by cystic acne, and he sported a fifties greaser-style haircut. Despite all of this, he was by far the most accomplished and seasoned with the girls in the sophomore class, and he made sure to remind his comrades of this constantly. Shiloh Robertson, on the other hand, was the whitest of white trash. He was of proud Scottish descent and would unrelentingly quote Groundskeeper Willie from "The Simpsons". Shiloh was tall and of average build, and for as long as the other boys could recall, he always donned the same dark brown buzz cut, and once his dirt mustache began to take root, it was pure ginger. Shiloh's father was a drunk and had been evicted from Erik's own trailer park multiple times. He always found his way back in. Someone somewhere would loan him a small sum, or his gambling addiction at times threw him a bone in the form of some winning scratchers or picking the right players in a sports game. Although he was a drunk and a gambler, he certainly loved his boy. Upon Shiloh's mother's passing away, it seemed as if Kurt Robertson may have scraped his act together. However, this was very short-lived. He was soon back on the bottle and at the horse track in Fort Wayne on the weekends. Shiloh has always shown empathy for his old man. There was love in that beer-can-littered mobile home, even if its tenants were soon to be out on their asses, once again. Shiloh loved Dad, and Dad loved his Shiloh. The three boys commenced their usual babblings and jokes and bullshit before the five-till bell sounded.

"The hell was you down there for," Shiloh directed at Erik, in his dopey, twangy bellow. "Thought you wasn't in math till the end of the day." Erik started but was cut off by Damien and his vulgar hand gestures.

"He was under Daddy Dwayne's desk, working that calculator, weren't you, homo?" Erik gave a sarcastic chuckle and grabbed both of Damien's dainty wrists, and soon had him face-first into Shiloh's locker. "Ahh, quit it, wrestle with Dwayne, not me, fag!" Erik didn't let go, not until a series of desperate 'uncles' were uttered by Damien. He finally released his grasp on his small friend and began to laugh. Damien was quick to smooth his hair and fix the sleeves of his jacket. He was looking around to ensure no girls saw the altercation. "Ease up, man. Damn," Damien began to pout. Shiloh and Erik mocked him, both looking around erratically and smoothing their hair. Although Shiloh had next to no hair, this didn't deter him in the slightest. The final bell rang, and all hallway stragglers knew they had a mere sixty seconds to make their way into their home rooms. The trio of goofy, lifelong pals scampered into Mrs. Crockett's classroom to officially commence this lovely autumn school day at Castalia High. As Erik, Damien and Shiloh settled into their seats and opened up their copies of Leaves of Grass, which they all lied about reading, another member of The Club was escorting his mother to one of her numerous appointments. Maron Calhoun was watching his mother, Gloria, die a little more each and every passing hour. Gloria had achieved remission status only a year prior, but during her follow-up only a month after, the doctors had found yet another tumor in her left breast. In short, due to other medical conditions which compounded on top of one another, this tumor was not removed swiftly upon detection. Chemotherapy, up until this point, was a very effective treatment option. But within the last twelve months, it hadn't proven to be too effective in treating this new malignance. Maron had all but given up hope. He prayed in Jesus' name every night. He held his mother through her sobs and whimpers until she eventually exhausted herself into a restless and pained slumber, each and every evening. Maron took it all on the chin. School, football, the guys, his pursuit of losing his virginity all took a backseat to Mom, and whatever it was she needed that day. Mom was above all and everything in Maron's young life. Dad left some years back, and Maron accepted this as most men would accept a late fee on their credit card bill or discovering a hair in their Burger King order. He accepted it, dealt with it, and quickly moved on. Focus was never shifted from Mom. She never dropped on the list of priorities. She was always number one. Maron kept up this routine and this outlook throughout most of his high school career, and it did not come without a cost. The boy was already a pack-a-day smoker and was lucky to pack in a solid four hours of sleep per night. His fair blonde hairline was already giving the inkling of recession. The dark rings under his eyes graduated to bags. His grades certainly reflected his recent lack of attendance at Castalia High School. He looked malnourished as ever. In certain poses, his ribcage was clearly visible through whatever unwashed t-shirt it was that he chose to wear that day. In practicing the preservation of Mom and by trying to extend her lifespan, Maron seemed to have cut his own in half. This once tall, handsome, strong defensive end was reduced to a walking corpse, at the tender age of fifteen. But he loved Mom. And in this life of ours, if a man truly loves something, he waters it. He tends it. He ensures its growth and safety and preservation. And if that thing which had expended all of his love, if it has filled all of the void that was his once lonely heart, then it is the purest and holiest of things in this man's mortal existence. Mom and Maron could not afford to lose. To Maron, it was simply not an option. He helped Mom put her boots on that morning, just as he did any other. They were her Doc Martens which he bought for her only last Christmas. He laced them and tied them for her. Her skinny, pale little legs dangled from the stool which was situated at the kitchen island. This was always Mom's favorite room in her whole home. In her youthful and healthier days, Mom was a nuclear engineer at a nearby power plant. She once led the charge on many projects and a handful of experiments alongside some of the more notable scientific figures of the twenty-first century. It was then that she met Dave Calhoun, some twenty-plus years ago. Dave was no scientist, nor was he an engineer. He possessed no formal certificate or degree confirming his attendance and completion of a course of study at an institution which offered a higher education. Dave started in data entry at Navarre-Clarke Power Station and that is the same insipid department in which he remained. Dave was quiet and awkward. Had Mom never made the initial move on Dave, he never would have had the courage to talk to her, to court her. He never would have been ballsy enough to ask her to dinner at Burke's and go see a movie at the cinema in Norhauk. He never would have had the courage to propose. And he clearly didn't have the fortitude to raise a son with her, as he elected to split once the going got tough. As far as Maron was concerned, Dave was but a fleeting glimpse in the rear-view at this point. Considering Gloria was the owner of the family's home, Dave was essentially left with no choice but to remove himself once he decided his wife and son were no longer worth staying for. He moved to Michigan, and the only time he made the effort of initiating contact with his son was to call and wish him a happy birthday, a week late, nonetheless. None of this was real or mattered any longer. The desertion by Maron's father was just a ghost. It was an event that came and went, just as this second bout with cancer will be. What was going on currently was what was of significance, and that was Mom's appointment with Dr. Stamm, an oncologist in the area that came highly recommended. Maron and Mom were both a bit apprehensive, as this would be their first visit to Dr. Stamm due to the previous oncologist, Dr. Munoz, retiring. The change of healthcare provider left the pair feeling optimistic, though. It was as if a different doctor delivering the same news would somehow be better. After so long of hearing the same bad news from the same man, it was as if Dr. Munoz himself had become bad. With a new doctor came new test results, right? And the only way to go from here was up. Mom knew it; Maron knew it. The two held each other in their moment of prayer and embrace, which they shared together every morning. After they were through, Mom looked up into Maron's baby blue eyes, and weakly but confidently uttered something Maron needed to hear.

"Let's go get 'em." A weak smile spread across her thin lips. Although her looks waned in the eye of The Town, and in the eye of the general public, she never looked so fierce and vibrant to her son as she did then.

"Kick ass, Mom," Maron responded, with a forced level of vigor and enthusiasm. He helped Mom off of the kitchen stool and trailed her as she shuffled out of the spacious kitchen and down the hallway to the front door. She exited her picturesque home, with her son in tow. The duo made their way to Mom's Acadia, which Maron would never pass up driving, despite the fact that he hadn't even obtained his learner's permit yet. The two buckled in, gave the car a minute to heat up, and they were on their way. They were on their way to hopefully hear the best news they had heard in some time.

Chapter 3

The lunch hour rapidly approached, and the boys all knew they would soon be united in the overcrowded cafeteria where the school's less than amicable lunch ladies slopped out trayfuls of the finest cuisine a public school's budget would opt for. The cafeteria workers prepped the lunch for the day without much urgency, despite the fact that students would be filing in within five more minutes. The women who ran this eatery could have easily doubled as exterminators. Whichever lady was privileged to have opening duties was always greeted by a colony of insects each and every morning, if that fact attests to the level of effort that goes in to keeping the place clean says anything. The crew was more comfortable with a can of roach and ant spray, which they were always sure to keep out of view of the students and other faculty, than they were with a spatula in hand. These ladies, like the vast majority of the staff, just droned on with the mindset of getting through one day at a time, and that's exactly what they did. This was the name of the game for some of them for years now. The lunch bell sounded, and within the next minute, the first few patrons began trickling in. They formed a chatty little line at the stack of half-ass washed trays and each picked one up. Among the first wave of the lunch rush were two more companions to Erik and The Club. They were Durand Desmond and Reginald Bousher, who were, in a way, the founding fathers of the boys' little clique. Durand and Reg were the first two friends, having met one another in kindergarten. The boys knew one another long before befriending Damien and Maron, and while they knew of Shiloh, they were both a bit standoffish to him upon his first impression in early grade school, but soon after embraced him with open arms simply due to just how goddamn funny the kid was. Despite being the founding members, it was Erik Serling who led them. Erik had this polarizing charisma that provided a sense of camaraderie and protection for the other boys, especially at their times of vulnerability, which with this small group of best friends occurred frequently. Erik was the ringleader of their little shit circus, and it would forever remain so. He soon shuffled in. He must have weaseled his way into the thick of the preppy bitch bubble. In front was Connie De La Rosa, who Erik admittedly always had a thing for. Although he was sure to not stand too close to her to avoid making these feelings obvious to the entire sophomore class, he could still pick up an aroma of Pantene conditioner wafting off her long, raven-colored tresses. She wore it down and natural that day, which made Erik absolutely crazy. He always favored the loose curls over the artificial straightened look on her. Still, he played it as cool as he could, as he knew she was always surrounded by her friends, which were, in truth, just followers and copycats. And all of these girls were quick to notice any type of staring or attention being given by a male classmate, especially if that attention was not showering them. Right behind him was Clarissa Thomas, along with a handful of other girls just cute and popular enough to interact with Connie and Clarissa. They were just as capable of noticing Erik's casual glances and would have been more than happy to make a big scene of it as well. Clarissa wasn't always a pretentious mean girl, however, as Erik and most of the others of The Club knew very well. She was actually, up until middle school, a very polite and inclusive girl. Erik actually was able to kiss her at the sixth grade "graduation" dance. A parent chaperone was sure to halt it there, but he recalls fondly that she walked back to her table of little friends, blushing and grinning from ear to ear. But even Clarissa's poor treatment of her classmates now didn't allow Erik to hold a jaded view of her. He knew that sweet girl with braces and a Cheetah Girls backpack wasn't entirely gone. She just needed the encouragement to emerge from the fake, preppy swamp that bogged her down. She could still breathe, somewhere in there. The line advanced and the pleasant fragrance of Pantene and pretty girl now mixed with the smell of soggy barbecued beef. Erik's interest did not waiver. He tailed Connie through the line and filled his tray with processed food, paid for his meal and joined Durand and Reg at their usual table in the corner. They struck up conversation and Shiloh and Damien soon joined. The only missing member, of course, was Maron.

"Did Maron's mom have another appointment," Damien quietly asked, as if the topic itself was deemed forbidden.

"Yeah, he's probably gonna be gone all week again," Erik replied. "Depending on the news, you know. Usually when things aren't great, he stays home with her a few extra days at least." The boys sat in silence for a moment. They all even took a break from their food. "But, on a better note," Erik continued, "I did score some more weed." The boys smiled, nodding their heads, all but Damien.

"You went back to Bose, didn't you?" The small celebration stopped.

"Well, yeah, Dim. It's not like I know anyone else."

"I've told you before that piece of shit broke into our store. Why are you giving him money for shitty weed every week?"

"You're pretty sure it was him, there's no concrete proof, just your own suspicion. And second, you don't complain about any of this when we smoke. I don't see you putting your ass on the line meeting with anyone and buying. It's always me or Shiloh, why is that? Let the trailer trash risk it, right?" A noticeable cloud of tension began swelling over the dingy little corner table. Erik began getting a little heated but was sure to keep his voice down due to the subject matter.

"Goddamn, okay," Damien snapped back. The table fell silent for a few more moments, until Connie passed by the boys to exit the cafeteria on her way to the restroom.

"Hi, Connie," Shiloh bellowed, with a mouth full of green beans. All of the boys looked to her, including Erik. She kind of smirked, paused, and did a frilly little feminine wave.

"Hi, guys." Shiloh mimed the wave she did, which caused her to roll her eyes before exiting the cafeteria. All of the boys got a good chuckle while Erik covered his face with both of his palms to hide his embarrassment. He let out a string of obscenities before looking at Shiloh.

"Was it fucking necessary?" He glared at The Club's own class clown. Shiloh's laugh began to trail off once he realized how pissed Erik actually was. The awkward silence began to manifest itself once more. It was Durand who fended it off this time.

"Well, Coach wants to meet with us all today. I think we might as well knock that out now, right?" He looked across the table to Reg, who nodded and proceeded to scarf down the remainder of his lunch and began chugging his Gatorade. The athletes said their goodbyes to the remaining three friends and the tension which surrounded them as well. Reg and Durand cleared their trays and stacked them on top of the pile of dirty ones. They retreated back the same way, passing Erik, Shiloh and Damien once more. Damien seemed to be on one of his infamous rants, as he was talking with his hands and looking from Shiloh to Erik sporadically. The pair made their exit and stepped out into a vacant hallway.

Chapter 4

"It's always goddamn something man," Durand sighed, half laughing.

"Yeah," Reg chuckled. "Damien is always the instigator though, like just looks for shit to be mad at. Then Shiloh just being his usual dumbass self. Gets old, man." Durand nodded in agreeance. The boys reached Durand's locker, which he opened to deposit his change from lunch. He glanced into his little magnetic mirror, which was mounted on his locker door. He smoothed his eyebrows and goatee before shutting it. Durand had the look and build of a D1 quarterback at the age of fifteen. While the image came naturally to him, due to what The Club joked about being "black genetics", he still lacked the skill and on-field performance in the eyes of many. However, his coaches and teammates, especially Reg, reassured him that he would grow into the role. He did manage to make the varsity roster as a sophomore, which was a rare feat for the school and its football organization. Durand was eagerly awaiting his first start, and considering only two games had come and gone, he was still optimistic about the remaining eight. It wasn't that he was hoping for Marshall Gibson, the Castalia Ice Cats' senior starter, to succumb to injury or illness to allow him the opportunity to start a varsity game, but he was fully prepared for this situation should it arise. Durand was tall and built more like a linebacker than most of the slimmer and toned quarterbacks in the school's conference. He was half-black and white, and after participating in a family genealogy research project, he recently found out that he was Scottish on his mother's side. He proceeded with the utmost caution regarding this information, to ensure Shiloh didn't find out, for he knew he would never hear the end of it if he did. Durand had two younger sisters, who showed up each game and preseason scrimmage, home or away, to cheer on their big brother for simply riding the bench. He remained hopeful, though, and his level of discipline and work ethic clearly showed this. Reg was a running back, and certainly possessed the stature of one. He was short and broad. After football season wrapped up each year, he went on to wrestle in the winter, which he tended to fare even better at. He had shoulder-length blonde hair and steel-gray eyes. Although he came up to five and a half feet on a good day, this did not detract from the intensity of his appearance. Reg was adopted as an infant by his parents. His father was diagnosed with a number of conditions which became apparent in his own adolescent years. And as a result, Mr. Steve Bousher and his wife, Jessica, were incapable of conceiving naturally. Reginald was the absolute apple of their eye, and, his mother, at least, reminded him of it every day. Steve was an accountant and Jessica was the owner of the sole salon in town, The Mane Station. She was there for its grand opening shortly after graduating high school and worked as a stylist, and over the decades she scaled the ladder and attained the title of manager as well as owner. Alongside Reg, it was her proudest accolade. Though things haven't always been gravy between her and Steve over the years, they both managed to hold it all together for their little boy. The best of best friends made their way to the coach's office, which was located in the athletic complex next to the football field. Coach Grenslait took time each week to meet with all varsity boys. He prioritized the young men's health, both physical and mental. Mr. Grenslait was never a father himself, but sometimes played the part for members of his team if required, Durand being one of several. Grenslait was good to them. Reg and Durand reached the building, a long, single-story rectangular structure. All school sports coaches had an office here and the weight room was also located within. The duo entered and proceeded down the hall through the men's locker room and eventually reached Grenslait's room, where he was alone.

"Hey, guys," his baritone voice boomed. He was a mountain of a man. These days he was a little more flab than muscle, but still strong as hell. "I have some news I am sure you'll both be glad to hear." Both boys took a seat across his desk. "No point in sitting down," he said with a sly smile. Durand could feel butterflies in the pit of his stomach. Reg glanced at him. He looked like he was on the verge of throwing up or shitting his pants. "Durand, you will be starting from here on out. I can't divulge the reasoning of why with you yet, but just know, you've got the job the rest of the season." Durand was on his feet, bug-eyed. He didn't know whether to scream or cry. He had to do one of the two as he was at a complete loss for words. Reg was ecstatic. He was jumping out of his seat, congratulating his best friend on his biggest sporting feat yet. Grenslait let them carry on for a bit before hushing them. "Now, like I said, this is under some, I guess, unusual circumstances, but it is what it is. You've busted your ass since I first met you in seventh grade. I'm glad to be the one to tell you this." Durand finally spoke.

"S-so, is Marshall good? Is he hurt?"

"Marshall Gibson is no longer a part of this team, that's all." Grenslait's expression shifted subtly, but in a way so Reg and Durand knew not to push the question any further. A brief silence fell over the room, which Reg broke.

"Marshall let me get plenty of touches, don't forget." Reg's comment directed at Durand made all three of them laugh.

"Yeah, you'll get your thousand-yard season, all-star, don't you worry." Durand was over the moon, as was Reg, who may have been even happier for him. The boys were sure to shoot the shit with their favorite coach for a while, at the expense of being late for history. They exited the athletic complex and were sure to put some of their ability to use while trying to beat the bell for fifth period. They couldn't wait to share the news with Maron and the rest of the guys. It was a good day for The Club.

The final bell rang and the students of Castalia High were set free. Free to run amok, free to socialize. Free from what many of them relied on as the main source of structure and organization in their lives. Sadly, the school served as the only safe place for many as well. All too many. Erik reached his bike at the rack outside the entrance. It was one of the last remaining few. He unlocked his chain and slung his leg over the little bike, beginning his commute home. The rest of the schoolday went alright, albeit uneventful, which wasn't always a bad thing. Erik cruised past Limerick Park, with not so much as a passing glance to Bose, who was in his usual spot, sure enough. He reached the carport outside his home and instantly heard yelling. This wasn't too atypical, as Erik's father was probably plenty drunk at this hour in the day. As Erik walked toward the door, he realized something was different, though, as he heard his mother yelling back. He hustled inside. The mobile home was a wreck, even by mobile home standards. Sarah was screaming in the back bedroom. Erik sped down the hall to where she was and found her bloodied. She stood on top of the bed, lamp in hand. She held it as if it was a Louisville Slugger, and Erik saw blood all over its crumpled shade. He looked to his left and saw his father, blood gushing from under his eye.

"Get your ass out now, unless you want whipped too," Jared instructed his son. Erik didn't hold back. Not this time.
Not now that he believed his mother to be bleeding at his excuse for a father's hand. The boy took a stand.

"Looks like you're the one getting your ass whipped, little bitch." He said it, standing tall. His voice quivered none. He uttered it in stone-cold confidence. Jared stood mouth wide open, aghast. In the silence that followed, Erik could decipher the situation. His father was bleeding, and at some point, his blood had gotten onto his mother's face and clothes, and clearly the lamp shade.

"Honey, go out. I'm going to follow you. Get your school stuff, wait for me in the kitchen," Sarah calmly, yet firmly ordered.

Erik was hesitant. He didn't want his mother left alone with Jared, even if just for a moment. His big boy voice came out yet again.

"No, Mom. You come down off the bed. Put the lamp back on the stand. Grab my bag for me." All the while, he never broke Jared's gaze. Sarah seemed dumbfounded at first but complied. She walked slowly out of the small bedroom, passing behind her son. She never looked away from Jared either. She exited and Erik could hear her slowly and cautiously proceeding down the hallway. Jared smiled.

"Thatta boy," he let out a drunk, moronic laugh. "Let's handle it like men, son." His speech was heavily slurred. The room stunk of sweat and booze.

"What the fuck happened? What did you do to her?" Erik was like a man possessed. This confidence, this show of strength was something he never had access to before.

"Why do you think it's always me?" Jared's voice gradually grew louder throughout the sentence. "Why am I such a bad guy to you, son? If you really knew about your mom--" Erik stopped him there. He let emotion take over once Jared wanted to start with his unfounded accusations.

"Leave her alone! You're talking to me now!" His voice cracked and he could feel his eyes begin to swell with tears. Jared detected this too. He was no longer dealing with Billy Bad-Ass, but rather, his scared and battered little boy once again.

"You cut that shit, right the fuck now," Jared boomed. He made haste, crossing the small room in a few drunk but swift steps. He grabbed Erik by his chin and single-handedly thrusted him back against the sliding closet door. "Where is the money you had in your room," Jared demanded angrily. Erik had it figured out by this point. His drunk father reached the bottom of his last bottle and didn't realize it was his last until it was already gone. It came as no surprise that he resorted to this, as Erik was fairly certain he had done it before. Jared's withdrawals of Erik's funds would start out somewhat subtly, but as of late, he noticed greater sums to be unexplainably missing. This was money Erik earned by mowing lawns and doing odd jobs. And while he had no problem putting some of this towards groceries or bills for the family from time to time, he certainly had his reservations about allowing this money to go to fund his father's most incendiary habit. Using both hands, he managed to free himself from Jared's intoxicated grasp.

"That's not for you to drink away! Fucking bastard!" Jared cocked back to swing, but Erik anticipated it. He side-stepped the blow and Jared cracked his knuckles against the closet door. The man voice came back, and Erik got into his best fighter stance.

"C'mon, punk bitch!" Jared was yelling, both in anger and pain. Still clutching his quickly swelling hand, he lunged at Erik and was met with a stiff left to the face. There wasn't much power behind it, but it was quick and effective. After years of being on the receiving end of his father's abusive blows, it felt good to deal one back. He followed this up with a sloppy combo which was comprised of two more stiff lefts and a full-force right hook across Jared's jaw. The first two punches were a bit lackluster, but the third was a haymaker. Erik delivered the shot and Jared's knees buckled. His whole body seemed to seize up in place, before losing his balance and toppling over on his right side. He was undoubtedly unconscious. Erik stood in shock. Sarah was now at the doorway, hand covering her face. Erik looked at his father, who was motionless and already snoring on the bedroom floor. Erik stood there in awe for a moment more before Sarah came to collect him. The pair shambled down the hallway, in somewhat of a shock or daze. Sarah opened up the cupboard below the kitchen sink. This was where all of the cleaning chemicals and supplies were stored. It was her safe place. To Erik's surprise, she knocked all of the cans of Comet and bottles of Dawn onto the floor, and reached as far back as she could, retrieving two small gym bags. She passed one to Erik, who started to piece it together.

"I packed these after the last time, honey." Her voice was quivering still, but she tried her best to hold it together in front of her son. Erik helped her to her feet, then they headed out the door together, Sarah swiping the keys to the old Cavalier on her way. They left the door wide open, the screen door swinging in the breeze.

"I hope the possums get in and scare the shit outta him," Erik muttered. Sarah cracked a weak smile and let out a little giggle. Her tear-stained cheeks glistened in the late afternoon autumn sun. She looked just as strong and beautiful to Erik as she ever had. The two hopped into the car and after a few sputters of the engine, Sarah managed to get the old goddamn thing to turn over.

"When I saw how much he drank and how fast, I decided to grab this," she reached into her hoodie pocket and pulled out a crumpled wad of bills, fives and singles mainly. She passed her son his money, and in doing so earned even more of his admiration, as if that was even possible at that point. Erik began to cry. He let loose what he felt he couldn't in the house, and his mother held him. After their brief embrace, Erik looked his mother in the eye.

"This is it. We're not coming back here. We're not coming back to him, ever." Sarah nodded, slowly but solemnly. "We can't come back, Mom," Erik repeated.

"I promise, we'll never have to," Sarah held out her pail, bony hand, extending her pinky finger. Erik returned the gesture, and the deal was done. And so, it was set in stone. The two were free. They were homeless, scared and without an independent income, but above all of this they were emancipated from a sick and unrelenting cruelty. They escaped abuse and degradation. They were free from unprovoked altercations for the first time in more than fifteen years. They were no longer victims, and they knew they never had to be again. The duo let the old Cav warm up for a bit before peeling out of the gravel driveway. They departed the shabby trailer park together in that old car and never once looked in the rear-view.

Chapter 5

Damien finished up a few more poems from Whitman's classic while riding with his father to Mazetti's Delicatessen & Grocery. He scribbled a few sloppy Post-It notes and carelessly slapped them onto the page, which was blessed to have "Passage to India" inscribed upon it. He slammed the yellowed old hardback shut with an exasperated sigh. This finally caught his dad's attention.

"Whitman," he said with a slight smile. "I remember reading some of him in school. I felt the way you do now, son. But in all honesty, there are a lot of beautiful things in here." Damien couldn't help but roll his eyes.

"It makes no sense, Dad. It's like he just goes off on some drunk tangent." Damien Sr.'s smile never wavered.

"You learn to view things in a different light as you get older, buddy." They pulled up to the deli and Sr. parked his new Enclave. "I certainly hope you do, considering this will be all yours some day!" Sr. did a corny jazz hands move and flashed an obnoxious grin while looking at his son. Damien rolled his eyes a little extra this time, although this one was accompanied by a genuine, loving smile. Although Sr. was a bit of a stiff, and always maintained a stoic image while at work, he always knew how to make Damien laugh.

"I'll appreciate it once I make all the money and don't have to do anything like you do," Jr. retorted. Sr. snickered.

"Well, that's not today, buddy. Today you get to change the blades on the turkey slicer." Damien let out an exaggerated and blatantly fake "Yippee!" upon opening the passenger side door and exiting the SUV. Damien entered the front sliding doors while his father circled around to the rear of the building. This entrance permitted the boss a more discrete arrival to his store. Sr. unlocked the door and settled into his office, while his son joined the ranks of his fellow deli workers. Business appeared to be on the slow side. Damien spotted a few regulars, mostly older people who came in every other day at least to buy trivialities. Mrs. Nesbitt was a crossword puzzle guru, and if she wasn't purchasing a puzzle book that would only take her a matter of days to complete, then she had a copy of The Times in her hand, whose puzzle would satiate her craving for a solid half-hour, if that. Another regular was the pretty, young brunette mother who Damien affectionately nicknamed, in his head anyway, "Cookies 'N Milf", due to her always purchasing something from the bakery to appease her screaming toddler. Apart from these two ladies, Damien just saw a crowd of faces. They were familiar, in a way, considering he's sure he'd seen them at least a handful of times in the store before. But the store in general seemed vacant, and not just due to a lack of customers as a whole, but it was the lack of regulars that was most notable. A Wal-Mart opened over the summer, just fifteen minutes away in the neighboring town of Norhauk. This certainly didn't do the family-owned establishment any favors. As far as Damien could tell, business was fruitful enough. Dad just bought himself that car, after all, and he bought Mom a ring for their twentieth anniversary. Speaking of Mom, she was making her way out of the manager's office, and she met Damien's gaze. At first, she looked detached, almost robotic. When she realized her favorite employee caught her in this state, she perked right up. She sauntered over to the little swinging door which led behind the deli counter. She was sure to flash a smile or blurt out an overexcited greeting to the few customers she passed on her walk. Raquel was the life and essence of the mom-and-pop shop. She was a warm, caring little woman, who came up to an even five feet in height. She was a fitness fanatic who never missed her four-AM workout before coming in and opening the store each and every morning. Because of her fit physique and pretty little face and frame, she never lost favor with any male customers. Because of her looks, Damien's friends always had plenty of ammunition in the form of rude and lewd comments as well. Raquel passed by her employees in the deli, exchanging pleasantries with each, before meeting her son. She was peppy as ever.

"Hey, honey! How did school go?" Damien was still in the process of tying his apron.

"It was fine, Mom. I have a reading assignment but that's it." She pressed both hands to Damien's face and gave his forehead a kiss. Damien rolled his eyes and smiled.

"Well, we won't need you too long, obviously."

Raquel motioned to the nearly vacant store. "Just a couple hours, okay?" She looked at Damien with the sweetest of smiles, tilting her head to the side slightly. Damien returned her smile and nodded in confirmation. Raquel thanked her son and departed the deli area to return to the office. Damien worked diligently, as always. He served a few customers, including Mrs. Nesbitt, who was clutching at least three puzzle books in her hands as she ordered her usual pound of roast beef. When there was no queue, he was wiping counters, sweeping or mopping. Damien felt good about work. As much shit as he gave his parents for it, particularly Dad, he genuinely felt a sense of purpose and satisfaction when performing his duties inside the little shop. Around six o'clock Sr. emerged from his office. This was the first time since arriving that Damien saw his father, which wasn't odd by any means. He had a habit of locking himself in the office, crunching numbers and making phone calls. He seemed to enjoy the solitude. He told his wife and son countless times that he accomplishes the most while alone. Sr approached the counter, with his usual close-lipped smile pressed on his face.

"Want to head out, buddy? I can drop you off at the house. We'll probably be closing earlier than normal any way."

"Sure, Dad. I'll wash up quick." Damien untied his apron, which, despite having dealt with very few customers that evening, had collected a fair amount of grease and dirt. He threw it into the near-full hamper in the supply room of the deli. He washed his hands and said his goodbyes to his coworkers, then exited through the back door. Dad was already outside, Buick running. Damien hopped in and the two pulled out of the deserted asphalt lot. Sr. was silent for some time, and it wasn't until the two were nearly home that Damien made an attempt to break the silence. "Everything good, Dad?" He glanced briefly at his father. Sr. seemed taken by surprise.

"Yeah, yeah, buddy. We're all good. A few slow days is all. You know how it gets. Starts cooling down outside and people aren't too keen on going out. With holidays coming up you know the place will be booming like it always is." He gave a cheesy grin. Damien nodded in agreeance, and they pulled into the driveway. Damien grabbed his pack and his copy of Leaves of Grass, bid his father farewell and let himself into the house. The house was a huge century home that looked as modern, if not more, than any other on Maple St. Only two summers ago Sr. put on new vinyl siding. And two summers before that he contracted Mozzier Construction to replace the roof. The elegant mansion loomed in the twilight. In its walls lived almost two decades of love and prosperity. This is where Damien took his first steps, where Raquel took an at-home pregnancy test to learn that she was carrying her first and only child, despite being told by multiple doctors that conception just wasn't possible for her. The home itself was a part of the family, standing as a testament to the Mazettis' work ethic and success. Damien stepped into the spacious foyer and hung his pack on the coat rack. He set down his book on the small table beside it and kicked off his Jordans. The entire home sat still and dark, with the exception of the small light over the kitchen sink being on. Damien followed the beacon down the long straight hallway until he reached the kitchen, where he flicked on the switch to the chandelier light. The kitchen, which many a chef would love to take a test drive in, was flooded with light, and Damien could reach the refrigerator for a snack without fear of accidentally kicking Bootsy or stepping on her tail. Bootsy was a haggard old tabby cat who arrived at 1708 W. Maple St. around the same time Damien did. She found her way to the back deck as Sr. was mowing the yard one morning and just simply never left. Sr. would feed her scraps of chicken or steak, and Raquel replicated the same behavior after some time. The winter which came that year came in full force as one of the worst on record for the area. The newlyweds couldn't bear the thought of leaving the poor thing in subzero temperatures and with some reluctance, brought her inside with the strict rule of her confinement to the laundry room and laundry room only. This rule was soon broken, and who was the first to break it depends upon which spouse was asked. The cat roamed freely, and the whole home was under her domain. She took a liking to Damien upon meeting him for the first time, and the two have been inseparable since. Bootsy weaseled her way into the family home out of sympathy and stayed out of sheer love. Damien retrieved a cup of yogurt from the fridge and was sure to give Bootsy a splash of milk in her bowl. He proceeded to retreat to his room upstairs and picked up his cell phone which he left behind to charge between school and work. It was flooded with group chat texts. This was nothing out of the ordinary for The Club. The content of the messages was a bit more serious than usual, however. There were no pictures of topless girls or cringey screenshots of classmates' social media posts. Erik described in detail what transpired only hours before. He was asking any of the group if they had vacancy for his mother and himself, and all members, save Shiloh, who, to be fair probably wasn't able to pay his phone bill on time as usual, gladly obliged. Maron spoke to his mother, and they agreed to move Erik and Sarah in temporarily, until other options became available for them. Damien felt instant remorse as he didn't reply sooner. He explained he wasn't near his phone when Erik reached out, and all was accepted and understood. Although the boys looked for all and any opportunity to rip one another a new asshole, sometimes for the smallest and most petty reasons, they all looked out for one another when the time called for it, without fail. Damien called and Erik recounted his tale of heroism. He may have omitted the parts when his voice cracked when yelling at his drunk father, or how scared he truly was in the moment, but apart from that it was fairly accurate. The two spoke for some time before Damien's parents came home. Damien excused himself from the phone call, as his mom's arrival meant dinner would be ready soon. He offered a few more words of encouragement to his friend before setting the phone down. Despite what happened, Erik sounded as strong and in control as he ever has. Damien had not the slightest of doubts that the leader of their little gang would persevere. He never failed to before. Damien trotted down the stairs and rounded the corner to see his parents at the small kitchen table. His father was speaking in a hushed tone, which he usually ceased once Damien came within earshot, but he continued his rhetoric in the same manner, not seeming to even realize his son entered the room. Raquel sat with her elbows resting on the table, palms pressed to her pretty little forehead. Sr. continued.

"We will have to decide soon; it just isn't practical. Ethically, it would probably be best to look at seniority, but some of the older ladies just can't move at the pace we would need. I don't know how we would explain or justify it without sounding shitty, and there's always the risk of an ageism suit if we did." Raquel looked up, wiping her tear-stained cheeks.

"Honey, you're going to be taking a pay cut," she could barely finish her sentence to Damien before breaking down again. Damien consoled his mother.

"It's fine, Mom. I don't need my own money right now. I just want the store to be okay." This only seemed to exacerbate Raquel's weeping. Sr. walked to his liquor cabinet and pulled a bottle of Scotch from it. He looked for a glass but thought better of it and just drank from the bottle. After a few sips he cleared his throat, and his eyes met Damien's, who still had his arm around his mother.

"Son, things are looking kind of grim. They've been like this before, and we always bounced back. This time will be no different, except for now we are going to have to lay off. We're having the meeting about this tomorrow. You'll be going without pay for the time, but I promise we'll make it up to you and then some once we're back above water." Sr. was completely stoic in his delivery. Damien didn't even see him blink.

"Okay, Dad. It's not a big deal for me. We'll do what we have to." Raquel seemed to gather herself, at least for the moment. Not much more was said on the matter, and Raquel started dinner as if this was just any other night. Sr. kicked back on the couch and found a baseball game. Damien debated joining him but wasn't sure if he was up for the awkward silence that would surely hang over the room. Usually, when watching anything, the two would joke and make cheeky comments about the show or game. Damien didn't anticipate that to be the case that night, so he retreated to his room again. Bootsy was plopped down at the top of the staircase, and he scooped her up on his way. He carried his oldest friend into his room and closed the door, save a small crack allowing the hallway light to filter in through. He crashed on his bed with Bootsy at his side and picked up his phone. He contemplated sharing with The Club the knowledge he was now unfortunately privy to but thought better of it. They were already dealt a substantial blow that day, and when one suffers, all suffer. Damien put on a movie and awaited the dinner bell. He joined his parents briefly at the table. The topics of conversation shifted to much more lighthearted matters, which everyone was okay with. Damien finished his enchiladas and soon turned in for the night. He fell into a mostly restless sleep before getting up to relieve himself shortly after midnight. Bootsy had left and he saw no lights on downstairs, meaning his parents must have passed out as well. He shuffled back into his room and didn't even bother with putting something else on his TV before lying back down. He was unconscious within minutes, and before he knew it, his alarm was rudely chiming. He awoke to the smell of bacon, which was fragrant enough to permeate every square inch of the massive old home. He slid into his slippers and made his way into the upstairs bathroom. He splashed some water on his face and proceeded to pop a fresh pimple. He washed his face once more and trudged down the decadent staircase. He turned down the hall and arrived at the kitchen, where he found his mother cooking quite the feast. English muffins popped out of the toaster as soon as Damien reached his spot at the kitchen table.

"Morning, honey," Raquel blurted out, turning to face her son with a plastered-on smile.

"Hey, Mom. Did, uh, Dad head in already," Damien weakly responded, his hand on the back of his chair.

"Yeah, hon. He had that meeting. I suppose he wanted to get it over with sooner than later was all." Raquel's smile never faltered. "There's plenty of eggs and bacon, too," she continued, rather over-enthusiastically. She heaped a breakfast buffet onto Damien's plate. Damien paused for a moment longer before taking his seat and digging into the most important meal of the day. Raquel kept busy as her son enjoyed the meal. Damien recognized this trait in his mother. When she succumbed to extensive stress, she felt obligated to stay busy. She had to move about. She had to be occupied with some task, even the most mundane, to keep her mind off of whatever it was that was troubling her at the time. Damien paused to take a sip of his juice, but before doing so, he was able to bring himself to pop the question.

"Is everything okay, Mom?" Normally he'd stop here, but he knew if he did, he would get a generic and affirmative response. "After last night I've just been worried. I couldn't sleep good. I just want to know if everything is good with the store. But I also want to know if it's not. I'm old enough to know. If I'm going to take over one day, like Dad keeps saying, I need to have a handle on these things. Just please, be honest about it." Raquel turned from the section of countertop she began to wipe down. Her smile finally began to crack a bit. She set the rag back down on the counter and made her way to the seat across from Damien. She opened her mouth to speak but paused once more. She finally came out with it. Being secretive would only make matters worse.

"Well, Damien, things don't look great now. It's never good when people are told they have to go without a job until further notice. We've had. this feeling for a while now but after reviewing the quarterlies the other day it really resonated with your father. He knows if we don't act now, it's a possibility that we would go under. We're doing everything we can to avoid that, and one of the first steps in that is cutting those who we could manage without. It's stressful, dear. But we're going to fight our way out of it." Damien sat silently for a moment, English muffin frozen inches from his mouth. Despite the severity of the situation, he felt at ease. He felt that there was no sugar-coating anything. His mother pulled no punches, and for that, he was grateful. It was a relief to hear the unadulterated truth from the person he is most near and dear to. It meant the world. He finally felt capable of responding.

"Thanks, Mom." Raquel looked puzzled for a moment until her son clarified. "For giving it to me straight. I kind of picked up on hints the past few weeks but it's good to hear it from you. I appreciate being let in on these things, is all." Raquel's smile returned. This time, however, it spread across her lips organically, as opposed to before. She began to slow her pace, without speaking a word. She made herself a little plate and sat across from her son and was able to somewhat enjoy the moment. Sr., on the other hand, was not reveling in the moment. He faced his staff that morning with a deep sense of reluctance, and a deeper sense still of shame. The small bunch retrieved some chairs from the break room and assembled them in a circle a few feet in front of the deli counter. Excluding Sr., his wife and son, eleven other hourly workers composed the workforce at Mazetti's. Of the lot, Sr. had selected four to take to the chopping block. The first who was up for elimination was Glenda Alder. Glenda was an older, plump woman. Upon her hire date, she requested specifically to work no more than two to three days a week. She was mainly utilized on weekends, and even then, didn't always manage to pull her own weight. She was sweet but notably lazy. She was the recipient of a rather hefty inheritance a few years prior to starting work at Mazetti's, and her earnings at the shop were more geared towards "fun" money than anything else. Sr. truly felt that the news of her cessation of employment would be somewhat of a relief to her. Her children were grown, and she was divorced. She simply worked to keep busy and earn a bit of spending cash. The next one to be taken to the slaughter would be Marvin Mayle. Marvin was a stout, older gentleman who took more of an interest in scoping out the pretty young women who came into the store as opposed to his work. He was a short, stocky man who shambled around with a bit of a limp. His bald head was always glistening with beads of sweat, even when he was not exerting much effort or energy. Marvin was a lazy employee overall, but he was always good for a laugh, and he managed to catch a few shoplifters in the act before. In both instances, he reverted to his days as a defensive lineman, which is how he spent his college football career. When apprehending his first suspect, Marvin hit the young man with such force that the back of the perpetrator's head bounced off the tile floor, inducing a seizure. Blood flowed from the suspect's nose and ears, and the Mazettis' concern over a shoplifter shifted to a potential count of manslaughter. The would-be thief, who was apparently a drifter-type just passing through, ended up being fine. The eggs which he had concealed in his hoodie, however, were not. Sometimes loss prevention has a counterproductive effect after all. The second suspect apprehended due to Marvin's intuition was an elderly widow who, when alive, came into the store quite often. Her name was Beatrice Affle, a former teacher at the high school from when Marvin attended. Mrs. Affle was caught boosting several pounds of ground beef as well as a few ribeye steaks. When she was found out, she went so far as to fake a pulmonary episode, which no one was buying. After agreeing to never come back to the store, lest the cops be called, Mrs. Affle lived out her last few months in her small home on the edge of town. Sadly, it wasn't old age that claimed the life of Beatrice, but rather, she fell asleep while pan-frying a small sirloin steak, of all things. She awoke in time to extinguish the kitchen fire, and after doing so she collapsed on her Davenport. It was determined that a heart attack actually did her in, for real this time. This never sat right with Marvin. The third employee to be laid off was Geraldine Mowzer. She was a polite older black woman. She had all the pep of a twenty-year-old and all the wisdom of one of the ancients. Geraldine was the only employee to match Raquel's pace and enthusiasm. She served as a motherly figure to almost all of her coworkers, never hesitating to do so, as well. Geraldine worked to occupy her time, mainly. Her husband retired from the railroad years prior, and she just liked to keep busy and feel a sense of purpose. Unbeknownst to Sr., Geraldine and Raquel spoke of this very matter weeks prior. Geraldine sensed something was amiss when the two sat down for their first break one day, which they always took together. Raquel spilled the beans. After listening and consoling her employer for the better part of a half-hour, Geraldine gladly threw herself on the fire.

"Honey, I'm only here to feel needed. Hank spends all day in his garage, my girls are so busy with college, my son is still in jail. I'm just here to feel some kind of purpose. I have all this energy to burn and this was the place for me. But knowing you and yours need to make these cuts, I'm more than happy to contribute to that, too." Hearing this only made Raquel cry harder. She hugged Mama Geraldine, who had been more of a mother to Raquel than her own, for a long while, before agreeing that she would be put on the list. The two ladies conceived the idea that Geraldine applied for a job at the new Wal-Mart and was hired in, and Raquel caught word that Geraldine intended to issue her two-week notice in a few days following the meeting as well. When discussing the chopping block, Raquel was sure to feed her husband her rehearsed speech about, inarguably, their best employee, and Sr. went along with it, although understandably shocked. The fourth and final candidate up for termination was Ralph Reirke. Ralph was an unmotivated twenty-something who still resided with his mom and stepdad. He was a short, wiry young man with greasy black shoulder-length hair, a face riddled with teenage acne still, and he always donned very thick coke bottle glasses. One lens was a different prescription than the other. Ralph was both near and far-sighted. This gave the illusion that his eyes were a different size from one another, only adding to his general creepiness. Ralph was your run-of-the-mill stoner burnout who never really left high school. It was understood that he was good friends with Bose, as well. Of all the employees being let go, this was the one Sr. didn't feel an ounce of remorse for. He knew for a fact that Ralph had more than a hand in the robbery of the store that occurred only over the summer of that year. However, the camera which had the cash register in question in frame was coated in dust. The lens was no exception. The only thing that could undeniably be determined was that two figures, one large and husky, the other small and thin, were prying a register open and helped themselves to several pounds of deli meat. No fingerprints could be detected, and the camera outside never recorded a vehicle. The thieves were smart enough to park elsewhere and break in around the back. All in all, they made off with a drawer prepped for the following morning which contained no more than one-hundred and fifty dollars, a good deal of it was change, and an estimated eleven and a half pounds of prosciutto, salami, ham, and thin-sliced turkey. Sr. would take joy in telling Ralph, who he fully intended to save for last, so this whole meeting doesn't leave an entirely sour taste in his mouth. He stood in the opening of the now semi-circle which his employees composed. He had his old clipboard in hand and remained motionless for some time while his crew settled in their seats. The scooting and scuttling finally ceased, and the chatter among the employees began to fizzle out. He knew it was time.

"I thank you all for coming in a little early for this, as you all always do. Please, everyone be sure to make yourself a sandwich or grab some coffee," Sr. motioned to the small refreshment table set up, which had already been raided. Most of the staff was finished with their food and drink. He hated this. He detested every last second of it. He just wanted it over.

"So, we'll get right down to it today, as it turns out," Sr. stopped to clear his throat and wipe the sweat which was already pooling and would soon drip from his brow. "It turns out, some of you will be without a job for some time. I apologize with the utmost sincerity, but it's something that will have to be done. A necessary evil of running a business, if you will." He nervously glanced up at his audience, whose faces displayed a montage of mixed reactions. "Those people are Marvin, Geraldine, Glenda, and Ralph. I'm terribly sorry," he began pacing the exterior of the circle, before realizing the proper thing to do would be to shake each now freshly former employee's hand and give them a well wish. He approached Marvin, who was in the process of climbing to his feet. "Marvin, I'm sorry for this. It's been a pleasure." He extended a slightly shaky and clammy hand. Marvin glared and waved Sr. off with both hands before shambling towards the door.

"Goodbye, to all. And a 'fuck you' to you, Mazetti." Marvin paused and turned for a double-barreled salute before finishing his exit. Geraldine stood up. The sweet familiar old smile never left the woman's face. She's a saint, Sr. thought to himself. She walked to Sr. and wrapped him up in a warm embrace. She rubbed his arms and gave her usual reassurances.

"It'll be okay, baby. You take care of that pretty wife of yours and your boy; it'll all be okay, honey." Sr. returned her warm hug. It felt so nice and genuine. Mama Geraldine was the best thing to ever happen to the store. Losing her just felt like a crippling blow.

Sr. let go of the sweet old woman, and she stopped by the table for a splash more of juice before making her rounds to all remaining coworkers, excluding Marvin, who was already firing up his old Trans Am and peeling out of Mazetti's for the final time, as a worker anyway. Geraldine walked out of the store, making sure to fold and leave her apron neatly on the counter upon her departure. She blew one more big collective kiss before leaving. And suddenly, a peculiar sadness engulfed the remainder of the staff. It was as if some kind of vital force or fuel had leaked out of the tank of the store, and nothing would ever move or operate the same way again. Next up at the plate was Glenda. Sr. simply motioned to her with his gaze, and she seemed to have known.

"I'm sorry, Glenda. I wish it didn't have to be this way." Glenda nodded and gave a slight smile. She hit the table for yet another sandwich. Sr. had no objections; the old girl had earned it, not necessarily for her work ethic or better yet, lack thereof, but simply because she was a sweet lady who meant well. She said her goodbyes and was wished well by the remaining crew. She left the store and silence again washed over the room. Throughout all of the departures, Ralph grumbled to himself and was outwardly sarcastic in attempting to mock Sr. in his dismissal of a chunk of his workforce. By this point, Sr. knew he would no longer take any joy in it. Perhaps he was wrong to assume he would have to begin with. "Ralph, I'm sorry. I fully intend to call everyone back once we're situated to do so." Ralph stood slowly, and Sr. could tell he was high.

"Save it, man. I can make more money working anywhere else. Fuck your shitty store. I hope you go under." Sr. expected some level of conflict, but not quite to this extent. Something within the man snapped. He smacked Ralph's goofy glasses right off of his smug face. The blow had Ralph staggering and surprised all of the employees watching as much as it did Ralph. Sr. couldn't believe it himself. He recoiled, beginning to apologize when Ralph struck back. The shot was square on Sr.'s nose, and a trickle of blood immediately streamed out. "Fuck you, fuck this!" Ralph exclaimed. "I'll knock this place off a hundred more times now. I'll make damn sure you go under now! Your bitch of a wife is going to get a new job on the corner, you fuck! Just to make sure your weak cuck ass can eat! Fuck you!" Sr. could feel the anger welling up once again but managed to contain it this time. It was clear that Ralph was fighting back tears as he scooped up his glasses. He made his exit, but not before toppling over the gift card display. Sr. took a moment more to compose himself before turning back to face what was left of his staff, all of which were evidently jarred by the interaction.

"Alright, show is over. Business as usual, before I decide to make any more cuts," he belted out with a confidence that evaded him the last twenty minutes, at a time when he needed it the most. The workers scattered, beginning their daily routines in the store. Sr. looked on for a moment more before retreating to his office. Raquel would be in soon, and that was all he could think about in that moment.

Chapter 6

Shiloh slept through all three alarms. His father was nowhere to be found. Even if he was home, he would probably be too tanked to drive his boy to school anyway, which was a good enough reason to stay home as any, in Shiloh's mind. He scavenged the cupboards and found a pack of Pop-Tarts. The expiration date of the pre-packaged breakfast was not of concern to him. He threw them in the toaster and grabbed a paper towel to serve as a plate. Many would look at Erik's home, what was his home, and think that the Serlings were slumming it, but in comparison to the Robertsons, they were living in a penthouse suite on Park Ave. Shiloh chowed down his breakfast pastries and decided to try to locate Dad. It was very possible he was still at the track in Michigan, or at the residence of a certain lady of the night. Either way, it would only be a matter of time before Shiloh began to worry. Shiloh kicked around the piles of laundry on the floor of his bedroom, looking for something that could pass as clean. He found a pair of ripped jeans and a hoodie. He threw them on quick and slipped into his boots, hand-me-downs from Dad. He laced them and grabbed a cigarette from his stash before stepping outside.

"Dad!" He called from the small stoop. A few neighbors were also out smoking, one being Mrs. Hadley. Upon hearing Shiloh's call, she waved him over. Shiloh scampered down the cracked-up concrete steps and jogged toward the sweet lady. Mrs. Hadley was an old, plump woman. She recently lost her left foot due to her diabetes, but that didn't even seem to deter her from her contributing habits, such as smoking and ordering a pizza five nights a week. She was kind, and Shiloh and Dad would often help her with small repairs around her trailer. She was like a grandmother figure to a lot of the trailer park kids.

She lived not truly alone, as she enjoyed the company of her four cats, but she had not cohabitated with another human being since her husband, Dud, passed away due to the unrelenting wrath of lung cancer just three summers prior. Shiloh approached her small porch, and she pushed her wispy gray hair out of her face.

"Hey, honey," she said, almost out of breath despite the fact she had been sitting down for a solid half-hour.

"Hey, Mrs. Hadley. How we doin'," Shiloh responded, plopping down on her steps.

"I'm fine, I just heard you calling for your daddy was all. When I got up, I noticed him out the window. He was getting into a big white truck, like an Explorer or sumthin'. Was barely dressed, still had his slippers on, I think." She began to wheeze and took another puff of her Pall Mall. Shiloh tried to recall any of Dad's friends who drove a white truck or SUV, but nothing was registering. He asked Mrs. Hadley to use her phone and she gladly obliged. Shiloh crushed out his cigarette and stepped inside. The cats, who first suspected their mom to be the one to enter, scattered upon seeing the boy. Shiloh made his way to the corded phone which was mounted near the fridge. Although his own phone was out of service due to not being paid on time, like always, he still rummaged through his pockets for it to retrieve his father's number. He dialed it and after the seventh ring he heard his dad's voice, somewhat garbled on his end.

"Hello, hello!" Kurt demanded sharply. Shiloh hesitated for a moment before speaking.

"Dad, it's just me. I'm at Mrs. Hadley's. Where are you?" More jumbled garbling on his father's end. "Dad, what? What's going on?" The response was much more clear this time.

"I just had some friends pick me up, bud. I had to go to the bank and pick up a few things, was all. Car's alternator is fuckin' up or something, I don't know. I'll look when I get home. I won't be long, bud. I'm okay. It's all okay." Shiloh felt a moment's relief.

"Okay, Dad. Well just so you know now I'm missing school today."

"Sorry bud, I know. When I'm home we'll cook up a real convincing doctor's note together, like we always do. It'll be alright." Shiloh chuckled slightly.

"Okay, Dad. I'm gonna walk to the store and get a few things, you want something?" An uneasy silence fell on the phone line. Shiloh was about to repeat himself when his dad finally answered.

"No, son, just take care of yourself. I'll be home soon, kay?"

"Alright, Dad." Shiloh was moving the phone from his ear to hang up when he heard, 'I love you, Shiloh.' Shiloh was torn between hanging up and responding. He pulled the phone back to reciprocate but got a dead tone in return. Dad hung up. Shiloh hung the phone up as well and turned to make his exit. Mrs. Hadley was standing in the doorway, a display of concern was evident on her wrinkled, chubby old face.

"He seems okay," Shiloh told Mrs. Hadley, trying to convince himself as well. Mrs. Hadley shuffled back out onto the porch. Her prosthetic foot and cane clicked simultaneously on the yellowed linoleum on her way out. The pair arrived back on the stoop and Mrs. Hadley hugged Shiloh, reassuring him of his worries. Shiloh said his goodbyes and skipped back down the porch steps to his own trailer. Once he was inside, an idea crossed his mind. He reached for the key hook and snagged the keys to his dad's Dodge Avenger. He hustled back outside and made his way to the rusty green car. He unlocked it and sat in the driver seat. Hesitantly, he slipped the key into the ignition and turned. The car started and turned over with no problem. He let it idle for a bit before shutting it off, and he continued to sit in the beat-down car, affectionately nicknamed the "Green Goblin", for a few more minutes. His level of concern multiplied after discovering that his father blatantly lied to him. He retreated back into the trailer once more and retrieved some money to make a trek on foot to Mazetti's. An entire twenty-seven dollars was scraped together before Shiloh departed for his shopping trip. This would easily cover the cost of several boxes of Ramen noodles, a handful of snacks, and a few two-liters of pop. The young boy began his mile-long voyage and lit up another cigarette. His route was very simple. After exiting the trailer park and taking a right onto Buchanan Road, he would stay on that for a half-mile or so, before taking a left onto Main. From there, he would continue another half-mile before reaching the store on his left. The entire trip he kept replaying his conversation with Dad. He sounded so uncomfortable, which just wasn't characteristic of him, ever. Shiloh tried his best to brush it off, but a lingering concern kept intruding his thoughts. He couldn't help but feel that Dad was in some shit; he almost knew it. After some time, Shiloh arrived at Mazetti's, which looked barren as ever. He grabbed a small cart and began cruising the aisles for what he needed. Within a half-hour, he accumulated all that he came for, and then some. He made his way to the only open checkout lane, which was indeed open, as there was no other customer in line or remotely near it. The cashier, a college-aged girl named Holly, leaned at the register, immersed in her phone. Shiloh saw her a handful of times before and thought she was simply gorgeous. She was petite with shoulder-length wavy blonde hair. Her summer tan was beginning to fade, but she still had a noticeable sun-kissed bronze to her complexion. Her blue skinny jeans, which had a few rips above the knees, really accentuated her round little bubble butt, not that it needed help from a pair of pants in the first place. She looked up from her game of Words with Friends momentarily to give Shiloh a generic and disinterested greeting.

"Hi, find everything ok?" Shiloh nervously piled the contents of his cart onto the checkout conveyor, now slightly embarrassed that his purchases were a clear indicator of his level of white trashiness, as if his dirty and tattered clothing wasn't already a dead giveaway.

"Uh, yeah, I think so." He internally cringed at his reply. Holly set her phone down and gave a slight smile and began ringing each item up individually. She already saw the month supply of Ramen noodles, so Shiloh threw caution to the wind and reached for the candy display above the conveyor and threw a couple of Reese's Cups on the belt as well. Holly smiled once more.

"Those have always been my favorite." Shiloh looked up, making direct eye-contact for the first time during the whole exchange.

"Oh, yeah, mine too. Me and my dad could survive on those things." Holly giggled and began bagging the boxed Ramen and Mountain Dew. Shiloh glanced up at the total on the register display after a few more items were scanned and began to feel a bit apprehensive. Nineteen dollars and eighty-seven cents and counting. Granted, math was never the boy's strong suit, but he felt fairly certain that his funds would have covered everything upon reaching the register. After the Reese's, the total read twenty-six seventy-nine, and this thankfully included tax. Shiloh felt that he could finally unclench his ass cheeks. Holly read off the total, and Shiloh confidently reached into his wallet, pulling out the cash. He handed it over and Holly counted it and got him his change. She placed it in his hand, and at that moment, Shiloh felt as if he was on a higher astral plane. Even though it was only fingertips, it was something. "Thank you." She smiled at him as he was loading his purchases back into the cart. The next challenge would be to escape the store with the cart. Whenever Shiloh made a trip on foot and it was more than he could carry, Mr. Mazetti was always more than understanding about Shiloh pushing the cart back to his house to deliver the groceries, so long as the cart was returned, which it always was. Obviously, Holly couldn't see this. Shiloh was as cool as possible about it. He began to depart the checkout lane when he heard that angelic voice once again.

"I think eggs are the best." He turned back around to face Holly.

"Huh," he was clearly confused. Holly reiterated.

"The eggs that they make around Easter, the Reese's. They have like the perfect ratio of chocolate to peanut butter. Those are my favorite." She flashed her pearly white smile once more. Shiloh stood for a moment, just admiring all that she was. He finally responded.

"Yeah, I've always said that too! It's like the perfect balance, isn't it?" He sounded almost too excited. Holly giggled again.

"Yeah, they definitely are. Well, bye, uh," she paused, clearly hinting for Shiloh to give his name.

"Bye," he cluelessly responded. The boy turned and pushed the cart to the exit, before realizing his error. "Fuck," he mumbled. Against his better judgement, he returned to Holly's register without his cart to introduce himself, only to see her walking toward the "Employees Only" door, and Lord Almighty, her backside was equally as pretty. "Fuck it," Shiloh muttered under his breath, before belting out, "Shiloh! My name's Shiloh." Holly paused right as she was about to push the door open. She smiled at him again, and Shiloh felt some kind of tremor in his heart, one that he had never felt in his nearly sixteen years.

"I was just going to call you "Reese's Guy", but I think I like "Shiloh" better. I'm Holly." Her smile never wavered as she entered the break room. Shiloh's never vacated his face as he exited the store. The trailer trash lover boy made it a good quarter mile away from the shop with only thoughts of Holly

47

and her curvy caboose in his head before stepping back into reality. That reality was his father seemed to be in a sketchy situation, and Shiloh was left in the dark about it. The late morning autumnal sun warmly cast its light upon Shiloh's pale face. Despite the friendly weather, Shiloh was plagued with ominous thoughts. Dad never sounded so strange, even when heavily drunk. There was just an overall dreadful tone and aura in his speech. It was something completely foreign. Kurt Robertson may not have amounted to much in the eyes of many, but he was at least a man of confidence. And he was especially bold with this confidence when speaking to his boy. The trailer park was within sight now, and Shiloh quickened his pace a bit. He pushed the cart through the gravel and grass, arriving at his trailer. To his surprise, the door was open, but the screen door was still shut, and he knew he shut both before departing for the store. A figure swayed in the darkness, just beyond the reach of the light which shone through the door's window. Shiloh began to pump the brakes before coming to a complete halt with Mr. Mazetti's cart just feet before the porch steps.

"Dad," he called out. The shape ceased its back-and-forth motion and stood still. A few seconds passed and Shiloh was about to repeat himself when whoever was inside the house shuffled to the door. A familiar face appeared in the window. It was Dad after all. Shiloh felt the weight of the world suddenly evaporate from his shoulders. He completely neglected the cart of groceries and leapt up the stairs, throwing open the screen door all in one motion. Kurt took a step back and a wide, absent-toothed smile spread across the old hillbilly's face. His unlit cigarette dropped right out of his mouth, but he didn't seem to mind. The two greeted one another with a warm embrace and Shiloh began to cry. He absolutely hated to, especially in front of his father, but there was no helping it. Quickly following the feelings of relief and gratitude for his father's well-being, Shiloh felt somewhat angry. He brushed this aside and held his father. A few moments passed before Kurt decided he should be the one to speak first, as he had something to explain. Kurt lit his cigarette and began loading his son's excuse for a grocery haul into their home. The duo decided to walk back to Mazetti's together to return the cart, and this would be the ideal time to talk. However, after multiple steps out of the trailer park lot, neither had so much as spoken a word. Kurt finally broke the silence.

"So, son, I'm in some hot water now. Long story short, I borrowed a lot, I mean a lot, of money. For the gamblin', for the bottle, even to pay our rent. I'm not proud and I don't 'spect you to be either, but I'm just givin' it to ya straight." Shiloh slowed his pace, handle of the shopping cart still in his grasp. Kurt took the cart in an attempt to alleviate some of the burden he was placing on his son. He decided to answer the question Shiloh had without being prompted, verbally, anyway.

"Just over thirteen grand." Kurt glanced down at his shoes through the grating of the rickety little cart. He was far too ashamed. This news stopped Shiloh in his tracks. The anger resurfaced, and he made no effort to conceal it this time.

"You're fuckin' kiddin' me? Dad, how could it get so bad? How?" Kurt paused as well. He knew the cat was out of the bag. The time for transparency was then and there.

"I have these vices, son. Ones I hope to God that you never inherit. I don't know how to make 'em go away. When I win big, I feel like it's all alright. I feel like ain't nothing wrong with the world. Some kinda high that beats everything else in life. But when I lose out, it's just the opposite. I just dig the hole deeper and deeper each time. I know I do. I know I gotta stop, too." Shiloh clasped his hands and placed them on top of his head. Kurt stood in silence for a while. He didn't know what else he could possibly say. He let down the most important person to ever exist in his life, and he never felt worse about anything before. Shiloh finally brought his hands back down to his sides, taking a deep breath in the process. He knew his father was going through it, and he could either try to help the best he could or stay pissed off and make them both even more miserable. He elected the former. He wrapped his pale skinny arms around his father, and the two stood together for a few moments. Kurt couldn't help but let out a small laugh, out of sheer relief. He had enough on his plate without his son detesting him. Having Shiloh in his corner was half the battle in the broken-down father's eyes. The two knew they didn't have much, but so long as they had each other, it was always enough. The pair resumed their walk to return Mr. Mazetti's cart together. They soon approached the store and Shiloh briefed his father on the interaction he had with a certain young lady earlier in the day, and asked Kurt if he would be so kind as to return the cart himself while Shiloh hung back a bit. Kurt had no qualms with this, and he naturally had to try to get a peek of Holly as he was bringing the cart back inside. Shiloh stood at the far end of the parking lot, out of view from any of the front windows. Kurt emerged with a pack of cigarettes and a smile on his face. He began packing the smokes onto the palm of his hand, his smile never leaving. Shiloh felt a little nervous.

"That little blonde thing, huh boy," Kurt chuckled as he opened his pack and flipped his lucky cigarette upside down, sliding it back into its place.

"What'd you say, Dad," Shiloh groaned.

"Nothin', nothin'!" Kurt reassured him. "She didn't even see me. Lucky for you." He gave Shiloh a playful shove which invoked one in return and resulted in both of them laughing together. They began their walk home together. Both men were scared, but both knew they had no other option but to face what was coming, whatever that may be, head on. They made the most of the rest of their day together.

Chapter 7

Reg was awake earlier than any other sophomore at Castalia High, and that could be attributed to a number of reasons. However, Reg convinced himself it was due solely to pregame jitters for the task which awaited him on Friday night. Each morning, he woke at four at the very latest to get his first workout in. This consisted of mainly heavy weights for low repetitions and a cool-down period on his stationary bike. The finished basement at 151 Tubult Lane housed quite the impressive home gym, which Mr. Steve Bousher was still financing. The sole member of this gym certainly got his use out of it, though. Reg was finishing up on the bike and going over all of the messages from Erik in the group chat. It was hard to feel glad for his friend escaping such a tumultuous situation knowing he now had no place to call his own home. At least Maron and his mom have some extra help around their house now, Reg reassured himself. Maybe Maron can actually show up to school more than once a week now. The young running back finished up his workout just after 4:30, which left him plenty of time for a shower and breakfast. His parents were still not up, so he was sure to be as quiet as he could. He showered off and threw on some jeans and a band t-shirt. He came downstairs and shuffled around in the fridge for his breakfast, which was prepped days ago. Reg heated up the two burritos and reached for his whey powder on top of the fridge. As he finished mixing up his shake, the microwave sounded and he pulled out his food. He carried his meal up to his room and sat down to enjoy it while scrolling Twitter. Durand was usually awake by now, but Reg held off on texting him. He really should start taking his workouts a little more seriously, Reg thought, and spared him any distraction. He finished his lukewarm breakfast burritos and took the plate down to the sink. His father joined him in the kitchen shortly after.

"Morning, son. You been up a while?"

"For a little, yeah. Are you or is Mom taking me?"

"Uh, I can, if you want. Let me get some coffee going and we'll head out." Steve was not much of a morning person, and Reg could never help but wonder if his biological father was. Mr. Bousher lackadaisically got his coffee supplies around as he fired up the Keurig. The longer Reg watched him sluggishly move about with no real intent or purpose, the more irritated he became. Steve was not a very active man. He lived a sedentary lifestyle, worked a boring job, and never really did much to win over the respect and admiration of his son. The two didn't share much common ground at all, but that isn't what really caused the divide that they both felt. It was the fact that Steve Bousher was a complacent loser, and his son had all the drive in the world to be a success. Of course, this is what any father wants to see out of his child, but witnessing these traits in his own son was some kind of alien and unrelatable concept to Steve, as he never possessed any of these attributes himself. This was undoubtedly the root cause of the strain in their relationship. They got along well enough, though. They interacted with one another amicably enough. Both of them put on the act that they were interested in one another's lives and activities, when in reality neither one was. In a way, Reg had a better realization of this fact than Steve did. But nonetheless, he played along. Steve brewed a cup of generic coffee, added his cream and sugar and sat across from his son. The two made small talk while Steve sipped his coffee and Reg his Gatorade. Reg discussed the changes in the Ice Cats' starting lineup while Steve gave his piece on prepping for the upcoming tax season. Once finished with their beverages, the duo packed up and headed out to the car. The commute to school was mostly quiet and uneventful. Steve wished Reg a good day as they pulled up to the main entrance. Reg returned the remark and exited the car, slinging his pack over his shoulder and closing the door. The custodians usually kept an eye on the entrances to let students in early, the ones who weren't reputable troublemakers, anyway. The entrance was unlocked, and Steve verified this before pulling off and potentially leaving his son stranded. Reg threw one last glance at his father, a look of contempt disguised as thankfulness, and walked into the school. The school was scarcely occupied at this hour, save for the janitorial staff and a handful of teachers. Reg was typically the only student arriving at this time. He liked to utilize this peaceful stretch to complete his assignments, as he's usually too busy after school each day. It is not uncommon for Durand to arrive this early as well, but he typically starts his day in the football team's weight room. The small apartment he occupies with his mother and siblings isn't spacious enough to accommodate a home gym, like Reg's, and his mother's salary certainly isn't capable of providing the equipment. Rather than bother Reg's parents to come over each day, Durand opts to train his mornings away in the school's facility. He usually joins Reg in the library after he showers off. On Reg's itinerary for the morning was a packet of questions for his biology class, and if after completing this he has the time or motivation, he intended to work ahead in reading his copy of Leaves of Grass. Reg made his way to the school's spacious and generously stocked library. He liked it there. It was clean, quiet and everything that is typical of a library. When he felt up to it, he would grab a yellowed old paperback off one of the dozens of shelves, usually at random, and just submerse himself, oft times halfway or later, into the story. Reg enjoyed reading, but felt he never had sufficient time to start and finish something cover to cover. He just liked to get his toes wet with it, and with no real intent of ever finishing an entire book, he engaged in this strange practice. There was no real commitment. Upon reaching the main entrance to the vast collection of Knowledge, he noticed that Durand was already seated at their usual spot. Reg entered and took his chair across the table from his very best friend but was greeted with a concentrated silence. Durand was hurriedly scribbling the final answers in the same biology packet that Reg was yet to conquer. With a prompt and exasperated sigh, Durand folded the packet back to its original state and pushed it across the table for Reg to copy. Well, almost copy. The boys were too wise to allow their answers to look too similar to one another's.

"Dude," Reg began, "How much coffee did you have this morning?"

"None, actually. Just been too hyped since yesterday," Durand replied. "Barely slept, just been too excited. Now I have that much more reason to stay on the eligibility list. Biology has been kicking my ass and I gotta maintain that "C" average. I found this page on Quizlet though and it had all the answers for this very same packet. Just change a few and we should be good." Reg rolled his eyes and was able to summon a half-smile. He copied roughly three-quarters of Durand's plagiarized work and threw a couple of multiple-choice questions to not look too suspicious. Biology was one of his strongest subjects, so he could afford a "B" from time to time. If he really made an honest attempt, he would've had an easy "A", but at the moment, he just couldn't force himself to care enough.

"You hear from anyone yet," Reg inquired.

"Just that Erik and his mom are staying with Maron. Sounds like his fucking psycho dad got out of control again. When I hear shit about him, I'm almost glad I never knew my own father, you know," Durand replied.

"I can completely relate. Fucking Steve, man. Dude is the most bland and ordinary guy to ever live. No interests, no passions, just goes through the motions of being an accountant, making enough to cover bills and buy groceries, going to bed and waking up only to do it all over again. Like he's completely fucking fine with it. If I was never told I was adopted, I think I would've discovered it on my own by now. Like, wouldn't you want and expect more out of life? Just the same routine day in and out would kill me. My biggest fear is becoming that." Reg looked around the room, after noticing he began to raise his voice as he spoke more excitedly about the topic. The only other person, the librarian, Mrs. Acox, seemed to not notice. The pair rambled on a bit longer, regarding a variety of topics ranging in seriousness and severity. They carried on this way until it was almost time to head to first period. After visiting their respective lockers, the boys were astonished to see Erik walking towards Mrs. Crockett's English class, with Shiloh in tow. Then came Damien, and the greatest surprise of all, Maron. It seemed it was the first day in quite some time where all boys were present and accounted for. A small stream of mostly cheerful bullshitting erupted amongst the six, until the warning bell rang, and everyone went to their first period class. It appeared to each one of them, in so many words, in one way or another. But a pleasant thought passed through each boy's mind, which more or less was, 'It can't rain forever.'

Surely enough, the gang reunited for lunch. They congregated at their usual table. Connie De La Rosa made her usual snooty pass, and Shiloh did something gross to hurry her along. Erik wasn't even the least bit irritated this time. Everyone was just glad to feel a sense of normalcy once again. Shiloh went into great detail of his flirtatious encounter with the hot blonde at Mazetti's. Damien interjected several times before finally calling bullshit on the entire story.

"It's true, you ask her!" Shiloh began getting defensive.

"I'm not going to ask her about an entirely made-up story of yours just so she can look at me like I'm an idiot. Never happened, just drop it." Damien often got jealous upon hearing of his comrades' romantic endeavors and conquests, especially coming from Shiloh, who was inarguably the least charming guy in The Club. Banter continued, both witty and not so witty. Erik opened up about the altercation between himself and his father. Maron's turn came and he shared that his mother was not in the worst of shape, and the pair remained hopeful. Damien casually mentioned that his father had to lay off due to slow business. Upon hearing the news, Shiloh became alarmed, worrying that the lady he was now courting was out of a job and possibly he would never see her again. But Damien reassured him that bubble-butt Holly was safe. Reg and Durand cut in with their sports segment, and the group collectively congratulated Durand on the starting spot. As usual, the athletes of the group cut lunch short to meet up with their coach with a few minutes to spare before the bell. Coach Grenslait confirmed that everything would go according to plan, and Durand would definitely start that Friday's game. It was almost as if Durand had to hear it multiple times. It wasn't real unless it was reassured daily. He refused to believe it if it wasn't. After this brief conference with Grenslait, the boys left for their next class. The other four convened in the main hallway after school was dismissed as Reg and Durand headed out to the locker room to get ready for practice. Damien received a text message from his mother stating that the store closed early that day, and he was free to do as he pleased on his day off. This was all he needed to hear. Plans were made to go back to Maron's house and pack a bowl. His mother would surely be asleep. The quartet made their way swiftly down Limerick Road. Erik and Maron were generous enough to lend their bikes to Shiloh and Damien after so long, and they trotted along to keep up. The boys approached the park and as sure as the sun rises each day, Bose was in his usual spot, shitty music blaring out of his speakers. He completely silenced this once he saw them coming. He waved them over.

Erik, who was still on foot and assumed he meant only him, began to trot towards, but when Bose shook his head and irritably waved him away, Erik stopped in his tracks. Bose raised a pudgy, tattooed brown hand and pointed to Damien, and Damien alone. He rotated his hand a hundred and eighty degrees and made the "come here" gesture with his four fat ashy fingers. Damien pumped the brakes on the bike and now stood as still as Erik. A few seconds had passed when Bose finally became vocal.

"Get your greasy goomba ass over here!" The Club, with its share of ethnic diversity, often cracked light-hearted jokes about one another's background, but Bose wasn't joking. He never was. Damien slowly dismounted the bike, and neglecting the kickstand, he let it fall to its side. He slowly trudged to where Bose was parked. Another vehicle was parked beside him. In this second vehicle sat Ralph Reirke. Damien recognized him instantly. He knew damn well what had transpired between Ralph and his father but was fully prepared to play the dumbest of the dumb. He reached Bose, who was now shuffling to meet Ralph after exiting his own car. "You know this man," Bose gruffly barked out while motioning to Ralph. Ralph crushed out his cigarette on the gravel and walked around the hood of his beater, so he was in full view of Damien.

"Uh, I uh, think he works at our store." Damien began to feel his legs shake. He hated confrontation.

"You thought incorrectly, little man. He did, emphasis on 'did' work at your store. Your old man gave him the boot today. Even hit him." Bose began taking his rings and watch off. This didn't bode well for The Club.

"I, uh, didn't know anything about that. That's pretty fucked up, I'm sorry guys." Damien tried his damnedest to sound sincere with the apology, but it wasn't in the least bit passable.

"You are, huh? Why don't you go over and shake the man's hand, then? Something your father wasn't man enough to do." Damien could feel the anger swelling inside him but had to play it safe. He didn't like the chances of the four of them beating down Bose alone, especially not Bose and a friend. He cooperated, and at a more quickened pace than before, walked over to Ralph, who already had a hand extended. He looked him in the eye, through those Coke-bottled lenses, and extended his own sweaty and trembling hand. Ralph took it firmly and shook it twice. But he didn't let go. He pulled Damien into a bearhug and applied a tremendous squeeze on the boy's upper back until Damien could feel things pop. Shiloh jumped off the bike he was on and darted towards Ralph as he released Damien, who crumpled to a heap on the gravel, trying his hardest to suck back his tears and regain his breath. Shiloh threw a wild right which missed Ralph by fractions of the inch. Ralph laughed heartily and motioned for Shiloh to repeat the move. Shiloh threw another haymaker and this time connected with Ralph's already heavily taped spectacles. Erik and Maron were on the heels of Bose, who was scurrying around his own car, trying to make it to the driver side door. Any alliance between Erik and Bose was terminated at this point. Seeing his best friend endure pain, even indirectly, at the hand of Bose was more than enough for Erik. He knew he could find shitty weed elsewhere. Bose turned to backpedal, and eventually tripped thanks to his baggy sweatpants. Maron took the opportunity to pounce on his much larger foe. Meanwhile, Ralph lay folded up next to Damien, and Shiloh delivered a series of vicious kicks to his torso. Shiloh was by far the boys' greatest weapon. He didn't possess the speed that Erik did, or the strength of Durand, but the boy was just plain fucking crazy. When he saw red, he simply meant to inflict pain. And nothing induced this condition quite like seeing a friend or member of his family being hurt. Maron delivered a few downward fists into Bose's face, and Erik played his part with a few kicks and spits as well.

"Fuck you, fuck your garbage ass weed! Hurt my friends again and I swear it to God, I'll fucking kill you!" The leader of The Club tugged at Maron's shirtsleeve, and he ascended from his full mount position over Bose's fat and battered body, who was now bloodied and near tears himself.

"Well fuck you little bitches too! Buncha pussy faggots. Not over! Fucking know that!" Bose propped himself up on one elbow and quickly wiped the start of tears from his eyes. All this time Shiloh acted as a man possessed. Ralph was turned over onto his stomach and Shiloh had his knee driven into the small of his back, while clutching at Ralph's left arm. He would have detached it from its socket had Erik and Maron not pulled him off. Damien was on his feet now as well. He spat on the back of Ralph's head without a word, and Erik carried him off. He acted as a crutch for Damien, while Maron and Shiloh gathered the bikes. They climbed on, and the boys were barely across the street when they heard the roar of Bose's car starting up. Ralph lay in a bloody heap, and the Chrysler was put into motion. All four of the boys had the morbid collective thought of being ran over. But both traffic and passersby prevented this from happening. Had there been no witnesses to the whole ordeal, it was a very highly likely possibility that Bose would've committed vehicular manslaughter on children. Eventually an older man out jogging, who Damien recognized as a semi-regular at Mazetti's, stopped to see if the boys were alright. Shiloh was the one to reply, with his usual goofy grin.

"You should be asking the other guys." He motioned back to Ralph, who was just now stirring. Bose and his car were nowhere in sight.

Chapter 8

The boys hobbled the entire way to Maron's house. His mother was, thankfully, asleep in her room. The wounded patched each other up with gauze and ice and went down into the basement to spark Erik's bowl. Damien certainly received the worst of it, on The Club's end, anyway. He was still short of breath and felt a bizarre sharp pain in his upper back each time he tried to deeply inhale. The other three boys were just nursing minor scrapes and swollen knuckles, which were the best possible injuries to result from such an altercation. Shiloh's right hand was badly swollen. Ralph's glasses broke and cut into his fingers.

"Wait till Daddy sees this shit!" Shiloh said with a grin, holding up his puffy hand. He could stand tall that day with little explanation to his father. The Robertsons were scrappers, and such an injury would illicit a proud pat on the back from Kurt. The other three, however, were not as fortunate. They would have to go to great lengths to hide their ripped clothes and battle scars from their parents, or else face a long line of interrogation. Damien definitely had it the worst, both as a result of the fight as well as in the explanation to Mom and Dad department. The gang plopped down on the couch in Maron's basement. Erik lit the bowl and upon finishing his toke passed it left to Damien, who inhaled deeply, despite the pain. The boys knew they were safe here, as Maron's mother never came downstairs to what she called "the cellar". Aside from the porch steps, she avoids stairs altogether. If, and grimly, that's a big "if", she ever got better, the smell should surely clear out by then. The bowl made its rotation several times and the boys sat mostly in silence.

"Imagine if we had Durand and Reg there. Shit, just Reg alone," Maron said with a smirk. "Boy is a fuckin' pit bull." After a few moments Damien chimed in, almost wheezingly.

"Durand could've done some damage too." Shiloh now.

"Shit, he's too much a pretty boy. I mean I know he would've fought for us, he's our best friend. But he don't like getting his hands dirty. Lookit the way he plays. He don't get down and dirty 'less he has to. Reg on the other hand, Jesus. Y'all think I'm crazy, I wouldn't wanna trade hands with that boy. He can get mean as fuck. Glad he's on our side." Shiloh concluded his monologue by choking on his puff. He passed the glass bowl back to Erik, who cashed it out and repacked it.

"They'll be glad to hear about it, I'm sure," Erik spoke quietly before lighting the fresh bowl. The boys burned through most of Erik's stash, before scaling back up the basement steps. Erik's mother was interviewing for a position at the new Norhauk Wal-Mart and would be due back shortly. Although she had no business going into the basement of a house she was a grateful guest at, Erik and Maron went through the Febreeze routine, spraying thoroughly. Damien made it a habit to sneak a couple bottles of the stuff out of storage at his parents' store weekly. As it wasn't cheap, comments would often be made by his parents when a whole bottle would mysteriously come up missing. Damien and Shiloh departed, both having to foot it home. Damien rehearsed his greeting to his parents and tried his best to hide any inkling of pain or physical injury. The reefer he partook of helped to ease the pain, but this relief wouldn't last forever. Moments like these, he envied Shiloh in a way. He didn't have to explain much, he wasn't expected to explain much. He was a simpleton with a simpleton father who probably would've been too drunk upon hearing the news that his boy was in a fight that day to react with the least bit concern. How the other side lives, Damien thought. Raquel nearly shits a brick if Damien struggles to finish dinner and Sr. is ever the quickest to cast blame on too much television or spending too long staring at a computer screen if the boy complains of a headache. They worry because they care, Damien recited silently. The two parted ways once they reached Maple. Damien ventured on toward the Victorian-style homes of the old section of town and Shiloh in the direction of a shell of a trailer park. All was right with the world. And both Durand and Reg were soon wise to the feat which their brothers in arms had undertaken that afternoon. In fact, before it was fully dark that evening, a good percentage of the school was aware of the smackdown that Erik and company left lay in their wake. And as it is in small towns, the parents of all those affected would soon know too. Despite this and whatever repercussions or restrictions the boys would face at home, they knew that publicly, they could wear this one with pride. Erik greeted Sarah upon her return from the interview. She was beyond excited. Gloria was even sure to be awake to greet her friend and listen to her recount the tale of her first job interview in years. Neither mother paid hardly a thought to the fact that, despite it being rather warm in the house, both of their sons donned hoodies and sweatpants. The boys suffered the warm discomfort, a small price to pay to conceal the multiple abrasions and scrapes which they had sustained in battle only hours prior. The four of them sat down to a fried chicken dinner provided by Sarah, which she picked up, rather discretely at that, at the deli counter after her interview was over. Maron found a movie on Netflix and Gloria and Sarah each poured themselves a glass of merlot to enjoy the flick with, while the boys retreated to Maron's room to play on his Xbox. It was not uncommon for Reg to join them a little later in the evening, but that night they were not so fortunate. Damien would sometimes join the party as well, but not on this particular night. When Damien arrived home, he found it odd that the house was so quiet, despite both cars being in the driveway and most of the lights on. There was no indication that dinner was underway yet, either. This was always easy to distinguish as Raquel's culinary masterpieces possess the power to make their presence known throughout the entire dwelling. Just the week prior, their neighbor, Mr. Martin, paid his compliments to Mrs. Mazetti and her baked ziti when he visited the shop the following day.

"I was outside raking leaves and all I could smell was that pasta cooking," he praised. Raquel thanked him and smiled as she noticed that his cart was full of pasta sauce, spices and noodles. His would not come out nearly the same, Raquel thought, but she encouraged him regardless. Damien ascended the staircase, rather gingerly. His parents' bedroom door was open but a crack, and he approached it with the stealth of a foreign assassin. He peered in, hesitantly at first, but reassured himself that his parents most likely were not in the act of making whoopee at the time. He saw Sr., bottle in hand, and Raquel skimming the pages of one of her magazines. They were laid out in bed with the lights dimmed. Damien didn't so much mind that his father drank at times, but he hated seeing him with a whole fifth in his palm. He at least wished when his father got drunk that he gave off the appearance of a sophisticated man. He may as well have been Kurt Robertson in that moment. On second thought, Kurt Robertson most likely couldn't come up with the funds for a bottle that night and probably spent the evening sober, much to his own dismay. This troubled Damien. He stood in silence at the edge of the room, waiting for someone to speak. After several minutes of complete silence, besides the flicking of pages on Raquel's part, Damien decided to enter. He gently pressed the door open and was greeted by the smiling face of his father.

"Heya, son! You out with your buddies," Sr. slurred. Raquel didn't bat an eye. Damien instantly grew uncomfortable.

"Uh, yeah, Dad. We went to Maron's to play his Xbox. It was a lot of fun." Sr. smiled and bobbed his head in somewhat of a nodding motion, pretending to comprehend what his son just told him.

"Did you speak with Mrs. Calhoun, dear," Raquel inquired. Her eyes never lifted from her copy of Good Housekeeping.

"Yep, she even had a glass of wine with Mrs. Serling. She seemed pretty happy. Maron was even at school today." The tension in the room felt like a lethal, noxious gas. Such an unauthentic level of conversation with his parents was not something Damien was used to. He was praying to God that Bootsy would make an unwanted appearance in his parents' room, and he would have an excuse to leave by picking her up and escorting her out.

"That's good, hon," Raquel replied dryly. "There's some rotisserie chicken downstairs if you're hungry. We'll be turning in soon. Don't be up late, okay love?" Sr. cackled at whatever it was he was half-watching on TV. Damien gave a weak smile in response to his mother, who never once made eye contact throughout the whole exchange. He backpedaled through the bedroom door and quietly shut it. Bootsy came scampering up the steps now, too little too late. Goddamn cat, Damien thought to himself. He scooped her up and slowly approached his room. Despite feeling the munchies kicking in, he just didn't feel up to eating. He crashed out on his bed and stripped off his clothes, which he intended to change before seeing his parents, as they were considerably dirty due to the fight. He caught a break, however, as this didn't matter in the slightest, considering Raquel couldn't look at him and Sr. was too drunk to even realize their condition. He checked his phone, hoping to see multiple new messages in the group text. All his screen greeted him with, however, was one message in the chat from Durand, inquiring if everyone was alright. Damien typed back a generic affirmative response, plugged his phone in for the night and drifted off. It was around this time that Shiloh Robertson was out on the stoop with his father, smoking his bedtime cigarette. The topic of their now greater financial struggles was only kicked around a couple more times that day, and both men decided it best to just sleep on it for the night and mull it over the following morning. Durand, too, was restless. He lay on the couch. His sister, Ramona, a tender-hearted little girl of four, rested her head on his chest and snored quietly. Durand's other sister, Breanna, age six, slept in her mother's bed with her. That was the only bedroom in the overcrowded apartment. It was quite common, when Durand was younger, for him to join his little family in bed with Mom. This was no longer typical. Durand's mother's name was Beatrix, and she was the youngest mother of any boy of The Club, barely in her thirties. She had Durand young and struggled plenty throughout his early childhood. Durand's excuse for a biological father was nearly twice Beatrix's age at the time of his conception. If the math adds up, it is clear she was taken advantage of as a young teenage girl, and the father, who Beatrix only ever knew as "Daryl", soon skipped town upon hearing the news that he knocked up an underage girl. Beatrix left it at that, and never once tried to get into contact with him. Rumors did circulate, however, that he overdosed when Durand was around Ramona's age now. Rumors, to many who reside in a small town, may have well been as credible as what is published in the local periodical, the Castalia Register. Regardless, Beatrix never shed a tear. Breanna and Ramona were fathered by the same man, Winston Cunningham. Winston was a younger black gentleman, a couple years Beatrix's junior, but was overall a decent guy who maintained a forty-plus hour per week job. He even took it upon himself to act as a fatherly figure to Durand, as well. He was initially responsible for piquing Durand's interest in football. He drew up simple routes for the two to practice at Limerick Park. They watched the Browns each Sunday afternoon in autumn; Winston even began a fund to purchase tickets to attend a home game together. This fund was depleted, however, largely in part to Winston getting behind in child support payments regarding his firstborn daughter by another woman. The whole idea was squashed shortly after its inception, but Durand appreciated the gesture anyway, as did Beatrix. Winston wasn't bad at all. But his undoing came over the summer that Durand was set to start middle school, three years prior to Our Story now. Winston had struck and killed an adolescent boy with his car and was found to be driving heavily impaired. He blew nearly three times the legal limit, and police found a substantial amount of cocaine in his vehicle as well. He is serving a thirty-year stint as Our Story unfolds. Beatrix and Durand both knew they would never forgive him had he ever got out. That is neither here nor there; what's here is Durand's jitters, the nervousness of finally starting a varsity game. If he hoped to get some amount of considerable rest, he knew he had to omit his morning workout, which he half-planned to do anyway to ensure he was amply rested for the showdown that following evening. The clock marched on, and the Ice Cats' newest superstar finally felt his eyes getting heavy. He slumbered a restless, dreamless sleep, and when he awoke at six in the morning, late for him, he carefully repositioned Ramona on the old GoodWill sofa, tiptoeing to the bathroom to start his day. After some serious anxiety shits and a hot shower, Durand emerged to try to eat a light breakfast. This was composed of two scrambled eggs and some wheat toast, which he struggled to finish. Beatrix was soon up and prepping herself for work. She was employed as a health inspector and made a semi-livable wage. Had she not three children to solely provide for, it would have been a fully-livable wage. She knew she had an easy day ahead of her, in the sense that there would be plenty of obvious violations to spot at the local Burger King.

"I promise you," Beatrix began once she saw her son in the tiny living room, "I will leave early if I have to. Me and the girls will be there, baby," she spoke as she pressed her hands up to Durand's handsome face, which he usually hated, but seemed to be just what he needed in the moment. He smiled at his mother, and she flashed her identical, beautiful pearly whites right back. The two hugged only for a moment, as Ramona saw and got jealous and interrupted with a squeeze of her own.

"Make room for me!" She wedged her little body between her two heroes and all three laughed. Breanna, who tried her hardest to give the appearance of disinterest, peeked her little head out of the bathroom door, as it was finally her turn, and was caught. She was ushered over by her family, and with a shy smile, she joined in as well. This transformed into a family huddle and break, with Ramona leading the chant. "Ice Cats on 'free', ready," her little hand was at the bottom of the pile.

"Ready!" All three replied, each putting a hand on top.

"Ready?" She repeated, as if she couldn't hear and wanted to illicit a bigger reaction.

"Ready!" The others repeated once more.

"One, two, 'free', Ice Cats! Whooooooo," she exclaimed, twirling about the little home. All members of the Desmond clan got a kick out of this and collapsed on top of one another on the raggedy old sofa, Durand's big frame on the bottom of the pileup, of course. It's crazy how days of nerves and borderline nausea can be remedied so quickly, with such a simple act of purity and bliss, Durand thought to himself. He wouldn't let his girls down.

Chapter 9

Reg only had a slight case of the pregame jitters that morning. He was considered the team's RB2, but saw a considerable amount of varsity time, even as a freshman the year before. He worked in with John Delks, a senior, who was considered, at least in Grenslait's mind, the stud running back for Castalia. Delks often missed practices and, in Reg's humble opinion, was riding on his past glories of his junior season to maintain his starting position. It didn't matter much though, as Reg got the ball often and after this season, he would be the big dog on campus. Delks was easy enough to play alongside. He was a nice enough guy, albeit not the brightest. He maintained straight "C"'s, with some help from Grenslait strongarming and, even once, bribing a teacher. He was hanging on the very edge of the eligibility list and had been doing so for the previous three years of his football career. Reg just worried about himself. That morning, like most others, he went through his routine of holding a dull conversation with Steve, waiting for him to make his damn cup of coffee, and then proceeded to suffer through another painfully dry car ride to school. Steve, however, did manage to throw a curveball during this commute. He noticed the new Hardee's burger joint was finally open as the family car turned onto Route 30. It already had a wraparound line waiting for breakfast sandwiches. He would recount this news to anyone who was kind or pitiful enough to pay him any attention at work that day. Reg arrived at school and headed straight for his usual seat in the library. Durand was just setting up shop there, slinging his backpack from his shoulders and hanging it from the back of his chair, as he always did. Reg entered the vast room of printed word and assumed his spot. Durand gave his usual greetings and, for the first few moments, both boys just sat there in silence, staring at what seemed to be the same piece of faint graffiti on the tabletop. Reg saw a very botched version of the video game character Kirby riding on his star, while Durand seemed to notice a misshaped cloud with oblong eyes. Finally, one boy decided to break the apprehensive silence. "You good," Reg inquired, half-smiling. Durand finally glanced up and the best friends made direct eye contact.

"Yeah, just nervous as fuck is all. I almost miss starting on JV, honestly." Durand slightly shook his head and began to smooth his goatee.

"Same fuckin' thing, man. JV, varsity. It doesn't matter. It's the same game we're going out to play. You wouldn't have got the call up if Coach didn't feel like you deserved it. And, believe me, you deserve it," Reg reassured his closest confidant, while rummaging through his pack for schoolwork that he was surely behind on.

"That's the thing, though. I got the call up because Marshall fucked up. I got the call up because I was the next best thing, not because I was first choice. Word around the campfire is dude got busted with coke. Henry Higgins said he saw him railing a line in the locker room two weeks ago and said something to Grenslait. Next day, they had him piss and he popped dirty for a bunch of shit, not just coke or weed. His parents fought it and he managed to not get forced into the rehab program at the church that the school "requires" to stay enrolled, at least. But word spread quick and Grenslait knew he had to do something to contain it all, so he kicked him off. I got here because of the better guy's bad choices. Not because of myself." Durand leaned back in his seat and clasped his hands on top of his head upon finishing his piece. Reg sat silently for a few seconds.

"I mean, I didn't know the extent of it. But it doesn't matter now. You're the face of this team, now. You're our leader. It doesn't matter how Marshall went out. It doesn't even matter that he's out of the picture now. You're here, he's not. Circumstances are irrelevant. You're it. You've got people counting on you to go out and do everything you can. I don't give a fuck if that means a blowout loss to Norhauk. All I care about is you giving everything like you always have. Sacrifice your all for our team and you win the game, each and every time in my eyes. Otherwise, last year on JV and riding the bench this season was all for nothing. You didn't put in the work to amount to that, and you know it. Let's man up, go out and put it to 'em." Reg concluded the pep talk by spilling a few drips of Gatorade on himself as he went to take a sip. Durand stared at him for a solid minute before finally shifting in his seat, then digging in his pocket for his phone. He turned around in his seat to face Mrs. Acox.

"Mrs. Acox, I hope you don't mind," he spoke with a smile. She smiled back, and before awaiting a verbal reply, Durand began to blast "Lose Yourself" by Eminem as loud as his Wal-Mart brand phone would allow. Reg could even swear that he saw the friendly, timid old widow bobbing her head to the song. Durand was never one for words, but responding with this action was all Reg needed. After all, he was a man of action, and he vowed to prove that on the football field that very evening. The duo pencil whipped as much as they possibly could of their history assignment before exiting the library together in the hopes of catching a glimpse of their other four friends before class commenced. Erik and company were spotted by Reg and Durand at their lockers. The six convened at Erik's and each began their briefing while there was still time. Shiloh was inquiring about cryptocurrency, and, admittedly, none of the boys were too knowledgeable on the topic, but they all agreed it was probably in Shiloh's best interest to just avoid it altogether. Erik shared that his mother was speaking with a landlord about an apartment on the outskirts of town later that afternoon, and all wished him well. Damien disclosed that his father was drunk as a skunk only the night before, and his mother has acted completely artificially regarding the family business taking a dive. He was no longer wheezing, at least. Maron told his friends that having Erik and Sarah in the house almost seemed to reinvigorate Gloria, and how for the first time in a while she managed to stay up past ten o'clock at night, as she chatted with Sarah and both mothers offered heartfelt words of strength and encouragement to one another in their own respective plights. The main collective focus for Reg and Durand was that night's game, and Durand's preparedness for it. All of the boys promised their attendance, including Shiloh, who would rely on the charity of Damien or Maron to purchase his ticket for him. Maron vouched, as Damien was generous enough last time. The Club proceeded to attend their classes and soldier on through their day, meeting again at lunch, which was uneventful. Each boy mustered all he had to scrape through the afternoon, before finally enjoying a taste of weekend freedom. Damien's father picked him up in his shiny new Enclave and reassured his son that he would be out of work in time for the game. Fridays could prove to be moderately busy for Mazetti's, and Sr. was hoping for it. Reg and Durand made their way to the locker room to meet with the rest of the Ice Cats' finest athletes. Durand felt that his first start being a home game was extra special. Reg agreed. Maron, Shiloh and Erik traversed Limerick Road without an ounce of fear. Since Bose was on the receiving end of an ass-whooping, he hadn't been seen by anyone. Sure enough, his car was absent from the park's lot. The three boys went to Maron's house and found Gloria asleep soundly in her room. Sarah was tidying up around the place and was ready to burst at the seams upon delivering her good news to her son of getting the job in Norhauk. Erik was ecstatic, displaying his emotions and affection by hugging his mother tightly. Shiloh's goofy ass joined in, wrapping them both in an unexpected embrace.

Soon Maron joined in as well. Gloria received the news upon awaking. She shed tears of joy for her friend's accomplishment. Despite Sarah's profuse and insisting attempts to be the one to shell out fifteen dollars for the boys' tickets, Gloria reached into her purse to cover the cost. There was a little extra, as well, because she knew that Shiloh would get hungry. The women sat down over a small glass of wine to discuss the cheerful news, and the boys soon headed out, all walking this time.

"Your mom didn't have to do that, man," Erik murmured to Maron, almost in an embarrassed tone. "I have some lawn money, just try to sneak it into her purse for me, okay?" Maron knew there was no use trying to contest it.

"You got it," he smiled at Erik. Genuine smiles and moments like this were few and far between for the boy. Erik always felt some deep sense of accomplishment when he knew he could be the one to induce it. After a half-hour or so of walking and bullshitting, the boys reached the high school parking lot, which was already beginning to fill up. They walked along the chain-link fence which encompassed the football field and its bleachers. Soon after entering and purchasing tickets, Erik was quick to spot Connie De La Rosa in her cheerleading uniform. She wore her dark hair in loose curls and put on just a touch more mascara than she typically did for school. Even from this distance, Erik recognized the radiance of her perfect smile, as well as noticing the plumpness of her ass cheeks as she did a little twirl mid-chant. He must have made this blatantly obvious, as Shiloh commenced his lewd remarks and gestures soon after. Erik gave him a shove and the two followed Maron, who was texting Damien for his whereabouts.

Shiloh pillaged the concession stand with Gloria's charity money and soon walked away with a bag of popcorn and his trademark Reese's Cups. He waved them in Erik's face before attempting to commence his story once again.

"Hey, did I tell you guys 'bout," but was cut short.

"Yes, Christ, we know," Erik snapped. Shiloh seemed offended.

"Well, just so you know, she was way hotter than Connie and actually nice. Not a stuck-up mean bitch who waves pompoms around." Shiloh poorly mimicked a cheerleader's routine, spilling some of his popcorn in the process.

"Goddamn it, Shiloh. She's a cashier. She's paid to be nice to people. She'll get fired if she's not." Erik's response seemed to have his friend puzzled. Shiloh contemplated the validity of it while the trio tried to locate Damien. The sun was now setting below the low row of trees behind the scoreboard. A brisk, dusky autumn twilight was enjoyed by nearly half of The Town's population here at Don Steyn Stadium. Damien finally responded. He was just arriving, he explained. He and Sr. were stopped at the train tracks, which wasn't too uncommon an occurrence for a Friday in Castalia. They finally got around, and Damien was dropped off at the gate. Sr. even offered to drive all the boys home so they wouldn't have to walk in the dark. None had any objections. Damien soon reunited with his crew and the four climbed the old steel riser steps until they reached the student section of the bleachers. None of them were too thrilled by their seating arrangements, but student-priced tickets meant student-quality seating. The student section was loud, crowded and filled with obnoxious peers who really didn't give a shit about what transpired on the football field, while the non-athletes of The Club certainly did. Erik, Damien and Shiloh weren't really too big on sports as a whole, but they always showed out to support their friends. Maron, on the other hand, despite losing out on playing this season due to bigger obligations, still had a burning passion for the game. He could have watched four quarters of two random schools from two random divisions from two random states and still would've been content. The cheerleaders sauntered over to the stretch before the student section, and Erik's heartrate drastically increased. He was in full view of Connie, jumping, bouncing and shaking everything she had. He was utterly transfixed. The cheerleaders performed on the eight-lane track which circled the football field. The football field doubled as a soccer field. And, if the quirkier crowd at Castalia High had their way, it would soon triple as a LARPing field. There just simply wasn't enough room on school premises to designate a separate area for so many different activities. The cheerleaders finished their little routine and began throwing small plastic footballs to the mostly bored student section. Shiloh reached for one but only managed to lay fingertips on it, spilling more of his popcorn in the act. The kernels fell to the cold metallic bleachers beside him. When his companions weren't looking, he fully intended to come back for them. Waste not, want not. All rose as the playing of the National Anthem commenced. A local Gulf War veteran by the name of Corporal Christopher Busdeick stood front and center on the field, giving his rendition. He was a portly middle-aged man who still sported a high and tight Marine-style haircut. He never so much as blinked as he belted out the tune in his bellowing baritone pitch. His singing was honestly quite good.

"So cool to see some of these boys from Two are still around," Shiloh spoke barely above a whisper.

"Shut the fuck up, Shiloh," Maron uttered a hushed reply, elbowing his friend in the ribs for the disrespectful comment. It later became apparent to Maron that it was possible that Shiloh truly believed the man singing served in the second world war, and he almost felt bad for the dig to the ribcage. He decided it best to just let it go. The crowd applauded, which prompted two of the band members to run onto the field with the team banner that the art club had slaved away over, only for it to be ripped to shreds by the home team upon their exit from the locker room and entrance onto the field. The percussionists stood several yards from one another, pulling the paper banner tight, both somewhat nervously peering into the mouth of the tunnel. The school fight song sounded, minus the parts of these two, and the Ice Cats stormed the tunnel, Durand leading the pack. With a great ferocity, he ripped through the team banner and had more motivation than ever to put in work against the Norhauk Strikers. He slowed his pace a bit, unable to even hear his own whoops and hollers over the sound of the crowd's. He instantly scanned the audience and found his mother and baby sisters. All three were standing on the risers, hands raised in triumph and pride. Beatrix was rummaging through her purse for her phone to capture the moment her baby boy got his first varsity start. Durand's eyes quickly darted to the student section. Without surprise, The Club was ecstatic. He couldn't hear their cheers very distinctly, but he knew without a doubt they were present and would be so throughout the entire game. Reg met him on the field and the two slowly walked to their own goal line as the crowd began to calm.

"Let's fuckin' go, let's fucking go baby boy," Reg delivered a few slaps to Durand's helmet with him returning the favor. The team exited shortly after, save the Ice Cats' special teams receiving, which stayed on to take the ball. Moses Arias, kickoff returner, caught the Strikers' kick with ease and managed a several yard gain on the play. It was time. Durand didn't even bother to sit during kickoff, as some teammates opted to do. He trotted onto the field with the line of scrimmage in his sights.

"Now, taking the field for your Castalia Ice Cats, in his varsity debut, number thirteen, Durand Desmond!" The school sports commentator, who doubled as a freshman English teacher, Mr. Roshay, came booming over the microphone. Durand quickly got to work. The offense huddled around their new leader, many with a reasonable sense of doubt in their hearts.

"Let's get this moving and let's get it moving fuckin' fast," Durand commanded. "Starkey, get in slot. Run a basic slant and I'll try to hit you. If I can't, I'm pitching back to Reg. Fuckin' go, guys, c'mon!" Reg couldn't believe that he was listening to the same nervous man who he was speaking to in the library only twelve hours ago. Durand lined up behind the center and called for the snap instantaneously. Corwin, his center, who was being heavily scouted by nearby colleges, delivered it perfectly. Durand caught it and pedaled back, looking for Starkey, who did as he was told. Durand fired a bullet just barely over his offensive line and Starkey pulled it in, managing to gain a few extra yards after the completion. Durand began his attack, which consisted of virtually no huddle and a smashmouth short-pass offense, along with a few handoffs and tosses back to his favorite running back, of course. Ice Cats were short only two yards of the first down, which prompted Durand to hand the ball off to Reg, who ripped through the middle before the defense's secondary had enough time to even get set. Reg picked up six yards on the carry, sufficient enough for the first down. The first five minutes of gameplay continued in this fashion. Durand aggressively commanded the field, and all teammates played their role. At the three-yard line, Durand opted to keep the ball for himself and squeezed between two defenders with a quarterback sneak touchdown. He was hit a bit late on the play, which prompted Grenslait to become vocal in hopes of being rewarded a penalty, but none was given. Durand didn't even care. He scored on the opening drive of his debut varsity game, promptly spiking the ball before being swarmed by his offense. The crowd erupted. He located the touchdown ball before an official could retrieve it and swooped it up. He jogged over to the stands and Beatrix and the girls hustled down. Little Ramona extended two tiny hands and took hold of her big brother's greatest accolade to date. Beatrix had tears in her eyes and Durand was fighting back his own. He skipped back to the bench where he was further congratulated. This was how the matchup continued. Durand dominated, and Reg scored six points of his own. The defense held up as well, only allowing a pair of field goals early on in the game. The Ice Cats emerged the victors by a margin of twenty-one points. The Club was on cloud nine.

Chapter 10

Erik, Damien, Maron and Shiloh were among the last to file out of the student section once the game concluded. They finally rose from their seats and walked to the steel staircase, Erik bringing up the rear. He was sure to throw a parting glance in Connie's direction, who was still in somewhat the same location on the track where the cheerleaders performed for the past hour and a half. She was taking pictures with her girlfriends, and Erik saw her parents approach her with a bouquet of flowers right as he was making a left turn to descend the stairs. He pondered the idea of gifting her a single red rose after the next home game. He could swipe it from Mrs. Calhoun's neighbor's garden, but almost as soon as the thought crossed his mind, it was pummeled and rejected by a more level-headed way of thinking. Best not to roll those dice, as it would result in an insurmountable string of ridicule, he thought. Erik thought it wise to just keep biding his time. Maybe after Connie popped out a few kids by multiple men in her late twenties, she would reflect and truly appreciate what a great guy Erik really was, then she would be all his. The leader of the ragtag bunch concluded his daydream and followed his boys to a sparsely populated section of the chain-link fence, where they could speak of the accomplishments of their athletic cohorts. The boys recounted the game. Maron only had to explain a few rules or plays throughout the whole exchange, much to his surprise. After reveling in the shared glory brought on by Reg and Durand, Damien received a message from his father stating that he was waiting outside the main gate. The boys jogged over, dodging a slew of parents and smaller children alike, who stayed up past their bedtimes to witness their beloved Ice Cats seal another victory. Upon approaching the turnstile, Erik spotted Connie, who was walking with Clarissa to attend the "feed-the-team". She still clutched her red roses in her dainty brown hands. Erik pumped the brakes and took a page out of Shiloh's playbook. It was now or never, he thought.

"You looked beautiful out there, Connie," Erik stood upright, shoving his hands into the pockets of his jeans as he punctuated his compliment with his beloved's name. Connie stopped in her tracks, as well. She met Erik's gaze. Even under the poor lighting, a distinct blush could be detected upon her sweet Hispanic complexion. She appeared to grasp her flowers even more firmly still.

"Thanks, Erik. See you in English Monday?" Her response was lightly glazed with an element of curious surprise, as if she couldn't become any more adorable in Erik's eyes. Erik stood nodding for a moment, not thinking he would make it quite this far, before snapping back into consciousness and replying. "Yep, I'll be there!" He continued his slow and rhythmic nod as his buddies pulled him away. Clarissa did the same to Connie. The boys exited the stadium's fenced-in perimeter before engaging in the ball-busting of the century.

"You're so pretty, Connie! Can I have one of your flowers," Shiloh mocked, accompanying his jab with kissing noises. Damien and Maron couldn't stifle their laughter. Erik didn't care. He took it all on the chin, right up until entering Mr. Mazetti's SUV, which is when the boys finally ceased their teasing. Sr. had the local station playing on the radio, which was highlighting the Ice Cats' victory.

"Sounds like Reg and Durand kicked some ass, huh, boys," Sr.'s attempt to sound like one of the guys. All boys cringed slightly, especially his son.

"Ha, yeah, Dad. They looked really good out there. Durand must've got over his nerves," Damien dignified his father's attempt at a conversation. Sr. made his rounds, dropping Shiloh off first and then Maron and Erik. After the passengers reached their destinations, the silence crept right into the fancy car. Damien decided to attempt to discuss the outcome of the game, trying to recall some of the terms Maron introduced him to an hour before. He was blanking. It was Sr. who broke the silence. That silence suddenly seemed far easier to face than this particular topic of conversation for Damien.

"So, I know things have looked rough, son. I know that I've looked rough. I know your mother has probably seemed a little strange. It's just that we are not the kind that are used to this kind of stress." Sr. pulled into the drive and threw the car in park, leaving the engine running. He continued, "I'll be flat out with you. I've never struggled with money. I bought shit on a whim since I was your age, probably younger. A lot was handed to me, thanks solely to your grandfather and great-grandfather. I was spoiled, Dim. And maybe all of this is some kind of karma, or something. I was reckless. I didn't plan ahead enough, and I didn't work hard enough. I coasted on my family's success, and this is where it got me. I'm not a business owner, I'm not a manager. I'm just an heir. I took something over as my birthright, and I didn't care for it enough. I failed it, and now, for the first real time in my life, I have to dig myself out of a hole that I created through my own negligence." Sr. sounded as sober as a judge. It was good to have him back. This fact slightly eased Damien, who was reaching, grasping for something to say in the moment. Nothing came to mind. "Son, we are thinking of selling the business and all assets. After speaking with several people, we've found that we can get three-hundred, or so, thousand for everything. We can pay off the house, car, still live modestly, and your college fund has remained untouched throughout all of this, I promise. I'm sorry if I've disappointed you in any way. I love you, Dim." Sr. killed the ignition and exited the car. Damien sat statue-like in the passenger seat.

Erik and Maron settled into their usual routine that evening. One boy rounded up the snacks and iced tea while the other fired up the Xbox. Maron had the luxury of staying in his room and starting up the console, while Erik gathered a supply of Doritos, Chips Ahoy! and some cans of Arnold Palmer from the fridge. Gloria and Sarah just laid down. Sarah was on the sofa, starting a Lifetime movie she had seen a dozen times before, as Erik was returning to Maron's bedroom with his haul.

"Don't be up too late, mister," Sarah put a wise emphasis on the 'too' in her command. She smiled at her son as he paused with his collection of junk food. Erik returned the expression. "Love you, mama. Have a good first day tomorrow." After the events of the evening, regardless of how insignificant they may seem to the outsider looking in, he felt a burst of happiness and pride swelling within him. He choked back a single tear. Sarah shifted her eyes to the TV screen, smile still present. Erik continued his stride to the room, discretely wiping a solitary tear from his cheek as he reached Maron's door. He entered to find his friend joining the lobby for their multiplayer match. This was a real treat for Erik. He could only play through all of the levels of Donkey Kong Country on his ancient and dusty Nintendo so many times within the confines of his old mobile home before going insane. The pair sat down and enjoyed some mindless virtual violence together while munching on snacks. Between matches, Erik finally found the words.

"Dude, I know I've said it before, but I just don't feel like it can be said enough. You and your mom are seriously too good for us. My mom has a job, finally. Something that she's wanted for herself for years. Your mom and her charity made that possible. I know what our name is like around town. I know how my dad fucked up so many things for himself and for us. But you always stuck by me. You always have been so good to me, and I just honestly can't see why. You're a winner, Maron.

You were on the football team. You had girls asking for your number. You have a big, beautiful house. You're truly the best guy that I know. Like, yeah, all the other guys in the group are great, I love them all. But you were always special to me. You're special to everyone. I just wanna say 'thank you'. You're the best friend I've ever had." Erik could feel the tears climbing back up from deep down in the pit of his gut. It was inevitable this time. Silent tears ran down the boy's face as he commended his greatest friend in this life. Maron could only look at him. The match had started, and he already died twice, but that was not of importance in the moment.

"Dude, everyone in our group wants to be you. Damien and Reg were telling me how they wished that they had reached out and offered a place for you first. You're the best. You're our leader. You always know how to fix things. You always know what to say, how to act. Your helmet does that 'WHOOSH' thing!" Maron cracked the tired old joke, as it originated from both the boys' favorite childhood movie. Erik let out a weak laugh. "You know you're always welcome, man. Your mom too. We love you guys." The two set down their controllers and embraced one another, Erik leaning over and partially crushing the bag of cool ranch chips. It didn't matter.

"I'm sure glad the guys can't see us like this," Erik confessed. Maron laughed and pulled his brother closer. After a few more moments, they picked up their controllers and began playing. Erik reminded Maron of his smooth-talk that he laid on Connie, and Maron encouraged him, mostly because he was happy to see his friend so excited and less so due to the merit of the girl or the probability of him and Connie actually becoming an item. The two played on well into the night. Meanwhile, Shiloh walked into a once-again vacant home. Kurt was nowhere to be found. The phone bill was paid now, however, and Shiloh was quick to wrangle his buddies in the group chat. Maron and Erik responded between killing zombies and discussing Connie's juicy ass, while Durand and Reg sporadically replied, understandably celebrating a big win over rival Norhauk. Damien was completely unresponsive.

Shiloh presumed he was already passed out in bed. He peered out the window in his bedroom and caught a glimpse of a cherry on a cigarette. Mrs. Hadley was up. He pulled his Vans back on and trotted over, knowing she would have a square waiting for him. The night suddenly grew chilly. Shiloh could see his breath in the air. Mrs. Hadley had her thick robe on, which was a clear indicator that fall was in full swing. Shiloh arrived at the steps of her porch and plopped down. On instinct, he reached a hand back toward Mrs. Hadley and she handed him a cigarette and her lighter. Shiloh took a long drag and simply shook his head.

"Left an hour before you got home, dear," Mrs. Hadley's raspy voice sounded. She shuffled her foot slightly and coughed. "Left on foot this time, though."

Shiloh thought of every bar within reasonable walking distance, even by alcoholic standards, and could only come up with two. Dad was either at The Alley or The Arrow, both a twenty-minute walk from home.

"He say anything to you," the boy inquired.

"Just 'hello'," the old woman responded. Shiloh's worst fears began to occupy every inch of his mind. He chiefed the remainder of his cigarette and asked for another. Mrs. Hadley provided. "Hun, my son came over to look at one of my 'lectrical plugs, I can have him drive you to the bars if you want." Shiloh immediately stood to his feet.

"That'd be good, Mizz Hadley," he responded, not fully excitedly. Mrs. Hadley slowly climbed out of her chair and went to fetch her boy, Alvin, who emerged a few moments later, stuffing a screwdriver into his back pocket.

"Ya look too young to set down at The Arrow for a drink, boy," he cracked a light-hearted comment. Shiloh gave a polite smile in return. The two hopped into Mrs. Hadley's old Taurus and peeled out of the trailer park lot. Alvin had Shiloh there in next to no time. Shiloh pushed the passenger door open and stepped out, nervously shuffling toward the bar's entrance. He pulled the heavy old door open and was greeted with blasting music and a thick cloud of cigar smoke. The bar seats were packed full of regulars, seeming to take turns in tipping their mugs or shot glasses back to take a swig. None looked like Dad. Shiloh glanced to the four booths which sat in the pub and saw no sign of him there, either. He approached the bartender, a middle-aged gal who was pretty but looked awfully tired and haggard.

"Uh, you seen a guy with a buzzcut and probably wearing a wifebeater, sorry, uh, white tank top," he inquired of the blonde server. She tilted her head back slightly before replying.

"Honey, there's been ten guys in here looked just like that. He have tattoos, earrings, or anything?"

"Um, he has a barbed wire tattoo on one arm and a name on his other, says 'Leah' on it." The bartender proceeded to think a little harder. She rapidly tapped her nails on the countertop, which aggravated Shiloh slightly.

"There was a guy like that, kinda, left with two others, just a little while 'go. One black, one white. They was big, and one of 'em yelled at him a couple times. Was about to send my man'jer over there but they calmed down, sort of. Who is he, hun, he your daddy or somethin'?" Shiloh didn't dignify the question with a response. He hurried back out the front door of The Arrow. Upon stepping outside, he was welcomed by a hearty and audible gasp and stopped to pay closer attention. Alvin Hadley shouted something from the open passenger side window, but Shiloh couldn't decipher it. The gasp repeated itself, which seemed to emanate from the rear of the building. Shiloh booked it down the alley which lay between The Arrow and the pizza place next door. He reached the end of the narrow alleyway and stumbled upon a scene of violence. The flood lights behind The Arrow illuminated a gruesome display. The men the bartender described were both present, one black and one white. The black man held Kurt double chicken wing-style while the white man delivered a series of fierce blows, both punches and kicks.

"You've had time, you've had fuckin' time, Robertson," the white guy bellowed before dealing another strong punch to Kurt's gut which caused him to crumple to a heap, still in the black guy's grasp. The belligerent stranger reached for the knife attached to his belt and clicked the button. The blade extended. "Shame, 'cause I really liked you, man. But boss needs his money, and we don't get paid 'less he gets paid!" Shiloh sprang into action. He darted toward the black guy, still undetected by either assailant. He dropped to one knee with greater speed and agility than he had ever utilized before in his young life and delivered a hard low-blow, which stunned the man enough to loosen his clutch on Kurt. Kurt took the opportunity and crawled a few feet to his left and popped up to his feet. The knife-wielding man was in shock and temporarily immobilized. Kurt definitely didn't look it, but he could throw and take punches with the best of them. He was nearly six feet, and a hundred and eighty pounds, a good deal of which was made up of beer-belly, but the man knew how to fight, and he hit hard. Quite a handful of townsfolk would gladly attest to this. Kurt squared up with his armed opponent, assuming his boxing stance which he learned and practiced so well in his youth. The man faked a quick stab at Kurt, who didn't so much as flinch. Shiloh took a few cautious steps towards the attacker, before being called off by Kurt. He disobeyed.

"Ain't two-on-one now, is it, bitch," Shiloh asked. "Already took out your nigger," he proudly declared, glancing back at his groaning foe, who was fighting his way to one knee.

"Fuck you say, you fuckin' country ass hick," the black guy responded, combatting the intense aching in his loins. Shiloh, ever the opportunist, took advantage and landed a swift kick to the black guy's chin as he raised his head up to see who called him a nigger. His face smacked hard on the asphalt surface after receiving the blow. He was out cold. A small but prompt stream of crimson gushed out of either his nose or mouth; Shiloh didn't spare the time to figure out which. He redirected his intense and bloodthirsty stare to the man with the weapon.

"Ain't nuthin' but a fuckin' pussy with a pigsticker now, are ya, boy," Shiloh resumed his taunts. The enemy was distracted by his much younger opponent's shit talk and completely neglected Kurt, who made a beeline and tackled him. The back of the violent stranger's head smacked hard off the pavement and the knife went sailing before hitting the ground and skidding another couple feet. Kurt commenced a series of vicious and unrelenting hammer fists, knocking several teeth out instantly. Shiloh ran over to retrieve the knife, which he clutched tightly in his hand, in case the black guy somehow miraculously woke up. Kurt continuously wailed until he was punching the pulp of what was once a man's face. After another stiff right hand made contact, an audible pop could be heard throughout the frigid, autumnal night atmosphere. Kurt let out a short stream of obscenities before continuing the beatdown, using only his left fist now. The man did not stir. By now, a small crowd of onlookers gathered at the back stoop of The Arrow. Only the unconscious black guy seemed to be within reach of the dim flood lights. Shiloh, Dad and the other man, better yet, what was left of the other man, were just beyond the stretch of illumination and stayed protected by the anonymity of the night. None of the voyeurs dared advance closer. Shiloh shuffled over to Kurt and tugged at his tank top, alerting him that they were at risk of being seen. Kurt rose to his feet, still standing over the man. He summoned up the biggest loogie he could in the moment, despite his dry mouth, and hacked it into the remainder of the man's face. The duo scampered off, Kurt rather tenderly, into the blackness of the night. They made it down Race St. a decent way before finally slowing their pace to catch their breath. Both men slumped over, hands on knees and panting. Shiloh was the first to address the violent and frightening altercation.

"Dad," he uttered between gasps, "what the fuck is happening?" Kurt continued to catch his wind. Nearly thirty seconds elapsed, and he dignified his son's very valid question with a response.

"Bud, I told ya I dun fucked it up. Borrowed money from some strangers and couldn't pay it off." Kurt slowly straightened his back out and stood upright on both feet, wiping a large amount of sweat from his brow with his dirty and bloodied hand. "They some mean fuckers, alright. Told me come out here or else they was gonna come to the house. Couldn't have that happenin', so I listened. Came out here and sat down inside with 'em. Had two sips of a beer and the negro said, 'hey, let's go outside for a smoke.' So, I listened then too, and we walked on out. Black fella said he had a joint and wanted ta go out back, so I followed. He reached in his pocket and pulled out a fuckin' shiv. Fucker jabbed it at my face and I ducked it, then raised a knee and caught me between the eyes. Think I was out for a few seconds, I dunno, 'cause then I was wrapped up and the white fella was yellin' and hittin' me. That was when you showed up. And just what in the fuck is you doin' here anyways? Why the fuck are you comin' over to this place and how the fuck did you get your ass here?" Shiloh had had enough. Sometimes parents need guidance too.

"You can fuck yourself, you know that? Been pissin' away all our money, got these crazy fucks comin' 'round the house for you! These ain't guys to be played with, Dad! They 'bout had your ass done in till I showed up! Talm 'bout what I'm doin' here, what are you doin' here? Gittin' yourself fuckin' killed, is what!" The young hillbilly hero let his old man have it. Kurt stared, completely silent and dumbfounded. Shiloh was about to resume his rightful tirade when his father took a step towards him. He wrapped his boy in a sorrowful and profound embrace, silencing him. Kurt began to sob. He apologized for his reckless behavior which was responsible for landing the two of them in this situation. Shiloh returned the gesture with some reluctance. The two held each other under the yellowed streetlight for a while. Kurt vowed to right the wrongs which he committed. Shiloh only half-believed. Several police sirens could be heard by now, only somewhat distant. Both father and son returned to the beat-down trailer park, Kurt limping the entire way. They remained undetected, as far as they knew. They stopped first at Mrs. Hadley's, as they were fairly certain she would have first aid supplies on hand. She welcomed her neighbors in, pelting them with a concerned bombardment of questions. Alvin already left after completing his work, so discreteness was out the window for all parties.

"The hell happened to you, Kurt, Jesus," Mrs. Hadley dragged Kurt behind her by his good hand. She was travelling as fast as she possibly could. The two made their way into the bathroom while Shiloh crashed on the tobacco smoke-yellowed loveseat. Mrs. Hadley reached into the medicine chest for rubbing alcohol and a gauze wrap. Kurt held his shaky hand over the sink, as if he was a five-year-old having a splinter removed by his mother. Mrs. Hadley gave the warning and dumped the isopropyl onto the wounded warrior's knuckles and right palm. Kurt winced and followed up with a loud laugh. Crazy old bastard, Shiloh thought from the other room. Mrs. Hadley cleaned up Kurt's face and examined his torso, where he was thankfully not bleeding from but was already showing the signs of heavy bruising. After being patched up, Kurt stood over the dirty toilet and released a stream of vomit. He rinsed his mouth out in the sink. He emerged from the tiny lavatory to find his son resting his head on the lap of Mrs. Hadley on the tattered little couch. She was massaging his scalp and whispering words of comfort to the boy. Kurt knew he was not finished with his explanations for the night.

"So, them boys you been seein' here are into some pretty heavy shit, and I guess I let myself get roped into the same shit, too," he started. Mrs. Hadley made eye contact, never removing her hand off Shiloh's head. "I met 'em at the track one night, up in Fort Wayne. They in'duced me to their boss, older Mes'can man named 'Juarez'. Guess that old bean been involved in the cartel trade for some time. Nice enough guy, till he's not. Loans money out to drunks and gamblers. Guess I fit both his markets. Gave me a thousand dollars one night, said, 'it's yours, we're amigos now. You place the bet on Marshmallow, win, and you give me half, 'kay?' So, I placed the bet, and I won. Marshmallow came in first, and I got paid out eight grand. I gave him the four like we 'greed upon, and all is good. Couple races go by, we just watch. I drank a few beers and even bought for them boys, too. After about five or so races, and beers, this crazy ole spic says, 'put it all on Toro, believe me! He warms up after a few. I've seen him do it plenty of times.' So's I go down and place thirty-nine and some change, after the beers, on Toro. Kid taking the money looks at me like I'm some kinda fuckin' retard. I go back up and Juarez got a bunch of food for us all. He bought the next round. We watch the race, and wouldn't ya know it, sumbitch comes in first by a nose. By a fuckin' nose! I'm in disbelief at this point. This ole boy can't not pick a winner. I collect the money, come back up and he says, 'that's it for the night, amigo. El fin!' I won over ten grand at this point and can't figure out for the life of me why he wants to call it. We leave the track and head out to his car, big ass Caddy on rims, fresh paint job, inside smells like it just came out the plant. Ole boy says to me, 'You made a great friend tonight, borracho. You come back next Saturday and you'll make a best friend.' I look at him and shake his hand. Hopped in the avenger and swerved my way home. This was all 'bout two months ago, or so. Still warm out. So, I go back the followin' weekend, and he picks 'em and we walked out with ten thou a piece. Ten kay! I couldn't figure out how this fucker done it. Like he was some kind of wizard, or god, somethin'. I meet him this third time, and he tells me, 'you been reapin' the rewards from my knowledge long enough, you tell me now. Pick a winner.' I don't fuckin' know what to do. I been losin' out for years now! You seen that weekend after weekend, Mrs. Hadley. So's I go back to what I knew. I picked Marshmallow, jus like he told me to that very first time. Wouldn't I be a son of a gun, ole shit finishes last. After that flag was waved I just looked at Juarez and his goons, same ones me and my boy beat down, right, son?" Kurt looked to Shiloh with a big grin, hoping for one in return, but Shiloh lay motionless, possibly asleep. Kurt's smile faded and he resumed the story. "They was all pissed off. Only put a grand down, ain't nuthin' but peanuts for this Juarez. But he says, 'scuchame, gringo, lightning don't always strike twice. Do better.' And the next race I put on Woody, tough ole fucker, got some years and some miles on his ass but he would still pull one out time to time. Next race, and two grand more, fucker finishes dead last. Like whatever I picked was the wrong fuckin' answer. Woulda been better off jus pickin' a name out of a hat at this point. And so, the night went on like this. Sometimes my horse would finish sixth or seventh, sometimes get a small return on investment, but never good enough. I kept tellin' this ole shit just to pick 'em. Then we all stood a better chance. But he wouldn't. Like he just wanted to see me lose. He cared more 'bout that than he did himself winning. After the final race I was broke. Wasn't just broke, I was in debt with Juarez's money now. But he kept listening to me. Kept giving me money on my picks. Like he was almost just lookin' for a problem. Weeks go on like this. Ask Shiloh, I been at that track every weekend since, right, boy?" Shiloh quietly snored and tossed slightly upon hearing his name. Mrs. Hadley prompted Kurt to continue. "Right, anyways, this was how it kept goin' down. I would get it right once in a while, but not enough to pay back Juarez. All in all, cost me 'bout thirteen thousand. Stayed my ass away from the track a couple weeks and his boys come lookin'. They found me, alright. Never told 'em I lived in Castalia, never even said I was from Ohio. But they just knew. He knew. First meeting they was kinda nice. Told me to pull my head from outta my ass and get the money paid back. I could only afford five-hundred, and they wouldn't even accept it. Second time was this confrontation tonight, and, as you can see, Mrs. Hadley, this is how it played out. This is what happened." Kurt felt another wave of vomit surfacing but choked it down. He continued pacing the small living room and managed to dig up his old habit of talking with his hands while doing so. He finally found a fitting seat on the floor, resting his tired and battered body on Mrs. Hadley's old oval throw rug. Mrs. Hadley finally ceased the stroking of Shiloh's short-haired scalp, who was fully asleep at this moment and no longer faking it to avoid conversation with his father. The tired old woman rose to her feet; rather, she rose to her foot and her artificial one, and traversed the short length to retrieve two beers out of her musty old refrigerator. She dug through a crammed kitchen drawer to locate the bottle opener and cracked them for herself and Kurt. She handed him his upon her return to the couch. She took a gulp, as did Kurt, before she finally spoke.

"Honey, I wish I knew what to tell ya. But truth be told, I ain't never been in a jam like this, no sir. Kurt, you fucked up. You fuckered it up and you gotta fix it somehow, baby. Beating them boys to death ain't gonna correct nothin'. Just gonna cause more of them to be after you." Kurt almost choked on his sip.

"Mrs. Hadley, I ain't say nothin' about beating them boys that bad." Mrs. Hadley reclined proudly in her weathered old furniture.

"Your boy whispered it to me, when you was pukin'. Says you mighta even killed him with your bare hands, Kurt. It's more than just sharks, now. You're in it with the law, too, boy." Mrs. Hadley sucked down more of her cheap beer and slightly shook her head. Kurt knew, that by one hand or the other, his goose was cooked. He had been in some scraps before, more than a few. But none of those ever posed implications of such severity. His boy was present, after all. Kurt's own child was in immediate danger, potentially at the hand of a knife-wielding maniac. Kurt knew that what he did, in his heart, anyways, was morally justified. By the law of Christ Almighty, he was protected. By the law of his fellow sinful men, some of those secretive and proper to the public view, and others just as blatant as he, he was guilty as sin. The weathered, Celtic-blooded father inhaled the rest of his drink before carelessly tossing the empty container onto the tarnished carpet. He rested his face in the palms of his hands, elbows digging into his knees. He cried not, for he knew it would not benefit anyone in the slightest and would only succeed in making himself, as well as Mrs. Hadley, even more uncomfortable in the situation which he presented her with. A few moments passed before Kurt prompted the million-dollar question.

"Do I run away? Do I take Shiloh? Do I just up and leave, and write him a note 'splainin' why I had to get away? The fuck do I do, Mrs. Hadley? If that boy's dead, and believe me, I felt it, he's dead, what happens to me? The people watchin' at the bar probably couldn't see the best, but I know they heard, and they saw me and my boy running through the streetlamps. Had to've. What can happen to Shiloh?" An entirely new wave of fear gripped Kurt by his mortal and impure soul. His boy could potentially be implicated in a crime and mess that he himself directly created. Mrs. Hadley was no attorney, but the old bat was wise enough. She sat to ponder the predicament for some time, before finally uttering her piece of advice.

"Shiloh was never there. It was an old friend. Give him some imaginary name, Kurt. Masgrow, or Moscow, something, Jesus. Just do not put your boy into that mix, or it'll spell out the rest of his future. Some other brown-haired kid, just do not confess to it bein' Shiloh. You just may be in the thick of it, boy. What you done is done. I can't say that it was right or wrong, not my place. But you don't involve Shiloh in any way. That damns the both of ya, and I know you don't want that for him. I don't want it for him." Mrs. Hadley glanced down at the sleeping teenager who rested his exhausted head on her lap. Kurt slowly nodded in a sign of understanding and agreeance. The two of them carried on that way throughout the night; Shiloh not once stirred.

Chapter 11

That same evening was more than gracious to Reg and Durand. The pair celebrated amongst their teammates, heading to the local Burger King to partake of yet another "feed the team", where Durand was held in the highest regard by all attending. The boys chowed down on Whoppers and fries and loudly boasted and congratulated one another. Two of the three on-duty employees at the establishment were also juniors at Castalia High, and upon their recognition by none other than the man of the hour himself, they were invited to come and feast with the football team. The cashier, a boy who was known to be quiet and artsy, and suspected to be a homosexual, was grateful to join his classmates in the gluttony. The girl, who was running the grill and packaging orders, was a transfer student who was yet to make any real friends, up until that evening. All were included and actively participated in conversation. Starkey managed to put away forty chicken nuggets, much to the astonishment of everyone. Jokes were cracked and laughs were had, and upon the arrival of a small string of customers, the employees had to resume their positions and bid the athletes a farewell, along with a well-deserved congratulatory statement. The team wrapped things up while Durand slipped a ten-dollar tip to his new friends behind the counter. They thanked him incessantly. Reg and Durand both confirmed with their parents that it was fine for Durand to stay the night. The boys all piled into the cars of the upperclassmen who attended the fast-food feast and were dropped off at their respective homes, save Durand, who was sleeping at his best friend's house that evening. Reg retrieved spare changes of clothes for the both of them before they took turns to hose off in the shower. Once squeaky-clean, the boys joined Reg's parents in the family room. Steve was watching a black-and-white episode of "The Twilight Zone", which, secretly, Reg very much enjoyed and highly approved of, but would never convey that feeling to his emotionally detached adoptive father. Durand and Reg sat for a few episodes before Jessica decided to call it a night and rushed all three boys up to bed. Everyone settled in. Durand made a cot on the floor of Reg's room. Both superstars got a kiss and a big 'congratulations' from Jessica before she turned out the light, retreating to bed herself. Steve never once made an appearance. The athletic duo lay in silence for a considerable time before Reg broke the seemingly eternal quiet.

"Dude, you put on a clinic. That was incredible. When Marshall did win us games it wasn't with that type of authority. It was almost always a single-score difference. You dominated." Durand propped himself up on an elbow to receive the praise of his long-time friend. He took some time to think of a worthy reply.

"Couldn't have done it without you, man. You made this special for me. You know what I'm like. It's not just something anyone can do. You believed in me when I doubted myself. That will forever stay with me. I love you, man." Reg naturally returned the sentiment. Both fell quiet for a minute more.

"So, uh, you think Shiloh's gonna nail that girl at the store," Reg proposed. Both boys laughed, as silently as they could, for a solid half-minute, before Durand replied negatively. What was meant as a light-hearted topic evolved into a considerably more serious conversation.

"I just don't feel like I could do it with any old girl, man, you know," Durand said. "Like, she's gotta be special to me. Until then, I'm just fine being a virgin. I mean, I know Damien has his stories, and some of them are farfetched, you know? But I feel like he's probably the only one of us to not carry that V-card anymore. But all for what? He's not with those girls. They don't want to show him off or do anything for him. They don't love him, and he doesn't love them. Just like Erik being hung up on Connie. Dude is a saint and she's a tramp. These boys simpin', man." Reg couldn't help but chuckle at the crass conclusion of Durand's observation.

"Yeah, man, it's almost not worth it. You're risking getting her pregnant or her turning around and saying you raped her. It's risky for guys, too. I'm fine waiting for a while, too." The same previous silence settled in once more. "And I definitely feel you on wanting someone special. It's a special thing, it shouldn't just be handed out to any girl. I mean, look at us, we deserve better than Castalia girls," Reg added, inducing more laughter between the two of them.

"Yeah, bro. Someone special," Durand seemed to trail off, as if envisioning this special person who was to lay claim to his virginity, even better yet, possibly his love. The boys lay in silence for a long while, during which time both were trying to determine how to proceed with the sweet yet somewhat awkward topic of conversation. Reg was brave enough to be the one to break the silence.

"You know, you're the most special person to me." Durand turned his head from the sheets on the floor to meet Reg's gaze as he stared down from the bed. Durand nervously chuckled. "Man, don't tell me you wanna go all Brokeback Mountain in here. You know I ain't with it." Reg was silent once more. "Like, yeah, you're a handsome dude, but this ain't it, you know?" Reg turned to face his friend again.

"You think I'm handsome? Dude, look at you. You're like Adonis. Every girl wants you. You could have your pick of them," Reg's volume slightly increased. Durand pondered the compliment for a few moments.

"Yeah, but, like none of that sounds special to me. None of that would mean anything." Durand was now sitting upright. Yet another silence befell the bedroom.

"Do you want to see if I could be special," Reg posed the most apprehensive question of his life. Durand soon obliged with a great hesitation that was soon washed away by tender and physical contact. He climbed into bed with Reg and the two began kissing and touching. They soon progressed. When all was done, Durand was sore, and Reg satisfied. Both returned to their respective beds. Neither spoke a word until daybreak. Reg was the first to wake. He stepped over Durand, who still slumbered away on the floor. He made his way to the upstairs bathroom with a hundred thoughts running wild within the confines of his mind. Guilt, happiness, contentment and fear all did battle within his head. He didn't know if what he did was right, but it didn't feel like it was wrong either, even in the present moment and standing and washing his face in sunlight's sobriety. He kept checking on Durand, who continued to snore. His mother was already gone for work, as Saturdays were her busiest day, seeing as how most women had off from work to get themselves groomed on this day. Steve was downstairs, attempting to troubleshoot the noisy, hissy toilet that could be heard from the upstairs hall. This would be his weekend project which most likely failed to be concluded. Reg ascended the staircase once more and turned to enter his room. He was relieved, somewhat, to find his friend rubbing his eyes in an upright position on his floor bed. Reg struggled to find the words.

"Hey, man, uh, wanna grab breakfast at Gary's?" Durand seemed startled at the normally ordinary question. He sat, mouth agape for a moment, before responding affirmatively.

"Yeah, man. That sounds good. Let me hit the bathroom quick and we can go." Reg nodded in confirmation and smiled slightly, before disappearing back into the hallway. He waited downstairs for his friend. Steve was watching a YouTube video to hopefully guide him in his task. Durand descended the decadent staircase and hollered a 'goodbye' to Steve before exiting the front door, Reg following. The pair made their way down the street, in silence at first. Both had the idea to break this silence simultaneously, and both hesitated upon the other's start. Reg formally began. "Look, man, I know last night was great and maybe got kind of weird, but I just want you to know that I don't think any differently of us, or you. I love you. You're my brother, and you always will be. Sorry if I seemed pushy about the whole thing; I was just curious." Durand kept his pace on foot. He pulled his vape out of his hoodie pocket and took a long toke before finally replying.

"I mean, I don't think it was weird. Like, yeah, a little different, but I liked it. I don't know, man; I never considered myself to be the type. But since it was you, it just felt right. I don't feel wrong about it, or regret or anything, and I hope you don't either. If it happens again, great. If not, okay. I love you too, man. And I guess I love you a little differently after last night." The star quarterback flashed a little wink at Reg, who slowed his pace and almost blushed. He was so preoccupied with Durand being uncomfortable that he himself began to feel the tension that he created. He returned the charming, picturesque athlete's smile, picking up his pace slightly.

"I just always had these thoughts, I guess. Like I look at you and then at Connie De La Rosa, and there's no comparison," Reg laughed, and Durand joined in as well.

"You're beautiful, Durand. I want to be you. All the guys want to be you. And just to have you as a friend, and then, well, like that, was like some kind of dream come true for me. I love you. I always will." Reg extended a sore right hand, and it met his quarterback, and lover's, fresh left one. The two interlaced fingers for a moment before realizing they were traversing a highly public street in broad daylight. Both seemed to notice the fact simultaneously, and released their grasp upon one another, but not in heart and in mind.

"You gay as hell, man," Durand muttered with a smile, quickening his speed to a light jog, forcing his favorite running back to try to keep up. Reg matched the trot, giggling the entire while.

"Not as gay as you," he tossed back, as Durand loudly and sarcastically laughed while bursting into a full-on sprint. The boys reached Gary's Diner sooner than they anticipated and sat down to order two huge omelets, which Reg was more than happy to pay for. Durand was generous enough to dig in his pockets for a two-dollar tip. Once finished, the duo set off for the community park, which boasted a large duck pond that was quite active during this time of year. Reg snuck back into the house to retrieve a slightly stale loaf of bread and to microwave a bag of popcorn to bring as appeasement. Steve had a puddle of water on the bathroom floor. Durand eagerly waited outside the front door, reassuring, via text message to his mother that he was fine, and with his greatest friend, about to venture to the park to feed a bunch of ungrateful mallards. Reg emerged from the home, empty calories in hand, which the ducks were sure to love. The two spent the fine autumn morning in this fashion. Both never felt more at ease and at peace within their own minds. One of The Club who did not pass a peaceful and relaxed morning, just yet, anyway, was Damien.

Damien remained in his room with Bootsy for some time before finally emerging to face the daylight and undoubtedly awkward conversations with each of his parents. He freshened up in the upstairs bathroom, pinched his usual morning loaf, and made his way down the staircase to an empty house. The driveway was vacant of both vehicles, as he discovered by peering out the living room window. He continued toward the kitchen, where he found a note in his mother's handwriting. 'At the shop, hun. Didn't want to wake you for breakfast. Money on the counter for food. Love, Mom'. Damien found a crisp Jackson by the toaster, pocketed it, and sat at his usual spot at the kitchen table. He was sure to check his phone, as he did any other morning, and sent further congratulations to his more athletic friends. Maron and Erik were unresponsive, as was Shiloh, which was typical. Damien doordashed a small order from the local Wendy's. He sat back at his same spot, letting his breakfast get cold. He finally indulged in the fried goodness before getting dressed and walking down to Mazetti's to observe the present state of business. To his surprise, the small delicatessen was rather packed. He quickly made his way behind the deli counter and threw on his apron before serving a slew of customers. He saw, in the distance, his mother cleaning up a broken-jar spill in aisle three. Sr. was nowhere in sight, surely secluded in his office. Damien served several regulars and a few unfamiliar faces before sneaking off to his father's headquarters. He performed their secret knock, which Sr. taught him as a small child: three small knocks left followed by a more dominant knock to the far right of the heavy door. Damien could hear the rustle of papers, followed by quiet footsteps. Sr. cracked the door a hair and peered into his son's eyes. A wide grin invaded his tired face. He welcomed his boy in. The two plopped down in the comfortable leather chairs, facing one another from across the heavy oak desk.

"Just what the hell are you doing here on a Saturday morning," Sr. prodded his son. Damien couldn't fight off the proud smile which crossed his young and fresh face.

"Coming to check on you geezers, I guess." Sr. instantly permitted an over-the-top bellow of a laugh at his son's smartass reply. The two bullshitted for some time before Raquel let herself in. The pretty, young mother had a streak of yellow mustard on her smock, and her hair was unkempt. Sr. wished more than ever to bend her over his desk, as he had so many times before, and to fuck her senseless. His son's presence was the only factor preventing this. For a moment, as slight as it was, he wished Damien would leave. He regained his professional senses and the urges passed. Raquel reported that the store was packed, and by glancing at the register totals, a profit of over a grand was already surpassed. Business was not at this pace for at least a year, even for a weekend. Sr. sat in amazement. Damien couldn't help but stand. He quickly rejoined his comrades on their tile battlefield. The owner of Mazetti's himself stormed the floor. A line of over a dozen flooded the small deli counter. Sr. hopped on the vacant register to aid Holly in her mission. The old man's dream and legacy were granted at least another day to live. Sr. rang up eight customers, all loading orders of forty dollars or more onto the weathered old conveyer belt. Holly had nine, at least by Sr.'s count, most with large hauls of groceries. Nothing could account for this surge of business other than an all-out miracle. Sr. praised Jesus after every customer happily passed to exit the generational shop. Raquel assisted on the sales floor. She guided old ladies to what brand of olives they preferred. She helped a young man locate the meager hardware section Mazetti's had to offer. She also threw a few free samples of sugar cookies towards a screaming toddler, whose mother came in for the bare essentials of milk, bread and eggs. The state of the shop remained this way well beyond the noon-hour. It wasn't until one-thirty that Damien finally felt comfortable enough to relieve himself in the employee restroom and scarf down a small deli sandwich. After that, it was back to work for the exuberant youth. He relieved Holly for her break, not after throwing a few sly compliments in her direction, however. He watched her apple-bottom jiggle away towards the breakroom before assuming his register duties. Disturbingly enough, he briefly considered Shiloh in this moment. Several more customers came through with substantial purchases. In his head, Damien calculated nearly three-hundred dollars in combined sales within only ten minutes on a single cash register. This figure only doubled as he turned around to view the machine that his father still manned. Sr. still had a line five-deep at this point. And so, business continued for the mom-and-pop shop.

Customers filed in, and the Mazetti family was able to stay afloat. If business proceeded in this manner for another month, Sr. would heavily consider calling back his laid-off employees, the benevolent ones, at least. Mazetti's opted to stay open nearly an hour after their traditional closing time of nine in the evening that particular night. An old man by the name of Dorobek, a semi-regular, was the last customer to reach the register on that fair autumn evening. He had but a puzzle book and a six-pack of Budweiser in his hands. Every sale counts, thought Sr. He rang the old gentleman up for a grand total of a whopping twelve dollars and seventy-six cents, before moving towards the store's 'Open' neon sign to click it off and then to the only doors accessible to the public, before promptly locking them. The formerly drunk and struggling father hustled back to the freshest cash register. Raquel counted and double-counted over twenty-eight hundred dollars on that drawer alone. The plastic and steel container was practically bursting at its bolts. This one was changed out twice throughout the day, and by Sr.'s quick and business-minded brain, he calculated five-grand on this one alone as a ballpark estimate. The old man let out a whoop and holler that was quite rare to his wife and child. They soon followed suit, after their initial shock. Holly mopped a small area near the checkout and Sr. dismissed her pretty little self. The trio of father, mother and son retreated to Sr.'s locked office with two register drawers in hand and, combined with the ones that already were placed in the safe, ended up totaling, after nearly an hour of counting and recounting, a sum of over twelve-grand. This would easily cover payroll and the electric and gas bill of the small operation, with a chunk leftover. The small family of dreamers sat marveling for a short while before Raquel finally rose to break the collective trance. She marched her cute little behind to Sr.'s door and swiftly exited, returning within a minute's time with one of the store's earnest attempts at a premade birthday cake. She nabbed it right out of the cooler and, kitchen knife in hand, sloppily cut out three chunks of the chocolate circle to serve to her boys and for herself. All dug into the artificial coolness of the small cake, laughing and high-fiving one another. Sr. and Raquel shared a messy and frosting-laced kiss, which Damien groaned at upon witnessing. Sr. calculated, then recalculated, and left the store with not only his family, but just shy of four-thousand dollars in take-home money. The Mazettis arrived at their lavish old home on Maple at nearly eleven-thirty at night, yet none felt even the inkling of drowsiness. They stayed up a little while later. Sr. and Raquel enjoyed sips of Moscato, and Damien was sure to sneak a few of his own from both his mother's and father's glasses, not caring if they caught him or not. Eventually, he was allowed to pour his own relatively small cup of the sweet wine and partake with his parents. Sr. seemed to have unlocked an entirely new mode. A year prior, he was antsy. Eight months ago, anxious. Three months ago, frightened. A week ago, desperate. The olive-skinned and handsome middle-aged man who sat before his beautiful family now portrayed the lively image of one freshly baptized in the Jordan at the hand of John. The rejuvenated and determined father felt completely at ease for the first time in a considerable while. The three drank a bit more and shared a handful of laughs pertaining to the busy day they had just conquered. After a tipsy silence engulfed them, Sr. decided to speak on the recent uneasiness which was obvious to all present. He felt he owed it to his boy and his wife.

"I know I haven't been myself lately, and the wine probably isn't helping any. But this is cause for celebration," the shopkeeper half-enthusiastically raised his glass in the air. The other two mimicked, both bearing polite smiles, knowing a deeper topic was soon to fall over the cheerful celebration. "I didn't do it for long, but, Damien, looking at you now, I drank too much because I was stressed. It wasn't right, and I hope you never fall into that same trap, son." Damien nodded in understanding, taking yet another sip of his wine, contradicting his father's sermon. Raquel looked on with admiration and forgiveness. Her Mediterranean complexion glistened with sweat from a hard day's work. Sr. noticed her small and perky breasts lift as she inhaled upon receiving the start of his apology. She had never looked more beautiful to him as she did in this moment. Sr. continued, "I was scared. I didn't know if, in a year from now, we would have this house, or even be able to eat. I was scared for my wife and my son, two of the only things that I hold sacred anymore in this desolate world." Damien could sense his dad's use of prose and poetry already. The man read all of Whitman's work, after all, and heavily pushed it upon his only son, well before he was required to read it for school assignments. "My point being, we are far from over. That was clear tonight. If we can have two to three nights of that level of business per week, we'll be just fine. And to be frank, I don't know what brought it on. Maybe the new Wal-Mart caught fire, who's to say?" Raquel let out an adorable little snort with her slightly intoxicated laugh. Damien simply shook his head and cracked a close-lipped smile at his father's morbid attempt at humor. Sr. was undoubtedly a stiff, there was no argument there, but the old boy had his moments. Even Damien had to admit this. "I just want to thank God for this day. If He allows it to continue further, fantastic. If not, I understand. It wasn't meant to be. But since I was a boy, this was my dream. I wanted to run a booming, busy little deli like my father. Only time will tell, and only God will decide if that is what I'm destined for, I suppose." Sr. finished his monologue on a somber note while looking down at his now nearly empty glass. Raquel noticed and stood to top him off, but Sr. stopped her. He dumped his remainder into Damien's cup, who, as the most inexperienced drinker of the bunch, was already feeling the effects. Sr. stared into his son's eyes before speaking once more. "To you, son, and your prosperity. Whether it's this business or selling keychains at the Sandusky mall, I just want you to make it. And I want you to make it longer and better than me. And for your boy to outdo you, and his boy him. I want our name to live long and to live strong. And it all starts with you and your will. Please, son. Do it in my granddad's honor." Sr. raised his now empty glass in a toast, and Raquel and Damien clinked their chalices with his. The evening continued in this grateful and somewhat quiet manner. Sr. motioned his little family into the living room and dug through his collection of DVDs before finally selecting one. He popped "Mrs. Doubtfire" into the dusty and, nearly at this point, archaic disc player and proceeded to zap a few bags of popcorn in the microwave. He returned with the snack and Damien shot his attempt at sneaking another glass of wine but was promptly cut off by his mother. His father saw no harm, but as Raquel gave him a stern stare, he jumped on board with his wife's denial. Damien rolled his eyes and threw a cheeky smile in his parents' direction before digging into his bowl of Redenbacher's. His little smartass glance meant more to his father in that moment than the boy could have fathomed. The trio shared a few laughs, when two-thirds through the flick, Raquel noticed Damien dozing off at his little spot on the living room floor. She got up from the couch to try to wake him, but it was in vain. The wine had done him in for the night. She looked at her husband and that sly, pretty little smile passed her sweet lips. Sr. could already infer her old question she had loaded just by the grin. The shopkeeper shook his head incessantly.

"Nope, nope. Not even gonna try it," the old man couldn't help but return a smile of his own. "He's way too big now. Look at him, Raquel, Christ's sake." Raquel let out the same little tipsy chortle that was heard at the table earlier on in the night. She, unlike her boys, had not stopped drinking. This was a rare treat for her, the petite fitness guru, and it would prove to be a very rare punishment for her in the morning when she would make her vain attempt at rising and readying for Sunday mass.

"C'mon, honey, I know you still got it in you! What if you grab his arms and I grab his ankles," the brunette bombshell cracked herself up beyond belief at her own suggestion, and Sr. was nearly in hysterics now, as well. It wasn't just Raquel's drunken commentary that got him; it was the overall disposition of the day which had just passed. Unbeknownst to Sr., as it shall forever be, but a piece of proud and sentimental knowledge to the omnipotent narrator, the man had outscored, in a manner of speaking, all three of the most popular fast-food joints in town in combined earnings that day. The Town pumped Mazetti's full of blood and hope on that quintessential autumn afternoon. What transpired in the flesh was something of Sr.'s greatest dream. It was granted, by simple townsfolk, at that. These were the people who worked at the rivaling and predatory Wal-Mart just twenty minutes east. They were the people of manufacturing plants that presided in The Town. They were the type who packed the same ham, pastrami and rye sandwiches for lunch each day, most of the ingredients obtained at their favorite local grocer. They were simple people with simple minds who pressed the same simple buttons on a machine or scanned the same familiar items for minimum wage at one of the many convenience shops in The Town and Its outskirts. They were a well-doing and honest, God-fearing and unadorned race. This was Sr.'s greatest aspiration; he desired to live like them in a mixture of simplicity and the decadence he was showered with as a boy. He wished to shed the stress and bearing of his managerial duties and to still the same reap the rewards and the income. If he had known on this particular day that he could earn the same income he was accustomed to by taking one of the many mundane jobs offered in the area, he would have sold the business in a heartbeat. The man was not equipped to handle excessive stress, nor alcohol, nor sex nor any other type of pleasure or discomfort and the vices that may accompany it. He was a simple man who was too early thrust into the expectations of the high and mighty, by community and family standards, anyway. Sr. brushed all notions aside and returned his wandering focus to his beautiful bride.

"Honey, let him sleep there. He's damn near as big as me. I won't be able to budge him." Raquel finally abandoned her hopes of seeing her husband carry their first and only up the stairs to his bedroom as he had done so many times before when Damien was but a lad. At the sound of footsteps, Bootsy scampered her old ass down the beautiful staircase and met Raquel at the archway to the luxurious living room. The cat whined and Raquel swooped her up, initiating a stream of baby-talk. The beast would only hear so much of it before fighting out of Raquel's grasp and sticking a well-coordinated landing on the unoriginal but still stylish floor of the home's lower level. She pranced over to Damien, who still slumbered on the cold floor, and licked his forehead in hopes of reviving her oldest and dearest friend. Damien stirred not, and the cat just as swiftly dashed away to the litter box and food bowl. Raquel and Sr. retreated for the night and didn't fully retire until Sr. delivered a few rounds of passionate and dominant lovemaking. Raquel squealed and moaned in the same fashion she did so many years ago. She sounded just the same after the senior prom, the event Sr. was fortunate enough to be her escort to, as well as her lover at the unofficial afterparty. The businessowner hadn't felt more content in a considerable length of years, all from one day. He leaned out the large bedroom window to burn a Romeo and Juliet, as Raquel still lay nude in bed, yet to move from the position in which she was just priorly savagely fucked in. She dozed as the man contemplated. He knew not what brought on the prosperity, albeit just a day's worth. Having just one solid day, in a sense, put pressure on the old man, though. Would his family come to expect this to be a regular occurrence? Did this freak incident instill a sense of hope and optimism that the Mazettis would most likely not get to enjoy again? Sr. waited until Raquel peacefully slumbered before throwing his boxers back on and slyly creeping down the hall to his home office. Bootsy tried to join but was shooed away. The old man went to the drawing board in an attempt to reel people into his family's little legacy of a shoppe. After a few more sips of wine, the ideas began to flow freely. He drew up plans for customer-friendly deals on soon-expired items, BOGOs on produce, and even frivolous plots such as 'wear a funny hat and get a free deli slider' day. This particular idea may have seemed foolish to some, many, even, but the man was desperate to stay afloat in a certainly tumultuous time.

Chapter 12

Erik and Maron rose earlier than their mothers that Sunday. Both boys pitched in to tidy the house as well as make breakfast. Each son served his mom a plate of scrambled eggs, bacon and wheat toast, all bedside and with smiles on their faces. Neither Sarah nor Gloria had ever enjoyed this luxury until this day. The boys chowed down on some stale cereal in the kitchen and soon departed on their bikes. They waited a while before trying to contact any of the others. Damien would surely be at mass, Reg and Durand would be sleeping in to compensate for the overall lack of rest they get throughout the week, and Shiloh would still most likely be knocked out at this hour as well. The boys rode down Limerick, and all-be-damned, Bose himself had resumed his usual spot. Erik gave a cold stare in passing and Bose returned it. No words were had, and the boys carried on. This was a typical Sunday. Well, it was for some time, until Gloria began to regress and Maron opted to stay at home rather than bike around the small town with his pal. The two hit the AmeriStop and picked up a few energy drinks and some beef jerky before eventually landing at the community park, which was still overrun by ducks. They sat for some time, babbling and bullshitting with one another on a tarnished bench. They took note of the hot mom who jogged by on the asphalt track which encircles the duck pond. She flashed a friendly smile and both boys were entranced by the way her ass bounced in her black leggings as she trotted away. A large buzzard circled in the distance, and both speculated as to what it was that died that could have piqued the disgusting animal's interest.

"So, homecoming's pretty soon," Maron was the one to make the initial shift to more serious topics. "You gonna finally nut up and ask Connie, or just keep staring at her tits in the hallway?" Both erupted into a fit of laughter, which concluded with Erik silently shaking his head.

"Yeah, sure. So she can say 'no' and tell all her dumb, preppy bitch friends. Sounds like a solid plan, man," The Club's golden boy again fell silent.

"Just ask, man. So what if she says 'no'? At least you have your answer, and you can move on with your life. If she doesn't like you, she doesn't like you. Forget her and find someone better. And believe me, there are a lot of better girls, even at our school." Erik remained silent regarding the insults directed at his lifelong crush. He decided to prompt Maron on the issue.

"Who are you gonna ask?" Maron leaned back on the park bench, the one which Reg and Durand had occupied only the day before.

"You know Hannah Lada, the Mexican girl in band? I'm gonna try with her." Maron answered with a confident smirk, the one which seemed to vacate his face for as long as any of his friends could remember.

"Oh, I gotcha," Erik chuckled. "You're gonna ask 'A'Lada Booty' to the dance?" Maron couldn't help but giggle as well. The girl's nickname certainly was a fitting one. "She's cute, man. When are you gonna ask?"

"Tomorrow, at school. She has our same lunch period. I'm just gonna go over to the band-geek table and ask her. She broke up with that one kid over the summer, and her friend, Ashley, told me she thought I was cute the other day in study hall. And just like you, man, if she says 'no', so fucking what? You've gotta take these chances in life. Getting a flat-out rejection is better than going on, not knowing." Maron's words resonated with his friend. Erik decided to pose the same question to Connie De La Rosa that following morning, as well. The boys each lit up a cigarette and sat in comfortable silence for some while. The ducks congregated before them, in hopes of being tossed some stale bread, which the boys came without. A light wind rippled the surface of the green pond and soon kissed the faces of Erik and Maron. After a few more moments of deliberation, both hopped back on their bikes and began to pedal toward Mazetti's, in hopes of Damien being present to sneak them a couple of cold cuts. The ride there was uneventful, and, as fate would have it, the Mazettis pulled up in their fancy car just as the cyclists rounded the corner to see the shop. Damien popped out of the SUV to greet his friends. Raquel, sunglasses still on her pretty little face, despite it being a rather overcast day, walked gingerly in the direction of the office entrance. She threw an unenthused and less than authentic greeting to Erik and Maron. Sr. handed her the keys and made time to shoot the shit with his son's pals. Maron reminded Sr. of his upcoming sixteenth birthday, and again expressed his interest in landing a job at the store. Sr. explained that after the cuts he made, he was obligated to call the laid-off employees first, but he could almost guarantee that most, if not all, would refuse the offer to return. Ralph would not be getting a call. Maron took it as a promise. Erik and Maron followed the Mazetti family inside and laid claim to what would be lunch for the day. Erik got a Reuben sandwich, which was doused in hot sauce. Maron played it safe and went with the turkey club. In exchange for their meals, they owed Mr. Mazetti an hour of cleaning and prepping for the store's opening. Maron gathered the cigarette butts which amassed in the parking lot, while Erik dutifully scrubbed the bathrooms, which were neglected in the shock and awe of the previous night's successful turnout. Damien had a workload of his own. He thawed several pounds of chicken and stocked the depleting meat cooler. Sr. was in his office, while Raquel feinted a busy step at dusting the deli counter. Even in her hungover state, Damien's friends couldn't help but spare a glance at the Sicilian goddess. Erik and Maron vacated the establishment five minutes prior to opening the doors to the public. The pair headed north on their bicycles, with the intent of catching Durand at his cramped apartment. They caught his mother heading out for a surprise inspection at the Applebee's in Norhauk. She ushered the two in, who were then pelted with greetings from Breanna and Ramona. Maron was roped into a game of Battleship with Breanna, while Erik made his way to the sole bedroom of the dwelling to speak with Durand. He knocked twice before entering, finding his friend laying on his stomach with a book spread open in front of him.

"Hey, dude, didn't see you guys yesterday," Erik softly spoke, as if the topic was somehow offensive. Durand propped himself up on an elbow while closing his book.

"Yeah, sorry, man. Just kinda caught up in the moment, you know?"

"It's cool. Just wanted to say 'congrats' after that great outing. You looked perfect out there, man. Reg, too. It was a great game." Erik slowly nodded as he dealt his compliments to, inarguably, the most physically admirable one of his best friends. Durand never stopped grinning. Coming from this particular friend, it meant something different, something greater.

"Yeah, man. We just really vibed out there. The whole team did great, but especially Reg, you know?" Erik continued his slow, stupid nod in agreeance. Durand hopped out of bed and led his friend back out to the living room, greeting Maron, who was throwing his match with Breanna and pretending to be frustrated in the process. Once his destroyer was sunk, he was able to exchange a few words with Durand, compliments, mostly. Reg's name was brought up so frequently that the only next logical destination for Erik and Maron was the star running back's home. They bid their farewells to Durand and his sisters, before hopping back in their saddles and cruising to Reg's upscale home. Mr. Bousher was trimming the hedges out front while Jessica gossiped to one of her stylists on her phone, sprawled out on the front porch with a half-drank mojito in arms-reach. She paused her conversation to tell her young guests that their friend was most likely in his basement-gym. The boys passed through the impeccably decorated Halloween-themed door and advanced down the hallway to the basement's staircase. The sound of free weights clattering to the concrete floor emanated throughout the swanky home. Erik was first to descend, a bit timidly, however, as he knew how Reg could get if a workout was interrupted. Maron was two steps behind. The hulking athlete paced in front of his squat rack, quietly singing along to whatever it was that streamed through his cordless earbuds. He resumed his position under the bar and squatted well over four-hundred pounds for a solid five repetitions before racking the weight, huffing considerably throughout the whole process. It was when he stooped to pick up his water bottle from the floor that he noticed his visitors. He took one earbud out to mutter a less than amiable greeting before guzzling half the bottle and continuing his set. Erik and Maron sat quietly by and waited for their friend to conclude his grueling leg routine. Ten minutes elapsed and Reg showed no sign of slowing down. He finally grew visibly irritated.

"You guys need something," he again pulled his right earbud out to bark the question. Erik and Maron were somewhat shocked.

"Uh, just wanted to check up, man. Haven't talked to you in a bit, just wanted to say, 'congrats' on the win on Friday," Erik started his explanation of his and Maron's presence in an oddly shaky tone but recovered halfway through. A strange expression swept Reg's face. It was one of annoyance.

"Are you my fuckin' girlfriend or something? You gotta 'check up'? I see you guys every fucking day, Jesus. Well, you, at least," Reg nodded to Erik, making a slight to Maron's lack of attendance in recent weeks. This hurt Maron and infuriated Erik, who now returned Reg's sour tone.

"What the fuck, dude? We came to see if you wanted to hang out and you wanna throw insults and get all shitty? For what? Fuck off, then," Erik didn't restrain. He motioned for Maron to exit the basement before continuing. "I don't know what's up your ass today, but whatever it is can crawl right out so you can stop being a salty little bitch!" Reg shook his head and shouted for his friends to leave. Erik reached the top of the stairs and gave the door a good slam as one last testament to Reg's unwarranted rudeness. He and Maron went back outside with not so much as a word to either Steve or Jessica. They mounted their bikes once again with the intent of contacting Shiloh. Their country bumpkin friend was found en route during his return from Mazetti's. He had with him a two-liter of pop, some discounted bread and a single pack of bologna. Even for the Robertsons, this was a meager plunder. Shiloh almost seemed to pretend to ignore his friends as they arrived behind him, as if they were just unknown passersby on the road. Erik and Maron dismounted their bicycles once more and walked them behind their downtrodden friend. Erik decided to be the first to pipe up.

"Hey, uh, man, doing some shopping, huh," he tried to inquire as lightheartedly as he could. Shiloh didn't immediately slow his pace, and he took a while to look back at either of his friends.

"If you wanna call it that, sure," he paused for a few moments. "You guys heard about it yet, my dad, I mean?" Erik and Maron traded curious glances before their friend built upon his obscure question. "My daddy's in some hot shit right now, alright. Got into it with some boys at the bar the other night. I got there in time to save his dumb ass. They was gonna kill him. I distracted one and my daddy beat the other one almost to death. Word 'round the campfire is boy is braindead. Probably gonna be a fuckin' potato the rest of his life. No cops or no one showed up to the house, yet. But I know when they do it's gonna be hell. Guys, my dad is gonna be goin' away. He fucked up and can't pay some real mean motor scooters back the money he owe. They sent for him and he fought back, and won, for now, at least. That boy he beat is alive, in the fis'kal sense, I guess. But my daddy took his life as he knew it. Might as well've put a bullet in his brain." Shiloh finally ceased his stride and realized there was no avoiding his oldest and best friends. He laid out the seriousness of the situation before them both, even omitting his own bravery during the encounter, for the most part. Maron and Erik were dumbfounded. Neither knew what to offer or how to console the boy. Just after hearing the tale recounted, all seemed to be of the understanding that Mr. Robertson would face some sort of repercussion, and hopefully one he saw to live through, even if that spelled out a life behind prison bars. The three resumed their journey to Shiloh's shack and once there, all helped to put his few items away in the fridge for him. Kurt was home, drunk as hell in the wee excuse for a backyard. He half-slumbered in a rusted-out lawn chair, bottle of Scotch in his clutches. Shiloh felt that he had disclosed enough for the time. He gave the option to his friends of either jumping to another topic or they could be dismissed. Erik announced his grand scheme of proposing to Connie at school that week, while Maron bragged about the compliments he received, secondhand, which were addressed from Hannah Lada. Shiloh was relieved to hear the news and displayed an authentic happiness for his boys in their romantic endeavors. He confessed he was not too focused or preoccupied with a homecoming date, at the moment, all things considered. However, he admitted that if he was in a better state, he would undoubtedly ask Holly to be his escort. Although the boy was in the thick of a rough patch, Erik and Maron couldn't help but express how imbecilic the plot sounded to them. She was, after all, an alumnus of the school and far out of any of The Club's league.

"Man, c'mon, she's like twenty-two," Erik could still not stifle his laughter. Shiloh even joined in.

"She's nineteen, fucker. She was a senior when we was freshmen. It's not crazy. Plus, if y'all saw her flirtin' and shit at the store, you would know. Yeah, buddy. Gonna ask that girl to marry me one day and I'll be 'Mr. Holly'," Shiloh waved his left hand, where a wedding band would go, daintily in the faces of his pals. All erupted into a state of unrelenting laughter, so much so that Kurt stirred from his drunken daze. Shiloh motioned the others to commence their return of Mr. Mazetti's cart so he wouldn't have to dignify his father's consciousness with any type of greeting. All three marched back with the small shopping cart, taking turns pushing it down the narrow backroad. The trio finally arrived, after several cigarette breaks between them, to find the parking lot of Damien's inheritance to be packed to the seams. Cars were circling the pavement in the futile hopes of finding an open spot. The boys were astonished to see the usually deserted business in such a booming state.

"Good thing we didn't drive, huh, boys," Maron cracked the joke, receiving a small smile from his friends, which he soon recognized to have stemmed from their realization that Damien's family was prospering in the moment and not necessarily from his wiseass remark. The group walked the cart into the store, and it was soon snatched up by a middle-aged woman to serve her own grocery-shopping purposes.

"It was busy an hour ago, but goddamn," Shiloh murmured. "Hey, I wonder if I round up some carts if Mr. 'Zetti will give me a sandwich." Shiloh always, without fail, butchered the surname. However, his friends encouraged him to do so, as they knew he only had cold bologna as well as a Styrofoam cup of off-brand Mountain Dew to look forward to as dinner upon returning home. Shiloh reemerged from the store and onto the asphalt, munching on a ham and cheese sub, and once finished, made good on his bargain. The young clod of a man made haste and retrieved several abandoned carts, which were carelessly scattered throughout the lot. He made decent time and every shopping cart, including his own, was accounted for and now present within the walls of the store. Shiloh returned to the deli counter to inform Raquel that his duty was done, and he was promptly and generously gifted a total of five more footlong sandwiches, ranging in types. He ran back out of the store to show Erik and Maron his reward. It was agreed upon that Shiloh would keep the spicier and stranger concoctions for himself, and Erik and Maron would lay claim to a chicken teriyaki and BLT, respectively, for their hardworking mothers as their dinner. Half of The Club made a brisk return to Shiloh's mobile home, where Erik and Maron said their goodbyes and saddled their bikes for a final time that afternoon, returning with a convenient supper for each of their moms. Kurt was in the main room of the small home, and Shiloh presented him a tuna melt, which the old Scotsman was eternally grateful for. The tired and scared son packed the other two meals in the fridge for their breakfasts tomorrow, and Kurt would not accept his boy's refusal to partake in the fishy sub with him, although tuna was not something Shiloh was particularly fond of. The two sat and dined in the dingy, green-carpeted living room while watching a Browns game together. Nothing of graveness was discussed amongst the pair, and a certain air of comfort and love and trust seemed to wash over the shabby little trailer.

That Monday morning, which always dreadfully and certainly reared its gruesome head, hit all of The Club like a sack of bricks. All seemed to arrive later and more tired than usual at school that day; this was the hangover of a good weekend, wisely spent with the people one cares for the most in life. And as far as hangovers are concerned, Raquel managed to bounce back after hers, swearing off wine until at least the holiday season of that year. The boys flocked around Erik's locker, all talking seemingly at once of the events which transpired over the previous forty-eight hours. Reg and Durand abided by a certain and unspoken pact to not disclose too much of their Friday night's festivities together. They won the game, they were heroes in the eyes of their peers, and that was it. The Mazettis' business flourished. Erik's mom started a new job for the first time in years. Gloria was in good spirits. And Kurt, while this often goes without saying, was in some shit. The little clique soon scurried off to their designated home rooms upon hearing the warning bell. With each step toward first period, Erik felt his anxiety and excitement rise and swell within him, soon dispersing as though it was all a tidal wave which crashed upon the white sands of a wholesome and romantic beach in a distant land. This land, of course, would have been ruled by Connie De La Rosa and all of her fierce and imposing feminine might. She was a goddess in Erik's perception, and there was no telling him otherwise. For a few hours more, he contemplated his plan of attack. After a few pep talks to himself in the upstairs boys' room mirror and following one close call with nervously vomiting in the sink, he landed on the decision of popping the question to his dusky-complected and raven-haired maiden at the lunch hour, which still gave him a short while to prepare. Lunch soon approached and hungry pupils filed into the well-used cafeteria. Erik was sure to arrive as soon as he could and only opted to grab a lemonade from the cooler, as he was still too apprehensive to feel even the remote signs of bodily hunger. His heart and his soul, however, were both famished, and they could only be satiated by a glimpse of Connie and her immaculate teenage beauty. Erik took his place at The Club's usual table and popped the lemonade open, taking frequent, nervous sips. A string of nameless and insignificant faces lined up to receive a slop of bland and borderline expired cafeteria food on the greasy trays which they clutched. Clarissa was spotted, trailed by a pretty transfer student who was cute and shapely and foolish enough to fall into the preppy bitch circle. Connie was not in the mix. Band geeks, stoners, The Club and all other sorts took their spot in the lunch line, yet the Latin damsel was nowhere in sight. Erik felt a wave of concern as well as relief wash over his anxious being. He knew he had spotted her before English, and in the halls, why would she skip lunch? The plan had to be executed before his friends were present to bear witness to his bold and romantic plot. Regardless of Connie's response, having all the guys there during the buildup and the question itself would prove to be too awkward for both the asking and answering parties. Erik held off another ten minutes before joining the lunch rush himself, figuring it was now safe to eat. Maron reached the table just as his new roommate was rising to grab a tray of mediocre food. The rest of The Club soon occupied the table as well, all in their "arbitrary", as Mr. Steinn would call it, assigned seats. Young Mr. Serling soon rejoined his posse, hoping to receive no questions as to breaking the routine habit by first taking a seat and waiting for the lunch line to reach maximum capacity before deciding for himself to dine as well. No such inquiry was posed, while Connie's pretty face was still yet to be picked out of the crowd of chattering peers. The boys carried on in their usual manner. Each expounded upon his weekend's occurrences, all taking their own turn to do so. Generally speaking, a pleasant disposition rested over the heads of The Club in its current state, save Shiloh, who seemed to be holding up well. For only one of the six familiars to require some minor counseling during the lunch hour was considered a victory for the little group. All swore solid vows to provide all they could for their most lowly, in terms of socioeconomic status, anyway, member's well-being. Damien went so far as to offer to explain to his folks the circumstance in hopes of Shiloh being allowed to bunk with him, which Mr.

and Mrs. Mazetti would more than likely oblige to. The contents of the ugly green trays dwindled down, on all accounts but Erik's, and Reg and Durand made their typical early excusal of themselves, while the other four still sat, picking at the remains of their lunches. Within the span of a minute, Damien, Shiloh and Maron all took their scraps up to dump into the large rolling wastebin at the head of the cafeteria. Erik remained, twiddling his thumbs in a sense. He wished, oh so badly, for Connie to step into the ragged and cramped eatery, and for her to make her dainty and most welcomed way over to him at the now vacated table. Alas, it was time to return the plastic tray, most of its own contents still uneaten, and hit the restroom once more before resuming the school day. The lunchroom's population decreased by the minute, and soon, only Erik and a single hand's count remained. He rose to return the cheap, plastic platter. Halfway through his stride to the stack of soiled dishes, he beheld the most beautiful sight of both astonishment and admiration that could ever be fathomed by the developing mind of an adolescent boy. His beloved, Connie, in the flesh, emerged from the locked employee door of the cafeteria, hairnet still crowning her angelic head. She had a trayful of lukewarm taco salad, which is what was proudly advertised as that Monday's entrée on the weekly lunch schedule. Erik's steps faltered, and he quickly made a recovery to avoid a rude impression.

"Hey, uh, you're a lunch aid this year?" Connie slowly nodded in reply, and Erik could sense the embarrassment which now flushed her pretty face. "Oh, that's cool. Yeah, I was one freshman year. It got me out of the first half of math each day, plus free lunches, which was pretty awesome." She never looked prettier to the young lover boy. The pigtails, the sultry cheerleading outfit, her designer clothes which she incessantly flaunted each morning at her locker, none of it could stack up to this humble and modest grace which she now displayed in Erik's sole and private view. Connie daintily cleared her throat, while motioning for Erik to join her at an abandoned table.

"Uh, yeah, my parents are kind of in hard times right now. So, every little bit helps. Daddy lost his job, or is laid off, I guess, and they found out about free lunches and signed me up for it. So now, here I am, Lunch Lady Connie," she squeaked out an embarrassed little giggle, which Erik would surely replay in his mind a thousand times that afternoon. The two were now seated across from each other, what some would even venture so far as to call a "date". Erik couldn't suppress his smile.

"It's nothing to be embarrassed about, Connie. My parents just went through some stuff, too. I don't know if you heard or not. I'm staying with Maron right now. We don't even have a place to call our own. Mom just got a job though, so that's something positive, I guess. Hey, let your dad know that Wal-Mart in Norhauk is hiring like crazy. I'm sure it's not as good as what he used to do, but at least it's something, right?" The charming young lad brushed his auburn hair from his face, and the motion sent unexpected ripples through Connie's delicate frame. For the first time, ever, she felt the same intrigue and passion for he, who for so long carried a candle in her own name. The two youths sat a minute more as the final bell rang throughout the school. The boy didn't show the slightest concern. The girl was yet to touch her lunch.

"I know I haven't always been the nicest person. Maybe that's what all this is, some kind of punishment for my own shitty behavior, I don't know," Connie trailed off, ashamed at even having to acknowledge the theory. Erik appeared to wince and shook his head.

"No, you're not a shitty person. These things just kind of happen, you know? I've never hurt anybody, Maron has never hurt anybody, yet here we are. When bad things happen, it isn't always for reason or punishment to us to have to repent for past sins. Sometimes these things happen. Our parents' actions, our friends' actions, sometimes they carry repercussions for us to face, and because we love these people, we oblige and take it all head on. Sometimes we have no choice. We can't choose our parents, obviously, or else I would have chosen my mom and a guy who had all the qualities of my mom. But we can choose our friends, which I did long ago, with those five goofballs," Erik motioned back to The Club's deserted table. "What I'm saying is, we don't always choose our problems and our fights, sometimes they choose us. But, on the other hand, sometimes we do choose those struggles. You always hear, 'life is full of choices', but that's only true some of the time. Truthfully, we can't fully elect our own destinies. Some other external factor or factors will always have a hand in it, in one way or another." Connie, enamored by the boy's deep speech and sentiment, could only gaze dotingly into his eyes. Erik's sweet smile returned.

"You've been reading that Whitman book, haven't you," Connie questioned, a small grin of her own passing her lips. Erik was now at bat for facing some level of embarrassment. He looked down at the edge of the table, smile never waning.

"Yeah, I mean, it's interesting to me, I don't know. I like it. I like poetry, I guess." His gaze returned to meet the eyes of the girl of his dreams. Connie giggled again, this time much more profoundly. The artificial concoction of low-grade beef and corn chips grew cold, while Erik grew later still for his next class. A detention, nay, a year's worth of detentions would be well worth the outcome he prayed to God for. "So, uh, I'm sure you've already been asked, probably by fifty cooler guys than me by now, but I had to at least try. Would you want to go to the homecoming dance with me?" The question prompted Connie's heart to mimic the backflips she performed at each Friday night's game. She answered with a rapid and repeated nod of her head and wide glimmer and shine of her picturesque smile. She knew the boy was well worthy of a formal and verbal response.

"Yes, Erik. I would love for you to take me to the dance," the great tension between the two could finally be sliced into smaller and safer pieces. Erik could finally depart, knowing full well he faced some level of punishment for missing over a half-hour of class, and Connie could finally nourish her flat and growling stomach. Erik jotted down and slipped his number, and Connie reciprocated. He wanted so badly to kiss her in that moment; to send the girl's lunch sprawling to the wooden floor and to make passionate love to her on the dirty and yellowed tabletop would be one of his greatest dreams achieved. However, Erik settled for a quick and one-armed hug before trotting out of the lunchroom, leaving his freshly found and newly humbled love behind. The lovestruck Romeo arrived at his after-lunch class and was able to slip in undetected by the instructor but was seen by Maron. He flashed his friend a subtle grin and a quick thumbs-up motion, and all was understood.

Chapter 13

Shiloh made the pilgrimage home. The weather was fair, birds cawing faintly. A brisk autumn gust greeted him as he set foot onto the premises of the weathered trailer park. Leaves whirled in what seemed to be miniature tornadoes all around. Mrs. Hadley was on her stoop, smoking a cigarette with a plate of chips on her lap while skimming a magazine. Shiloh took his rightful spot on the upmost step and initiated conversation with the elderly lady. Grim news passed her thin, wrinkled lips.

"Police came today for your daddy, hun. I'm sorry. The coon at the bar was able to identify him by name. They came and he went quietly. He's just bein' questioned, no arrest or anythin' yet. He might even be home tonight." The old woman's words were of no comfort to the boy. He knew, in his heart, that something would amount from the conflict which transpired in the parking lot of the run-down bar; he just hoped it wouldn't have happened so soon. Shiloh accepted a smoke from Mrs. Hadley and sat quietly for a few minutes more. He understood full-well that what had happened had happened. No one or no force had the capability to fight the fact of the matter and win. Tears began to swell in the boy's eyes as he fought to find the words.

"Was he brave, Mizz Hadley?" Shiloh choked back a stream of tears and was proud to see Mrs. Hadley nod her head in an affirmative motion. There was no stopping it now. The dam which the young delinquent hoped to maintain had more than a crack in it, and the river of salty sorrow flooded forth. He cried long and hard in the arms of the tough old woman while she consoled him as best she could. The pair eventually went inside for supper. Mrs. Hadley had a hearty stew brewing on the stovetop. Shiloh knew it would be the last true homecooked meal he would be able to enjoy for some time, lest he learned a culinary skill to support himself. Kurt Robertson was no saint, but God Almighty knows the man could make miracles out of scraps in a decrepit kitchen. The son vowed to learn the ways. The beef and potato soup was served in Styrofoam bowls, both diners eating more than their fill. Shiloh confided all his worries and concerns in his haggard neighbor lady, while she tried her damnedest to reassure him. Kurt sat and slept not a wink behind his own iron bars until very late that night. Throughout his entire confinement, he could only think of his son. Both wished worse than anything that evening to be reunited, even if it meant living in a dusty trailer park together forever. Kurt made the most of his own meal, scarfing down his toasted cheese sandwich at suppertime. Admittedly, it was one of the better meals he had enjoyed in recent weeks. He made shy conversation with the guard, a young boy of maybe twenty-six, until his shift was over. After him came a grizzled veteran of the occupation who was looming on retirement. Little conversation between the two was had early on in the evening. Lights were shut off and Kurt was ordered to bed. The mattress was thin, as well as stained. It had a damp smell of a wet dog to it. Kurt detested the odor the beasts emitted. For this reason, no dog ever roamed the Robertson household. Just one more reason for his son to loathe him, Kurt supposed. The entire jailhouse was only occupied by a total of three prisoners that night. One of which was a drunk driver. The other was accused of domestic violence by his well-known and highly esteemed cheating wife. The third was Kurt Robertson. The old and tired guard whistled a tune, which Kurt quickly picked up on as the theme to "The Andy Griffith Show". The watchman finally ceased his noise and Kurt sprung at the opportunity at conversation.

"Ya know, Barney was always my favorite. That fucker would split my sides, I tell ya. Me and Pa used to watch it all the time. I 'member when he first got the television, all the guys at his job was talkin' 'bout this great show, and Pa brought it home and was so excited to watch it with me. Ma didn't care for it, but we watched it in the den as long as it was on. That Barney Fife, man, always got me goin'," Kurt earnestly spoke, in hopes of some positive reaction from the old man. He received one. The officer cracked a slight grin from his desk.

"Yep, Barney was the best of 'em. My old man got to watch the show too, before he passed, an Opie always tickled him pink, you bet. Ole bastard always said he reminded him of myself," the guard chuckled shamelessly. "Guess I kinda looked like him when I was a lad." Kurt finally felt more at ease.

"'Lad'? Ain't common to hear in these parts, friend." The guard now set down his sudoku puzzle and faced his captive. A sly smile crossed the geezer's face once more.

"Daddy was a Scot, Mama was an Englishwoman. Been called 'lad' all the best decades of my life, son." The old man was fully engrossed in the conversation at this point.

"I hail from the Great Clann Donnachaidh. Full-blooded Scot here, sir. Grandaddy came over on a small steamer and worked in construction way over in Virginia. Built a bunch of office buildings over there, on Broad Street. We finally settled up here. My daddy picked up the family trade, and I worked 'longside his best men after he retired, up until I fell off a roof and damn near par'lized myself. He died of lung cancer just before my boy was born, Shiloh. I don't know how it works. I swear to God it skips a generation with men. But he has all the handsomeness and confidence of my own father. Two bastards never met one another, yet they're identical. Same temperaments, same eyes, same exact sweetness that's masked in this rugged and cold outer shell. Almost makes me believe in reincarnation. My daddy died three months before my boy came into the world. I ask you, where did his soul go? Did it only rest for ninety days before attaching to another body? To another fleshly vessel? Is that how it all works? Do I come back as my boy's firstborn? Do I come back fifty years from now, when he's old and gray? Do I come back at all? What becomes of us, my man? What does it all mean?" Kurt's unexpected philosophical dialogue left the old gentleman in a contemplating daze. He did not expect such an ardent commentary from a common crook. The ancient guard was named McDougall, as Kurt came to know. He had but four months left of his tenure at the county jail and prayed that they passed easily and uneventfully. These last hundred and some days were like a kidney stone to the experienced sentinel. It may not be gentle, but it, too, shall pass. The two carried on in this manner for hours. Detainees who mirrored Kurt's behavior made the job somewhat easier for McDougall, though those men came few and far between. It was well past three in the dawn of the proceeding day when Kurt finally shut up to try and grab what few precious hours of sleep that he could. The old guard resumed his puzzle, after many stories and laughs were exchanged. He hoped and prayed the best for the comparably young father; he wished a peaceful outcome for his new friend. Daybreak came and Mr. McDougall left his post. A new and unfamiliar face assumed the duty of babysitting the incarcerated. This man was much younger. He sported a high-and-tight hairdo and wore the attractions of a conventionally handsome man. He was named Berstromm, a United States Marine who was discharged under hazy circumstances. As a military police officer, his methods were questionable, at best. As a corrections officer to civilians, he was downright cruel. A generous plate of scrambled eggs and bacon was dished out to each prisoner. Kurt chowed down and swiftly reclaimed his cot, attempting to compensate for the lack of sleep he missed out on at the expense of speaking with Mr. McDougall throughout most of the night. Berstromm immediately took note. He rose from the heavy oak desk with nightstick in hand. He broke into a loud racket upon the bars of Kurt's cell. The inmate, understandably displeased, shot straight up into a sitting position, looking at his antagonist with an offended scowl. Berstromm finally ceased his taunting, smiling at his animal in its cage. Kurt rubbed the Sandman's kiss from his face.

"It's seven in the morning, boss. Just what the hell do you think you're doing by sleeping away a gorgeous day like this," the caretaker inquired, motioning to the only non-barred window of the chamber, which was located behind his cushy desk. "I think some pee-tee would do your body good, you old drunk," the young enforcer goaded his prisoner with a cocky grin that nearly touched both of his earlobes. The guard barked out orders consisting of one-hundred push-ups, two-hundred sit-ups, and five minutes straight of wall-sits. Kurt's feet did not touch the floor upon such rigorous command. Kurt had dealt with the type before: a young hard-ass who had something to prove to himself and his superiors. Berstromm was a bully, plain and simple; Kurt Robertson tolerated no bully. He realized his crime, he accepted his punishment, but he refused to be further demeaned in such a manor for a sick young man's cruel satisfaction.

"I'm doin' my time, son. I know I fucked up, s'why I'm here. But I'm not your fuckin' circus pony. Now you pull that stick outta your ass, you take that stick outta your hand and put it back in your belt and you leave me be. Got nothin' to say to one another. This is the first night I spent sober in some years, and I'd 'preciate it if you'd just let me sleep it off, if you know what I mean." Berstromm failed to pick up on Kurt's clever irony, which only fueled his disdain for the man.

"Get your ass up or get knocked out, you little piece of stinking shit," the guard's voice boomed, awakening other still-sleeping suspects, all yet to even touch their breakfasts. All of whom he cared not to antagonize. His hands felt for his keyring, itching for any sign of disobedience. At this point, Kurt's head hit the flattened and stained pillow and he casually pulled the ragged and itchy covers over his hardened, alcoholic, and weathered body.

"So, if I don't cooperate, you're gonna knock my ass out anyway, which is what I want? Junior, you run a strange operation, let me tell you, friend. Go right 'head. Bring your candy ass in here and I'll stomp you silly. Thank I give a fuck for an assault on an officer charge? My boy hates me, my life is done. Boy I stomped in the back of the bar might as well be dead. Hell, I'll probably catch murder charges even though he's still livin' and is just a potato. I welcome you. I invite you in this little six-by-six cell with me, boy," Kurt's voice carried further than Berstromm's had just a moment before. The blood of every Highlander and bagpiper coursed through the tired and constricted veins of Kurt Donnachaidh in that courageous moment. He was now on his feet, proudly. "Fuckin' get in, you pussy-ass little bitch. Call me old and drunk, you're goddamn to hell fuckin' right! But I'll beat your ass six ways from Sunday. Prove you're man enough. Go on, step in, you fuckin' girl! I'll bend you over my cot and fuck you in your sweet little asshole. I bet it feels better than your mom's pussy, don't it boy," Kurt was straining to fit his head in between the metallic bars to try to take a bite of the face of his foe at this point. The boy shrunk back in a cowardly fashion, phoning his commanding officer from the comforts and protection of his desk. Kurt's taunts were unrelenting. The first twenty-four hours of Mr. Robertson's incarceration resulted in some serious introspection of the life of a drunk and irresponsible man, a new friend made, and a young and barbaric guard's serious consideration of a change of career paths.

Chapter 14

The following day at school was largely uneventful for The Club. Durand and Reg went to practice. Erik and Maron went to and from their classes. Damien lent a hand at his family's resurrected store. Shiloh sulked. Aside from Connie hanging out at the lunch table after her shift as a dishwasher, which must have appeared strange to more than a few students at Castalia High, nothing truly out of the ordinary occurred. A silent tension brewed, however, between the two most physically outstanding of the group of boys. Reg was, for the most part, besides on the practice field, cold toward Durand, who quickly grew tired of the immature and insecure game. After practice on Tuesday, a confrontation was initiated. Durand met Reg at his place in the locker room, after a hot and revitalizing shower.

"Hey, man. You all good," Durand kicked off the conversation. He waited a few silent moments before continuing, "You just seem, off, I guess. Like you're all pissed off about something. Couple other guys, like Starkey, noticed it too. I just wanna make sure all is good, dude. You cool?" Reg half-considered dealing out the rude and unexpected response that Maron and Erik received days prior, but he thought better of it. The key piece of Castalia's run game lightly sighed and slowly relaxed his broad shoulders. He cleared his throat before speaking.

"Yeah, man, I'm good. Just a lot going on now, you know?" Durand didn't know. This cold demeanor from his greatest friend was something completely alien to him. He nodded his head in silence before prompting an honest and inquisitive reply.

"So, I can't help but notice that you started acting this way after 'that' night. Erik and Maron told me about it, how you acted, I mean. Is there some kinda guilt or anger about it? If that's the case, I understand. I won't ever say anything; I haven't said anything. I just hope that's not it. It's cool, man. Nothing's changed, for me at least. We can move on, if that's what you want." Reg swiftly and forcefully reached to clutch Durand's thick wrist. His cold eyes met Durand's with an almost sinister glare.

"You don't talk about that, not anywhere. But especially not so anyone can hear," Reg's voice passed in just above a hiss. The pressure on Durand's throwing hand was increasing to nearly the point of pain. He pulled his hand out of Reg's grasp in disgusted fashion. The unexpected reaction, although not entirely worthy of one, was dignified with an answer.

"Look, I don't know what your problem is. Something happened. It happened. I liked it, you seemed to like it in the moment, and now you can't deal with it. Get over yourself, man. Until then, don't think of me as a friend," Durand, out of courtesy and secrecy, managed to keep his words under the faintest of whispers, but he was largely disappointed and hurt by Reg's level of conduct. The quarterback for the Ice Cats exited the steamy and smelly locker room, not once looking back. A crisp October day kissed his darkly-complected and handsome face with the affection of a thousand ethnic grandmothers. The boy walked across the mostly deserted parking lot and his secondhand Jordans met the pavement of the freshly redone sidewalk that adjoins the schoolhouse. Some days, Beatrix got out of work early enough to gather her children from school. Some days, she missed the mark and was kept over with her work. On these days, Ramona and Breanna caught the bus, while Durand would walk home. The beautiful young mother was always sure to call ahead and forewarn both the elementary and high school of her circumstance. A message was, without fail, promptly relayed to all of the Desmond children. These shortened autumn days always tantalized Durand on his walks home, which were quite infrequent, for what it was worth. It was so deceiving to step out into a bright promise of sunshine and radiance only to have it yanked away a few hours later. Durand anxiously and irritably trudged on through what was otherwise an ideal fall afternoon. A few kids on bikes passed him on his left, one of them congratulating him on his seemingly stale and long-ago victory just that previous Friday night. Never breaking pace, he called out a thankful response. He soon met the brass knob of his home. Breanna and Ramona were sprawled out on the couch, eating little packets of goldfish crackers and slurping Durand's Gatorade. Both little angels were ecstatic to see their brother walk through the door. Durand picked them both up, one in each arm, kissing their sweet little foreheads with a persistence that he never exhibited before. The girls begged to play Battleship, and Durand laid the strict rule that he was not on anybody's team, but rather a referee in the showdown. The girls concluded two games, both racking up one victory. Beatrix entered the humble domicile with sandwiches from Subway, and Durand was relieved that things wouldn't have to get ugly with a tiebreaker. The family sat down, Durand and his mother on the couch, the little girls on a blanket spread across the floor. The footlongs were devoured and Beatrix shared her events of the day. The McDonald's did not store their meat properly. Mazetti's passed all examinations with flying colors. The Subway was not on the docket for that day, but sounded good, so Beatrix decided it was what was for dinner. The young mother already neared forty hours on the timeclock that week, despite the fact that it was only Tuesday. The overtime was always welcomed in the Desmond household. The little family got on the topic, by one way or another, of sharks and their devastating capability. Durand had the bright idea of scrounging through the DVD collection and finally picked out the classic titled "Jaws". Throughout the flick, Ramona shrieked unapologetically, while Breanna put on her best brave face, insisting she wasn't the least bit frightened of the movie. The girls' tummies were full of sandwiches and off-brand popcorn. Their minds were occupied with an aquatic terror that, realistically, never posed any true danger to either of them in their lifetimes; but such is the way of the minds of children to wander and dream. Bedtime rapidly approached. The girls hunkered down in Beatrix's room while the mother stayed up a while longer to speak with her only son. Both were seated on opposite ends of the tattered couch. Durand had SportsCenter on the television. Beatrix cleared her throat and decided to prompt a simple, yet not, question.

"You okay, honey," the mother's voice was barely above a whisper. Durand was taken by surprise, nearly dropping the remote on the freshly vacuumed carpet. He fumbled for a convincing response.

"Yeah, Mom. Just a lot on my plate, you know? Between the season, all that's going on with the guys. It's a lot, I guess," the boy never met his mother's inquisitive stare.

"What all is going on with you? I hear so much about football and about your friends that I don't hear any real or personal news about my own son." Beatrix slightly shifted her position to have a fuller view of her eldest. Beads of perspiration began to form at Durand's hairline, a telltale sign that he was either lying or uncomfortable, sometimes both.

"Nothing, Mom. Just a lot to take in at once for a kid, you know? I have this big job in front of me with next to no notice about it and the whole locker room expects big things outta me, the kinda things Marshall was able to give them. I'm just stressed. I'm happy, but I'm stressed, too, is all," the young man finally gathered the courage to look his mother in her eye, in hopes that his explanation would be reassuring enough and he would not be prompted for any further commentary. Beatrix nodded her head slowly, which could mean many things.

"That Marshall boy, I heard he was caught with cocaine and steroids. Mr. Grenslait's wife is a waitress at Bob Evans. She told me all about it when I went to inspect them. There's not any of that going on with 'the guys', is there, Durand?" Durand let his cooler side prevail. He knew if he reacted in an offended manner, it would only further his mother's suspicion. He calmly collected his response before issuing it. He licked his lips several times and clasped his hands as if in devotion before answering.

"Mom, none of us do coke. None of us take steroids. To be honest, to be completely honest with you, we've smoked weed before, and Shiloh's dad's cigarettes. We never drank, we never did any crazy stuff. And I don't do it now, because I don't wanna end up like Marshall if they decide to test me. I haven't smoked since the summer, I promise you. And I don't plan on it again." Beatrix seemed satisfied with her inquiry. She still knew something was amiss with her boy, but couldn't quite place it. Durand's genuine explanation sufficed, as it was all true. He didn't smoke with Erik, Damien and Maron anymore. But this matter was not the root of his regret and on-edge temperament as of late. Beatrix shared a few more sweet words, along with stories of the dangers of drug abuse, as she had experienced this torment firsthand. She bid her son goodnight, as she joined her babies in bed. There was no harm and no foul, but Durand never felt more isolated in his struggle and attempt at understanding who or what he was. A restless sleep ensued, and the locally famous athlete was up and pacing the room every hour or so. He managed to string together at least two hours of uninterrupted slumber before the alarm on his phone chimed to alert him of the arrival of the present day and its tribulations that were to come. He arose and prepared himself just as he did any other morning. Much to his surprise, Reg and his father were awaiting him on the curb in front of the apartment. The three rode together and traded small talk.

Reg was exceptionally vocal, in comparison to recent days, that is. At least a few of Steve's jokes landed, and he knew he could set foot in his office that morning in an ostentatious manner. He would surely brag of 'paling around with the boys' to all of his coworkers at lunch. Reg and Durand met their stop and exited Steve's car, which sped away before either boy had even reached the door. As usual, the hallways were largely unoccupied, which ensured a peaceful certainty that the library would also be vacant as well. Both boys entered, Reg then Durand. They took up their usual table, each groaning courteous morning sighs to express just how tired they were. Durand's were far more genuine. Packs were unzipped and books were scattered upon the surface of the vandalized library table in a unison fashion. Leaves of Grass was almost at an end, sadly. Reg thoroughly enjoyed Whitman's classic. Talks of the upcoming game were had. Both boys were anxiously excited to square off with Edison that coming Friday evening. That team was, after all, ranked considerably higher than the Ice Cats. To pull off a victory, however slim the margin, would be phenomenal. All too soon would be the homecoming game and dance, which traditionally proceeded in that order. The first true awkward silence fell between the boys. Reg was first to act upon it, attempting to combat it. The time for splashing in the puddles of small talk was over.

"You know, man, it's not easy feeling this way. Something we made fun of from elementary school onward. I truly think, no, I know," Reg hushed his tone in fear that the librarian may overhear, "I'm gay. I know that I like guys. I like you. I love you. And I'm so scared about it all. What will my parents think? What will your mom say? I've heard all of them make comments before. I've heard my dad, well, Steve, say 'fag' before when he was drunk. What's gonna happen if this ever gets out, or if we even try to go to our own moms and dads about it? I'm sorry, dude. That's why I was so shitty. I'm just scared for what people are gonna think and say, is all. And I'm sure you are, too." Reg nervously rolled his pencil to and fro across the carved-up tabletop. Durand absorbed the explanation and was more than understanding. A few silent moments passed before a strange straggler wandered into the library. He was Butch Bernthal, a quiet and quirky boy who was always present in Reg's health class. He paid no mind to the pair of jocks and made his way quickly to the history section for reasons undetermined. Like a moth fluttering by a bright lamp, he soon dissipated into the labyrinths of printed word. Durand took the chance to respond.

"So, I'm fine with what happened. I accept it, and I think I might be, too. Or at least bi, I don't know. Like I see you and I see Hannah Lada and I want you both, if that makes sense. Well, not necessarily her, but girls like her. But I loved what we had and did that night, Reg. It just hurt me to see you so ashamed of it. I get it. You're this macho dude who has to uphold this tough face. But it doesn't have to be that way around me. I'm not saying that you have to be my boyfriend or something, or even that anyone has to know. But I loved what we had and what we did. I thought of it as a beautiful thing and you just kinda shit on all of it. It's not fair, man. What happened wasn't wrong; it was just a little different, is all. And I know, with girls, you're a full virgin. So am I. So don't give me any excuses or comparisons, because you have none. But what's done is done. If it never happens again, that's fine. But don't treat me and talk to me like some kinda stranger or bad guy when I went along with what you started." Durand was sure to keep his reply hushed. Nobody, aside from the two of them and God Himself could have been privy to the subject matter that was being discussed at the small table. Reg thoughtfully looked down at his own muscular thighs, which hulked and bulged in the confines of his blue jeans. He waited for what seemed an eternity before dignifying his friend's feelings with any type of sentiment. He cleared his throat and spoke softly.

"I just want things to be back to what they were a month ago. I want us to be excited for our future here. I want to feel excited for our team, and what you're able to do for it. I want to go back to normal. I'm not saying that what happened was a mistake or a regret, because it wasn't. I'll forever cherish it, even in secret. But that's how I think it should all stay, a secret. Maybe one day and maybe somehow, if we ever leave this two-star town, it doesn't have to be a quiet thing. But for now, as young as we are and because of who and where we are, I think it's just best that we keep it under wraps. I'm sorry if that's not what you wanted to hear." Durand received it all, hands clasped under his chin in a thoughtful pose. Truthfully, he was glad to hear anything at all in the moment. He brought his hands back down to his sides, slowly reclining in his chair.

"That's all I needed, man. You've been dodging everything the past few days when that's all you had to say. I love you, I always will. But you're right. Right now, there's other matters at hand. And you're right, too, on the whole 'one day' thing. If it happens down the road, maybe somewhere else, then great. If it doesn't, then I know I still have you in some way. We can just move on. As long as we're still friends and still together, then I'll always be happy." Both boys flashed a simultaneous and somewhat shy smile, just as Butch emerged and plopped down at a table a mere fifteen feet from them. He studiously plunged into a comprehensive work which spanned the entirety of the Revolutionary War. Both Reg and Durand knew that the conversation could be neatly packed away, as both boys had their answer. Class soon commenced. The presence of The Club was not very strong that particular day, as Maron and Erik were both unaccounted for.

Chapter 15

Gloria had an early appointment that morning, something which Erik and Maron both were aware of but failed to mention to the other boys. She was particularly apprehensive of this one. She was scheduled to meet with several doctors of different specialties, as her cancer happened to extend to other areas and caused other concerns in regard to her general health. Maron elected to stay home from school that day, as well as Erik, who used the defense of moral support when questioned by Sarah. Sarah had the day off from work and just assumed she would be the sole individual to drive Gloria to her oncologist and presumably and celebratorily grab a couple of drinks from Starbucks afterward. This plan was crashed once she found that the boys intended to play hooky and tag along. Neither mother could deny their request. The four of them loaded into the car at a rather early hour, earlier than they were all accustomed to, and drove first to the Denny's in Sandusky to grab breakfast before venturing to the distant township of Lorain. Gloria ate an abundance of food, considering her anxious state. Waffles and bacon slid down easily. She even asked the server for a slice of lemon meringue pie for dessert. She finished the sweet dish with ease. After scarfing down the feast, she made the remark that she wished that mimosas were served at the establishment. The whole table, as well as the one adjacent, got a chuckle from the comment. Behaviors exhibited by his mother, such as these, gave Maron a deep sense of hope and optimism. When the boy was in middle school, his mother still had this youthly and silly way to her, even at the age of thirty-five, at the time. Little acts such as the joke in Denny's renewed some sense of hope within the lad; he held onto the shine that maybe that woman from ancient times could make a return, and she would remain in place of this sick and frail shell. These aspirations were always short-lived, as Gloria soon began a string of coughs and wheezes after laughing at her own comedic statement. Such a display reminded Maron that this type of thing was just not feasible, not yet anyway. The little family unit soon packed it in, Sarah adamant to pay the bill. She was, after all, and after all these years, a working and independent woman once again. All four soon reentered the automobile and Sarah sped down the highway to Dr. Gatz's office, still yet a half-hour away. Gloria snoozed in the passenger seat while the boys thumb-wrestled in the back. Maron emerged victorious more times than not. A light sprinkle sprayed the windshield in a seemingly foretelling way. The car came to a gentle stop in a freshly paved parking lot before an upscale office. Gloria stirred from her catnap. All exited the shiny vehicle and Maron was sure to grab the front door for everyone. The dim and cool waiting room was mostly vacant, save for an older couple tucked away in a quiet corner near the magazine rack. Gloria signed in and took a seat beside her boy, immediately clutching his gaunt yet strong hand. The two began their routine prayer session while Erik and Sarah bowed their heads and remained silent out of respect through it all. The older couple, who were soon called in, took note of the ritual, and seemed to replicate the behavior. Their names were Behr, and the man walked with a visibly painful limp. His wife clutched his left arm during his strenuous excursion through the door, which promptly shut behind them. Several more minutes passed before another pretty young nurse popped her face through the doorway, inviting the Calhoun party to join in on the fun. The nurse was a svelte woman of Asian descent, nearly thirty, and had a pleasant and soft face.

She wore her hair in a neat bun at the crown of her head. Maron helped his mother to her feet while Sarah rose as well. She hugged Gloria dearly and a solitary tear ran down her cheek as she kissed her friend on her forehead and wished her the best of luck. The mother and son duo trudged through the doorway, which was held open by the womanly figure of Nurse Ling. The door closed, but not before a passing glance was thrown from Maron to be received by Erik. Sarah eventually sauntered over to the magazine rack and grabbed multiple editions of months-old "Good Housekeeping". She made vague and disinterested comments as she skimmed the pages. Erik half-heartedly responded to each before pulling out his phone in hopes of finding any form of distraction. He updated the guys of the current situation. Shiloh managed to swipe Damien's phone and typed back a heartfelt message of encouragement. Responses from Damien himself, Durand, and Reg soon flooded in as well. Erik felt a wave of relief wash over him. Somehow the positive sentiments from his closest friends were more profound than any doctor's diagnosis. These encouragements superseded a trained medical professional's observations. Nearly an hour had passed before a new level of anxiety took root in the hearts of Sarah and Erik. At nearly the eleventh hour of the day, Maron and Gloria emerged from the door, which was once again propped open by Nurse Ling, whose flawless face seemed to lack the luster and excitement that occupied it before. Gloria wore a cold and stoic expression. Maron fought back tears. Scans were administered. Tests were run. Blood was taken. All signs, as Erik and Sarah would soon learn upon entering into the privacy that the car offered, with intentions to soon depart, pointed to the worst. Gloria was given three months, optimistically. The car still sat idle as she delivered her grave news from the passenger seat. The tough old bitch concluded her sermon with a smile. All other occupants of the vehicle wept at varying degrees. Sarah was, by far, the worst. Nearly thirty more minutes of daylight wasted away after this deliverance of despondent news. The car had not budged an inch. Finally, in the most cheerful note uttered by anyone on that grim morning, Gloria suggested that the gang should head to Red Lobster for lunch. Upon their arrival, all parties visited the restrooms. Sarah came out, wearing even deeper tear streaks than before on her face. Gloria radiated the appearance of a woman who just went grocery-shopping but was too tired and lazy to cook any of the meals she would have just purchased the ingredients for. That same expression aligned with nearly half of the women who occupied the restaurant at the time. The party was called on and then seated. No one aside from Gloria truly felt any capacity for an appetite. The haggard mother ordered a platter of lobster tail and crab legs, along with the mimosa she had been craving all morning. The other three opted to share a pair of appetizers for the time. Gloria filled her withering stomach with the finest seafood that northwest Ohio had to offer. The mimosa was sucked down in two hearty gulps, followed by a refreshed "Ahh!". Gloria looked around her table and witnessed the sad and hungerless expressions of all of her favorite people. She knew she would, at some point, have to give another serious speech. No better time than the present. She took note of the attractive young waiter passing by and ordered another drink without much in the way of discreteness. As he went to fetch it, the tough old broad addressed the gloom elephant in the room. She cleared her throat.

"I see your faces. I feel the pain that you all feel for me, especially you, honey," directing the comment at Maron. "I heard the news. I know what's to come. I don't want to spend this time scared and sad. This is a time for celebration. People will say, 'she lost her battle with cancer', just as they have said about so many others. But that's not the case. The truth is, I won. I won my battle. Physically, it ravaged and killed my body. It took away my most womanly parts. It made my son, the holiest of things in my entire life, terribly sad and miserable. It made him scared. It even changed who he was. But I won't let it have that power anymore, and neither should any of you. This isn't a farewell dinner; it's a homecoming feast. And speaking of homecoming, hun, isn't that right around the corner? I heard through the grapevine that you wanted to take Hannah Lada! Goodness gracious, she's a doll! If you haven't asked her yet, I just want to tell you that you have my full blessing." Maron blushed a little at the mention of Hannah's name. A new atmosphere seemed to rise from the crevices of the restaurant's floorboards and permeated and hovered over the Calhoun table and the Calhoun table alone. Gloria continued, "When it's all over, I'll be better off. I'll feel better; I'll feel good for the first time in years. This isn't a sad thing. This is something that just had to happen. I'll be gone before my baby graduates high school. I'll be gone before I am ever a grandmother. I'll have lived a shorter life than most women, and that's just the way it has to be. We're not the ones to pick and choose. We're not the ones to decide in the end. This is all predetermined. It's all God's plan, and His plan, alone. You know, I had a cousin when I was younger. We were both twelve. He was an athlete, a football player, just like my baby used to be. One day, during practice in late August, he collapsed on the field. In the days and weeks up until this point, he was strong as an ox. He never gave off even the smallest sign of any kind of defect or weakness of the heart whatsoever. His coach ran out and scooped him up. Even though it was a ninety-degree day, he was cold as the grave. He was rushed to the Bellevue Hospital, which was very new at the time. Just before midnight, he was pronounced dead. His mother, my Aunt Judy, rocked back and forth in the chair, holding his limp body. She kept screaming, 'No, my baby can't be dead! He's strong! He can't die! He'll never die!' But my cousin was, in fact, as dead as could be. My family, my grandmother, that's Grandma Ruth, hun, I told you about her; you met her when you were around four, took it all so hard. But at the end of the day, what are we, as mere mortals to do? We can't turn back the hands of time. We can't interrupt this process which is far greater and more resilient than we are. We may be made in God's image, but this fact does not entitle us to bend and break His laws. What I'm saying is, what is going to happen will happen. We can only prevent and avoid so much. He will always have His way, and it will always be The Way that is meant to be. When I pass, which will be soon, it will only be yet another part of The Plan. And there's no sense in any of you being upset about it. Let these last months, weeks, maybe even days, let them be happy. Happy for all of us. You are all my family now. Sarah, you're my newfound sister. Erik, you're my second son. You're a brother to my baby boy, who I just love more than any and everything in the history of my life," Gloria broke her solemn character to squeeze Maron's face with one frail hand and deliver a stream of unexpected but most-welcomed Eskimo kisses. Maron had a soggy and tasteless bite of salad in his mouth at this time, which he nearly spat out at the sign of his mother's great affection, due both to his own surprise as well as the physicality of her action. Sarah and Erik both issued a light chuckle at the whole interaction. Lunch proceeded in a somber way for most of the party, save Gloria, who chowed down on her seafood platter. The tab was paid and all four made the commute back home. Gloria napped in the passenger seat while Sarah drove. The boys spoke not a word to each other the entire time. It was drizzling back home as well. Text messages continued to arrive in the inboxes of both Erik and Maron; The Club was eager to hear of good news, any news, at this point. Neither boy sent so much as a single reply for most of the evening. No dinner was cooked and served that evening. Gloria had gotten her fill at not one, but two, restaurants that day, and no one else felt even the remotest inkling of an appetite. The boys retreated to Maron's room and strained an attempt at playing video games together.

Maron finally responded in the group chat, sharing in vague detail, that things took a turn for the worse. All boys, including Shiloh, who stayed late at Damien's house, shared their utmost condolences and words of futile encouragement. Erik decided that he should say something, anything, in the moment.

"I'm just really sorry about all of it, man. You guys didn't deserve this, any of it. I've never had to deal with it before, so I don't really know. But I would give anything, my own life to The Devil, right now, if it meant that your mom was okay and lived to see another sixty years." Erik struggled to reach for more proof of his bold sentiment, which Maron knew already enough to be true. The run-down young man nodded his head slowly and almost rhythmically. A few minutes more elapsed before he said anything.

"Just like she said, who are we to question why? She's at peace with it all now. I guess that means I should accept it, too. It had to be some kid's mom, so why not mine, Erik?" Maron met Erik's intent stare with a cold and desolate one of his own. The boy was completely detached, and he arrived at this state in the most silent fashion possible. He sacrificed opportunities. He passed up on chances. His high school football career was sidelined, which he quite excelled at, in hopes that his mere presence and truancy would somehow be the reviving sip he so desperately wished his mother to receive. In his own damaged mind, all of it was in vain. The next match started and Maron gazed into the void of the television screen with the attention and ability of a corpse. Erik reluctantly picked up his controller as well and made a feeble attempt at vanquishing the opposing team. After several more rounds, the boys decided to call it a night. Both neglected to brush their teeth. Sarah, who was drinking alone at the kitchen island, did not receive a 'goodnight and sweet dreams' message from her son. The boys crawled into their respective beds and hoped to simply fade away into the soft and mysterious darkness of the rainy autumn night. The following day came quick, and Sarah was out of the house and on her way to work well before either teenager began to rub the sand from his eyes. Gloria dozed peacefully in her room, as Maron discovered nearly the instant he was awake and on his feet. He closed the slightly cracked window before tiptoeing from the master bedroom. God forbid Mother, in her frail state, should catch a cold now. Erik and Maron quickly took turns in the bathroom. Showers, shits, and the brushings of teeth between two boys were quickly completed. The not-yet shavers mounted their bicycles and made haste toward their schoolhouse. Bose was again parked in his reclaimed spot. An angry stare down, this time accompanied by words, was indulged by both parties. It seemed as if things were escalating, and Erik and Maron were not the type of men to be instigated in their current state. Both boys locked their bikes on the rusty and weathered rack with several minutes to spare. They soon joined their peers in the bustling hallways. Connie lingered around Erik's locker, and for the first time ever, she bullshitted with the guys before the final bell. With a seventh member in the morning discussion, each of the usual suspect's accounts was cut considerably short. Connie shared that Veronica went out to buy the same shoes she was gifted on her birthday, as well as the fact that Clarissa gained a considerable amount of weight since freshman year. She even went so far as to speculate that her friend was potentially knocked up. The boys, who were largely unfamiliar with this type of discussion, soon shied away completely from the topics Connie mentioned and directed the conversation to football, strange smells, and Damien's pretty mother. Connie couldn't help but roll her eyes at each topic and tightly clutched Erik's hand as he escorted her to English class upon the sound of the warning bell. Clarissa and company passed the couple, going the opposite way down the hall. Some girls threw a questioning look; others displayed faces of disgusted contempt. Connie proudly smiled in all their faces. They soon took their assigned seats and pretended to engage in the mandatory silent reading that kicked off every English class. Connie kept turning around to send Erik flirty glances. She was eventually reprimanded by Mrs. Crockett, who, at first, showed leniency as she was an assistant cheerleading coach. These times at home were grave for the boy; these times at school were extravagant. For the first time in his life, Erik preferred to remain in the latter location. He embarrassingly grinned at Connie's cute and puppy-like behavior. The two reunited as the dismissal bell alarmed throughout the large horseshoe of the edifice. Fingers interlaced once more; Erik was tempted more than ever before to plant a kiss on the object of his greatest carnal desire. He shyly resisted and resumed his day. The Club soon congregated at lunch. Connie donned her hairnet and scrubbed away at the plastic trays in a braver demeanor that late morning, as opposed to her previous days as a lunch aid. For the first time, without being interrupted by Connie's gossip, the other four boys were able to offer their sincerest sentiments to Maron in his bleak time. After all kind words were delivered, and halfway heard and understood, Maron spoke in a nearly indifferent manner.

"It is what it is, guys. I did everything I could. Mom did everything she could. These things kind of just happen sometimes," the grieving lad picked at his lunch at his best attempt at seeming disinterested and absent. The façade did not last too much longer, as he soon broke down in front of his most trusted confidants, the greatest friends he would ever be blessed with in his lifetime. Durand shed tears as well. "Why me, though, guys? I was a good son. I did everything for her. I do everything for her, even now. Even when now it's all pointless. You should've seen her yesterday, you guys. She was eating crab legs and even got kinda drunk. And the whole time she just had this way of not caring. Like everything just didn't matter even more. She even flirted with the waiter, if you can believe that. It's like she was eighteen years old again, and the whole world was her oyster. Here's me, Erik and his mom just sitting in this grim silence, and it's like she just won the lottery. It's selfish, man. She doesn't have to deal with it anymore, but guess who fucking does? Me! I hate her for it, guys, I really do. She won't have to be here when I am! She won't be an orphan, and I will!" The volume of Maron's monologue was rising to the level of an enthused and plastic politician's campaign speech. The surrounding nosy lunch tables soon hushed their own conversations and paid attention to the commotion that was going on in the corner. Maron was now standing and pounding his fists against the tabletop. Everyone's lunch spilled over onto the carved gray surface. The boys could only look on in awe and concern for their friend. He was in hysterics at this point. "I swear it to God, I'll kill everyone in here if it means my mom lives! You think I give a fuck about your lives? I fucking don't! This place, with all of you in it, can burn to this shitty ground!" The faraway tables' occupants now watched the scene in an uncomfortable silence. A school resource officer was soon notified of the disturbance and was dispatched to try to contain it. A husky man in his early thirties rushed into the cafeteria to find Maron standing atop the lunch table, cursing all, including his friends, to the depths of hell and back. The boy was finally broken. In front of God and everyone, his fracture proved irredeemable. The officer radioed for backup, and two even larger and huskier men stumbled onto the scene within minutes. It took all three of them to hold Maron down. He wailed this godawful scream that could never be forgotten by all those who bore witness to it. EMS was soon phoned, and the principal executed a direct order for all to vacate the cafeteria. The students assembled in the dark peace of the auditorium. Many were still famished. Erik took a seat amongst his buddies, and he couldn't help but wonder if Connie had caught a glimpse of any more of Maron's violent display. After the final bell, Erik met Connie, still teary-eyed from the shock at lunch, at her locker. Her pixies were dismissed so she could privately disclose all that transpired after the general population was segregated from the intense scene. Maron assaulted a school resource officer and managed to break free from their hold. He lunged for a real police officer's gun and was met with a violent kick and a blast from a taser. He still managed to rise to his feet and shouted out another stream of obscenities before being tased once more and quickly handcuffed. The next part, which would have been unseen by Connie and the lunch ladies, involved Maron riding in an ambulance and upon arriving at the psychiatric ward of the hospital in Norhauk, undergoing a series of examinations, with most reviewers glancing through a negative lens at the boy upon hearing of his abrupt and unexpected behavior. As a minor, he caught many major breaks and was, to his own dismay, at the moment at least, not afforded a suicide-by-cop. Connie, although not close to the accused, and truly not even close to her own newfound boyfriend, not just yet, anyway, sobbed into Erik's chest while he did what he could to comfort her. Truly, it was he who required the comfort. But he was plenty happy to provide his own for Connie's sake. The two clutched at each other and finally shared the passionate kiss which Erik dreamed of for years. He could feel her tear-soaked face on his own, and it all somehow made her more lovely and sensitive to him in the moment. Maron's sobs were drowned out. Jared's drunkenness, better yet, his whole existence was no longer a reality. Sarah was rich and Erik was four inches taller. He grew up to be a wealthy man of no reasonable explanation or trade. All of five-billion dollars just fell into his lap one cool October day. Perhaps it was the same day that Connie De La Rosa agreed to go to the homecoming dance with him. He had two gorgeous children with Connie, both fluent in multiple languages and could read Hemingway by the tender age of six years. Her unspeakable Magick was an essence that both haunted and blessed the boy until the day he died. It would be taken to his grave but would not die with Erik's earthly body. It was something Eternal. The two locked lips several more times before exiting the building, and Connie extended the invitation of Erik to be her escort home that day. She wanted no part of cheer practice, and accepted whatever consequence came of the decision. Romeo and Juliet skipped down the concrete steps as joyfully as they could, as cheerfully as the circumstances would permit. Erik unchained his bike from the rack and walked it slowly beside him. Connie, however, was quick to get out of dodge. She feared she would be spotted skipping practice to allow a strange boy, whom she truthfully never really spoke of around her usual crowd, to walk her home. The two reached the intersection, Erik having to hop on his bike to keep pace with the brown-skinned beauty. Her thick thighs and toned calves went to work and carried her quite a way and mostly out of sight from the after-hours participants. Connie's round, plump butt jiggled a little in her jeans with each secretive step. Her upper half was relatively thin; she maintained a flat stomach and small, perky breasts, but the lower half of the girl's body was what tantalized Erik beyond belief. Her mother, Adelwolpha De La Rosa, definitely did her daughter a service by passing down such heavenly genes. Mrs. De La Rosa was quite the fox in her day, as well, as any of The Club's still-present fathers would gladly attest to, under the influence of a few beers and so long as their wives weren't present. At this point, Erik truly knew very little about Connie's parents or family life as a whole. He understood, through recent conversation, that Mr. De La Rosa just lost his job while the family struggled and panicked. Such an impact, in Erik's mind, at least, seemed to alter Connie's ego for the better. She was not ashamed to be seen with The Club, even when Reg and Durand were not present. She was clearly not embarrassed to kiss young Erik in the hallway multiple times. The whole experience of potentially being one of the "poor kids" may have humbled the alluring beauty. Erik caught up as the two rounded the street corner. Once a considerable distance was put between the lovebirds and the school, the girl nearly tackled him off his bike for another thirsty kiss. Erik objected in no way. He let his bike fall to his left side, a behavior his father drilled into him from a young age to never be so careless to permit, but it mattered none now. Connie wrapped the boy up and her long locks tickled both sides of his face. Erik's own hair was quite long now, and Connie made several comments to affirm this appearance.

"Look at that mane," the Spanish beauty queen reached for Erik's scalp and tousled his auburn tresses. "Don't tell me you're one of those guys who has to look better than his girlfriend. You're not, are you?" Erik froze in a perplexed joy at the mention of the word 'girlfriend'. He stood statuesque and nearly let his bicycle topple over for a second time.

"Girlfriend," the boy questioned with what he thought was an obvious display of excitement in his own tone and facial expression. "You wanna be my girlfriend?" Connie suddenly felt a flushed sense of embarrassment at the question. She blushed and peered into the boy's eyes with an unusually nervous stare, for her, anyway.

"I just thought since you wanted to take me to the dance and all, that, you know, you wanted me to be your girlfriend," her apprehensiveness multiplied, and, admittedly, to see her in this strange and somewhat panicked state truly excited Erik. It was adorable to him. He let out a nervous laugh and began to nod his head profusely. The trademark, dazzling white smile once again occupied Connie's flawless face.

"Connie, that's all I've wanted for so many years. This is like my greatest dream, coming true as we speak. I would love for you to be my girlfriend. There's nothing I could ever want more, I promise you." Erik moved in for another kiss; Connie's smile never wavered. After another twenty or so minutes of walking, the new couple turned onto Merlin Lane, where the De La Rosas inhabited a healthy estate which rivaled even Damien's. Connie's father, Alonso, was at a job interview at a local plastics plant. Adelwolpha, more commonly referred to as "Addie", was cleaning the house. She met her daughter at the door, as well as her new boy toy. Addie was strikingly similar to Connie appearance-wise, despite not having a drop of Hispanic blood in her veins. The pretty middle-aged mother welcomed Erik into her home, remarking, as well, on the length and color of his locks, which Connie adored even more so now. The three made small talk in the freshly mopped kitchen while Addie tried her best to avoid embarrassing her child in front of her fresh love.

"Honey, Connie told me you were cute, but goodness, look at you! I saw your mom at the store the other day. Such a sweet lady. She was a couple years behind me in school, you know, so I never really got the chance to get to know her, but she is a peach! Invite her over for dinner this week, okay, dear?" Erik politely smiled and nodded while Connie seemed to shrink back from the kitchen. Addie went on further, prompting Erik with casual questions; the boy answered each in a confident and gentlemanly manner. The conversation became considerably more personal as Addie inquired about Jared, who she knew from school. At this point, Connie rather rudely interrupted, announcing that Erik would be helping her with their English assignment upstairs. Addie obliged and half-jokingly remarked that she hoped the boy brought a box of rubbers. Erik laughed, perhaps more loudly and uncomfortably than he should have, and the two youngsters ventured down the hall and rounded about to the old staircase. Connie was ahead, and her mother's remark about condoms soon went out the window as Erik watched the girl's backside sway and bounce up the staircase. The boy knew that if he was going to get any, protection would be out of the question. The pair made a left down the long and narrow hall as Connie opened the door to her room. Posters of boyband singers lined all four walls. The carpet was a clean shade of an obnoxious and loud hot pink. The faint scent of Connie's morning perfume still hung in the air. It was everything Erik had dreamed of. Connie attempted to discretely cover a crowd of teddy bears under a blanket, but Erik noticed immediately. He drank in all the glory that was his love's domain. Connie stood before her bed and nervously clasped her hands behind the small of her back. She toed the carpet shyly as the two stood staring at one another.

"So, uh, this is my room," she felt the need to offer up the obvious explanation. Erik couldn't resist the urge to smile at such a cute comment. At this point, he received multiple text messages from both his own mother as well as Maron's. The incident at school nearly slipped his mind at the prospect of escorting a goddess to her dwelling.

"I love it, uh, it's just like I imagined," Connie blushed at his response. "Listen, so my mom is freaking out, and so is Mrs. Calhoun at what happened today, you know? I-I think that I need to go because they're heading to the hospital where Maron's at, and they're wondering where I am." Connie ceased the shuffling of her feet and plopped down at the end of her bed in an almost disappointed fashion. Her hands now met at her lap.

"But you could stay for just a little longer, right," she prompted Erik, almost defiantly. Erik stared in a most tempted way.

"No, um, I gotta get going. They're leaving soon to see him and want me there, so I can't, sorry." Connie poutingly hung her head.

"It's not like it would take you long, babe," she raised her chin until her dark eyes met with Erik's. She slowly and seductively stood to her feet and wrapped the young man up once more in an embrace, this one far more passionate than the ones before. Erik had not the willpower to defy her. The two lustfully kissed and, within minutes, Connie was fully nude, legs splayed on the freshly laundered bedspread. Erik made full well on his thought from earlier: protection was simply not an option. He disrobed as well and mounted his damsel, delivering a series of soft and rhythmic thrusts, all of which spanned the entirety of five minutes. Once finished, Connie wrapped him in her soft, thick legs and planted even more fervid kisses on his lips. She continued to moan the entire time. Erik regained his sense of responsibility, though it took a while to emerge from the thick mire of temptation. He quickly dressed, and Connie reciprocated. He returned the way he came, and Connie followed up until the front door. Addie was on the phone gossiping to some girlfriend about another friend's recent new hairdo. Erik kissed Connie once more and promised to call later before mounting his bike and pedaling as fast as he ever had in the direction of Mrs. Calhoun's residence. He arrived at a vacant driveway and quickly, yet reluctantly, pulled his phone from his pocket. Sarah was livid; Gloria's most recent message was nearly an hour ago. The youth walked his bike around the back of the garage and let himself in with one of the spare house keys that his hostess was gracious enough to gift him. The house was as hollow as the driveway. Shortly after entering, Sarah called her son, just as she had attempted to since school dismissed. This time he answered. "Huh-hey, Mom," his voice cracked. Sarah remained silent at first, as if completely baffled by her son's ignorant greeting. "Uh, I got stuck staying over at school, I was late to-" Sarah would have none of it. Unbeknownst to Erik, she made the silent promise to herself to try to keep her cool. This was soon broken.

"Where the fuck were you? Your best friend was taken away in an ambulance today, in front of you, and you're out fucking off instead of coming straight home to see him? He's in the hospital, for Christ's sake, Erik! Gloria hasn't stopped crying. He had to be sedated. And you're out where? Smoking pot? Getting into more fights? A family who was generous enough to take us both in needs us right now, and you couldn't make it? I'm fucking disgusted. A move like this I would expect from your father, but never in a million years did I see it coming from you. I don't want to see you once we're all home. Don't touch Mrs. Calhoun's food. You can go hungry tonight, for all I care." The exhausted mother ended the call before Erik could summon so much as the vaguest of apologies. He still pressed his phone to his ear as if the conversation would resume and he would have a chance to say his piece. This didn't happen, however. He slowly pocketed his device and trudged upstairs to the bedroom which wasn't even his own. He wept for a long while. Connie was adamant in communicating but was, for the first and only time in her life, ignored by a boy. Erik finally managed a reply but kept it relatively short. Juliet exhibited some level of understanding and let the boy alone for the remainder of the night. Sarah and Gloria returned at nearly ten that evening. Erik heard the car pull in but dared not stir. He prayed that if he faked being asleep that he would be left alone. This was not the case. To his surprise, Gloria was the one to crack the door and peer into the darkness of the bedroom. She waited a moment, perhaps trying to find the right combination of words. She huskily cleared her throat.

"I understand that things happen, Erik. But my son needed you today. We needed you there today. Your mom is hurt, and that hurts me. Whatever it was, I hope that it was more important than your best friend's wellbeing. I'm not mad at you, and I hold no ill feelings. I'm just disappointed more than anything. Get some rest, dear. And, by the way, you can help yourself to the food in the kitchen. I'll talk to Sarah. Goodnight, honey." The door creaked shut as the sound of the frail woman's footsteps pattered down the carpeted hallway and slowly moved out of earshot. Erik's stream of silent tears was only magnified after such sentiment. Nearly an hour had passed when he crept to the bathroom, hoping to move undetected by his own mother. All indications pointed to Gloria being soundly asleep in her room and Sarah being awake and on the couch, sitting in front of the television as it quietly displayed one of her comfort movies. Erik was sure to direct his stream of urination to the sides of the toilet bowl to make as little noise as possible. He even opted to keep the bathroom light off. Feeling, once again, disgusted with himself, he dared not flush as he silently but briskly stalked back down the hallway to a room that belonged to his best friend but contained no such treasure at the time. Nothing got by the sly old mother. She was, after all, a professional in the "being discrete" business. A whisper, which escaped Sarah's lips in more so the shape of a hiss, beckoned to the boy.

"Get your ass down here, now," the command sent chills up Erik's spine. He complied immediately, somewhat relieved to not have to maintain his act of invisibility any longer. He descended the steps at a relatively quick pace and crossed the living room to face his mother. She pointed to the large vacant armchair in the corner of the room. Erik obediently took his seat, hardly letting his gaze shift from his mother's stern and pretty face. Throughout the entire interaction, Sarah's eyes never shifted from the screen. Much to Erik's surprise, she was viewing an adaptation of a Stephen King classic rather than a mushy and artificial Hallmark flick. The two sat in silence until the next commercial break. Sarah slowly turned her head to face her son. Erik felt like throwing up, both due in equal parts to pure intimidation as well as the guilt and resentment he felt toward himself on behalf of his negligence earlier that day. Sarah started, "Whatever it was you were doing, wherever it was you were, it does not take priority over them, do you understand that?" she calmed herself down considerably while interrogating her boy, in person, for the first time since Maron's episode. Erik agreeably nodded his head. Sarah returned her dagger-like stare to the screen once the movie resumed. "So? Where were you when you were needed most, Erik? Maron is spending the night in a psych ward, and all he asked for was your forgiveness the whole time we were there. What exactly did he say to feel the need to beg for your forgiveness?" The stressed mother really emphasized the "your" in her line of questioning. Erik gulped and finally took the chance to explain himself.

"So, Maron freaked out at lunch. He said all this stuff about being a good son, and always doing what he was supposed to, but still this all happened to his mom. I guess he felt like it wasn't fair, which I agree, but he just had like this meltdown. He said he hoped everyone in the school would die if it meant that Mrs. Calhoun would be alright in the end. Mom, I truly think that he's snapped. I mean, a kid can only put up with so much of this before he finally gives in. I just think that the news yesterday broke him. It definitely broke me. It hurt me to see, Mom. I'm not going to lie and tell you that that was why I avoided going to see him after all that went down, because that's not it. Connie invited me over and I just went, I guess. I know it's not a good excuse, and I know I'm a shitty friend for it. But that's what happened. I went to spend time with the girl I like instead of supporting my friend who needed me more now than ever. If he ever talks to me again, I'm going to apologize and do my best to make it all up to him. But, for what it's worth, I'm sorry to you, and when I see Mrs. Calhoun tomorrow, I'll tell her the same thing. I'm sorry. They helped us when we were at our worst, and I couldn't do the same for them. I'll never forgive myself for that, Mama. I guess I can't blame anyone if they decide not to, either." The gush of tears broke the dam once more, and Erik silently wept into his hands, slouched over in the armchair. Sarah contemplated her next move, before instinctively rising to drape herself over her baby boy. She caressed his hair and softly tried to hush his despaired whimpers. The actual conversation halted there; Sarah spent the next half-hour just trying to console her boy. He spewed line after line of unintelligible gibberish, and Sarah somewhat feared that her own son had succumbed to the same lunacy. She saw, genuinely, that he was truly remorseful for the gross and selfish behavior he exhibited that afternoon. She walked him back upstairs to Maron's bed and laid beside him for a long while. Eventually, the boy drifted off. Sarah was not far behind. It was one of those quick and restless sleeps that one must accept under times of extreme duress. No alarms were set before laying down to sleep. As a result, the caws and cries from the black birds which spanned the infinity of the blue morning sky was the beacon that woke mother and son. It was just past nine, which was excuse enough for Erik to remain home that day. Sarah did not have to be at work until three in the afternoon that day, as she volunteered to pick up an afternoon shift of a recently terminated employee by the name of Ralph Reirke. Erik stood to his feet, still shivering off his frigid slumber. Sarah had the habit of stealing the covers and denying any of the behavior once called out on it. Erik thought of making the playful accusation he always had when the two would share a bed, but thought better of it under the circumstances. Sarah visited the bathroom and instructed her son to peek in on Gloria. The lad quietly strode down the hall in case his hostess was still snoozing. As silently as he could, he turned the knob and carefully pushed the door open about a foot or so. Gloria was half-on the bed, her torso hanging over the foot. Erik urgently called for his mother. He rushed to the cold body and took note of the odor of stagnant vomit on the carpet, which he surely stepped in. This mattered none. Sarah came rushing in, still hiking up her pants midway through her frantic dash. She suppressed her scream and gently, with the help of Erik, dragged Gloria's body back into a normal resting position, gingerly and almost strategically situating the back of her head onto one of her fancy pillows. Erik dialed 911 while Sarah vainly performed her best imitation of CPR. An ambulance arrived ten minutes later, and the home was flooded with men in uniform. Two police officers stood at the front door, as if to keep watch for some invisible and malicious force. Little did these two buffoons know, at the time, that that force had already settled deep within the walls of the home they pretended to guard. Actually, multiple villains were at work inside the home. Cancer, regret, hopelessness, abandonment, the giving up of a young man's aspirations, just to name a few, all had a hand in creating the dismal atmosphere which hung heavy above the superficially beautiful domicile. It was only a matter of several more minutes before the county coroner arrived. All that could be done in Gloria's favor was swiftly and professionally executed, but it was all to no avail. The tough old bird was dead. Erik could only think of Maron, in his already dilapidated state, and how much more this devastating blow could cripple him. The body bag was brought into the room, while two sturdy young officers scooped up Gloria's corpse with the utmost care and sensitivity. She was placed inside and gently picked up onto a gurney. She was transported from her precious home, which seemed to have been blessed with a new freshness of life and vigor only twenty-four hours prior, and into an ambulance, which had no realistic purpose of sounding its sirens upon departing but did so regardless, perhaps out of respect. Erik and his mother stood in the doorway, tears streaking down their faces. The mother held her boy tightly. Both sobbed, and one remaining officer stood quietly by. He was a young boy of notable Irish descent by the name of O'Hare. He slowly paced to the pair of mourners and offered his condolences.

"When I was a little guy, still, I lived next door for a bit. Mrs. Calhoun would see me and my sister outside and she would always rush us in. Maron was still a baby, and Callie, my younger sister, would stand over his crib for an hour and talk and sing to him. Mrs. Calhoun was always baking something. Whenever I got home from school, off the bus, I would step outside and more nights than not, I was welcomed with the smell of fresh brownies or cookies, or sometimes a pie. Oftentimes I wouldn't even want to play outside, but I did so in the hopes that she would see me from out her back window and invite me in. So long as she was home, she always did. She was a sweet lady; she was the best. I'm going to try to pull the guys together, the firefighters, too, and try to kick up a benefit or bake sale or something in her name to help with the funeral costs. I'm sorry you lost such an amazing woman. I'm sorry that I lost such an amazing woman, as well as the best neighbor I've ever known." The rugged young man broke his fourth wall and wrapped his long and thick arms around Sarah and Erik with ease. He knelt, beckoned the two of them to do the same, and murmured a prayer in the name of the Virgin Mary. With tears welling in his striking green eyes, he hugged Sarah and gave her a kiss on her wrinkled forehead. He took up Erik's hand into his own tough and rugged palms and shook it profusely.

"Be tough, boy. Your family needs you. Maron needs you. Bless this house, and all of its members, understand?" The gruff and husky voice slightly stunk with the odor of black coffee. Erik nodded comprehensively. The young officer excused himself from the home, waiting until he was nearly at his cruiser before daring to wipe the tears which now streaked his handsome, hardened face. He sped off, leaving Erik and Sarah only further alone. The two hopped into Gloria's car and made haste to the hospital. They were present when the sheet was pulled over her cold body and they walked as closely as they were permitted to the morgue entrance. Maron was taken off the backburner and mother and son rushed back to the front desk to inform the chubby old receptionist that they would like to visit Maron Calhoun. She slowly stood, panting, and phoned for one of the orderlies. A tall, young black man greeted Sarah and Erik within a minute. Despite his line of work, he was exceptionally polite and peppy. He took the two of them to Maron's room, where a nurse was checking his blood pressure. Erik and Sarah knew not how to proceed. They wished, desperately, to just rip the Band-Aid off and pray for the best. Sarah led the charge after the nurse scribbled some jargon onto a clipboard.

"Honey," Sarah began, clearing her throat, "I'm sorry to say, but your mom passed this morning. We found her and she was already gone. EMS did all they could, but it was no use. I'm sorry, baby." Sarah again erupted into a plethora of silent tears. Erik stood near the door with hands clasped in front of him. Maron finally graced them with a dismal stare from his hospital bed. His eyes darted as if he tried to calculate some improbable figure. He shifted slightly before summoning a verbal reply.

"Yeah, that's really bad, huh, guys?" His gaze was reunited with the needle that was stuck into his hand, as it was before his visitors arrived. Neither messenger of grim news knew how to proceed. Maron slowly sat up from the stiff cot and performed a yawn accompanied by a casual stretch of the arms, as if he was readying himself for a typical day at school. He smacked his lips several times before continuing, "I knew it would happen. I knew it a year ago. For whatever dumb reason, I had this faint hope that she would come out fine. I hoped and I prayed so badly that it would be true. But in the end, I knew it wouldn't." The sick boy let out a small chuckle, as if to laugh at the fact that he knew he was right all along. Sarah and Erik's discomfort grew, undoubtedly visibly. "I just kept holdin' on, huh, Erik? I quit the team, I've quit my friends. Hannah Lada wants me to fuck her so bad right now and I couldn't even care. This isn't what life should be, you guys. This isn't what we were promised when we read that 'We were made in God's Image'. God didn't go through this, did He? So why am I?" A sad and uncomfortable silence befell the bleak hospital room before Maron continued his monologue, rather abrasively this time. "So why the fuck am I?" The boy shouted at his lungs' capacity and the same attentive orderly came bounding down the hospital hallway. "It's not fair, Erik. You still got your mom. Damien still has his. Reg and Durand still do, too. So why am I the only one to suffer? How is it fuckin' fair, Erik, my fearless leader?" Maron took up a spiteful tone at the conclusion of his questioning. Erik, as distraught as he felt, couldn't help but smell a bit of his own resentment at the bitter line of interrogation which he now faced.

"Don't you forget Shiloh. Don't forget what happened to his mom. Maron, I'm sorry that this happened. I wish that I was the one who would've died instead of your own mother. I swear it to God, man, I would give anything to be in the grave if it meant she came back from Heaven right now." Sarah winced slightly at the thought of her own baby being in the dirt but kept silent for the sake of his message. "This is what happened, man. I didn't do this to her, my mom didn't do this to her, and maybe you need to be reminded of this fact, but you also didn't do this to her!" Just as he did on the day of the conflict with his own father, Erik found his balls once again, belting out the harsh but necessary sentiment to his brother.

"Don't you blame God, don't you blame us, and above all else, don't you fuckin' dare blame yourself for what happened!" Maron slightly scooted up onto his pillow, as if attempting to keep the monsters at the foot of his childhood bed at bay. Erik wiped away several tears before carrying on.

"You've got to pull it fucking together, man. I know you don't see it now, and I don't blame you. But you have a full life to live still. What would Mom have wanted for you, Maron? Would she want to see her own son crippled and depressed and fucking miserable all the time? Of course, she wouldn't. Think of the woman she was. Think of her positivity the last few days. She craved life more than anything else. That was the greatest gift to her, and she wanted it for you, above everything else." The handsome young orderly stood in the doorway, watching the whole scene transpire. He vowed, to himself, to only intervene if the sign of physical confrontation made itself present. Erik waited in silence, hoping that his speech would prompt a thoughtful reply from his friend. Maron closed his eyes in a defiant display of being triumphed. All else that he had to say wouldn't be able to be conveyed unless it was screamed. Even in this damaged state of mind, Maron knew it was not the right move. He turned his back to Erik and his mother while the orderly finally felt at ease enough to take a breath. These three exited the room and a pretty blonde-haired nurse snuck in with a tray of hospital food. The orderly escorted Erik and Sarah to the door of the wing and wished them both the best of luck before dipping away into the nearest patient's room. The two of them shuffled, sad and defeated, to the elevator and held one another the whole ride down. Perfectly fittingly to the scene which just played out, a steady rain beat down on the cars in the parking lot. Sarah and Erik entered Gloria's vehicle and the mother hesitated to turn the car over. Both of the Serlings sat in stoic fashion, perhaps each awaiting the other to speak first. Neither did for quite some time, but nor did they shy away from the gushes of their tears. They held each other for a long while; Erik's head uncomfortably rested on his mom's bony shoulder. Sarah started the car and cracked the window, lighting up a cigarette before handing the pack to her son. He engaged in the behavior as well. Once their butts were flicked out of their respective windows, the mother decided to be the one to break the painful silence. She cleared her throat repeatedly, wiping her eyes as best she could.

"I love you, honey. Always know that. Always know that if that was me, instead of Gloria, up until my dying breath I would only be thinking of you. You're the greatest thing to ever happen to me: the only great thing to ever happen to me!" Her strained voice broke a little at the last sentence. Somehow, this folly provoked the most emotion out of the son. He continued to cry on his mother's shoulder. "What you said in there, baby," Sarah continued, attempting to stifle her own sobs, "was very brave. And I know you meant it wholeheartedly. I'm just so proud of you." She alluded to Erik's offer of a self-sacrifice if it would promise Gloria's earthly return. "You're wise beyond your years, hun. There's a reason all the other boys look up to you. I know you don't always see it in yourself, but you're the strongest of them. I know you don't run around on a football field. I know you don't bring home perfect grades. God knows your parents didn't inherit a grocery store all of their own. But you're you. You've made this image for yourself, like some kind of idol. I hear all the time, even at this new job now, from my coworkers and customers, how you are in school. Mr. Steinn came in and ordered a bucket of chicken last week and recognized me instantly. He says, 'Hey, Erik's mother, right? Your son makes my math tests look like third-graders should be taking them. He's just so quick about them. If I knew for a fact that the average teacher's salary would double in the next decade, I would push for him to pursue it. He's bright. A very bright boy you have, Mrs. Serling.' Sarah attempted her best imitation of the old educator, even soliciting a laugh from Erik in the process. "And then, honey, then, guess what," her voice seemed rejuvenated at the next tale of her son's greatness. "And then, that retar- sorry, that differently abled boy's mom came in that same night. Stephenson, right? His mom recognized me from when you and him played soccer together at the rec center, remember? She recalled the time that his shoes came untied right as you guys were going out onto the field, and you saw and stopped him before he tripped and tied them up real good for him, 'member?" Erik did, in fact, remember this incident, as his team went on to lose. However, he still prided his ten-year-old self on helping a little Robbie and preventing him from tripping (any more than he usually did) and hurting himself. Sarah absolutely gleamed with pride, even during such a desolate hour. Erik was somewhat confounded as to how a period of intense mourning transitioned to a speech of encouragement from his biggest supporter. Perhaps it was Sarah's best attempt at cheering up her son during the grimmest of periods in his young life to date. Regardless of her reasoning, the boy was able to strain a smile at the kind words. The two picked up a bag of fast food and hurried home. After lunch, Sarah phoned one of the local funeral homes. Arrangements were made and a final cost was agreed upon. Once hearing the dreadful, yet inevitable news, Gloria's lawyer contacted Sarah, and a lengthy conversation was held.

Chapter 16

School dismissed that day and Reg and Durand skipped practice for the first time in their entire sports careers. Steve picked the boys up and delivered them to the hospital's entrance. Reg thanked his father for the lift and hustled to keep pace with Durand. The boys announced their reason of presence to the lady working the front desk and were soon granted admission to Maron's room. The facility was positively booming at this hour. Grownups were just getting out of work; kids were freshly leaving school. Reg and Durand recognized a few familiar faces. Tommy Aston was visiting his grandfather who occupied his own deathbed as a result of decades of smoking. Marley Connenberg stopped in to see her older cousin, who was several years removed as a graduate from Castalia High. The young woman slit her wrists considerably deeply the previous night but was managed to be salvaged by first responders. John Brach, one of the geekiest of the band kids, was admitted after falling down his front porch steps and shattering his tailbone. This particular boy always looked to Reg and Durand with a heightened sense of admiration, even prior to the notable and recent victory over Norhauk. The boys were sure to stop and spare a few minutes in an attempt to brighten their classmate's day. After goodbyes were said, the pair ventured on to the uppermost floor of the building, hoping to catch their friend in a conscious state. The elevator ride was slow and quite delayed. Several occupants already were spread throughout the vessel when it was halted at Durand's pressing of a button. All who were already inside seemed to express disgust at how great an inconvenience it was to have two more, rather massive in relative comparison, members join their passage. The two most youthful of the transport expressed the utmost earnest and silent apologies.

The boys exited at Maron's floor and bounded down the clean and funny-smelling hallway. The same cute, bubble-butted nurse was checking Maron's vitals as the athletes reached the doorway of what seemed to be a prison cell. Maron slowly turned his head to meet the gaze of his comrades. All three remained in silence as the gorgeous caretaker muttered some words of encouragement directed at her young patient. She turned to face the visitors, smiling and greeting them. She jotted some notes onto her clipboard and pranced to her laptop, which was precariously set down underneath the paper towel dispenser at the room's handwash station. The boys shuffled toward Maron once the bombshell attendant was out of the way. They lightly conversed as she still lingered about the room. She soon received another call, making her exit. Reg and Durand both cast a look of sincere and profuse apology for not arriving sooner in Maron's drastic time of need. Maron silently, yet genuinely, accepted such penitence from his friends and shifted restlessly in his bed. All boys seemed to clear their throats simultaneously, all seemingly eager to be the first to profoundly speak.

"So, how you holding up, man," Durand was the one to attempt an initiation at a deeper-leveled conversation. Maron continued to stir under the thin covers before propping himself up onto one elbow to answer the prompt.

"Ya know, man, truth be told," he slowly started, "I've been a lot fuckin' better, Durand. In fact, I have never felt so bad, man." The guests of the hospital room expected a less than enthusiastic demeanor from their host, however, this response absolutely floored them. Durand struggled to find an appropriate reply.

"Uh, yeah, dude, I understand completely. I mean, I've never lost a parent or anything like that, but I understand that what it is that you're going through is something big, and if you need anything, or if you just want us to leave right now, we can do that. This time is about you, brother. Whatever it is you want or need, just name it. We can make it happen, okay?" The clutch and normally collected quarterback never in his nearly sixteen years had ever felt as uncomfortable and displaced as he had in that moment. A single bead of sweat formed at Durand's hairline and began to trickle down his milk-chocolate forehead, taking a turn at his thick left eyebrow and continuing to pass down parallel to his sideburn. He casually mopped it away with his massive non-throwing hand. Reg appeared to be on the brink of a sincere sentiment but withdrew his remark just as it formed at his lips. The room filled with a stagnant and nearly painful silence as Maron struggled to his feet. The weathered lad staggered to the bathroom and released a stream of yellowed urine, half of the load spilling onto the tile floor. He made a half-assed attempt at washing his hands and wiped his damp paws on his hospital gown. Reg and Durand advanced to the two vacant chairs, which sat several feet from Maron's bed. They took their respective uncomfortable seats as Maron plopped back down onto his stretcher. Nearly another minute passed, which was utter agony to Reg and Durand. Maron seemed as calm as could be throughout it. He exerted the effort to roll to his left side to face the boys.

"You know that Erik came by here, guys? He came by after abandoning me yesterday. I did him and his mom the biggest favor ever by inviting them to stay with us, me and Mom, I mean. And he couldn't even make the effort to come see me my first day in here. I thought we were best friends, but something more important must have come up for him." The cynicism in Maron's voice was quite obvious to his listeners' ears. They glanced at one another nervously. Maron continued, "I know you guys have shit going on. Practice is no joke, I remember. From middle school onward, practice was held at a higher standard than gameday. And I bet the two of you skipped it today just to come see little ole me, huh?" Maron's voice took on a sudden and unexpected cheerful pitch, and Reg and Durand nodded in a brief but swift fashion. "See, that's my big thing. You guys actually sacrificed something else, something important that you were both dedicated to, just to come and see me. That's what matters to me. From now on, that's the kind of thing that I'll look for to determine if someone is a true friend or not. What else did Erik have going on? Sending love letters that'll never be opened to Connie De La Rosa? Smoking some more of Bose's shitty weed? Crying about his piece of shit dad? Still trying to learn to play the guitar after years of sucking at it? What the fuck did he have that was so much more important than what I was facing? Huh?" Maron's voice fell just shy of a boom now. The hot nurse was expected, and not completely unwelcomed, to hurriedly dash back into the room at the slightest sign of disturbance. No such pretty view graced the trio, and they were forced to look at and speak to one another for at least a little while longer. Reg found his voice and put forth his damnedest effort to calm the young mourner.

"You're upset, clearly, Maron. I would be, too. I think of things, sometimes, bad and scary things. I wonder, sometimes, what it would be like to lose my own mom. While I can't possibly know exactly what it is you're suffering through, I can at least equate it to my own hypothetical but painful notions of having my mother taken from me, and it terrifies me beyond belief." Reg was truly a fan of Whitman's greatest work and read it nearly three times through, while his friends still struggled to finish it for the first time. The jock made his best attempt to duplicate a similar prose to something his favorite author would spew. Truthfully, his imitation sounded, to the simple ear, at least, quite compelling. Maron seemed to catch the slightest whiff of bullshit in it, though. He repositioned himself again and took a swig from the oversized hospital cup he was supplied. He slowly nodded his head affirmatively.

"Yeah, those are pretty scary thoughts, Reg," he wiped a droplet of water from his lips. "Thank God, though, they're just thoughts for you, right? It sure would fuckin' suck to actually live through that, huh? Man, I couldn't imagine. Some poor bastard out there is probably going through it right now. Think so, boys? Goddamn, would it suck to be that kid." Maron slightly tilted his head back and a laugh, which toed the line of sounding maniacal, escaped his mouth. This was ultimately the straw that broke Reg and Durand's backs. The boys stood to excuse themselves, Reg pushing the red button on Maron's remote, less than discretely, at that. But it mattered not at this point. Nurse Sweet Cheeks came strolling in, Maron still cackling, tears streaming down his face. The boys passed her and threw a sorrowful glance back at their brother, who may have taken that opportunity to become combative with the nurse. The orderly from earlier was spotted in the hall. Durand flagged him down, nervously requesting him to remain on standby. The young man complied with the request, and the boys went back the way from which they came.

Chapter 17

Erik was not the only one of The Club to neglect a prompt visit to Maron's bedside. Damien was among the ranks, Shiloh too. However, Shiloh had a very valid excuse in the fact that his father was locked up, and he could not yet legally drive. Damien prayed he would receive a pass as well by reasoning of the store's continuous and seemingly miraculous level of unexpected business. Though Raquel and Sr. extended the offer, multiple times, of a day off so the boy could visit his friend, Damien insisted he would rather stay and man the cannons at Mazetti's. The whole prospect of mental illness and breakdowns utterly terrified Damien, though he would grow up to be diagnosed with multiple conditions himself. Hospitals scared him. Discomfort and awkward conversations scared him. Death absolutely mortified him. And, quite truthfully, Maron scared him. Though the avoidance of visiting an unwell friend made Damien feel completely ashamed and, at times, physically sick, he continued to justify his lack of a visit with Mazetti's out-of-the-blue boom in business. 'Mom and Dad need me, right? The Store needs me. I'm important here. Nobody makes sandwiches like me. Nobody mops a floor and leaves it looking glossy and new like I do. Yeah, I'm important. Maron will get it, right?' With his morning Hail Mary's, the boy was sure to squeeze in the request of Maron's understanding when addressing, presumably, a very busy God. Around the time that Reg and Durand uncomfortably exited the hospital and awaited Steve's arrival to retrieve them, Damien was serving up a pastrami on rye, multiple turkey clubs, and the largest plastic container Mazetti's offered of potato salad, to Mr. Rabinowitz. Mr. Rabinowitz was a kind old Jewish man who was speculated to have escaped Nazi capture with his family and caught a ride to New York. This was, of course, merely a rumor, perhaps. If Damien's comprehension of math and history added up, this would put the man at ninety or so years of age, assuming he left Poland as a young boy. The smiling elder always donned a Yarmulke on his bald and spotted head. Occasionally, he would slip Damien a fiver or sometimes even ten dollars as a tip. When doing so, he would always command that the boy kept it secret from his dad, in only a half-joking way. The sweet old gentleman surely broke the stereotype with his monetary generosity to the youth. Mr. Rabinowitz was great. If the whole store was filled with a bunch of Mr. Rabinowitzes, all the time, clumsily bumping into each other with their carts and carefully selecting kosher items off the shelves, it would make Damien's job a piece of cake. Right now, it was not a piece of cake by any means. However, dealing with a slew of impatient customers still beat the alternative of having to face Maron and say something to the effect of: 'Sorry your mom died. This whole topic makes me uncomfortable, so I'm just gonna linger around your lonely and desolate hospital room out of politeness and concern and hope you don't freak the fuck out again.' The selection of deli meats was becoming scarcer by the order. The delivery was supposed to arrive before noon, yet still no sign or call from the driver at well past four in the afternoon. Sr. was livid. Such an unlikely surge in commerce couldn't be halted by a slow and lazy delivery driver. The old man wouldn't stand for it. At half-past five, a chubby young man in a box truck backed into the sole loading dock of the grocery store. Sr. unloaded a frenzy of curses and condemnations while, nearly violently, prodding the driver's flabby chest with an olive-skinned pointer finger. The driver, quite possibly baked out of his mind, took it all in stride and wheeled in the cases of salted meat, unloading each box into the cooler for an angry Mr. Mazetti, who swiftly grabbed several of the cases and rushed them up to the deli counter, proudly announcing the freshness of the product to his herd of hungry and too-lazy-to-cook-that-night customers. There was no time for a snack or bathroom break that evening for young Damien until after seven o'clock. The young boy stripped off his apron and made a beeline for the facilities. He thoroughly washed his hands, considering germs are another source of heartfelt trepidation for the young worker. Damien was relieved to see, for the first time in hours, not a single customer waiting in line for a BLT. He wisely took the time to scrounge up some roast beef on two buns for himself and went to town. In five minutes, the sandwich was vanquished, and the lad returned to a small congregation, all scanning the chalkboard that was suspended from the ceiling. This displayed the staples and specials the deli offered, all in Raquel's flawless handwriting. Things carried on this way up until closing time. Holly was exhausted, as the register was every bit as busy as the deli counter that evening. After the girl's drawer was accounted for, she swiftly made her exit, but not before whipping herself up a small bowl of pasta salad. The whole day generated a sum of just over fifteen-thousand dollars, shattering the previous record by several grand. Sr. danced around his office, his moves soon spilling out onto the floor as Raquel and Damien tidied up. The old man let out a string of whoops and hollers of pure ecstasy, and the late delivery no longer mattered in the slightest. Damien continued to sweep debris off the floor as his mother ran into his father's arms. The two shared a passionate kiss, much to the disgust of their son, and Sr. made his way over to Damien, yanking the broom and dustpan from the boy's hands and carelessly tossing it into the canned food aisle. The two spun around in a clumsy embrace, Sr. planting a multitude of kisses on his boy's forehead. Damien laughed as he wiped away the stubbly smooches of his father. Nobody knew how or why, but the Mazetti family continued to win.

Accompanying this triumph, however, was a sad and nauseous feeling of complete remorse for Damien. He knew he had to visit Maron the following day. He asked to be excused from school tomorrow, which Sr. promptly granted. The Mazettis locked up, and Sr. double and triple-checked that all cameras were functioning as they should. The three sped away in the Enclave, swinging by the Wendy's for a late dinner. Much to the family's surprise, a familiar face near the establishment's dumpster was picked up by the bright beams of the luxury SUV as it rounded about to the voice box of the drive-thru. Shiloh was approaching the trash receptacle, and the whole family could assume why.

"Honey, go get him, now," Raquel demanded. Damien was already in the process of opening his door. He jogged over to his friend, who still stood frozen by the shock of the headlights, as if he was part deer. Shiloh looked to the ground once Damien got close enough.

"Dude, hey, you don't have to do that. Look, come in the car with us and my dad will get us all some dinner, okay? Come stay the night with me tonight. I'm skipping tomorrow to go see Maron. You can come with, okay?" Shiloh finally summoned what was left of his pride and met his friend's eye contact. He anxiously toed a broken-up piece of asphalt, while wishing to disappear into the abyss of everybody's collective memory forever.

"Right? Dude, a Baconator sounds fucking amazing right now, doesn't it? Come on, Shiloh." Damien ushered his friend toward the vehicle, but he did not budge. Shiloh finally found the words.

"Look, man, I'm fine. I'm just out on a walk, is all. I been staying with Mrs. Hadley. Like I'm good, I don't need to come and crash at anyone's place. I'm fine," Shiloh flashed an unconvincing grin. Damien suspected he hadn't eaten since lunch on the day of Maron's meltdown.

"So, staying with Mrs. Hadley, huh? So, I guess you've eaten nothing but cigarette butts for days?" Damien's attempt to lighten the mood with humor fell flat. In fact, Shiloh displayed the visage of a boy who was at least mildly offended.

"I'm good, Dim. I don't need handouts. I just wanna walk, alright? Git back to your mom n dad, leave me be," the boy's normally goofy conduct showed no trace of itself throughout the entire exchange. Damien shot a glance back to his parents, who were now holding up a line of at least three cars. He slowly raised his palms to his earlobes, as if to signal to his mother that his invitation wasn't working. She reciprocated the motion before unfastening her seatbelt and crossing over to the two boys. Honks commenced and Raquel feistily waved the impatient line-waiters off. She strutted over to Shiloh, extending her slim and tan arms and wrapping the boy in a hug around his neck.

"Honey, what's wrong? Just get in the car, we'll get you some dinner and you can stay the night. I know Bootsy misses you! Come over tonight, baby. Damien's skipping tomorrow. You guys can go see Maron together," Raquel's enticement proved to fail as well. Shiloh pulled free and took a few subtle steps backward.

"Uh, no, Mrs. 'Zetti. I just gotta get goin', okay? Thanks, though." Shiloh strode past the dumpster he was hoping to retrieve some scraps from only moments earlier and continued his shameful stalking through the night. Damien and his mother slowly reentered the car. Raquel was sure to throw the finger at the hangry line of cars who continued to honk and swear at her. She had had her fill of lines that day. The family picked up dinner and drove home. Sr. took a rather roundabout way in hopes of catching a glimpse of his son's displaced friend. After twenty or so minutes of cruising the east side of town, the Mazettis succumbed to their hunger and soon found themselves parked in the driveway of their comfortable dwelling on Maple Street. Shiloh had vanished, quite literally, like a thief in the night. The family sat down in the living room together, and in the spirit of Raquel's favorite and rapidly approaching holiday, Night of the Living Dead was selected for their viewing pleasure that evening. Damien, tech whiz extraordinaire, set up the DVD player and the trio soon indulged in some greasy hamburgers and a black-and-white classic together. However, during this family movie screening, Damien did not pass out on the floor. He nearly concluded the movie when he looked back to see his parents asleep, Raquel resting her modelesque head on Sr.'s shoulder. Damien retrieved a blanket and carefully draped it over his mom and dad's laps. He clicked off the lights and scooped up Bootsy, who was lazily lounging at the foot of the stairs. The fat old cat revved up its purbox like a hotrod, and Damien could feel the comforting vibration against his chest. The two entered Damien's room, where he left his phone to charge. Much to his surprise, several unopened messages awaited him: 'Hope all is good. Talked to some of the guys besides Shiloh. I honestly feel like you're my only friend left. Might be released tomorrow. They couldn't get ahold of my POS dad, shocker. My Aunt Dot is coming from Pennsylvania to stay with me. I would love to see you soon Dim. Love u bud.' Although the message was only received an hour ago, Damien made haste to scribble back a reply in hopes that his wounded friend was still awake. He was. Maron's reply read, 'Mom did them another favor. Tell you about it tomorrow. Come see me if they don't release me, ok?' Damien replied affirmatively, adding an encouraging message of his confidence that Maron would soon be back in his own home, with his relative who may as well have been a complete stranger, Aunt Dot. The boys wished one another a good night and Damien soon drifted off into a well-deserved slumber. He awoke to the smell of French toast that morning. Raquel took the day off for herself as well to escort her son to see Maron, and hopefully treat herself to a little spa trip since the two would already be in Norhauk. Sr. was already at the store. Raquel served up a hearty helping of French toast and hashbrowns to her son. The boy opted for a coffee in place of orange juice that day, something Raquel wasn't fond of but never outrightly objected to either. The pair conversed for a while, Damien speaking through mouthfuls of scrumptious breakfast food. Once finished, he hit the bathroom for a dump and a quick shower, and mother and son were on their way. The weather proved to not be such a factor on this day. A cool breeze welcomed two-thirds of the Mazetti clan once they exited the car. The sun shined from just above the rooftop of the hospital, kissing the visitors' faces with a warm and promising benefaction. The two made their way in and were promptly directed to Maron's room. The sick young man was out of bed and in a chair, facing the shatterproof window. He quickly turned his head upon hearing footsteps. He stood with a smile and outstretched arms, welcoming Damien and his mother to his room of confinement. Damien wrapped his friend up in a bearhug and couldn't help but notice that he had lost even more weight. Maron was lean as hell to begin with. He now teetered on the edge of starvation. Damien ignored the troubling observation as Maron repeated his embrace, this time in the direction of Raquel. The young mother wept into Maron's bony shoulder as if she was the one who lost her most beloved person in this godforsaken world. All things considered, Maron seemed rather enthusiastic. Damien guessed it was some type of overcompensation to prove his sanity before witnesses and his caretakers. Staying, for a prolonged length, in a dreary and bleak hospital room often produces the opposite effect of the initial intention for the admitted. Even those of the tender age of fifteen could deduce this simple fact. The three conversed lightly, at first. Maron brought up the plans for Aunt Dot to come and stay for a while. This led to Raquel's questioning of the long-term scheme; what would become of Maron once Aunt Dot had to return to the suburbs of Philadelphia to resume her spinster lifestyle? Those cats can't feed themselves, unfortunately. Maron dropped the bombshell news of Gloria's plan: Sarah got the house and was to adopt Maron as her son. Damien and Raquel practically jumped for joy, knowing that the boy would be taken care of and would have a legal guardian. Better yet, he had a legal guardian who was freshly reemployed, had a house which was paid off, as well as a newer model and reliable vehicle, as his real mother willed the car to Sarah as well. Even more handouts, huh? Maron mulled it all over in his head since he was admitted. Throughout the miniature celebration on Damien and Raquel's part, Maron seemed rather stoic. He forced a smile, at least, but didn't exhibit his visitors' ecstatic behavior. The lack of his participation stifled, but not entirely silenced, Damien and Raquel's blissful display.

"You know that I'm not gonna call her "Mom", right, guys," Maron quizzed the two that sat across from him. Both looked confused at the remark. Raquel rose and walked over to Maron, kneeling and grasping his fragile kneecaps before verbally responding.

"Of course, honey. She's not your mom. And she won't ask you to think of her as such. Legally, though, you need an adult in your household, or you could be moved to the system. It's for the best, babe. Believe me." The kind and beautiful woman's response invoked only a slightly relieved feeling within the orphaned young man. He slowly nodded, mostly out of courtesy, and Raquel removed her hands from the boy's lower thighs, much to Maron's dismay. The conversation shifted back to a lighter range of topics.

"So, I hear that cutie by the name of "Hannah" wants you to take her to the dance, huh," Raquel inquired, in a nearly flirty and jealous tone. Maron forced an embarrassed smile.

"Well, that was before I freaked out in the cafeteria. I'm sure she's not interested anymore," the boy modestly responded.

"Oh, stop that," Raquel waved her dainty little hand in Maron's face, eliciting a more profound grin this time. "She could only be so lucky, baby. Right, Dim?" Damien nodded in confirmation of his mother's sentiment. In fact, much at the behest of his mother, Damien pulled some strings and managed to procure Hannah Lada's phone number, which he offered to Maron. The nervous Count Paris spent nearly thirty minutes typing and then deleting his proposal. He finally pressed 'send' after an anxious battle within his own heart. He received a reply within seconds, and a positive one, at that. A genuinely happy expression soon spread across Maron's face, this being the first one since Mom died. He announced the confirmation that he would have the pleasure of escorting a cute, awkward, big-butted girl from the school band to the formal. Damien and Raquel recreated their joyous celebration from before. This time, Maron joined in with sincerity. The troubled lad was released later that same day into the custody of Sarah once she was dismissed from work. Erik was shyly in tow. The sick boy exemplified an entirely opposite display which he wore only the day before. He proposed to Erik and Sarah that the three of them meet up with Damien and his mother for dinner that evening. No demand was too great to grant, not on his behalf, anyway. The boy who lost all gained something many of us have had and do have today. The potential promise of another woman to love him and cherish him loomed on the horizon. Granted, this one would not have the culinary skills that Mom did. This one would not recount embarrassing but comical stories that Mom did, as this one didn't really know him, not just yet. This one would smell different. She would use a different shampoo, conditioner, or perfume that would fall short of The Greatest and Hers, which She kept in Her bathroom's medicine cabinet. However, this one was also cute and youthful. Her breasts and most womanly parts were not yet ravaged by a sick and unrelenting disease. This one was fresh. She still had years and many-a-mile in the tank, as The Greatest was riding on faith and fumes for quite a while. Such is the mind of a young boy. Some may speculate that his outlook was selfish, lustful, and shallow. Others, such as myself, recognize the optimism and vitality that were not completely buried with Maron's mother's precious memory. For I know that life goes on. If you don't move with it, you will soon be buried with the peels which once enveloped it and the shells which once protected its sacred fruit.

Chapter 18

Shiloh slept at Mrs. Hadley's residence, but this did not necessarily mean that he called it his own. Indeed, her home was largely similar to his. It was cramped. It was dusty. The perpetual yellowed stench of tobacco smoke seeped into every surface within the domicile, but it was not home and would never be. Kurt awaited his court date, still. So much for a swift and speedy trial, thought Shiloh. The boy visited his father several times, sometimes twice in a single day. He confirmed with Kurt that the trial would fall on next week's Thursday, the night before the homecoming game. Despite threats of officers paying a visit to the delinquent's doorstep due to truancy, Shiloh mostly remained absent from school. He would go on to make two appearances that particular week, completely neglecting the other three scheduled days. The youth mostly passed his days alone. This day, however, he managed to scrounge up whatever spare change he could and paid a visit to Mazetti's. He was sure to thoroughly scrub his face that morning, as well as brush his teeth. He snagged his dad's stick of deodorant, which wasn't touched in weeks by either of the Robertson men and applied a thick layer onto each armpit. Even Kurt's cheap bottle of cologne wasn't safe. Shiloh sparingly sprayed himself and rubbed the final dose behind his ears, which was an area he often neglected to wash. 'Just a dab'll do ya, boy,' Kurt's advice rang in Shiloh's ears. With his hopes to God Himself, the boy left on foot in the pursuit of purchasing a bottle of cheap pop and getting one more conversation with a beautiful cashier. The voyage was uneventful, save for seeing a dead and stinking cat in the road.

Shiloh entered the thriving shoppe with a renewed sense of confidence. After all, what was to lose at this point? He spotted Holly at her usual position. A customer was price-matching a package of name-brand paper towels. What a pleasant concern to have, Shiloh bitterly spoke in his head. He strolled the store before landing in the bargain aisle and picked out a jug of Peak's Crisp soda. He casually meandered to the packed checkout line. Holly rapidly scanned her current customer's purchases and bagged each item herself. She was the epitome of allure in her tired and hungry state. Shiloh patiently waited and quietly devised at least a dozen opening lines. He was at the plate, and Holly's demeanor drastically shifted from that of an exhausted and underpaid seasonal worker to that of a proud owner of one of the most lavish estates in southern Italy who was desperate to sell just before vacation season.

"Reese's Guy," her effeminate voice rang, nearly shrilly, at her recognized customer's approach. Shiloh couldn't help but beam at the inside joke. He slung the two-liter onto the conveyor belt, as close to Holly as he could manage, in an attempt to lighten her workload. The blond beauty scanned and bagged the singular item for a hopeful young man. She half-jokingly tried to upsell a package of Reese's chocolates, which Shiloh politely rejected, insisting he had to watch his figure while pointing to his gaunt ribcage. Holly giggled, insisting he could afford to indulge in some empty calories. If only she knew. As Jack handed his beloved Rose a handful of quarters and dimes as payment, he finally found his courage.

"Holly, I know we don't know each other real well, sorry, 'very well', but my homecoming dance is soon, and I would be honored if you would be my date for it," he blushingly glanced down at his tattered shoes just after prompting his six-million dollar question. Holly stood, mouth agape, for several seconds. The girl got a grip on herself and realized she had to verbally answer. As much as it pained her, even more so than it did

Shiloh, she had to let him down easy. She explained the age gap, as well as being a graduate from Castalia and returning as a date for some random kid just wouldn't look right. She sorrily denied the boy's gentlemanly advance, not due to looks or status, or even to the fact that Shiloh was mixed up in some pretty heavy shit at the moment, unbeknownst to her. Purely and morally, she rejected him. And Shiloh was able to justify that as soon as his trip home.

"I think you're really sweet and cute, but you taking me just wouldn't be right. Oh, if you were a few years older, my God!" Her voice did the same girly squeak as before, nearly causing her suitor to faint. Shiloh confirmed that he understood and no hard feelings existed between the two. He vowed to pay another visit for some Reese's Cups and off-brand pop in the near future. Despite not receiving the result he had prayed for, the boy walked a little taller that day. In minutes he arrived back at the trailer park. One of the first signs of life he observed was Mrs. Hadley making her best attempt at a pace across her microcosm of a lawn. She hobbled over to the boy as soon as she caught glance of him. Despite her commute only being a dozen or so yards, the old woman was practically wheezing when she attempted to deliver her news to the nearly orphaned boy. She paused for a moment to try to catch her breath and instinctively reached for her pack of smokes she kept stored in her bra.

"Honey, that boy," she started, sucking down a long stream of cigarette smoke, "that boy at the bar, he's s'posed to make a recovery, the doctors said. My cousin is an ass-wiper at the hospital. She been carin' for him and says he's gonna live and should return to somewhat normal, I guess. This means your daddy ain't gonna face no murder charges now. Been lookin' shit up, Kurt might do some prison time but could be as little as a year, baby. Your daddy could be back here before you graduate, even. That sure beats the hell outta him doin' years or even life in prison." Mrs. Hadley chiefed the remainder of her square and lit up another, Shiloh partaking as well. The young man's initial reaction, which he fought like hell to stifle, was to jump for joy. Upon hearing the news, he could've planted a big wet kiss on old Mrs. Hadley as if she was the beauty queen that his favorite cashier was. But there was something about the old hag's phrasing and delivery of the announcement that just put him off to any type of positive reaction. Kurt would have another felony stuck to his name like glue. What would this mean when he got out? It would be even harder than before to find honest work. That's what it meant. Simply the fact that it was not a death sentence for the single father was not good enough for Shiloh. It was not good enough anymore. What would happen five years down the road? When Shiloh, hopefully, would take Holly as his bride and start a family, would the grandfather even be present? Would he be incarcerated once more? Or, worse yet, in the grave? The young delinquent often looked to the family lives of his best of friends and made bitter comparisons to his own. Sure, Durand never knew his own father, but he at least had a father figure that wasn't drunk constantly. Reg shared the same case to a slight degree. He at least had a man he could call "dad", who did love him, although struggled to show for and act on this sacred bond. Erik's father may have been worse, considering he became belligerent when drunk and often took out his frustrations in his own shortcomings in life on his wife and youngest son. Maron's father may have split early on, but that didn't impede his quality of life at home. He was loved and sheltered by a sturdy and beautiful single mother for most of his years. Then there was Damien. Perhaps Shiloh's relentless teasing and taunting of this particular friend stemmed from a burning and intense jealousy that took root early on in life. Damien not only had a father, but he also had a winner. Sr. coached little league for years; Shiloh was fortunate enough to play for his team at the age of ten. The man gave back to the community when he could. He was present at every blood drive. He donated books to the library. He drove a fancy car and had a pretty wife. His son was well-fed and always sported the nicest clothes ever seen by any Castalia student. One year, around the holidays, Damien got a new pair of Nike Cortez's and gave his beat-up pair of Adidas high-tops to Shiloh. It was the greatest Christmas gift the boy had ever received. That year, the only gifts he unwrapped that were addressed by his own father were a pair of jeans from GoodWill, which were two sizes too big, and a weathered and heavily crayoned Superman action figure, which Kurt didn't actually even purchase from any store, but rather found in the neighbor kids' yard, so he snuck it home after it got dark. Forgotten trash and pre-worn clothes were all that Shiloh was worthy of that year, at the impressionable age of twelve. It would seem that Mr. 'Zetti was the model father that any boy should be given the shot at. Isn't that what a dad should be, anyway? Successful, present, encouraging, and sober were just a few desirable traits the middle-aged man exhibited. Shiloh had never felt more jealous than he did in that moment. Throughout all of his life, he didn't ask much of the world, or his friends, or even of God Himself. But to have a dad like Mr. 'Zetti would just be aces. Another strange feeling eclipsed the weary youth's mind. Though Shiloh could never recall his mother, or what she looked like, or what she smelled like, or how she sounded when she certainly spoke sweet kindnesses into his infantile ear, he deeply missed her. Rhona was killed six months after bringing Shiloh into this world. She struck an eighteen-wheeler head-on while coming home from her late shift at Fontana's in Norhauk. Of the more cynical theories as to how the accident unfolded, some supposed she was drunk and drifted across the center line. Others, her coworkers and friends, mainly, backed the idea that she was simply dog-tired from a seventy-hour workweek and dozed at the wheel at the worst possible time. When suspicions take hold of such a small town, some of which manage to flourish in the form of parasites and deceptively grow into what is widely believed to be God's Honest factual truth. The hunch that Rhona was intoxicated or stoned out of her mind was the explanation that pervaded most of the minds of The Townspeople. Many of Rhona's own family blamed the possibility of postpartum depression. The tragedy was further smeared and painted a suicide by those who were supposed to be closest to her. Here was a young and, at times, unstable girl who unexpectedly became pregnant by a man largely a stranger to her. She was poor, as was the father. 'Lass knew she cuh-int hannel it awl', Aunt Gwenn, Rhona's next of kin, spoke the words on more than one occasion. The "lass" was barely nineteen. Shiloh returned from his infinitely deep ponderings and self-reflections to finally respond to his neighbor. The cherry of his cigarette nearly scorched his knuckles now. He carelessly tossed it into Mrs. Hadley's gravel driveway.

"Mizz Hadley, I'm glad that he's not doin' life. I love my dad. You know that. But just 'cause I'm glad don't mean I'm happy. This whole mess, this whole shit show, right here, is all 'cause of him and his choices. Them boys would never've messed with us if Dad didn't get mixed up in their shit, and you know that. We wouldn't be so goddamn poor if he could keep a job and put the bottle down. You know that's right, too. Mizz Hadley, he ain't got a life sentence hangin' above him, which I thank God for, but I'm also thankin' Him for handin' out some type of reaper-cushion for my dad to have to face. Maybe it's what he needs, ya know? Tough love, or somethin' like that. He needs to learn how to be a grownup, 'cause I'm tired of havin' to be one to myself. I'm headin' in, come in if ya want." Shiloh stepped forward to hug the flabby and flabbergasted old bird before turning around to enter the sad and solitary shack. Just as he crossed the threshold of the front door, the cheap plastic bag which contained his bargain brand pop ripped open, allowing the two-liter to hit the floor and fizz up and rupture through the seal of the cap, leaking out onto the surface of the entryway. This did the boy in. Shiloh loudly proclaimed that he was 'done with this fuckin' day', and, as politely as he could, revoked his invitation for Mrs. Hadley to come in. He left the sugary and artificial mess on the floor and, before breaking down completely in front of his neighbor, swung the door closed in her face and crumpled into a defeated heap on the dirty floormat. He remained in this position for nearly two hours. After finally achieving some sense of composure, Shiloh swallowed his pride and crossed back over to Mrs. Hadley's front door. She cleared his spot on the old, tarnished couch, but the boy insisted he only wanted to make a phone call. His wish was granted, and he soon dialed Mazetti's landline, the business, not the home, as it was the one listed in the phonebook, and Shiloh never made the effort to learn by heart his friends' cell numbers. He barely remembered his own old landline, considering it wasn't operational for years at that point. He was put through to Sr. and he humbly inquired if the offer of a sleepover at Dim's was still on the table. Sr. obliged with a sense of audible relief and satisfaction as if he was thrilled to have a dirty, ill-mannered white-trash youth such as the Robertson boy take up residence in his mansion. The two made arrangements for Shiloh to be picked up that evening. The dinner plans with Erik, Sarah and Maron were also announced. Shiloh, as forward as ever, asked for Reg and Durand and their parents to be invited as well. 'Whoever wants to, kay, Mr. 'Zetti? Durand's lil sisters, too. Everybody! Let's all go out!' Sr. could not deny the boy his wish. Sr. excused himself to tend his shoppe and Shiloh, for the first time in what felt like years, was looking forward to spending an evening with the people he could always rely on. Mazetti's closed around seven that evening. All members of the household hurried home and showered and dressed and were in Shiloh's dusty driveway by eight o'clock. Shiloh promised Mrs. Hadley a plate to go. The old bat's eyes lit up. Shiloh climbed into the middle row of the expensive SUV, clicking his seatbelt and looking around the cabin with a blatant sense of admiration. Damien couldn't help but smile. In all, four vehicles were taken to the Suzuki Grille and Steakhouse in Norhauk that evening. Sarah drove Erik and Maron, who conversed with his new family members as if nothing uncomfortable had ever happened between them. Beatrix took all three of her children, despite the fact that the late reservation was already toeing the line of the girls' bedtimes. Reg's commute with his parents was mostly silent, nearly to the point of feeling pained and strangled. And, of course, Shiloh wore the armband of "Honorary Mazetti" that evening. The four cars convened relatively nearby one another in the packed parking lot. Everyone got out to greet one another, all the boys flocking around Maron. Collectively, they all were given the impression that almost felt sinful to even think, much less to make a verbal observation on; Maron somehow looked years younger and degrees healthier. The parents noticed it as well, all seeming to try to meet Sarah's glance at once. The less astute restaurant-goers that evening, Ramona and Breanna, fought over who got to ride piggyback on Shiloh first. The young man managed to sling both little girls on his back at once and hauled ass for the door as they were deceptively heavy. The silly act invoked quite the roar of laughter from all who were present in the party. The four families entered, Durand holding the door for all, aside from Shiloh and the girls, who were the first ones to rudely crash into the swanky restaurant.

"Mazetti, party of fourteen," a young hostess politely questioned. One could tell the girl was nearing the end of a long and thankless shift, as her soft voice was faintly tinged with a particular note of exhaustion and anxiety. Sr. confirmed, and a line filed behind the hostess to the largest table at the center of the restaurant. Beatrix waited for the hostess to leave before bringing her fellow mothers in for a little mom huddle and proceeded to dish out all of her gross findings at this particular establishment in recent years. Granted, she hadn't been back, on-duty, anyway, since the place changed ownership and became "Suzuki's". The men, too, initiated their own conversation, Sr. doing most of the talking. He was excited to hear of Reg and Durand's on-field conquests, as the old man was a star player back in his own day. Damien couldn't help but feel the slightest bit jealous upon seeing his father's face glow and beam at hearing all about his friends' accolades thus far into the season. This petty sense of envy evaporated once appetizers were delivered to the table, however.

"Yep, have Clyde tomorrow then homecoming the week after," Durand spoke between bites of his salad, receiving a stern look from his mother as he dabbed dressing from his goatee with his fancy napkin. Sr. was no better. A stream of broth from his soup trickled down his stubbly chin. He drank up the news of the football team much as he did the contents of his small porcelain soup bowl. Raquel rolled her eyes in embarrassment. The mothers split two sake flights amongst themselves. The little girls, Shiloh, and even eventually Maron began tracing through Ramona's and Breanna's kids' menu mazes. The boys helped the little ones with their word searches, Maron on Breanna's team and Shiloh on Ramona's. Entrees soon arrived. The Club and Its Family carried on in this way for the next two hours. They all ate, drank, and laughed with a carefree and innocent sense that none of them, save for Breanna and Ramona, had truly experienced in years. At long last, Maron stood with his peach iced tea. He held the glass high and proposed a toast in not only his own mother's precious name, but in Kurt Robertson's as well. Shiloh reciprocated, holding nothing but a glass of ice cubes. The little girls, with their plastic take-home cups, followed suit. The tipsy moms, most of which now brought to tears, raised glasses of merlots and cabernets. All the other men at the table joined in as well. No spoken words expounded on this toast, but none were needed. Maron and Shiloh reseated themselves and the party got ready to pack it up for the night. It was well past most bedtimes. Sr. discreetly indicated for the waitress to directly hand him the bill when she brought it. He also footed a four-hundred-dollar tip, much to the other parents' objections. Steve meagerly offered up fifty dollars of his own money but was completely ignored by Sr. Damien smiled as he recounted his petty jealousness from before. What had he to be jealous of? He had great friends. He had the best parents he could ever hope for. He took note of each and every child and woman at the table and counted his fortune of blessings. He had it all. Sometimes he just lost sight of that simple fact.

Chapter 19

Shiloh bunked with the Mazettis that evening, as he would continue to do for the foreseeable future. Reg and Durand salvaged what few hours of sleep that they could squeeze in before gameday. Durand's baby sisters passed out in their booster seats on the ride home. Reg was silent while Jessica blabbed about some snooty new client at the beauty parlor. Steve pretended to listen, still feeling like a punk over dinner. Erik and Maron lightly conversed in the backseat of what used to be Gloria's prized vehicle. The funeral would be that Monday. The elephant in the room, or rather, in the car, was soon addressed by Sarah. She vowed, solemnly to God and all of His angels, that once Maron turned eighteen the car and home would all be legally his, just as Gloria had intended. She promised, in the meantime, to 'work like hell' to find her own home for herself and her son. Such distant events didn't typically concern the average teenage boy. These events were so far-off, they may as well be put on the backburner and completely forgotten about. One concern not on the backburner, but rather very much present and worrisome, was the dark figure slinking around the side of the house, which Sarah just caught view of in her headlights. She and Erik knew instantly. Maron was left, quite literally, in the dark as Sarah shut the engine off.

"Honey, call the police right now. Tell them there's an intruder at the house. Keep the keys in here and keep it locked," Sarah's firm instruction sent a chill down both boys' spines. Erik only had "9" typed into his phone before starkly objecting to his mother's reckless wish. Sarah exited the vehicle, ensuring it was locked before slamming the door shut, as if to announce her presence. Maron was up to speed now. Erik's crazy fuckin' dad, at MY house? At MOM's house? The boy's anger began to swell. Erik had the police on the phone and was told to stay on the line. Sarah disappeared alongside the home. Maron swiftly unlocked the car from the driver's door and exited, much to the objection of Erik, who soon followed. Sarah felt the crunch of glass under her light and timid footsteps. She looked up to her left to see all four windows on this side of the home were shattered out. A deranged laugh sounded from the decadent backyard. The sloshing of a liquid could be heard. Maron went the other way with Erik at his coattails. He noticed no indication of vandalism on this side of the house, at least. He was the first to see Jared, who was dumping gasoline in a sloppy trail right up to the steps of the back porch. All of the anger reignited within the lad, much quicker than Jared could ignite his own flame. He belted out a fierce and horrendous scream as he made large and quick strides toward the drunken bastard. A single match struck the box and was dropped. Maron tackled his much larger opponent with a ferocity and vigor not normally seen out of a scrawny and withered one-hundred-thirty-pound boy. The stream of gasoline went up and burnt hot. Sarah and Erik panicked, desperately scanning the area for something to extinguish the blaze, but the back porch was engulfed within seconds. "Get the fire department! He set a fuckin' fire! Fire department, hurry," Erik demanded into the phone. He knew this was no longer a covert operation. He quickly joined Maron in the relentless beatdown of his own father. Jared was too sloppily drunk to fend off two attackers, regardless of their size. He was taken to the ground. Maron delivered repetitive blows. He threw combinations of hammer fists and short elbows into Jared's teeth, several of which popped right out with a sickening crack. Sarah ran for the garden hose and tried her best to contain the blaze. Sirens soon boomed throughout the cool night air. Within minutes of Erik's call, three cruisers and two firetrucks were parked on the lawn of Maron's mother's home.

Jared lay unresponsive under the full mount of Maron. Erik pushed his friend off, rather abrasively. He wanted to get his licks in, too. Erik stomped the face of his greatest tormentor. He felt bone-crunching creaks and cracks under his foot, but he never slowed down. In front of six men of the law, eight firefighters, his best friend, his own mother, and in front of God and all of Heaven Itself, the boy just kept stomping and punting. Blood gushed from every pore, every orifice of Jared's face. His nose was a crimson faucet. His eyes rolled back into his skull, and the once-whites of them leaked tiny rivulets of a jelly and blood mixture. The firefighters, the ones who were not violently puking into the bushes, anyway, extinguished the last of the cruel and evil remnants of arson. A police officer, barely out of the academy, strode over and pulled Erik off. "Fuck him! Fuck him! Dead isn't good enough! I want him to be a pulp on this fucking lawn! Shoot him! Make sure he's really fucking dead," the boy was in hysterics. Maron could no longer claim the title of the craziest friend in the group. I know he was breathing, at least, when I last hit him, Maron thought as he looked down at his shaky and blood-soaked hands. He stood to his feet and slowly found his way into Sarah's arms. She was sobbing.

"I just couldn't let him destroy Mom's house, right, Mrs. Serling? I didn't mean for him to die, but he shouldn't have been doing that, right? Right, Mrs. Serling? Right? Mrs. Serling?" The sound of Maron's repetitive stream of her name, along with the sound of sirens and the stench of burnt wood and lacquer, would haunt Sarah's dreams for years.

Chapter 20

Small towns are vastly different from many communities in which plenty of people grow up within and are accustomed to. A town or a village, or even a hamlet with a miniscule population does not necessarily constitute a "small town". Small towns have their ways. The Town keeps its secrets. Sometimes, often, in fact, these secrets protect its evil doers. A prime example is the upbeat, likeable middle-aged man who lived in the ugly blue house catty-cornered to you in your youth. He lived a long and publicly celebrated life. His family, members of his community, the boys from his old scout troop, the oblivious ones who thought so highly of him, anyway, all congregated at his funeral. They wept in his name, and he escaped this life smelling as sweet as a rose, never having to answer for any ill deed. He was branded a saint as he was lowered into the ground. But several former cub scouts were not in attendance at the funeral; they did not make an appearance at the showing. Sure, some of them, now grown men, many with families of their own, had prior obligations. Others moved too far away to justify coming back to the Podunk town where they once played little league ball, or caught frogs in its community park, all to say their farewells to the scoutmaster they barely remembered from their boyhoods. One particular former scout, by the name of Burl Bartlett, wept a river of his own tears, but the falling of such drops was not rooted in sorrow, but rather pure bliss and relief upon receiving the news. As a child, Burl Bartlett was a runty little boy with a less than ideal family life. His father was present, in the physical sense. Burl was not too unlike our fearless Erik, but Burl never managed to find the courage to stand up to his adversaries, whether it was his own father when he mercilessly beat down Mrs. Bartlett for starting dinner late, or his scoutmaster, Bismuth

Goldschmidt, whenever he requested to play 'the game' with Burl. Mr. Goldschmidt had a pool in his backyard. Plenty of times, the boys would convene at this spot after meetings. Goldschmidt would whip up some snacks for his guests and many boys would stay late into the evening. After all, it was summer vacation. Burl was always one of the night owls. He looked for any and every reason he could to avoid returning home to a surely angry and belligerent father and a cowering mother. One day in late August, the pool party concluded at a comparatively early hour. All troop members but Burl saddled their bikes and pedaled to their safe and secure houses for a homecooked meal. Burl always felt the utmost jealousy towards the other boys. They had fathers who weren't angry at the world. They were birthed by mothers who had a backbone. Granted, Mr. Bartlett never physically lashed out at his own son; he reserved such brutality for his wife exclusively. However, the verbal abuse directed at Burl would cause irreparable damage to his psyche, even as a grown man. Over the span of several months that year, since joining scouts, Burl made this fact well-known to Goldschmidt. The scared little boy confided in the only adult he truly cared about or trusted. He confided in a monster. Just like a shark indulging in the bloodlust, the scoutmaster began to circle his prey. After the others had departed that night, Goldschmidt took Burl inside. He offered the nine-year-old boy a glass of sweet wine, which was reluctantly sipped. Burl couldn't stomach the thought of disappointing another grown-up; worse yet and above all, he didn't want to be screamed at. Once mildly intoxicated, his Batman trunkies were pulled off of him and Mr. Goldschmidt disrobed as well. The boy was led into a well-kept bedroom and was shown pictures of nude children his own age. In some of the vile Polaroids, the boys were kissing and touching one another.

"I can show you what that feels like, Burl. But it's gotta be a secret, okay? I don't show just any boy this," Goldschmidt whispered excitedly into the inebriated child's ear. A variety of the most depraved acts were performed on the boy. Such perversion was capable of making any halfway decent father's blood boil. This continued for nearly four years. After Mr. Bartlett beat his wife to the point of brain damage, child protective services finally intervened, rehoming and rescuing Burl. He quit scouts the same day. "God, make me whole again, please" was the lad's bedtime prayer each night, which he still utters to this day. The boy spent most of his adolescence with an older couple, who were nice enough but incredibly strict and devout Catholics. He would graduate and join the United States Army, where he would attain the rank of sergeant. He would lose most of his left leg fighting barbaric zealots in Afghanistan. He would marry the prettiest girl of the largest sorority, who he met at the college he attended, thanks to his G.I. Bill. She would bare him two beautiful and healthy children, who Burl would father in a firm, but gentle and patient manner. He would cry like a baby upon checking his mailbox one Saturday afternoon and receiving the invitation from Mrs. Goldschmidt, God bless her, as she was just as oblivious as the other boys or even Burl's own parents to what wicked acts truly went on inside her own home. She worked afternoons as a home nurse in Norhauk any time "the game" was played. Big Burl broke down into his wife's slender little arms that night after his own babies were sound asleep in their twin beds. Through a painfully embarrassing admission, his dirty little secret lost all power over him. The Town often masks Its Own evil and proudly displays Its good for all to admire. It lets us see what It wants us to see; It keeps up Its picturesque and charming postcard image for all outsiders to adore. But sometimes, much like Its own citizens, The Town gets drunk and forgets what should be seen and what should be hidden. Sometimes Its evil comes to light; sometimes the good gets mistaken for bad and is promptly and automatically swept under the rug. This is what happened in favor of Erik and Maron.

Chapter 21

Jared Serling did not die that evening. He was indefinitely comatose, however. Doctors estimated that he would never react to external stimuli so long as the remainder of his cold and cruel life should permit. The baby-faced cadet who plucked Erik off of his own father formulated a specific and bulletproof tale: Jared Serling was mercilessly assaulted by an unknown attacker that night. He was drunkenly wandering The Town, as he often did, and his assailant assumed the front yard he was passed out in rightfully belonged to him. A dispute existed between the two men, most likely regarding a debt that was yet to be paid. The phantom attacker, who was still at large, by the way, beat Jared into his current and vegetative state. This imaginary lunatic proceeded to torch the home from its ass-end before the heirs of the estate returned and chased him off. Nobody got a good look at the man. They found Jared clinging to life and called the authorities to report the bizarre and violent scene. The dispatcher, who was an aunt to the strapping young cadet, corroborated the tale. Fingerprints were wiped. Promises were made. Castalia's boys in blue were the good guys. This truth may have been good enough for The Town, but Erik, Maron and Sarah knew God's Truth, and what actually occurred on that horrendous night. Sarah got a motel room for herself and a separate room for her two sons. News soon spread, not just within The Club, but throughout The Town as well. Connie was worried sick, soon contacting her newly beloved. Hannah also reached out to Maron. Damien, Shiloh, Reg and Durand all kicked up the group text conversation, eagerly awaiting answers to the same question: what the fuck happened? The boys were quickly filled in. Erik maintained the story the young officer settled on and delivered this tale verbatim to Connie. Maron followed suit in his conversation with his girl. Messages from strange and unsaved numbers began appearing on both boys' phones. All were ignored. The fewer times either boy was expected to elaborate on what transpired, the better. None of the three which occupied the Motel Six slept a wink that night. Housekeeping visited both rooms at eight o'clock sharp. The three headed home, rather, they headed to what was left of home. Police and an assortment of workers were present, along with the usual nosy neighbors. Upon inspecting the damage in broad daylight, the kitchen appeared to be unscathed. The back porch was too far gone, however. The workers, some from Geardon Lumber, the other half, roughly, from Stowitz Hardware, were already busting ass to construct a new deck. The ash and debris were already cleared out, thanks to Cyclone Removal Services. Mr. Geardon and Mrs. Stowitz both swarmed the family upon their arrival to the backyard. Both business owners proudly declared that their services were free of charge, and they were both glad to help in a time of such dire crisis. Sarah went inside to cook up a breakfast, enlisting the help of both of her boys. Within an hour and a half, fifteen plates of French toast, bacon and hashbrowns were dealt out. Such a feast wiped the refrigerator nearly clean, not that it mattered under such circumstances. The helpers took a very grateful break, some of which attempting to pull some morbid details from Sarah, guising their efforts as small talk. Sarah spoke as little as possible while still maintaining a polite demeanor. It was quite rude for some of the younger guys on the crew to, in a sense, make her relive such a hellish scene, she thought. After breakfast the crew got back to it. Maron and Erik lent a hand where they could, whether that was in the shape of hauling lumber from the pickups or fetching water for the workers or directing a few of them to the bathroom. Both companies strictly prohibited either young boy from picking up a power tool, for liability purposes, of course. This was, in fact, a real shame, as Maron was quite skilled in woodshop and hoped to go into either the construction or electrical fields once he graduated. Sarah cleaned up and the boys managed to sneak in a cigarette break of their own. Both were reluctant to speak on the more serious matter at hand between drags of their Marlboros. Erik decided that he was the one who should bear the uncomfortable burden.

"Look, man, I'm sorry for all of this. I'm sorry for being shitty and not coming to see you that first day. I'm sure that was the hardest day, too. I'm sorry for coming from this weird, fucked up family, and that my, well, Jared tried to torch the fuckin' place. You didn't deserve any of this. I know that me and my mom made your life a thousand times more stressful, and I just want to apologize for all of it. You're my best friend, and I haven't even been anything close to that to you in a long time. I'm sorry, Maron. I wish none of these past few weeks had never happened." Erik crushed his cigarette butt out under his raggedy shoe and lit up a fresh smoke. Maron nodded slowly throughout the whole deliverance, then snatched Erik's cigarette from his hand as his own. Both boys started to giggle as if all that needed to be said between the two was already said. Erik snuck inside for another one of Sarah's smokes and rejoined his friend. It was finally Maron's turn to speak.

"It wasn't your fault. None of it. You didn't light my house on fire. You didn't give my mom cancer. You didn't make my dad decide to move away. You didn't do anything wrong. You're not guilty for why my life is how it is. I guess if anyone has to be guilty, it would have to be God, I suppose. He controls everything, right? He could've stopped my mom's cancer. He could've prevented your dad from doing what he did. He has the power and the knowledge to stop so much bad shit from happening, Erik. But He chooses not to act on it. I'm not mad at you or Sarah. I'm glad you guys are here. God, though, He can fuck right off. You know?" Erik was apprehensive to respond, partly due to fear of Maron having another emotional episode and partly because of his friend's level of blackhearted blasphemy. He simply nodded at Maron's sentiment, and the two boys crushed out their last cigarettes. They walked around the house to aid the laborers once more. The work was nearly done that day, structurally, anyway. Geardon promised to return the following day and sand, stain and paint the new deck, which overshadowed the old one by a considerable length and width. Sarah was quite pleased by this fact, not only because it looked good but because it meant less yard for her to have to mow. She didn't necessarily dislike mowing; the act itself was simple enough, and it improved the appearance of something around the house, which she was all about. But she hated being sweaty. She hated feeling dirty. Above all, she detested the smell of fresh-cut grass. A bigger deck was an improvement. The workers packed up into their vehicles and left, half of them assuring their return at the apple skin hours of the following day to prime and polish what was left of the workload. Sarah took to her few social media accounts to sing the praises of both companies and screamed from the mountaintops, virtually, at least, of the small businesses' wholesome generosities. The three ordered a pizza that evening and stayed up late watching decades-old slasher films together. They understandably missed out on witnessing Reg and Durand shut down Clyde's defense, but would hear enough of the highlights the following Monday to the point of feeling as if they had attended the game in person. The same morning that Maron and Erik arrived home to see an assortment of generous townsfolk working diligently to repair their home, Reg, Durand, Damien, and Shiloh all arrived at school with a collective pit in their stomachs. This was more than pregame jitters for the athletes. The day dragged on as it usually did. The lunch table was mostly silent. Connie and Hannah, unlikely friends, to say the least, joined the boys in their corner. Connie managed to pull a day off from her duty as a dishwasher in hopes of finding out more about Erik's predicament. The girls both felt as if some vital piece of information was being withheld from them, and rightfully so. The six spoke softly when they did speak. They all promptly dismissed themselves once the bell rang. Damien enlisted the help of Shiloh at the deli counter that afternoon, only for a few hours, as it was gameday, after all. Much to the Mazettis' astonishment, the displaced boy busted his ass serving customers. He's devoured every type of sandwich at least six times before; it only makes sense he knows how to make them by now, Sr. thought to himself. Shiloh kept the line moving, despite frequently throwing lustful glances in Holly's direction at the register. The blonde cutie even made her way over to converse several times that afternoon. Just before six o'clock that evening, the owner pulled Shiloh into his office and offered him a sum of one-hundred and fifty dollars for his impromptu labor at the store. Shiloh grasped the three fifties in his sweaty hands and exalted to God Almighty as if he had just struck gold in his own backyard. He ran around the old desk and hugged "Mr. 'Zetti" as a scratch-off junkie would embrace a gas station clerk when he stumbled upon a lucky prize that would justify his recent and indebted spendings. Sr. was nearly brought to tears at seeing the boy jump and swivel and skip. Once Shiloh finally settled down, Sr. prompted the topic of working after-school hours at the store a few days a week. The agreement stated that Shiloh's room and board were paid, and until his father's release, he would live under Sr.'s roof and abide by Sr.'s rules and work three days a week at the thriving delicatessen. Sr. was sure to mention that Shiloh's hourly rate of what equated to fifty dollars and some change, untaxed that day, would be reduced to roughly ten dollars per hour and would take effect the next workday. The boy agreed without hesitation, as he had everything to gain and nothing to lose. A job, a clean room, three hot meals per day, along with everything paid and accounted for? Shiloh Robertson knew he would live like the ancient Kings of Alba that he had heard so much about from his own father. The boy practically signed his name in his own blood at Sr.'s proposal. He agreed to return the next day, bright and early, exiting the office, still skipping. He wrapped Raquel up in the sweetest of hugs and pulled Damien out the door, announcing their permission to leave for the football game. Damien hadn't the time to even untie his apron. The two began their journey in the form of a sprint, which regressed into a jog, then a trot, then a winded and gasping-for-breath walk. The fact that the first half of the high school football season consisted of almost all home games was a bittersweet feeling for all. Reg and Durand knew the team could pick up some momentum early on, which has been the tale thus far. The athletes' parents didn't have to concern themselves with shelling out gas money for away games just yet, anyway. And the rest of The Club knew they could walk, if need be, to the venue to see Reg and Durand deliver an ass-whooping to their challengers. The boys reached the small brick building which served as the ticket booth. Damien tucked his apron into the back of his pants, then quickly opted to leave it hanging on a post of the chain-link fence that circled Don Steyn Stadium instead. Pops could always order more, he thought. At this moment he felt a rush of panic, as he had no cash on him for tickets. Shiloh appeared to have been waiting for this very moment. His cheesy grin stretched across his freckled face as he pulled out a crisp fifty-dollar bill.

"Tix and snacks are on me, bud," he teased Damien by waving the note close enough to his face to tickle his nose. Damien rolled his eyes and made a half-assed attempt at snatching the money. Shiloh was too quick. The boys entered and swiftly raided the concession stand. To say that Shiloh Robertson slightly splurged that evening would have been a gross understatement. For himself alone, the lad purchased three hotdogs, a large bag of popcorn, a side of nachos and two packs of Reese's, on the off chance that Holly should show up and was hungry. Damien was content with a pack of peanut M&M's. The pair hauled Shiloh's platter up to the student section and managed to find seats with an almost decent view. The Ice Cats were warming up on their half of the field. Durand was throwing short and speedy bullets to his receiving corps. There was something vastly different from his on-field presence just weeks ago versus now. He was so much more commanding. It was as if he grew another three inches and packed on twenty more pounds of lean muscle mass since his varsity debut. Confidence can do wonders for a young man. It can make him or break him. Durand seemed to have struck the perfect balance for himself. Reg was pacing the backfield. He took several handoffs and sprinted up to the thirty each time before abruptly pumping the brakes. Kickoff was shortly underway. Shiloh already devoured two of his three dogs, munching on handfuls of stale popcorn in between. Let him have this, Damien justified to himself. Poor buddy has been surviving on off-brand pop and crumbs for weeks. He threw a little smirk in Shiloh's oblivious direction. Team captains went out to call the toss and Clyde won it. Castalia was set to receive the kick. At that moment, as if out of some long-ago and forgotten fairytale, Holly herself strode up into the student section. Damien recalled that it was alumni night, and football players and band geeks by the dozen were filing in, but none of which into the student section. This night of remembrance did not exclude the small squad of cheerleaders from Holly's graduating class, of which there were six. The poor girl wandered in through the wrong staircase, and thus, she would be subject to Shiloh's attention.

"Look, see, I told you! She's here! Is there mustard on my face? Hurry, get it off!" Shiloh barked the command and embarrassingly enough, Damien complied, brushing a speck of yellow sauce from his friend's wispy whiskers. Shiloh cleared his throat, "Holly! Hey! I got food! You comin'?" The question was too sincere and hopeful for the boy's own good. Damien suddenly felt as anxious as Shiloh. She better sit up here with us, Damien repeated in his mind while Holly took the time to look around and respond. Her gaze met Shiloh's. The love-bitten youth waved his Reese's Cups above his head as if trying to entice a puppy with its favorite treat. Holly squealed in excitement.

"Reese's Guy!" Her soft lips spread apart to reveal her dazzling white teeth. She rudely stepped over a high school couple's shared plate of pizza and began scaling the steel risers. Shiloh's heart bounced around in his chest with the tenacity of an elite gymnast competing for gold. The girl stopped just a step below her admirer and his friend. "Hi, Dim! Reese's Guy! You work with me and you follow me everywhere? Creep!" Her airheaded and girlish giggle pleasantly sounded and carried on the fall evening's gentle breeze. Shiloh laughed in return, as well as Damien out of sheer courtesy. "I have to find the other girls and our coach. It's our alumni night or whatever. We're supposed to go out at halftime, but I really just don't care, you know?" The girl's voice took an air of disinterest and boredom. She quickly glanced at her phone and looked back up at Shiloh, her smile shimmering once more.

"Uh, here, Holly, got these for you," Shiloh extended the candy which was nestled in his now shaky hand. The beauty queen graciously accepted, smile somehow reaching wider than before.

"You're just the sweetest, you know that? So, they're sitting over there or whatever," she vaguely waved her slender tan arm in the general direction to her left. "But here, let me give you my number for work purposes, right? Or if you have more Reese's waiting for me, Shiloh!" The annunciation of his name was the most majestic thing to the young suitor's ears. Upon hearing it, he melted quicker than the chocolates which he offered as they would on a blistering August afternoon. Holly swiped Damien's phone and keyed her number in. She looked to Shiloh to repeat her course of action, leaving the boy dumbfounded.

"Uh, he dropped his phone at work today. It won't even turn on now," Damien swooped in to save his friend. "When he gets a new one, I'll make sure he has your number." Holly nodded in understanding. She began to turn away before glancing back at the young man who was more devoted to her than any college boyfriend ever was.

"Remember, only contact me if it pertains to work or chocolates, okay? Or I suppose once you turn eighteen, Shiloh," she threw a sly wink. To a nosy onlooker, it simply looked like an exaggerated and goofy wink from a pretty girl. To Shiloh Robertson, it was a swear to God in blood that he had already found the woman he would one day marry. He knew the mother of his children well before he even got to third base with any girl. This may as well have been a promising hand on The Holy Book itself. He was in a transfixed stupor as his bride-to-be sauntered her jiggly little apple-shaped butt back down the steel steps. Damien felt a sense of genuine happiness for his friend while fighting off any level of jealousy of his own. Shiloh appeared frozen in place.

"I gotta buy me a phone, bud," the dazed Romeo kept repeating. Damien laughed and helped himself to the last of his companion's hotdogs. The game was soon underway. This one proved to be the most grueling challenge yet throughout the Ice Cats' still young season. Durand zipped passes into the hulking and cradling mitts of his receivers. Reg danced through tacklers and picked up multiple yards per carry. Durand ran a few sneaks himself, as risky as most of them were. The offense punched in several scores; it was the defense that couldn't maintain its side of the field. When all was nearly said and done, Castalia's punting team managed to force a fumble off of a sloppy giveaway on the freshman punter's part. With under ten seconds to play and the game tied, Durand took a snap from the opponent's fifteen-yard line. None of his comrades managed to safely free themselves from the opposing secondary. Reg went out to throw a block, in hopes of Durand zeroing in on a perfect spiral pass to Starkey. The quarterback kept it for himself and made a mad dash for the goal line. He turned on the afterburners as he crossed the line of scrimmage. A free safety remained in his way. Durand reminded himself that he was God on Castalia's homefield, and no buck-fifty-pound shrimp would stand in his way to glory. He not only trucked the defender; he forced him back into the endzone with him as he crossed the goal line. The crowd roared as Castalia's star put up six more points, avoiding a risky quarter of overtime. Durand noticed he dragged the safety into the endzone as well, as he clung to his ankles. He was greatly tempted to spike the ball into the boy's facemask in a display of dominance but was reminded of kind and humble words his own mother spoke daily, avoiding such a counterproductive and disgraceful penalty. Durand dropped the ball and let it roll to his left side. The safety finally made it to his own feet and scampered off in defeat. Durand pulled off his helmet and wedged it under his left arm. He waved to the booming spectators. Ice Cats pulled yet another one out of their caps. The team hit the showers as the crowd began to disperse. Shiloh caught one more glimpse of Holly before walking back to Damien's house that night. He was hoping to see some type of cheer or chant, or pompom waving display out of the girl. However, the alumni night event consisted of only a brief introduction of each former player, band kid or cheerleader as their name was announced. Damien led the trek back to the Mazetti estate, Shiloh recounting the interaction with Holly the whole way. They arrived at the house to find Sr. chasing Raquel around the kitchen with a snow crab claw, the latter of the two shrieking and laughing throughout it all. Shiloh quickly joined in on the fun, helping Sr. to corner his wife with not one, but two chomping crustacean limbs. Damien got a kick out of the whole scene as well but pretended to be annoyed by it. He grabbed a Disney movie out of the DVD collection. The old disc player was certainly getting its steps in as of late. Raquel prepared a delicious seafood bake, something which Shiloh was largely unaccustomed to. Damien showed his friend how to crack each leg. He advised his friend to dip each scallop in butter. He even shared half of his own lobster tail with Shiloh after the nearly starved boy wolfed down his own in record time. As well as things may have been going within the Mazetti family, Shiloh couldn't help but feel troubled, almost guilty. A big day was rapidly approaching. Within a week, Kurt would be handed down a sentence. This verdict would determine Shiloh's future for a considerable length of time. As the younger Robertson chowed down on a succulent lobster meal, the elder one made the most of a cold bologna sandwich and a small bag of dollar store chips.

Chapter 22

That weekend came and went. Reg and Durand hung out at the park again and felt safe enough to sneak a few kisses with one another. Shiloh was treated to unlimited access to Damien's Xbox. Maron and Erik profusely apologized for their absences from the game, which were promptly forgiven by the athletes. Reg assured that all was understood, and he and Durand only wished stability and recovery for Maron and Erik. Erik met with Connie again. This time he hosted. Sarah was thrilled to see such a pretty girl standing on her inherited doorstep, eagerly awaiting her own son to come out and kiss her. Sarah pretended to go out and check the mail, discretely spying on her boy as he wrapped the brown-skinned beauty in his arms. Maron was encouraged to invite Hannah over as well. The awkwardly cute and shy girl was dropped off. Soon, all four teens were on the couch, watching "The Twilight Zone" together. Sarah made up some buffalo chicken dip and soon joined them. Her interactions with Connie and Hannah proved to Erik that his mother was not as old as he thought. The girls gossiped and carried on as if all of them were old friends. Through suspicion, mostly, as well as a keen observation of body language, Sarah determined that Erik had already lost his virginity to the pretty cheerleader that sat on her couch. She only hoped that they used protection. Hannah came out of her shell as well. She constantly had her hand on Maron's lap, only removing it to scoop up a bite of homemade dip with a generic tortilla chip. The three ladies' conversation revolved around an upcoming season of a mutual favorite TV series. Erik and Maron were left in the dark. Connie brought up that her own mother was trying to relearn the art of sewing and crocheting. Gloria was second to none with a needle and thread, as Sarah proved by proudly pointing about the living room to some of her dear friend's greatest works. A checkered quilt, a lovely floral pattern encased in a glass frame on the wall, hand-stitched throw pillows, and the exterior of the recliner, which was actually completely refurbished at the once steady and strong hand of Maron's dear mother. The girls oohed and ahhed at the plethora of handcrafted beauty before them, in that room alone.

"Oh, and she kept this sketchbook! She showed me a few times. She was kicking around the idea of working on wedding dresses for a while. She drew out each one, they're gorgeous! Let me," Sarah's voice trailed off just as her excitement peaked. "Oh, honey, I'm sorry. It's not my place to be showing off all these things." Sarah embarrassedly looked at Maron, who was just as excited as she, if not more.

"No, Mrs. Serling, it's fine. If you wouldn't mind grabbing that, I'd like to see it too," Maron reassured her. Sarah smiled and nodded, tiptoeing her way into Gloria's old room, with the level of respect and caution one would exhibit at the threshold of Christ's tomb, where a large boulder once stood but was moved. Sarah's boulder was a creaky door on rusty hinges; the tomb, suitably enough, was the dying place of the greatest friend she would ever know. She retrieved the sketchpad from the top drawer of Gloria's bedside table. She realized that it wasn't until this point that the room was undisturbed by anyone since Gloria's body was removed. She brushed away any inkling of guilt over this as she returned with the book. The five of them carefully took turns admiring the dozen or so pages which were meticulously adorned with delicate linework and shading of various degrees. It seemed that Gloria excelled in whatever it was that she put forth any level of effort into. It wasn't until the thirteenth page that a drawing was left incomplete. Instead of signing this one with her own elegant signature, Gloria simply left the note, "BOB". Maron immediately recognized the old codeword his mother introduced him to when he first was learning to read. "BOB" stood for "back of book". It was in the back of Maron's childhood storybooks that Gloria would leave him funny, encouraging or, very rarely, serious sticky notes. He flipped to the last page of the sketchbook to discover a note addressed to himself, spanning nearly a page long. He got through a third of the manuscript before tearing up, which was Sarah's cue to take the girls home. Erik kissed Connie goodbye as Hannah gave Maron a peck on the cheek and a quick hug. The girls assured their presence at the funeral service that Monday. The three ladies left out the front door. Several minutes after their departure, Maron finally got a grip on himself. He finally passed the book to Erik, who silently read the message to himself, multiple times. The woman wasn't just a seamstress. She was not merely a scientist. She could do more than captivating works with charcoal and colored pencil than most. But her real knack was poetry, as this beautifully transcribed piece of Heavenword demonstrated. Between Connie's kiss, still fresh on his lips, and his exposure to such divine craftsmanship of the written English word, Erik felt completely intoxicated. This was better than any high he had yet to experience. It was as if God parted the clouds that Saturday afternoon and extended a massive hand, plucking the boy from The Town and showing him all of the cosmic wonders, providing swift answers for the most archaic and trying of questions. Erik felt the highest degree of enlightenment; this feeling only ever being rivaled when Connie would agree to marry him shortly after their high school graduation. It would only be undisputedly topped upon witnessing the birth of his own son, a year after he gives Connie her new last name.

"We c-can frame it, i-if you want, man," Erik managed to sputter out. Maron shook his head after a bit. Erik felt compelled to snatch the book back off the coffee table, just to be able to touch such magnificence and purity and love again.

He resisted the urge. Man was not meant to know such divinities, let alone at their age.

"I'll keep it in my room," Maron responded flatly. "Each anniversary I'll read it again. You will too, but just us, Erik." The sternness in Maron's voice sent a shudder rippling through his friend, who agreed to the conditions. Maron walked the book into his room alone, spending a considerable length of time with it and sobbing.

Sarah arrived back home and began cooking dinner, asking no questions. Rod Serling talked on the television. Maron and Erik were the only mortals privy to the contents of such angelic etchings. Not even I, the all-powerful wizard who spins this tale of gain and loss before you, could attest to the contents of the sacred final page of Gloria's sketchbook. Whatever sweet word it spoke seemed to fix Maron, though.

Chapter 23

On Monday it rained. Such weather was only exemplary of such a sorrowful morning. As promised, The Club and its parents, as well as the ladies of The Club, were all in attendance at the funeral parlor for the showing. Maron, Erik and Sarah stood by the casket and hugged or shook hands with each and every mourner who passed by. The level of sentiment and expression varied from one to the other, depending upon who it was approaching the casket and how familiar that particular person was to the family. A Lutheran minister presided at the pulpit of the showing room. Gloria never really expressed any true devotion to her religion during her adulthood, but was raised in a Lutheran home, as many in these parts were. Family, both distant and close, showed up. Aunt Dot, who was not the least bit saddened by the news that she would not have to play babysitter, sat by Cousin Sherm. Cousin Sherm had his three girls, ranging in ages of seven to seventeen. Admittedly, the oldest girl was quite the prize. On more than one occasion at family gatherings, Maron would tell himself 'real shame we're related'. Of course, his relation to the red-headed beauty meant nothing to Damien, who snuck glances at the girl throughout the event. Many more unfamiliar faces sat behind this row of attendees, and the fact that most of Maron's family were strangers to him finally began to resonate. However, others from school, including Starkey, Millie Mauvre (who was the girl who often got paired up with Maron for "study buddies"), Mr. Steinn, the mailman, the lady from the utilities office, several people from Mom's work, Mrs. Crockett, all the laborers who reconstructed the back deck, and the middle-eastern fellow who owned and operated the only gas station Gloria would ever visit in town, the Ameristop, were all present. The moment had finally arrived. This day, this event, which was pure unadulterated nightmare fuel for Maron throughout his entire adolescence, was finally born into existence. Mom's funeral was no longer a dreaded possibility; it was the cold hard reality that must be lived with until the end of time now. Until this realization set in, Maron resisted the urge to look at what was physically left of his mother. He finally mustered the fortitude to glance at her body, and regrettably so. She looked plastic, the boy thought. She looked as if she would melt in the sun or begin to drip in the light of a close candle. That's not her. Gloria Calhoun never looked that way, even as she was knocking on death's door in her recent dilapidated months. She never looked this bad. Could such a thing really be for the best? Could a painful and agonizing life actually hold more merit over no life at all? Gloria may have been put out of her misery, but misery, like energy, is never destroyed but only transferred. Maron inherited it just as he would one day inherit the home whose walls echoed the joyous sound of Gloria's young laughter, and whose halls carried the sweet note of her dinner call, accompanied by the mouth-watering aroma of a succulent homecooked meal nearly every night of the week.

"BOB," Maron quietly spoke. Erik picked up on it, but Sarah did not take notice. "BOB," Maron repeated. "This is her back of book. Her story's over now." For a moment, Erik began to feel on-edge, almost bracing for another mental health catastrophe out of his friend. He gave Maron's shoulder a squeeze but said nothing. The last of the guests made their passes and all were seated. Erik, Maron and Sarah had their reserved chairs in the front row. The old minister cleared his throat and began what must have been his eleven-hundredth funeral sermon. Maron picked up bits and pieces. Sarah listened intently. Erik was only mindful of his best friend in that span of fifteen minutes. When all was said and done, the congregation of about eighty or so people spilled out of the funeral home's doors and packed into their cars. There were enough procession flags to be donned on every vehicle. Maron insisted on closing the casket lid himself, not after a final goodbye to Mom, of course. The grim party made their way to the cemetery. Hannah and Connie managed to reunite with their boys. Erik squeezed Sarah's hand in his left palm, Connie's in his right. Maron could barely notice Hannah clinging to his right arm. The minister spoke but a few more words, and the casket was lowered. Many of the mourners adorned it with various wreaths, bouquets, and single roses. Maron paid his own respects with a mental reel of his fondest memories he shared with his mother, as well as a singular promise: to get better.

"Get busy livin' or get busy dyin'," Maron quoted Mom's all-time favorite movie. He would have uttered a line from "Happy Gilmore", which was a close second to "Shawshank", but thought it inappropriate for the occasion.

Chapter 24

Ralph Reirke didn't precisely know what his next course of action would be on that fateful Tuesday morning. Truth be told, he didn't even expect to get as far as he had come. Ralph knew where at in the house his stepfather kept his revolver. He knew buying a gun would be off the table, due to past convictions, and Bose was no help either. Bose had access to a range of firearms, but didn't particularly want mixed up in Ralph's vendetta, so he denied his friend when prompted to "borrow a pistol". Bose did, however, wish Ralph the best of luck, insisting he knew nothing of the whole ordeal. Once the house was empty that day, instead of turning to his usual vices of snorting Percocet and masturbating to hardcore pornography, Ralph took out the false bottom of his stepdad's underwear drawer of his dresser and swiped the Magnum. He stuffed it in a string bag and set off at a good pace in the direction of Mazetti's. He chiefed five cigarettes on the way.

"Just get him, Ralph. The kid's in school, so that's good. No kids, no kids, no bystanders, just Mazetti. No innocents. You're a bastard, but you're not a fuckin' bastard, right, Ralph?" The deranged young man giggled to himself, stifling his laughter upon realizing that a middle-aged man out jogging was coming up behind him on the left. Perfect time to practice, Ralph thought. Once the unnamed balding father of three was fifteen feet or so in front of Reirke, the maniac quickly reached into his bag and drew the weapon. The sidewalk sloped up and Ralph accounted for this. Looking down the sight, he maintained a steady hand, much to his own surprise. He felt a sick and invigorated sense of dominance and control in this situation. He could've easily blown The Stranger's head clear from his neck that very second. Realizing it was broad daylight and anyone could've seen, Ralph quickly holstered the weapon, this time into the waistband of his sweats for easier access. The Stranger trotted on, completely oblivious to the possibility that a sick young man could've blown his head clean off. He made a left down Race Street, probably for the best. As Ralph closed in on the store, he was overtaken with a wave of nausea and dread. He staggered off the sidewalk and loudly vomited into the yellowed grass to his right. Doubt began to creep in. "No, you came to do it, so just fuckin' do it! Don't pussy out now. You've always been a pussy, it's time to man up!" He reassured himself with a quivering peptalk. "Grease that goomba piece of shit. Fuckin' greedy Italian bastard. Then fuck that little hot slut wife of his, Ralphie. He did this to you. He deserves it, you deserve it!" Ralph fought off another shrill burst of disturbing laughter. The parking lot was now in his sights. The place was already packed with the usual older crowd. Ralph strode across the asphalt, deliberately knocking over a small display of pumpkins which was so carefully arranged by Raquel only days prior. He stepped through the automatic door, the nausea returning once more. Sr. was marching back to his office after handling a rather grouchy customer's demand for a refund over a slightly moldy pint of blueberries. The two made eye contact, which only worsened the shopkeeper's mood. Sr. pretended not to notice the arrival of, inarguably, his worst employee yet. He picked up the pace and Ralph trailed, catching him just before the door was swung closed. Ralph scratchily cleared his throat.

"Hey, uh, Mr. Mazetti, got a minute," Ralph inquired, nearly sounding polite. Sr. was quiet.

"What, Ralph? I'm pretty busy at the moment. I don't really have time." Ralph almost took the response and walked out of the store with it. He tried. Time to rail some percs and watch some hot blonde mom get fucked from behind. He talked himself out of what would have been a harmless but embarrassed retreat.

"Uh, I just wanted to talk to you about coming back, possibly. I know that kid started, and you said you would call us back, and," Sr. interrupted him.

"That was under unusual circumstances. I owe you nothing, Ralph. I know you're not going to buy anything, so you're just loitering at this point. Leave now, or I call the police." Sr. meant business. So did the young man with a thirst for revenge. He glanced quickly to his right, and the coast was clear. He quickly snatched the piece from the small of his back, drawing it to meet Sr.'s gut.

"Get in the office, old man. So we can talk like fuckin' gentlemen," Ralph spoke, nearly growling the order. Sr. turned white as a sheet but complied. He slowly backpedaled into the room that always served as his own personal sanctuary, until this day. Ralph discretely closed the door behind himself upon entering, locking it. Sr. slowly raised both hands above his head, maintaining a brave exterior.

"Ralph," he began, clearing his throat, "don't do anything you'll regret. I can't give you your job back, but I have two-thousand and some change here, in my safe. You can have it and this will be forgotten. Just never come back here again, and stay the fuck away from my family, and it's yours." Sr. motioned under his desk, where he did, in fact, keep his safe. The crazed youth took careful steps forward, never lowering the revolver. "It's yours, Ralph. Just take it, leave, never come back and all is forgiven." Sr. repeated, still remarkably calm considering the scenario. Ralph had to see for himself. He tried to fake Sr. out by purposely lowering the gun slightly while glaring at the metal safe, which was enshrouded in what appeared to be an old tablecloth. Sr. didn't so much as flinch. Ralph did believe the old man and would have been wise to take him up on the offer. However, some nagging voice in the back of his head reasoned with him that such a modest peace agreement was not good enough. This same voice commanded

Ralph to 'finish the job'. This was the most dominant of the half-dozen voices which regularly spoke to and elicited responses from Ralph. This voice was known as "Man". "Man" sounded quite similar to Ralph's biological father but was even more violent. This voice made its first appearance during Ralph's adolescence, which was the point of his youth when he fled with his mother to rid themselves of his cruel father's presence forevermore. Ralph's dad committed suicide just weeks before the boy graduated high school. Ralph regained his aggressive composure, declining Sr.'s bargain. He took two steps toward the owner, burying the barrel of the old hand cannon into his torso once more, this time in more assertive fashion.

"That's not enough, man. You fired me, you humiliated me! Do you know how many times my glasses have been smacked off my face in my life, Mazetti?" Discreteness was out the window at this point. Ralph was practically hollering. "And you went and did it, too. What's one more time, right? What's one more time for old Ralph, huh?" He kept repeating various phrasings of the question. A solitary tear streaked the acne-marked face of Ralph Reirke. Sr. knew he didn't have it in him, but he played along. "I'm gonna shoot you in the fuckin' head. Then I'm gonna bring your slut wife in here and fuck her on your desk, then I'll take that two-grand and everything you have in each register, Sr." Ralph seemed to have regained some level of poise and, in his own mind, some control over the situation again. Sr. was as cool as a man could be when a loaded gun was sticking into his gut, while held in the sweaty palm of an emotional and undoubtedly psychotic young man.

"Ralph, I'm going to open the safe, now. I'm going to hand you everything in it, and you're going to leave. I won't call the police. Just take the money and get out," the old man's voice didn't so much as quiver. Ralph only grew more uneasy upon hearing the offer of appeasement. Before he knew it, Sr. took a knee and threw back the sheet which covered his safe. He began to enter the combination with one hand; with the other, he reached for an object on top of the safe. Ralph paid no mind to this. Sr. popped the door open and stuck his left hand in, simultaneously drawing his own weapon and discharging two rounds into Ralph's left thigh. The would-be robber let out a shrill scream and fired two shots into the wall. He crumpled to a heap on the floor and Sr. snatched his gun away with relative ease. Each of his hands brandished a weapon at this point, Ralph sobbing on the floor. A fervent pounding sounded at the office door. Sr. backpedaled to it, never taking his eyes off his suspect. Raquel was understandably in hysterics, already on the phone with the police. Sr. stood over the lunatic, never lowering either weapon. Ralph was heavily bleeding. God, his femoral artery, Sr. thought. He's going to die within minutes. The delinquent made a feeble attempt at rising to his feet. He made it not so far as to a single knee. Officers arrived within ten minutes. Sr. lowered the weapons and complied with all of their instructions, being slapped with handcuffs, much to Raquel's ardent dismay. An ambulance soon arrived, and Ralph was still breathing. He was more than breathing, in fact. He was screaming and carrying on and threatening to sue and this and that and the other. He would be fine. This fact nearly relieved Sr. of any level of guilt, but it also concerned him. What if, years down the road, the boy would come back? Would he get that lucky twice? Sr. calmly answered all questions posed before him. Yes, it was an act of self-defense. Yes, the boy was armed. Yes, he was a disgruntled former employee. Yes, the only weapon discharged that day was legally registered to the man who defended himself. Upon the end of questioning, Sr. offered the security footage that would have been picked up by the nearly hidden camera in the corner of the room, which Sr. thought wise to install when he became aware of just how many teenage girls he had working for him, as well as the instances these girls came into his office with him for meetings, to complain, or to deposit a register drawer. The shopkeeper never would have guessed that camera would have come in handy under these circumstances. The sheriff's department glanced at the clip, as if any more evidence was required to determine how this incident played out. They saw the shakiness in Ralph's knees, as well as the calm and level-headed demeanor of Sr. Ralph went down. Sr. shifted out of frame to try to calm his wife. Then he stood over the perpetrator until the authorities arrived. It was hard to believe that the whole scene was dragged out over eight minutes. To Sr. and, presumably, Ralph, it seemed to take a whole day. Sr. was let go and was advised by Sheriff Undermeyer to contact his lawyer if he so pleased, but the whole case was relatively open and shut. Ralph was taken to the hospital in Norhauk but didn't spend much time there. His injuries, the physical ones, anyway, would heal within weeks. He would be sent off to Cleveland to spend a length of time in a psychiatric unit, being released after nearly a year, then faced a considerable prison sentence after being deemed mentally competent. He would follow his own father's footsteps and hang himself in his cell at the age of twenty-nine. The remainder of the present day was a blur. Raquel sat with her husband for a long while, making futile attempts to calm herself before erupting into fits of laughter and tears again and again. She finally composed herself in an attempt to retrieve Damien from school. She nearly crashed into the building, thinking the car was in reverse. Sr. called up Mama Geraldine, who was at the store in "two shakes of a lamb's tail", as she loved to say. Police rushed all employees and patrons alike from the store. An officer was posted up in the parking lot, dismissing would-be customers. Geraldine arrived in her little car, as calm as a woman attending a Sunday brunch with long-ago friends would be. The sheriff granted her access to see Mr. and Mrs. Mazetti. The sweet, graceful old woman peppily strode into the office to find two of her greatest friends in such a disheveled state. She crossed the room with her eyes locked on Raquel's; she never stopped smiling.

"Come on, honey, you know I got you," she squeezed and kissed Raquel, who absolutely let loose at this point. She wept into Geraldine's shoulder as long as time would permit. Geraldine smothered Sr. with hugs and kisses, as well. Raquel quickly stole her back for herself. She made soothing remarks and behaved as if the whole incident was nothing more than a child spilling his snack off of his little pop-up table on accident and making a mess which he feared his mother would be furious at. The kind old beauty realized the blood splatter on the hardwood floor and quickly made her way to the aisle which housed the cleaning supplies, returning with several scrub pads and bleach and various cleaning compounds. Halfway through her scrubbing, she glanced up at her former employer, "Just take it out of my check, baby." The owner of Mazetti's finally let a genuine laugh escape his lips, the first since the previous evening. Raquel teared up again. Geraldine took note of the hour and excused herself to fetch Damien.

"Gotta go get the baby, okay? Do not touch any of this; I mean that. I will drop him off at home, finish this, then I'm taking you lovebirds home, understand?" The sweet but sassy lady's command grabbed both Raquel's and Sr.'s attention. They agreed to her terms without the slightest argument. Geraldine drove to the high school to spot a confused and anxious Damien. Raquel, sometimes Sr., were always beyond early to pick him up. Geraldine was then forced to engage in a behavior she absolutely detested: lying. She sold her story of a surprise health inspection of the family's deli counter. This was then followed up by a visit from the local police department to inquire about a rash of break-ins at local businesses in recent weeks. She assured Damien that she was already in the store shopping and was humbly requested by Raquel to pick him up from school. She then informed Damien of his unexpected day off, as the police's presence seemed to drive off more than a few customers, and he would not be needed that afternoon. Geraldine really sold her sincerity with an impromptu trip to the Twistee-Treat, The Town's favorite, and only, ice cream venue. She claimed she had a real hankerin' for a strawberry banana split that day and couldn't wait any longer. Damien ate it up, albeit with a slight suspicion. The two visited the ice cream parlor. Mama Geraldine got her strawberry split and Damien modestly opted for a small chocolate cone, not before offering to pay, of course. After all, this was his first date with any woman, ever. Geraldine dismissed such chivalry and drove the boy to his home on Maple, where the two sat in the kitchen and polished off their ice cream. This ploy may have worked in the analogue era, but in the digital age, Damien was sure enough to see something online about the horrific attempt at his own father's life within five minutes of scrolling through his phone. News, more often the bad than the good, spreads like a plague in Small Towns. A lifelong citizen of Castalia could have constructed mansions for the poorer families at no expense to them, found and administered the cure to cancer to The Town's ill and frail at no cost, as well as picked up every empty beer can and cigarette butt which one could not walk or drive more than ten feet through The Town without spotting at least one of these pieces of litter. The news of this hypothetical Samaritan's acts of righteousness would not carry nearly as far as a relative stranger's unmerited claim that one of the girls at the middle school was pregnant. As the old song goes, "People love it when you lose, they love dirty laundry". Damien was in shock. Geraldine was largely unfamiliar with social media and cell phones as a whole, but she recognized the look of fear or worry on anyone's face, let alone on that of a child who was entrusted in her care.

"Dim, honey, I know. I'm sorry for making up the story. I'm sure you've heard from fifteen different kids by now what happened. Your mama and daddy asked me to do this. Believe me, sugar, I hate fibbing under any circumstance, but felt that I owed it to them. Your parents are fine, the store is fine. Everyone is juss shook up, is all. Baby, please don't be upset with me, or your folks. I know what it's like. Not even parents are perfect, babe. They tried, though. In a half-hour I'm gonna go pick them up. Then I'm gonna fix dinner for you all. Please, honey, pretty please juss wait in your room a while. Let them decompress before askin' them all kinds of questions, okay? For me?" Geraldine's beautiful brown eyes met Damien's, which were now welling with tears. She reached her caramel-colored dainty hands across the table and gave Damien's fingers a light squeeze. Despite nearing the age of senior citizenship, the selfless mother hen didn't look a day past thirty. Many people go through their entire lives without encountering such a physical embodiment of kindness and matronliness. The Mazettis were fortunate enough to have befriended such an angel in the guise of a woman that is Geraldine in their youth. Damien excused himself and headed up to his room. He truthfully wished Shiloh was present, although he would never admit that fact aloud. Shiloh took a trip with Mrs. Hadley to the GoodWill in hopes of finding "court clothes" for the boy, in the words of Mrs. Hadley. To many, these would have just been considered casual articles of clothing that the average middle-class American would have worn to a niece's birthday party or to a Sunday matinee with friends at the Paramount. Shiloh Robertson may as well have been shopping for his wedding-day attire in hopes of dazzling Holly. It was a big deal for the boy. Geraldine called out that she was leaving, and Damien made no attempt at a verbal response. He heard the little car turn over in the driveway and the squeal of overdue brakes in the street. Geraldine sped off to collect the rest of her children. Damien took this time to genuinely and whole-heartedly cry. It was a well-deserved feeling of release for the youth. He tried his damnedest, all the time, to act as stoic and statue-like as his old man. He attempted to be as peppy and upbeat as his vibrant mother. Sometimes, the boy felt like he couldn't relate to either parent in terms of emotions or physical display. Sometimes he just wanted and needed to cry and feel angry and scared and uncertain. He wouldn't be able to totally justify and accept these feelings of his own until he would become a father himself at the far-off and futuristic age of twenty-eight. Bootsy came to comfort her greatest friend in his time of despair. She stood on his chest and licked his forehead with her scratchy tongue. Damien usually found the act to be annoying and, at times, downright gross. But he laughed off this encounter and swaddled Bootsy in his blanket as if she was a newborn. He cradled the old cat and returned downstairs to pour Bootsy a splash of milk as a treat. He urged the beast to finish lapping up her serving of Toft's as he heard the car rumble into the driveway. Raquel and Sr. heavily frowned upon giving the cat any type of dairy or table food. At long last, the old girl finished up and Damien made haste to dispose of the evidence that was a Tupperware bowl with milk spots on the bottom. He would utilize the excuse that he made a bowl of cereal for himself if questioned. Bootsy pranced back upstairs as Geraldine led Sr. and Raquel through the front door of their own home. Geraldine gave the visual of a realtor trying to sell her first home to a young and timid couple.

"Sit on the couch, kids," Mama instructed Sr. and his wife. "Dimmy, put on a movie for Mom and Dad, 'kay, baby? Ooh, something scary! Halloween is juss 'round the corner!" Geraldine's smile illuminated the atypically drab home. "Rocky, I seen you seasoned some pork chops and got 'em in the fridge, atta girl!" Raquel proudly nodded in confirmation, as if reliving the greatest compliment she ever received regarding her culinary skills. That tip of the cap came when Raquel was eight and made grilled cheese sandwiches and tomato soup, all on her own, and presented her sickly grandmother with her resplendent spread. Raquel would recall till the day she would die the exact tone of Nonna's excited squeal upon being presented with perfectly sliced triangles of buttered and fried bread, which were glued together with a generous helping of melted Kraft singles. The finger sandwiches were served alongside plastic bowls filled to the brim with condensed tomato soup. The dollar store bowls served as ponds to their inhabitants, which were schools of Goldfish crackers. Every time Raquel served up a pint of Mazetti's own tomato soup, she could nary avoid the fondest of her own childhood memories, all of which Nonna was a key player in. Her father's mother cherished her far deeper than her own. Raquel would come to accept this fact years down the road. In the present day, Geraldine got to work in the kitchen. Damien located his copy of "The Nightmare Before Christmas" and popped it into the DVD player. Something lighthearted and whimsical would surely do the family good. As a bonus, Geraldine never saw the classic throughout her sixty-plus years on the planet. The lad paused the movie only seconds into it to rush to help his honorary grandmother in her quest to serve up a delicious meal for a haggard young family. Unlike many other adolescents, Damien was already quite advanced in the culinary field. Perhaps it had something to do with his "volunteering" at a local deli since the age of nine years. He was assigned to side dishes and got to work by hand-mashing the potatoes. He then opened multiple cans of green beans and sauteed them to Raquel's preference. After this, he made use of the toaster oven by sliding in a whole roll of peanut butter cookie dough, his father's absolute favorite. He was sure to adorn each glob of dough with several chocolate chips at their final stages. Geraldine whipped up a panful of homemade gravy to dress the chops with. Damien escorted Bootsy from the combat zone several times before finally giving in and carrying the old thing off to the couch to join their parents. Raquel dozed on Sr.'s shoulder. Not to be outdone, Geraldine swept and mopped the entirety of the kitchen floor. She took the garbage out, changed a burnt-out lightbulb in the garage, and swept the vast expanse of the front porch in a matter of ten minutes. The old woman finally announced that dinner was ready and pulled up a tall kitchen chair into the living room to enjoy what was mostly Damien's handiwork. Sr. insisted she sat on the couch with everyone else, but his star employee declined. She knew, in her heart, she could never forgive herself if she made even the smallest of messes on such an immaculate piece of furniture. Damien played the movie while the four watched and ate. Geraldine was amazed by both the plot and the animation. Raquel and Sr. forced a few chuckles at their favorite parts during their beloved classic. Halfway through, Geraldine began clearing everyone's plates, promptly washing each dish, much to the opposition of Raquel. She neatly put everything away and continued tidying up the kitchen. She stayed for the remainder of the movie and asked Damien if he would be so kind as to lend it to her, which he most readily obliged.

"I'm sure Hank's gonna be worried if I ain't back soon, babies. But you have my number, and you use it if you need anything tonight. I'll be right over," Geraldine assured her kids over and over. All said their goodbyes and Sr. walked her to her car. It was well past dark. Upon opening the door to her vehicle, Mama used the light of her car to find her pen and pad she kept in her glovebox. She scribbled down her eldest daughter's contact information. Naomi would soon graduate with her master's degree in psychology. The lovely young girl planned to become a clinical psychologist. Geraldine heavily encouraged Sr. to give her a call sometime that week. Mr.

Mazetti graciously accepted and made a nearly convincing promise to do so. Geraldine reversed out of the flawless driveway that led to a picturesque home which housed a freshly troubled family. That evening, Raquel took a triple dose of melatonin. Damien snuck a good deal of his parents' wine. Sr. would not catch a wink of sleep for the next two nights.

Chapter 25

On Thursday, Kurt Robertson made his appearance in court, as scheduled. Shiloh recited every prayer he had ever learned in Sunday school, or rather, what he could recall from them. He concluded this long overdue talk with God with a little ditty of his own. He made a promise, a child's promise, to God to be better every day if his earthly father was let off easy. This swear meant no more smoking of any substance. No more porn, in the rare instances Shiloh had access to internet and five minutes of privacy. No more swearing. No more dirty jokes. He vowed to take his studies considerably more seriously. He swore to treat Holly like the queen she was when she would eventually take the last name "Robertson" for herself. He pledged to go beyond expectations at his new job as well as duties around the home he was welcomed into. A mere boy, not very bright or worth noting, at that, confidently proposed these offers to the Highest Being of the Universe in exchange for leniency on his own dad. Mrs. Hadley drove him to the county courthouse. The boy had on a polo and black slacks, an absolute steal for only eight dollars. He wore his father's only pair of dress shoes, which were admittedly a size too big yet. All the other boys were in school that day. Maron had received multiple notices of truancy in recent weeks but was cut some slack due to Gloria's passing. He knew he couldn't afford further absenteeism. The principal himself almost denied Maron's permission to attend the homecoming dance. Sarah managed to sway his decision, however. The whole incident led to The Club teasing Erik, making the comparison to the scene of Forrest's mother's encounter with his own principal in the Tom Hanks classic. This joke ran for several weeks, even after the dance was over. The majority of The Club, as well as Connie and Hannah, flocked to Erik's locker. Erik kissed Connie as Maron did Hannah. Childish smooching sounds all emanated from the mouths of Durand, Damien, and Reg. A lot was discussed within the span of only several minutes. Erik and Connie's colors would be navy and white. This rule was decided by Connie alone. It mattered not in the slightest to Erik. Hannah didn't realize that couples typically pick colors and match for a school dance. She was considerably heavier during her freshman year and was not asked by any boy to be his date. Connie offered several suggestions and the girls landed on maroon and black as Hannah and her escort's colors. Maron had no complaints. Damien was scheduled to return to work the next day, on Friday, as would the rest of the Mazetti family and the entire staff. The deli was closed down for a couple of days so Sr. could get his head straight and manage at least a few hours of sleep. Additionally, police had some business to tend to at the location as well. Sr. was advised to close temporarily so all could be sorted out. The owner was generous enough to pay his employees for their scheduled hours during this furlough as well. Geraldine was at the house every day, even bringing her husband, Hank, for dinner one of those evenings. The Army vet had some colorful stories for Damien, and the lad introduced the old-timer to the concept of video games. Damien was somewhat concerned that playing a first-person shooter game would invoke some kind of bizarre flashback and reaction out of the old man. To his surprise, though, Hank really got into it, laughing the entire time. All in attendance would share a splendid evening together. Durand and Reg discussed the task that lay before them in the homecoming game, that being Sandusky's stellar defense. Throughout three games, this team only allowed a total of ten points against them. On paper, the offense as a whole was quite comparable to Castalia's own. On paper and in practice, Sandusky's defense was leaps and bounds ahead of the Ice Cats', as well as many other high school football teams at the national level. While most schools boast of a star quarterback with big dreams of going on to play at a notable college, it was Sandusky's defense that earned the vast majority of the school's wins. From a quarterback's perspective, being outmatched as a position player was not such a scary thing. The star of the team could rely on his defensive counterparts to get the job done on their end. When an offensive player is faced with eleven savvy and quick defenders, the picture is painted quite differently. Durand and even, to some degree, Reg, had a substantial case of nerves. The more serious topics of the roundtable were now brought up. All of the kids wished the best for Kurt and Shiloh. Connie insisted she knew exactly who the man Kurt pummeled was, at least by suspicion. Over the summer, some creep who fit the bill saw Connie sunbathing in her backyard and voiced several unsavory comments. He had a black guy in the passenger seat of his Challenger. The perv circled the block several times before Big Al chased him off with a loaded Remington 870. Connie would see the car several more times in the following months, neither driver nor passenger ever uttered a word more. Lastly, The Club commended Maron on all he had overcome in recent weeks. All of his friends, new and old, personally assured him that they would make themselves available should he need anything. It was almost as if a bandage was ripped off, allowing an old and festering wound to finally breathe. The boy looked and felt better than he had in over a year. The teenagers all made their way to class in hopes that the day would pass smoothly. Lunch came, and much to everyone at the corner table's surprise, Connie was not on tray duty. She explained that her father was a working man once again, having started at a nearby appliance vendor and reparation service. Erik was overjoyed at the news. After school dismissed, Reg and Durand followed their usual routine of attending practice, which would be a light day, composed mainly of watching film. Damien was picked up by his mother and father. He informed them both that Shiloh may need some space after the events of the day. Connie may as well have been kicked off the cheer squad at this point, considering her multiple unexcused absences from practice. Hannah's mother called the band instructor, conveniently ten minutes prior to school's dismissal, spewing some story about a made-up family emergency. She was just happy to see her daughter had made her own friends. This was a one-time thing, though, according to Mrs. Lada. Erik, Maron, Connie and Hannah all made their way to Mrs. Hadley's hut in hopes of getting the chance to speak with Shiloh. Both boys were gentlemen, opting to walk their bikes to remain close to the girls. This lasted until Hannah and Connie decided to playfully steal their boyfriends' bicycles, leaving the young men in the dust. The girls reached the sooty driveway of the trailer park in record time. The boys lagged a good fifteen minutes behind. The boys arrived to discover their ladies both slouched over the handlebars of their bikes, making loud and exaggerated snoring sounds. The girls couldn't stop laughing over the whole occurrence; the boys each forced an embarrassed chuckle. The quartet walked over to what was definitely the shabbiest of trailers in the whole lot; then, they proceeded across the way to Mrs. Hadley's residence. Her car was carelessly parked at a weird angle just feet from the front porch, which was at least a sign that she was home. The kids all crowded the stoop. Erik was naturally the one to knock. The sound of shuffling slippers grew louder as a figure emerged from the perpetual smoke cloud which permeated the home's interior. Mrs. Hadley was recognized by her shape and limp before her words or face. She wetly coughed several times before meeting her visitors at the screen door.

"Shiloh, your friends are here, hun," Mrs. Hadley hoarsely belted out. Her eyes shifted between both girls. "Now, which one of you beauties is Holly?" She spoke barely above a whisper.

"Uh, she's a different girl from work, Mrs. Hadley," Erik made the save. The old lady seemed somewhat surprised and smiled. Shiloh crept to the door. It was evident he had been crying.

"Uh, you guys can come in if ya want," he sniffled as he made the offer. "Where's Dim at, anyway?" Shiloh seemed slightly hurt that his roomie wasn't among the bunch.

"He figured you might want some space today, man. His parents picked him up. You know, with everything that happened, they're kinda extra clingy now," Maron stepped in this time. Shiloh nodded in understanding.

"Baby, why don't you go on with your friends a while, huh?" Mrs. Hadley again. "Guys, maybe take him down to the Wendy's, right?" All four nodded at the old woman's suggestion. Shiloh had never felt so belittled. He went into the bathroom and slipped out of his fancy court clothes, dressing himself in a set of Damien's name-brand hand-me-downs. He hugged Mrs. Hadley goodbye, not speaking a word. The old bag fought back tears. He stepped out onto the small concrete block with his friends, reaching into his pockets where his cigarettes would normally be, but remembered that he threw them out himself that morning upon making His Promise. He nearly regretted such an oath. No one spoke for a quarter of a mile. Erik finally piped up.

"So, uh, you just gonna leave us in suspense, dude," the leader inquired, gripping the handlebars of his bicycle with considerably more force than before. Shiloh simply shrugged and kept his pace forward. "Is it years, months? Tell us something, man." Erik made no attempt in hiding his perturbation at this point. Shiloh finally slowed his stride. He wound down to a halt and turned to face his friends at a snail's pace. He finally made direct eye contact since their arrival at Mrs. Hadley's house.

"Two years, Erik. He's in Mansfield for two years. Two whole years," the length of the sentence seemed so surreal to even Shiloh, still. He just kept repeating, "Two years." All of the youths truthfully expected a lengthier stretch, to be completely honest. Kurt's record certainly was feared to have been a factor in the judge's verdict, but it did not seem so. Two years of hard time seemed relatively lenient considering the man who was attacked sustained such gruesome injuries, not that anyone was complaining. Shiloh explained that the ruling was circumstantial, to a degree. Because a minor was present and was being protected by the accused during the act of the crime, it gave the judge something to mull over. This was a man who, after all, was a father himself. Despite Kurt's shady dealings and the events that set the stage for such an altercation, he did all he could in his power to protect his boy, which is undoubtedly one of the most just and upright things a man can do in this world. If it meant a damnable sentence of life in prison or even the consequence of lethal injection, Kurt would have thrashed his adversary all the same. Nobody threatened Shiloh's well-being, this being the holiest of pillars in Kurt's hard-lived life thus far. Shiloh would grow up to appreciate the sentiment after only a few months of his own journey into fatherhood had passed. A man grows what he can and cares for It the best way he knows how. To most of those present, the verdict handed down to Kurt Donnachaidh seemed nearly worthy of celebration. A man beat a fellow man to the brink of death with his bare hands and would only be locked up two years and some weeks. In a nation where people are incarcerated for marijuana-related offenses for decades at a time, such a scolding seemed to be quite generous. Shiloh initially failed to see this for what it was. The younger Robertson seemed to have held on to this confident hope that his father would walk free the very same day. He couldn't process the fact that Kurt had sinned and was just a few blows shy of committing murder. After adamant consoling from Erik, Maron and the girls, Shiloh was finally able to get a grip on himself. The five went out to eat at the Wendy's, following the advice of Mrs. Hadley. Hannah was in possession of her mother's credit card. She forgot to return it to her mom's purse after purchasing her outfit for the upcoming fall pictures; she was fitting in with the delinquents already. The cute and considerate girl from the school's band purchased five value meals for her friends, and the group spread out to occupy two separate booths in the dining room. The boys sat at one table and the girls at another, nearby, of course. Shiloh was hesitant to touch his burger and fries. Maron polished off his entire order within minutes and still felt hungry enough to take down a whole side of beef, saving room for dessert. He settled for a small order of chili. After months, his appetite had finally returned. The girls giggled and made faces at each drive-thru customer as they passed by the window of their booth. Erik nibbled at his meal, trying to think of the right thing to say. It was, of course, his job as the leader. He was responsible for any and everything that happened to any of his five boys, regardless of the severity of the occurrence. Shiloh began to pick at his burger, certainly a positive sign.

"I invited Dim," Erik prompted, almost shyly. "His dad is dropping him off soon. Just thought he should be here too, ya know?" Shiloh perked up at this announcement. Damien and Shiloh often butted heads for years. Damien was teased for being a square and having a hot mom; Shiloh was made fun of for being an uncultured and ill-mannered bumpkin. Since Kurt's incarceration, the two unlikely friends forged a bond that may as well have been ironclad.

"Yeah, Dim should be here, huh," Shiloh responded with a surprising level of pep. As if on cue, Damien stepped into the shabby and yellowed fast-food dining room. He glanced around, spotting his friends with ease, considering the room was only occupied by one other older couple and a solitary minimum-wage employee pretending to wipe down tables. Damien cast a smile at the boys and mildly acknowledged the girls' presence. He placed an order for a small chili and fry and received it within a minute. He joined the boys at their table, claiming the fourth and final chair. After persistent glances from both Hannah and Connie, Damien and Shiloh relinquished their seats so that the girls could sit across from their respective boyfriends. Shiloh and Damien moved to their former booth. Shiloh began to wolf down his sandwich just after the seat swap.

"I heard about it, man. I'm sorry. Your dad took out some bum off the street. Some guy, probably worse than Bose. He shouldn't have to pay for that." Damien's words carried the sweetest relief to Shiloh's ears. Shiloh nodded in agreement. His mouth was full of food and his practice of not talking with his mouth full, which he learned at the residence of the Mazettis', carried over to this rundown Wendy's establishment. He gulped down his bite before speaking.

"I agree, man. I know he fucked, sorry, screwed up," his freshly taught manners, which were vehemently instilled by Raquel, came into play once more, "but them boys was lunatics. If it was just me back there and I so much as looked at 'em wrong, they woulda killed me without a second thought. They're animals, Dim. My daddy shouldn't have to pay two years of his life for puttin' down a animal." Shiloh concluded by taking a large slurp of his Coke. "Least he'll be out before I graduate. If I graduate, I guess." The last comment was spoken with a notable and concerning undertone. Damien dunked a fry in his chili and sat back in his chair with a striking resemblance to his father.

"I know it's hard for you to see, but things will be alright, bud. My dad just shot a man. Could've easily killed him; I honestly wish he would've. My dad did nothing different than your dad. He protected himself. Personally, I think old Kurt deserves a medal," Damien said as he finally took a bite of his chili-drenched fry. Shiloh permitted a goofy grin. The girls laughed and shrieked about God knows what. Maron and Erik sat silently, trying to pick up on what they could of Shiloh and Damien's conversation. The six soon exited the dingy restaurant. Fortunately, Sr.'s Enclave seated seven. The girls were dropped off first; both Erik and then Maron escorted their women to their front doors and received sloppy and impassioned kisses for doing so. Erik and Maron were the next to reach their destination. Sr. then pulled into his own driveway, carrying both his son, as well as adopted son to the place they called their own. The three exited the vehicle and stepped into the decadent home to be greeted by the pleasant aroma of one of Raquel's home-cooked meals. Tonight's entrée was chicken alfredo. Despite eating within the past hour, both boys would happily agree to a second round. Sr. was famished. He skipped more than a few meals that week. The familiar smell of tender and perfectly seasoned chicken paired with the succulent fragrance of fettuccine pasta tantalized the man beyond belief. All ingredients, naturally, were brought home from the shop. Raquel spoke the blessing over the meal, as she usually did. The biological Mazettis conversed light-heartedly. Nobody prompted the honorary member of the family to speak about the elephant in the room. The topic arose organically.

"So, Daddy's facing two years for the assault. Sorry, the "aggravated" assault. I actually done, sorry, did some research on this partic'lar offense," Shiloh was trying. "It's not uncommon for the defendant, if found guilty, to face upwards of five years for such a crime." The boy recited his Wikipedia research from memory. "I guess he caught a break, or somethin'. I didn't expect him to get out on a slap on the wrist, or nothin'. I just hoped it wouldn't be as long, is all." The parents of the household solemnly nodded their heads. Damien continued to slurp his noodles. Younger people are, at times, better at recognizing feeling as opposed to words. Adults often base their thoughts and reactions on what is spoken; their younger counterparts respond to and resonate with what the afflicted is truly experiencing. Most of us lose a great deal of humanity as we grow older. This is not voluntary, necessarily, but just one of the many things that can happen to us when we stop believing in Magick. Raquel and Sr. were at a loss. Raquel made a meek attempt at changing the subject.

"Mom, I'm not sure if Shiloh's finished explaining," Damien piped up, politely dabbing his mouth with his napkin. The matriarch apologetically looked back to Shiloh, eyes as big as the dinner plates she served this delectable feast on. Her lips moved but she made no audible sound. Both adults may have found Damien's remark a bit out of place, but the boys certainly didn't.

"It's okay, Dim. Just wanted to report my findings, is all. It could've been worse, 'specially considering Daddy's record. What I'm gettin' at is that I'm not happy, but I am glad, at least. He'll be out before, if, I graduate," Shiloh looked up at the Mazettis with his dopey smile, all of them grinning back. "And I figure it'll be at least a few more years till I put a ring on Holly's finger." Raquel lost it at this. She was on the fence between crying and laughing. Surely Shiloh was capable of swaying her decision to the latter. Sr. got a chuckle out of it as well. Damien simply rolled his eyes and took another hearty bite.

"I knew it," Raquel exclaimed. "I see how you two are! Honey, she's adorable, but maybe a little old for you." Raquel ended this in a tone of a borderline question.

"That's alright, Mrs. 'Zetti. I like 'em older. Look at the woman I been livin' with the past couple days," Shiloh rebutted, referring to dear old Mrs. Hadley. Damien couldn't stifle his laughter, as hard as he tried. Sr. and Raquel were practically in tears. Dinner continued and concluded in this fashion. Shiloh entertained his hosts with an array of goofy remarks and stories. He displayed a semblance of his former self; Damien could tell it was genuine. Shiloh volunteered for dish duty but was adamantly dismissed by Sr., who encouraged the boy to catch up on his homework instead. The boys trekked the stairs to Damien's room and diligently hit the books for close to two hours. They took turns reading passages aloud from "Leaves of Grass". Shiloh demonstrated a keen knack for comprehension of the material and formulated quite a few sincere responses in a sloppy hand on his packet of questions which was the homework assignment that evening. Damien was astounded, to say the least. Sometimes all a kid needs is a positive change of scenery to outshine his past self. Once finished, the boys fired up the Xbox, both relieved to see Maron and Erik were online. The four engaged in several rounds of online-play together. Erik, as usual, carried the team. Texts from Reg and Durand were sporadic. The athletes required their rest, as all knew. Connie was, as any of the other boys would put it, "nagging", but Erik didn't mind in the slightest. Soon, all of The Club lay snuggly in their beds, dreaming of all that had happened thus far and what would one day come.

Chapter 26

Durand was the first of The Club to rise that Friday. Little Ramona was soon awake as well, tailing her big brother about the apartment. By now, the superstar had grown accustomed to being scrutinized. He answered her stream of innocent and curious questions sweetly, even through the bathroom door, as he took an anxiety-fueled shit. Breanna awoke soon after. Durand whipped up the best plate of French toast and bacon the girls had ever had, according to them. He was sure to put on a pot of coffee to share with his mother. Until only recently, Durand couldn't stand the taste of the stuff. Since he was a child, he loved the aroma of a fresh, hot pot of coffee, no matter the type or location of its brewing. But to take a sip was simply abominable to him. As he grew, his tastes changed as well. He now drank a large Thermos of it, black, each morning, much to the annoyance of Beatrix. Mother Bear was showering, and Durand prepped the toaster with her preferred light breakfast: two English muffins, sparingly buttered. She emerged from the bathroom, already in her work clothes. On cue, her son popped the toaster down and fetched a butterknife from the silverware drawer. Beatrix profusely beamed at the caring gesture. She quickly snatched the boy up in a loving embrace, making every second count as she knew it would soon be interrupted by two jealous little girls. The babies of the household interfered and included themselves in what was now a family hug. The muffins popped up from the toaster, but all were too busy to pay any mind.

"Ice Cats on three, ready," Durand bellowed.
"Ready!" His three ladies said in unison.
"Bree, lead it!" Durand encouraged.

"One, two, three, Ice Cats!" The curly-headed little beauty shrieked, and the family all raised their brown hands from the huddle, hooting and hollering and collapsing onto the old couch, piling atop one another. Beatrix threw her muffins onto a flimsy paper plate, almost forgetting her butter. Durand chased her to the front door with the tub of margarine and slathered some on each piece of the carbohydrate-loaded breakfast. Beatrix hugged and kissed her boy once more, as did the little ones. They rode to the office with their mother that morning. Beatrix would excuse herself from work temporarily to drop her babies off at the elementary. This commute only ever took thirty minutes at the most, roundtrip, that is. However, her manager, who presided over her for years, always insisted she stayed over to compensate for the half-hour she was gone. That man, Mr. Galloway, was only just recently terminated from his position after he was locked up for multiple child pornography-related charges. For this reason, among many others, Beatrix was always glad she never introduced any of her children to the man. Her new boss, Ms. Duff, did not make such strict demands of her people. On the contrary, the young, tubby woman brought with her a light and frivolous air to the office upon receiving the position. Beatrix liked Ms. Duff. Steve was sure to pick up Durand. Beatrix left her son with a generous sum of gas money, which was politely refused by Mr. Bousher. Now Durand was faced with the strenuous task of slipping the money back into his mother's purse, hopefully undetected. It was no easy feat as the mother of three was very aware of her credits and debits and kept a detailed ledger to account for it all. Reg, Steve, and Durand traversed to the schoolhouse together. Steve was making an honest attempt at understanding more about the game that his boy played and was so highly commended for. He posed a few vague questions for the boys, who did their best to answer them.

"So, son, you have eight touchdowns already? Wow! What's the school record?" Steve glanced at his son, who gave it his all to not sound perturbed.

"Uh, not really sure, Dad. I don't really keep track of stuff like that. I just want us to win. It's about the team's performance, not mine, you know?" Reg's response stumped his old man.

"Yeah, yeah, very true, buddy. We're gonna get some more touchdowns today, though, right fellas," Steve's attempt at a pep talk invoked an artificial answer from his boy as well as Durand.

"Yeah, Mr. Bousher, I'll throw a few of 'em just for you," Durand replied, overly enthused.

"Yeah! Hell yeah, boys! That's what I like to hear," Steve exclaimed in response, deciding to cut his losses and not reveal too much of the fact that he hadn't the slightest clue of what he was talking about. The three pulled up to the entrance, the youths exiting the car. The boys bid their driver a farewell as he sped off to face his own dull and monotonous challenges that the day would throw at him. Reg and Durand swung the doors open and took up their usual spots in the library. They chipped away at their assignments, unbothered. The two wrapped up their schoolwork before devising their own gameplan in the hopes of embarrassing the most unforgiving defense in the area. The boys packed up and soon met with their closest friends at their leader's locker. Connie laid her head dotingly on Erik's shoulder. Hannah excitedly presented Maron with a t-shirt that represented the school's band. The lovestruck lad slipped into the bathroom to change and came back out into the hallway sporting his new piece of apparel. The Club and its ladies all broke out in applause, some letting out a few cat-calling whistles. Reg and Durand kept the sports talk brief and to the point. Shiloh was unusually tame, despite Connie wearing what the boy liked to refer to as her "hooker skirt" that day. Erik and Damien were mostly silent. Class commenced at the bell. All eight youths were in good spirits and met at their normal lunch spot. Connie's title as a cheerleader, as well as "preppy bitch", was officially taken to the chopping block. It didn't faze her in the slightest. Everyone dined on an excuse for chicken parmesan, some partaking more than others. The remainder of the school day followed suit as it typically did. Hannah left for band rehearsal. Erik was invited to Connie's house as neither of her parents would be home. Reg and Durand joined their fellow teammates in the locker room. Damien and Shiloh were both scheduled to serve a three-hour sentence at the family store. This left Maron to his own devices. He stood at the chain-link fence which ran the perimeter of the practice field for a while, catching glimpses of his girlfriend rehearsing with the rest of the band. He discretely stole huffs of his new shirt, which wore the faint fragrance of Hannah's favorite perfume. After nearly an hour of being unacknowledged had passed, he left the practice field and headed in the direction of home. He soon took note of a Chrysler, blaring jumbled and unsteady music, circling the block which he walked. Maron soon grew uneasy and scanned his immediate area for a shortcut back to base. Bose was on the prowl. Granted, he didn't have his disturbed lackey with him, he still posed a threat to the young boy as a solo attacker. From behind, Maron could hear the music bumping once again, this time accompanied by the screech of brakes. The boy took this time to cross the street before the sound of a window rolling down made its presence known. A gross-sounding cough came from inside the vehicle.

"Hey, faggot! Yeah, you, bud! Where the fuck do you think you're goin'?" The stench of Bose's cigarette wafted all the way over to Maron's nostrils, even as he reached the adjacent sidewalk. The underweight and distressed teen kept walking. Bose slowly crept behind, trying to initiate some level of conflict the entire time. Maron finally threw a hesitant glance back, only briefly.

"Hey! Fuckin' listen when I talk, bud," Bose hoarsely cried from the driver seat. "Your little butt buddies got lucky that day! Then your little faggot friend and his bitch-made dad got my boy in some shit! Fuck you, you little prick! Better hope I don't hop out this car!" But Bose didn't push the matter further, physically, at least. Maron knew running wasn't an option at this point. He had to stare this bully in the eye, just as his mother did hers. Speaking of which, it wasn't until more personal remarks were being made that Maron would finally retaliate.

"Get away, man," Maron weakly warned his assailant. "It's done. Leave me alone." He finally stopped to face Bose head-on. The car shifted into park. The door cracked slightly, more for show than anything. An old woman was across the street, paying more attention to the altercation which was sure to unfold before her eyes than the sweeping of her front porch. She spoke not a word.

"You fucks outnumbered me and Ralphie. Now, when it's one-on-one, you wanna hide, huh? I see how it is, pussy," Bose continued to taunt from the comfort of his little car. "Yeah, I heard about your mom, too, junior. Too bad. I heard she was a real piece of ass in her day." The drug-dealing bum snickered as he crushed out his cigarette. Maron experienced an emotion that differed from fear at this point. He clenched his fists but still remained mostly motionless. "I guess I still got a shot if I go and dig her up, right?" Bose cackled at his own depraved comment, inciting what would truly be Maron's last meltdown that he would ever experience in his lifetime. The younger of the two stormed the car, but not before Bose could close the door. He forgot his window was all the way down. Maron snarled and slobbered in a heat of extreme fury. Bose clicked the button to roll the window back up, but Maron already had half of his body in the car. Bose landed a few short and stiff blows, but none of which matched the small boy's wrath. Maron was aware enough to unlock Bose's car from the door's panel, then opened the door up and dragged the man onto the littered asphalt road. After that, some kind of unsurmountable terror took over and simply possessed the damaged teenager. Bose was on hands and knees, frantically trying to stumble back into his vehicle. Maron dealt a series of swift and vicious knees into his antagonist's mouth. Blood spurted onto the pavement, along with what appeared to be a tooth. Bose whimpered, attempting to scamper back to the security of his car. Maron leapt on the man's back and locked in a textbook rear naked chokehold. Bose gagged and sobbed through his strangulation. Surely, now that Maron had the upper hand and no longer felt endangered, people wanted to show up and intervene. A middle-aged balding man, perhaps the same one that Ralph nearly considered shooting dead earlier that week for no particular reason, wrestled Maron off of the instigator.

"Get off, son! It's alright! Let him go," The Stranger pleaded. Maron finally released Bose from the hold. The scumbag crawled back to his seat, promptly vomiting all over the gas and brake pedals. The interferer continued, directed at Bose, now, "Get your ass outta here! Before I let him go!" A chunky rope of slobber hung from Bose's mouth. He turned to face his savior and nodded. The sclera of each of his eyes was completely red, most likely due to burst capillaries sustained during Maron's attack. It wasn't until Bose threw the car into drive and had covered a good hundred feet until the interferer finally loosened his hold on Maron, in fear of the boy running after the car and possibly catching up to it. Maron stared at the ass-end of the Chrysler, slightly teary-eyed himself. The man rubbed his shoulder in an attempt to console the boy. Maron finally made eye contact with his arrestor. He was in his middle to late forties, dressed in a jogger's attire and had a kind and calm face.

"Fucker's been terrorizing me and my friends for a month now," Maron weakly explained. The older man nodded in understanding. "He said something about Mom, and I just lost it." The Stranger wrapped the boy up in a sincere but unfamiliar type of hug, the more youthful of the two now sobbing into his new friend's shoulder.

"I know about him," The Stranger started, "I know he's bad news. I hear he's been messing around with one of my daughter's friends. Girl is only fourteen. Fucking disgusting." The man shook his head to emphasize his level of aversion.

"Audra Woulden, she's my girl, do you know her?" Maron thought for a bit. He finally put a face to the name.

"Yeah, I think she's in my study hall. Freshman, right?" The boy inquired. The more senior of the pair smiled and nodded. "Yep! She's a shy girl. A little on the heavier side, I'm sure you could tell. She gets picked on sometimes. I tell her she needs to stand up to those kids. It looks like you've already mastered that lesson, huh?" The Stranger permitted a warm and genuine smile. Maron returned the expression, nodding and slightly embarrassed. "Well, bud, my name is Mr. Woulden. As much as I would've loved to see you put that creep on a ventilator, I couldn't let you get yourself into trouble." The man extended a sweaty and pale hand. Maron accepted Mr. Woulden's gesture and introduced himself, as well. The two bid their farewells, not before Maron offered to speak to Audra and invite her to sit at his lunch table that following Monday, of course. Mr. Woulden was much obliged. The elder resumed his steady trot. Maron kicked his pace up from before, as well. They were back to back on the same stretch of sidewalk, both throwing glances at one another at different times, so neither one ever saw. Maron was nearly home before he discovered smeared blood on both of his forearms. He was relieved to see that the car was gone, meaning Sarah was still at work. He hurried inside and scrubbed Bose's grimy bodily fluid from his own person. He showered and slipped into a fresh change of clothes, which he intended to do anyway. Sarah pulled Gloria's old ride into the driveway. Despite a slightly neglected brake change, Mrs. Serling kept up quite well on the vehicle. Every Saturday, since moving into the Calhoun home, she hand-washed the exterior and vacuumed and wiped down the interior, quite thoroughly. The following Saturday would be no different. In addition to maintaining a clean vehicle, Sarah was on top of all the requirements the home itself posed, as well. Picking up after two teenage boys was enough of a task, but the woman went above and beyond in detailed fashion when it came to the yard, or the carpets, or the floors, or the kitchen. Gloria's old room was left nearly untouched. The only times Sarah ever intruded was to clean up Gloria's vomit off the carpet and to retrieve her best friend's prized sketchbook and return it to its place with the utmost care. Maron was pleased with the degree of upkeep Sarah maintained throughout the home. He was pleased with Erik's patience and selflessness since taking shelter at the home. He was largely pleased with what was dealt to him, considering the circumstances and conditions. Make the most of what you have. Maron greeted his adoptive mother at the bottom of the stairs. She carried with her three plastic grocery bags, all slung over one thin arm. Her free hand clutched an iced coffee.

"Hey, babe," she exclaimed, still sporting her sunglasses. "I picked up some sandwiches from work, want one?" Maron hesitantly shook his head but snatched the bags and drink from Sarah in an attempt to aid her. He carried the plunder into the kitchen. The mother doffed her shades and smiled at the boy before her. "You going to the game tonight?" Maron played everything as cool as he could.

"Yeah, but mostly just to see Hannah," he answered, rapidly raising his eyebrows twice. Sarah erupted in laughter, plopping down in a chair at the kitchen island.

"But to see Reg and Durand, too, right," she prompted. Maron jokingly shrugged his shoulders.

"I guess, if they're gonna be there," his smart-ass reply only invoked an even shriller laugh than before. The boy took a chair across from Sarah.

"Is Erik home," the mother questioned, somewhat disinterested by the tone of her voice.

"Uh, no. Connie's mom needed help with some gardening, or something. He went over there to lend a hand," Maron lied, but not entirely, as Erik was at Connie's house. Sarah nodded in surprise.

"Well, when he's done, he can weed the garden on the side of this house," the woman responded, only half-jokingly. Maron immediately nodded in affirmation. Sarah ate her sandwich, washed it down with two glasses of wine, and put on a movie for herself. Erik soon let himself in. He was sure to vacate Connie's home before Big Al returned from work, and in the nick of time, at that. His bicycle was laid carelessly in the center of the pristine lawn. Only seconds after closing the front door behind him, he was given The Signal from his friend. The Signal was composed of three simple motions, all from the right hand: two rapid points of the index finger to the signaler's left, followed by a clenched fist. The Signal meant something went awry and needed to be discussed. It was invented and utilized by The Club since they were but tykes. Erik gave a solitary nod to signify his understanding. He met with his mother, briefly, said his hello's and how-are-you's, then retreated with Maron to the boys' room. The door was barely shut behind them before Maron began his babbling frenzy. Erik managed to calm him, if only for a short time.

"Okay, so you fought Bose? Like, beat his ass?" Erik was scrambling to piece it all together.

"Yes," Maron hissed. "Crazy fuck was circling me, then got out and started talking a bunch of shit. I almost had him choked out till some guy, uh, Audra Woulden's dad, pulled me off. Fuckin' bitch was saying stuff about Mom. I just lost it." Maron sounded nearly apologetic, considering what his mother always thought of physical violence. He sat on the end of his bed, elbows on his thighs, bringing his palms up to his forehead.

"Hey, I don't blame you, man. That piece of shit has had it out for us long enough. Sounds like he got something long overdue to him today," Erik reassured. "He's got a record, man. If it comes down to it, it's your word against his. Guess who the police would listen to." Maron slowly nodded.

"I don't think he'll fuck with us anymore, Erik. Not me, not you, not Dim or Shiloh. Fuck, he was too scared to ever start shit with Durand or Reg. He knew they would beat his ass down. I guess I surprised him, huh?" A smile finally ruptured through the solemn frown which occupied young Mr. Calhoun's face since he arrived home. Erik returned the expression.

"Speaking of Reg and Durand, we'd better get going, huh? Dim and Shiloh will be out soon." Maron nodded in agreeance. He rose from his bed and followed his brother through the door.

"So, I told your mom you were busy gardening when she asked about you," Maron whispered. "You take care of that bush of hers, buddy?" Erik fought back silent laughter.

"Good cover. And if you must know, there is no bush. It's all freshly mowed." The boys giggled the whole way down the stairs, catching the attention of Sarah, who was still planted on the couch.

"Boys! Are you leaving now?" She propped herself up on one elbow. A good deal of wine had simply and inexplicably vanished from the bottle on the kitchen counter by this point.

"Yeah, Mrs. Serling! Heading out now," Maron called, still grinning.

"Well, just bring me some popcorn or something, okay? Also, be careful. That boy who stuck up Mazetti's has some pretty rotten friends, I hear. Just be aware of your surroundings, guys." Maron's smile only grew.

"Uh, I don't think that'll be a problem anymore, Mom," Erik boastfully spouted, as if he was the one to whoop Bose in a public street that afternoon. "Love you, bye!" The boys slipped out the front door before Sarah had a chance to digest the response and formulate one of her own. The two opted to travel on foot, out of consideration for the others. They swung by Connie's home first and were greeted by a grumpy-looking Big Al, Budweiser in hand. He surely had plenty of questions regarding why his daughter was no longer a cheerleader and why two scrawny kids were standing on his doorstep and asking for her by name. He let most of them slide, considering how intoxicated he already was. He did make some level of conversation, though.

"Which one of you boys is Erik?" The burly man gruffly spoke. Erik immediately raised his hand as if he was eagerly waiting to be called on for a response in Mr. Steinn's math class. "Addie told me about you. Connie's been doodling your name all over her notebooks, too. I'm all for doodling, son. Diddling, though, is something I won't stand for. Understand me?" The hulking man crouched slightly to make himself eye-level with Erik, who profusely nodded.

"Yes, sir. None of that, absolutely not," he lied to Big Al's face. He caught a glimpse of Connie skipping down the stairs, still brushing out her dark tresses. She saw the conversation taking place in the doorway and instantly grew annoyed. She rolled her dark brown eyes deeply into the recesses of her eyelids as she reached the bottom step. Suddenly, it didn't matter to Erik if Big Al broke that beer bottle over his skull and choked him out on the foyer floor. All that mattered to the boy was Connie and having her forever.

"Dad," Connie called out from behind, in her best attempt at a voice that didn't sound irritated, "I'd love for you to meet Erik, Daddy. And our friend Maron." Al turned his head as far as his beefy neck would permit to glance at his daughter, then right back to the boys. "Mom said she'll pick me up after the game is over." Al grunted in confirmation, knowing full well that he would be passed out when that time came.

"No funny business. I mean that," Al peered into the boys' souls, who both nodded in terror. Connie dramatically groaned and went to the kitchen to kiss her mother goodbye. She soon repeated the act on her father's cheek. Al extended a large, brown, hairy-knuckled hand and shook with both of the boys. His grip was firm and engulfed both Erik and Maron's bony fingers, covering well past the wrist bone. Without a word more, he turned his back and Connie closed the door. She threw herself onto Erik, giggling and squeaking as she planted a hundred kisses all over the boy's face. The three teens descended the porch steps and checked the time. Shiloh and Damien would be released in the next twenty minutes, so there was no sense in making the voyage all the way to Mazetti's now. Erik texted Damien and the five agreed to meet up at the field. He recounted the severe altercation with Bose just an hour prior, on behalf of Maron. Connie didn't seem the least bit surprised.

"Such a fucking loser. My older cousin's friend dated him for a little while and said she went through his phone and found messages from girls younger than me, even. I wish that guy wasn't there to save him." The boys silently agreed with the ill wish. Like clockwork, the trio met up with the deli employees just as all arrived at the stadium entrance. Shiloh still sported his apron, wearing it like a superhero cape. Damien was obviously annoyed at the fashion statement. All five were granted admission, and Connie treated her boys to the concession stand. Shiloh was not modest, to say the least. The Club found an unoccupied length of bleachers in the student section.

"Connie, shouldn't you be out there with the other cheerleaders," Shiloh teased, stuffing a stack of tortilla chips into his mouth, seeming to forget who it was that bought them for him.

"Fuck off, Shiloh," Erik snapped.

"I think you should be out there, Shiloh. You're definitely skinny enough to fit into one of my skirts," Connie retorted. Shiloh let out an obnoxious laugh, shooting out a chunk of half-chewed chips onto the front of Maron's shirt.

"Goddamn it. I'm gonna choke you out next if you keep being gross," Maron wiped the slobbery glob of food from his clothing. The National Anthem was played. Soon, the band took the field to perfectly execute the school's fight song. Maron knew right where Hannah would be. His eyes fixated on her the entirety of the tune. The school band cleared out and the banner was drawn out by two members of the spirit squad. 'Stomp Sandusky' was proudly painted on the front. Durand led the pack from the locker room's tunnel that connected to the field. This was the best that the Ice Cats would look all evening. Durand would throw four interceptions, two of which were taken back for touchdowns. Reg fumbled the ball twice during two sloppy handoffs. He managed to recover the first. The second, however, eluded him and was scooped up by a Sandusky lineman and brought back for a touchdown as well. The score at halftime was forty-two to seven. The home crowd was largely silent. Even Shiloh's snacks sat uneaten. Then came the coronation of the homecoming king and queen. Even under such bleak circumstances, the crowd was able to get into it, due to who the recipients of such illustrious awards were. The title of queen was awarded to Asuka Hayashi, a beautiful Japanese foreign exchange student who continuously outshone her American counterparts in academics. She was a shy girl who was encouraged to join the cross-country team by her host parents. She finished last in nearly all of her meets but was heavily cheered on by all of her classmates. She was somewhat of a celebrity at Castalia High. The winner of the king's crown was Albert Weishaim, a vibrant and exuberant boy who endured twelve years of special education. Albert was placed on a multitude of spectrums at a young age. But at lunch, he sat with the football players. He flirted with the prettiest senior girls. He was always picked first for a team in gym class, due mostly to his relentless and vocal trash talk of the opposing team. He was also a sweet boy. He passed all of his classes. He remembered his classmates' birthdays. At the start of Damien's freshman year, he found himself somehow sitting at the jock table during lunch, which was headed by Albert, formerly prince, now king. This year The Club's lunch schedule was considerably broken up and spaced out over all three lunch periods. Damien ended up the odd man out. Albert had the idea of going around the table and asking every boy's favorite color. Why? Because Albert had to know everyone's favorite color that day. Damien was silently praying that he would be overlooked; he was not.

"Hey, buddy! New buddy! What's y-y-y-your favorite c-color, my dude," Albert finally sputtered out. Damien looked up from the slop on his lunch tray to meet the collective and intent gaze of Albert, as well as ten varsity football players. He suddenly wished he had taken his lunch into the library to dine alone. He thought for a moment.

"Uh, probably red. Yeah, red's my favorite," Damien meagerly squawked. All of the jocks turned their heads to face Albert, as if waiting to see if this was even an appropriate response. Albert grinned, standing up now.

"Y-y-yeah! That's why the swooshes on y-y-your Nikes is r-r-r-red, huh?" Damien had to look down at his own shoes to confirm that they really were red. He truthfully didn't know.

"Yeah, that's why I picked 'em out! Good eye, man!" The table of meatheads erupted in jovial triumph, congratulating their leader on his supreme level of astuteness. Damien was relieved at the reaction, and that he was left alone and sat unacknowledged for the remainder of lunch period that day, but he still made the effort and succeeded in switching to a lunch period that his friends were in. Fast-forward a year and some days. Damien pulled a cheap red pair of earbuds out of his pocket and carelessly tossed them into his locker on the second or third day of sophomore year. Albert happened to be walking by.

"H-h-hell yeah, my dude! D-d-d-d-Dim's favorite c-color is red!" Damien's face lit up at being acknowledged by the coolest guy in school. The two shook hands and went their separate ways. That would be the last face-to-face interaction with Albert that Damien would ever be graced with. The young man with special needs would graduate that spring, only to be struck and killed by a distracted driver that following October. He was hurrying across town, on foot, of course, to pick up his little brother's insulin from the CVS before they closed. The light was red, and he saw the pedestrian sign light up to signal what should have been a safe crossing. A teenage girl staring at her phone blew through the intersection and collided with the young man, going forty, easily. His throat and chest cavity were ripped open. He gasped and gurgled on his back, bleeding out and dying at the scene. The girl, who was returning to Norhauk after visiting her boyfriend in town, served three months in juvenile hall and got her license back before the age of twenty-five. Such is life in a small town. It's those acts of God that really stick it in and break it off. But none of which is either here nor there. Albert was king in the present moment, and he knew it. The homecoming court was ushered off the field and play resumed. It resumed in the same fashion, as well. Castalia was beaten and beaten badly. Durand braced each play to either be sacked or have his pass batted down or intercepted. The charisma was a ghost now. The final score was fifty-six to fourteen. A considerable chunk of Sandusky's points came from their defense. A discouraged and heartbroken Ice Cats roster slunk off the field in utter embarrassment. Starkey shattered his helmet to pieces on the concrete slab in front of the locker room, slamming the headgear down repeatedly until it was no more. Grenslait had anticipated the outcome, truthfully, and already had a speech prepared to console his boys. The Club exited the stands, tail tucked between their legs. The non-athletes knew better than to try to initiate conversation with either Reg or Durand following such a devastating loss. The five of them sifted through the crowd to the band room door, where they awaited Hannah. The shy beauty emerged, remarkably happy, considering the outcome of the event. She wrapped Maron up in a big hug and planted a kiss on him. Suddenly, the boy forgot what it was he was sulking about.

"You looked beautiful out there, you know that," the troubled young man complimented his lady, barely above a whisper. This only caused a more passionate and frenzied reaction on Hannah's part. Connie's mom was eagerly waiting, having noticed a police officer was parked beside her and she had a nearly full twenty-ounce Thermos of merlot nestled in her car's cupholder. She honked to get her daughter's attention. Connie irritably looked to her left to make eye contact with her mother, who stared daggers through the windshield of the vehicle.

"She's probably hammered. If you guys don't hear from me tomorrow, you'll know I didn't make it," Connie joked. Erik was considerably alarmed by the real possibility that Addie was drunk and intended to transport his precious cargo, but he laughed it off just as the others did. Connie leaned in for one more kiss. "I love you. You know that by now, right?" Young Mr. Serling's heart skipped several beats upon the startling admission of passion. He stood, mouth agape, slowly nodding his head as most dumbass teenage boys would under such pretenses. Connie gazed, almost anxiously, into his eyes, awaiting the reciprocation.

"Yeah, uh, I love you, too. I always have," the startled leader stuttered out. "I love you, Connie De La Rosa. I always will." The second half sounded a tad more confident. Connie blushed at the sentiment and got her goodnight kiss, waving goodbye to all her friends, prancing like the princess she always was into the passenger seat of the family car. It wasn't just young men who schemed and plotted. The fair damsels of the same age did as well, if not more. The Latin beauty queen had waited all evening to make her confession, finally picking out the perfect moment to do so. Connie was so overjoyed to hear such soft and honest notes of the heart spoken in return to her that she forgot to even ask her mother to take Erik and Maron home. But Addie had already peeled out, nervously and tipsily speeding out of the crowded asphalt lot. Minutes later, Hannah's mother slowly crept her car just a few feet in front of the youths. Maron, being the gentleman that he was, hauled his girlfriend's bag into the backseat of the vehicle before being beckoned from the driver's window. Maron briskly walked around to the other side of the car. Hannah said goodnight to the remainder of the lot before taking her spot in the passenger seat. Maron held a brief conversation and threw out a wave before dismissing himself around the backside of the vehicle, rejoining his friends in front of the band room. The car cautiously drove off, in stark contrast to the one before it.

"What did Mrs. Lada want," Damien finally prodded.

"She just told me how happy Hannah's been since meeting me. She said 'thanks', in so many words, I guess. I told her I felt the same. That Hannah's been so good to me these past few weeks, and I wouldn't trade that for anything," Maron spoke with a slight smile. "I think I love her, guys. I know I do." Erik, Dim and even Shiloh all nodded in understanding.

"Make sure you tell her, bud," Shiloh nobly started, to the surprise of everyone present. "When somethin' good comes your way, don't let it pass you by. Tell her you love her. Tell her that her support since your mom passed means everything. Girls don't always get this kinda concept. We know that not everything needs to be spoken out loud. We can pick up on certain things without having to be verbally told. Girls are different, bud. They need to hear that kinda thing. They need that re'surance. Tell her tomorrow, just like Connie told Erik. Flat out, 'Hannah, I love you'." All three boys looked at Shiloh with such an obvious expression of shock. "What? I don't get school like you nerds, but I understan' how things work. I got street smarts, boys." Shiloh cockily popped the collar of his t-shirt before breaking out a cheesy little spin-move, nearly falling in the process. All erupted in laughter just as Sr. pulled the Enclave into a spot twenty or so yards away. The four trotted to the car. The weather had grown cold by this time of year, and all were happy to have their backsides greeted by the heated seats of the old man's luxurious ride. Raquel occupied the passenger seat, so the boys made use of all three rows of seating.

"Hungry, boys," Sr. posed the question, as if it had to be asked. The six of them made haste to El Ranchero, a quaint little Mexican restaurant that lay equidistant between Castalia and Norhauk. It was located on a side road, often overlooked by travelers, but a notable gem amongst the locals. Sarah gave permission on behalf of her boys' attendance in exchange for a take-home enchilada dinner. The Mazetti-Calhoun-Serling-Robertson party was seated and treated to a plethora of combinations of beef, chicken, seafood and tortillas, all drenched in salsas and quesos which varied in degrees of spiciness. Shiloh compensated for his wasted haul of snacks at the game by gorging himself at the restaurant. All in attendance ate until the point of bloat and borderline nausea. Sr. picked up the bill, naturally. Erik and Maron were dropped off at home. One carried a piping hot Styrofoam container of enchiladas and refried beans, the other a frozen blueberry margarita, which he was sure to sneak a sip of once the front door was closed behind him. Sarah, nearly unconscious at this point, was presented with the bountiful feast and beverage, never having to leave the comfort of the couch. The boys sat in the living room and talked with her for a while as she struggled to finish the platter. The drink, though, seemed to evaporate within only a handful of sips. Erik desperately wanted to address the hot and heavy topic of his final conversation with Connie that evening with his mother but thought better of it. By that point, his phone was nearly exploding with over twenty unread messages, all sent from his beloved. The boys said their goodnights and crashed out in Maron's room. The Mazettis made it home shortly after. Reg was picked up by Jessica alone that evening. He specifically requested his mother be the only one to retrieve him and made no excuses or apologies as to why he asked this. Durand was picked up by his girls, as usual. The little ones adamantly rubbed the sand from their eyes, but, seemingly within seconds, it always returned. Beatrix wore her warm and pretty smile that adorned her face throughout most of her life.

"I'm proud of you, baby," she spoke to her only son as he climbed into the passenger seat of the car. "No matter what, I'm proud of you. Nothing can change that in my eyes." A wild idea steered Durand's mind toward the unthinkable.

"Nothing could change that, Mom? You're sure?" He quietly returned. Beatrix nodded, smile never wavering. Durand knew now was as good a time as any. He already disappointed an entire town; what was one more person, even if that was his own mother? "Okay, then. I want to take this chance to tell you that I'm gay." The mother's smile and slow nod persisted.

"Oh, I knew for a while, baby," Mrs. Desmond replied, absolutely flooring her son. She pulled into a proper parking spot. The lot was largely vacated by now. Only a dozen or so other cars remained. "Honey, I knew for some time. I just wish it hadn't been kept a secret for so long. Look at you! You know how many girls have been lined up, just wishing you would talk to them?" The babies dozed in the backseat. Beatrix tried her best to not wake them. "By eighth-grade I was fairly convinced; you just had no interest. That's fine, Durand. Did you think I was gonna be mad about this? I'm more hurt than anything that you never thought to communicate this to me." A slight tear welled in Beatrix's left eye, which she promptly wiped away upon noticing its formation. Durand was at a loss.

"Mom, I just didn't know how to go about it. I didn't know what you'd think. I don't want the guys to ever find out that I'm like this! I have this reputation and this image I gotta live up to now. What school wants a gay quarterback? I'm already one of only five, that I counted, black kids in the school. I'm a fag, too, though. How am I supposed to explain that to anybody?" Durand's voice came in more than a whisper. He was now fighting back tears of his own. The little ones stirred in the backseat. Beatrix would often take them on drives when they were colicky infants, which is the trick she utilized now to keep them asleep. The car began to roll forward. She spoke not a word more until the family was out of the parking lot.

"Don't you ever call yourself that. You understand? You're not no nigger. You're not no fag. You're my son. You're my baby who is caring and considerate and responsible. You're a man who takes care of his baby sisters and his own mother in more ways than you could ever know. Don't ever think less of yourself, Durand." Once home, Beatrix continued her piece after the littles were snuggly tucked away in her bed. She emerged from the bedroom to find her son pretending to be asleep as well. "Don't think that's gonna work on me, boy. I invented that trick when I was the girls' age," Mama Beatrix sternly warned. Suddenly, Durand was reinvigorated. He immediately sprang to a sitting position on the sofa. "That's what I thought." Beatrix grabbed some leftovers from the fridge and heated both of them up a plate. She carried the day-old helping of baked spaghetti over to her son, who wasted no time. Four quarters of utter annihilation at the hands of a rabid defense sure made a boy hungry. "Friday Fear Night" presented an intense lineup that evening: "Nightmare on Elm Street", "Misery", and "The Shining" were all slated to air on the tube. The thrill and suspense of such classics paled in comparison to the uncertainty that awaited the remainder of this particular conversation, though. After both plates were cleaned, and during a commercial break, Beatrix decided to push the topic just a hair further.

"So, what made you want to tell me tonight, honey? Is there a boy, or did you just feel like you had to finally get it off your chest, or what was it, exactly?" The sweet woman inquired, lackadaisically reaching for her crossword puzzle which she had left on the small end table. Durand really wished he had saved his "fake sleep" bit for this moment instead. He cleared his throat.

"Well, Mom, there is someone. I guess that's what makes all of this so much more complicated for me, though," the young man said as he mindlessly scrolled through his phone. Beatrix readjusted her position on the couch, yet to make the slightest attempt at her puzzle. "I have feelings for one of the guys, Mom. I'm sure you can guess who. And he felt or feels the same way, but I know he would never go public about it. It hurts me that he feels the need to suppress his feelings about us and about me, but at the same time, I get it. Just feels like I can't be happy. I can't be like Erik or Maron and show off a girl, because I don't have one and I really don't want one. And the guy I do like, love, to be honest, is so far in the closet that he'll probably spend his whole life there. And that's not fair to him either. It's bad enough to lose the game, but to feel like I lost something bigger that I didn't stand a fair chance at hurts even more." A few more streaks of tears burst from Durand's beautiful brown eyes. Beatrix, at last, ceased her nodding, which seemed to have been infinitely present since her son first dropped his bombshell news. She scooted across the tattered couch to hug and console her oldest. "But, how did you know? What gave it away?" Durand was still perplexed at his mother's statement from earlier.

"A mother just knows, baby," the kind but tough woman's voice sang out as sweet as a lullaby to an infant's ears. "I just had this feeling that you were different, not that that's a bad thing to be. And I didn't love you any less then and I sure don't feel any different now, hearing it from your mouth. And your friends won't, either. You're still their best friend. You're still the star quarterback. You're still you. Coming to grips with this and telling me about it was the bravest thing you have done so far in your life." She gently massaged Durand's scalp, which was an act he admittedly enjoyed and was able to fall asleep to for years. "I do hope that you decide to tell your friends, but I hope it's on your terms and in your own time. As for the other boy, I can't tell him what I think is best, because I'm not his mother. But I hope he grows to see this for what it is and you both are happy together. Until then, all we can do is hope, honey." Beatrix reached for the remote and turned the volume back up on the television. The classic, which featured a young James Caan, was halfway through. Despite the fact that the mother and son duo had seen the film a thousand times together, the ankle-shattering scene never failed to make them squeamish.

"Just one of the reasons I'm not attracted to women," Durand muttered. "They're all crazy." He looked to his mother for a reaction, which he surely got. Beatrix playfully scowled, lightly smacking her son on the chest.

"Men are just as bad, baby. Believe me. You're in for a surprise," Beatrix replied, both erupting into laughter. They tried to stifle their giggling, but to no avail. Little Ramona awoke and wandered out to the couch, speaking not a word before collapsing into her big brother's lap. He played with her hair until she drifted off to sleep once again. He carried her to the room and laid beside both little girls, falling into a well-deserved slumber himself. Beatrix took the couch that evening and rose for work as she did on any given day, in her usual early manner.

Chapter 27

The day of the dance had finally arrived. The junior varsity team followed suit of their upperclassmen and were blown out in their competition as well on that brisk fall morning. Connie and Hannah went together for their hair and nail appointments. This would be the first time that Hannah ever had her hair professionally cut or her nails properly manicured. All six boys sat in Maron's basement, glued to the television as multiple college football games played out before their eyes. Damien snuck a case of beer from the store. Sarah had her suspicions of what went on downstairs but left the boys be.

"Spartans are getting knocked off today, for sure," a tipsy and excited Reg bellowed from the armchair. This prompted a great debate, and even the lesser of football fans present had their take on the topic. The case was killed by two that afternoon. By three, the boys suddenly were reminded of an important event taking place that day, that at least two of them were expected to be a part of. Connie was irritated that Erik hadn't been replying. Hannah felt the same with Maron but was much more reserved in her showing of it. The two lover boys had an hour to shower, get dressed, sober up and meet the girls at the park for pictures. They bounded up the steps, leaving their bachelor counterparts to their chips and brownies and football. Maron and Erik freshened up, both slipping into their shirts and ties that would match their ladies' choices of colors. Reg, Durand, Damien and Shiloh all went home to change as well. When all was said and done, the lads looked dapper as ever. The bunch cleaned up rather nicely. Sarah drove the boys to the park to meet their dates. All parents were present. Big Al looked slightly less grumpy than before. Connie was barking orders nearly immediately. The girls posed for pictures together. Then several solo shots were taken of each. Finally, the boys were included. Erik had to abide by the utmost rigid and demanding instruction as if following the command of a drill sergeant. Maron and Hannah simply muddled their way through it, seeming to have more fun with the whole process than their friends. Once finished, nearly a hundred pictures in total were taken. Connie appeared in more than half. Sarah drove the two couples to a chain steakhouse in Norhauk. Hannah was kind enough to compensate everyone's meal, the chauffeur's included. The boys chowed down, both of which had obtained a serious appetite after their drinking session. The girls were courteous and lady-like, but finished a strip steak apiece, nonetheless. Sarah was modest and ordered the cheapest chicken-based entrée on the menu, opting for a Pepsi instead of a glass of wine, much to Erik's surprise. Soon after, the four arrived at the school's main entrance, ready to dance the night away. The parking lot was flooded with partygoers. Dozens of pretty girls sauntered about in elegant dresses, some more modest than others. Erik was blind to all of it. Friends took pictures, they laughed, they chased one another and tickled and hugged. The only sight to behold, from young Erik's view, was Connie De La Rosa and her majestic, girlish essence. Maron felt the same toward his bashful date. The quiet cutie slipped out of the car and turned more than a few heads of her male classmates. Many of which never knew she existed a week prior. Maron held no feelings of jealousy in regard to the blatant gawks and stares. He was proud to show off something this beautiful that was all his own. The party moved inside. Connie forced Erik to take the floor right away. The two casually danced to an eighty's ballad, Erik's hands on his woman's hips. Hannah was much more reserved.

"Did you wanna dance," Maron proposed, lightly grasping Hannah's soft hand from across the table. The cute and awkward girl fumbled with her words.

"Uh, no, not yet. I guess my food's still settling," she cringed at her own response. Maron nodded in understanding, never releasing his gentle grip. The four bachelors soon made their way to the table that Maron and Hannah occupied. It was evident that they hadn't stopped drinking.

"Guys! Guys, I'm so glad to see you!" Shiloh stretched both arms out in a remarkably impressive wingspan. The boy wasn't incredibly tall but had these long, gangly arms that were often a teasing point of his friends. He enveloped both Hannah and Maron in a tipsy embrace. Both halves of the couple couldn't help but laugh at the innocent and sincere gesture. Shiloh took a seat alongside Damien. Reg and Durand broke off to chat with some teammates. A more modern and upbeat tune boomed throughout the gymnasium. Shiloh took his chance at the dance floor, leaving Damien alone with the awkward couple. The three poked fun at Shiloh as he exhibited his blatantly cringey moves. Erik was finally permitted to sit and grab some water. Connie sat and conversed with Hannah, finally convincing her to join her and some other girls for the next song. Reg and Durand made their way back to occupy the last two vacant seats.

"You guys look fucked up," Maron declared, rolling his eyes. Durand nodded in confirmation.

"We went to Damien's store and snuck some wine. I'm feeling it, man." Durand was engaged in an intense battle with "the whirls". Every seasoned drinker knows that for one to conquer "the whirls", he must plant his right foot, often several times, firmly and obnoxiously on the ground in order to keep the room from whirring around him. Durand was not an experienced drinker, however, and made the critical mistake of closing his eyes several times, only exacerbating his condition. Damien paced himself considerably better than his comrades. He was buzzed but not inebriated. Reg was caught somewhere between Damien's and Durand's levels. Shiloh was positively gone. The nature of his dancing amongst his peers was a dead giveaway. The girls returned to the table, and Hannah acquired the thirst for dancing. Maron escorted her onto the floor at the chime of "Time After Time". A more perfect first dance was never had. The geeky girl swayed slowly with the damaged boy in a rhythmic repetition to the tune. Neither spoke a word until the song was nearly through. Their motions did most of the communicating for them. Maron cleared his throat as the next song commenced.

"I love you. I can't tell you how much you've helped me. I was at the worst I've ever been until you came around. I can honestly say that I thought of killing myself after everything that happened." Hannah winced at the last remark. Maron continued, "But you showed me that I have a life to live. You showed me that it doesn't all end when someone ends. You've given me life, Hannah. And I just need to know that you'll always be there. I can't face someone else leaving me forever. Promise me that? Do you promise me, Hannah?" The shy and adorable band-geek doll nodded fervently. Tears dripped from her beautiful brown eyes, smearing her mascara ever so slightly. She made no effort to conceal this blemish of her otherwise flawless appearance. The two passionately kissed and remained on the dance floor well into the next song, neither making the slightest attempt to dance but rather just holding one another closely. Connie marched her date back out for several more songs, finally taking a break once the homecoming court took the floor. The principal walked to the center of the gym, microphone in hand. The king and queen were formally introduced, receiving a near-deafening round of applause at the announcement of their names. Asuka and Albert held hands and, as gracefully as they could, moved forward to claim the floor as their own. "Forever Young" dreamily drifted from the speakers which surrounded the deejay's table. The two shared the song and the night together. Asuka found Albert adorable and charming. This dance would sadly be the closest Albert would ever physically get to a woman in his brief and damned life. After the song's conclusion, dozens flooded the floor to gift Asuka bouquets of flowers and Albert handshakes and congratulatory remarks. In the slow and Magickal moment of the dance, Asuka truthfully fell in love with the boy. She honestly saw somewhat of a future with him. He was kind, strong and polite. He was not shy or avoidant as many boys of her homeland tended to be. He was confident and direct, which she found exceptionally appealing. The two would be in close communication with one another right up until Albert's untimely and cruel death. Asuka even managed to fly back to the states to attend his funeral and adorn his casket with a single red rose. The two most lovable students of Castalia High vacated the floor, signifying its return to a commonplace for the numerous peasants in attendance once more. The other teenagers wasted no time in rushing back out. Erik was dragged along by his gorgeous girlfriend once again. Hannah, too, had found her rhythm that night, as well as the youthful desire to be shown off as a young boy's prize and playfully demanded Maron to come back out at the sound of the "Cha Cha Slide". The lad was happy to comply. The couple forced their way into the space next to Connie and Erik and the four danced and laughed together, mainly at the boys' lack of comprehension of the direction of the song. A cute and rather largely unnoticed girl by the name of Sasha Bairck approached the table which the dateless members of The Club still gloomily occupied. She finally looked up from the floor to make eye contact with Damien.

"Do you want to go out there and dance," the blond-haired blue-eyed beauty tentatively requested of Mazetti Jr. This came as a complete and most welcomed surprise to the boy. The two shared study hall together, where Damien once lent a ballpoint pen to the girl. Other than that, no interactions were ever had between them. Little did young Mazetti know, Sasha would keep that cheap Paper Mate in her private desk drawer, holding onto the sacred relic of their love until the two would end up breaking up forever at the end of junior year. Damien was sobering up but still elected to give a slight and corny bow at the proposal. This act elicited quite a clamorous laugh from Shiloh. Damien turned to scowl at his friend and redirected his attention to Sasha.

"I would love to. Sasha, right?" The girl giggled and nodded in confirmation. Damien offered his arm, which she gratefully wrapped her whole self around. Another slow song began, just in time. Damien swayed with the girl, and she with him. This evening's Magick had bitten two more. It was not done just yet, however. Reg, as hardened as he was, extended his hand to Durand. The elite quarterback looked at his best teammate with such an expression of shock and awe in the moment. The stocky running back rose from his seat, looking taller than ever.

"I'm tired of hiding. Come on," Reg urged. Shiloh still sat, mouth agape. Durand graciously accepted. The two football brutes took one another, fingers interlaced, and paced out onto the dance floor. Many members of the team, most of which clumsily stepping on their ladies' shoes at the time, diverted their attention to the queer couple which began to slowly sway with the masses of their peers. Within a minute, all the kids present had taken note, erupting into a loud round of applause and cheering which nearly rivaled that which they paid to Asuka and Albert. The two jocks held one another as a boy did a girl: both their hands on one another's hips. Shiloh was soon to run out and make a fool of himself at the scene.

"Yeah! That's my two gay best friends, right there! Anyone has a problem they can kiss my white ass! You hear me! Who's got a problem? Anyone got a problem? Yeah, I didn't fuggin' think so!" The goofball jumped and hollered around the couple. Erik and Maron pulled their girls closer to the only pair of same-sex dancers on the floor.

"We always joked and had our suspicions but seeing this really ties it all together. And I just wanna say that I'm really happy for you guys," Erik paid his respects, with the most sincere and genuine smile on his face that was ever witnessed by any of the boys. Connie nodded in agreeance, tears streaking down her flawless, flushed face. She cast a great smile upon the boys and their act of confidence and love. Hannah and Maron beamed as well. The jocks, even the most close-minded and dim-witted ones, kept any and all disparaging comments to themselves. Many even applauded their team's leaders in their display of romance. The night carried on. The Club scarcely left the dance floor. Pictures were taken, kisses were had, memories were branded into the hearts and consciousnesses of all in attendance. The Club all left early, on foot, in the direction of the community park. The night was cold but not quite frigid. Nonetheless, all three girls, as Sasha tagged along, shuddered upon the autumnal night air's immodest kiss as the nine youths stepped outside. Erik was quick to drape his jacket over Connie, Maron following suit. Damien left his inside and insisted on going back in to grab it, but Sasha assured him she would be fine. The group moved in the direction of the park, all couples holding hands. This left Shiloh the odd man out, enticing him to pester each pair of lovebirds, one at a time, the whole way. The effects of his drinking were wearing off, but not soon enough.

"Yeah, Damien's a good guy. His folks have that store 'Zetti's. I'm sure you heard of it. I work there, too, now," Shiloh tried to chat up Sasha. "My girlfriend works there, but she thought she was too old to be my date, else she woulda come with me." Sasha was amused, Damien annoyed.

"Goddamn it, Shiloh. She's not your girlfriend. She's just a girl you like that works with us, and you don't have any kind of chance with her. Find a girl your age, man," Damien snipped.

"Wait, what's her name," Sasha curiously interjected.

"Holly. She's beautiful. She has blonde hair and is the prettiest girl I've ever seen. I wish I was just a couple years older. I swear to God, when I'm eighteen, I'm asking that woman to marry me," Shiloh dreamily explained, softly smiling at his own grandiose plans. Sasha, unexpectedly and almost rudely, burst into a fit of laughter. She stopped in her tracks, halting Damien as well.

"That's my sister! Oh, my God! She told me about some guy that comes into work that always flirts with her and is just so sweet. No offense, but I definitely didn't think you would be the kind of guy she was talking about," Sasha's comment did, somehow, despite issuing the 'no offense' prior to stating it, cause Shiloh some offense. "She calls you 'Reese's Guy'? Because you always buy Reese's?" Damien was holding back a ferocious bout of laughter. Shiloh felt two feet tall.

"Uh, yeah, that's her pet name for me, I guess," Shiloh shrugged out of embarrassment. Damien started to experience some level of sympathy for his obnoxious friend. However, Sasha's next few remarks would quickly bludgeon that feeling.

"Oh, well, she goes on and on about you. She said you're a little young for her, still, but she does like you. Since she's gone off to college, she just cries over these asshole guys who just use her for one reason then dump her. She was going on about one until a few weeks ago, then she just suddenly stopped. Like she stopped talking to him and the other ones and just seems happier. Don't get me wrong, Holly's a ditz, but she is a sweet girl, and she just wants to be happy. She likes you, Shiloh. Just be her friend and be there for her. In a few years maybe she'll come around." Sasha's words of encouragement were all the boy needed to hear. It didn't matter that he was dateless and kissless that evening; Holly Bairck (her last name was finally known) had some level of interest in Shiloh Robertson, which meant he stood a chance. Young Mr. Robertson counted this a win and marched on with his friends. His ego extended into the stratosphere. The park was dimly lit and, save for the few and intermittent sounds coming from giggling and horny teenagers who had the same idea as The Club, largely silent. Reg and Durand took up the first unoccupied bench they came across. They nestled into one another's arms, optimistically gazing up into the array of dying cosmic deities which littered the night sky. They dreamed, at least in that moment, of something bigger than what it was that they knew. Each boy desperately hoped to live this feeling out with the other. But teenage dreams are fragile; they often do not survive the rigorous tests of time and patience. The one they shared with each other that starry evening would fizzle out and expire just as all of the cosmic bodies before their eyes either already had or will one day. Just as so many aspirations before theirs, and even more after theirs would, this dream would fail to come true. Damien and Sasha strolled about the park, arm in arm. Shiloh tagged along, trying to pry more information out of Sasha regarding her older sister. She had not much more to offer, but this deterred the boy not in the slightest. Damien snuck a few kisses, all of which induced a slight bit of envy in Shiloh, but a greater deal of hope. The lad wandered as a third wheel behind his friend and his lady, concocting elaborate daydreams which all focused on the fair Holly as their main subject. Daydreams are dreams. And this one would happen to come true in the purest sense. Maron, Hannah, Erik and Connie all cautiously trotted down the crude concrete steps, which were haphazardly carved and embedded into the grassy hill which separated the park's upper and lower halves. The boys led the way, never lifting a finger off of their dates, assisting the girls in each and every step down the unrefined excuse of a stairway. Once at the bottom, both girls threw caution to the wind, adorably jogging ahead of their boyfriends and giggling, leaving Erik and Maron behind. The boys simultaneously rolled their eyes and caught up with a few swift strides. The four arrived at the larger of the two shelter houses that the park offered. The memory of Erik's sixth birthday suddenly seemed so fresh to him. Nine years and some days ago, the big shelter house was booked for a different event that was canceled at the last minute. Sarah called a week prior to her baby's special day but was denied, as the venue was already claimed. She received a call back saying that the shelter house was freed up as the other family unexpectedly pulled out. This unknown father's deposit was kept by the city as a late cancellation fee and was generously applied to Sarah's cost, so she essentially got the site for a fifty-percent discount. Erik recalled kids being there, but none of them would grow into his greatest friends he would cherish from the age of fifteen onward. It was mostly Jared's family in attendance. Jared was responsible for retrieving the cake, but carelessly returned it in such a crumbled and smashed state as to match his own. Upon seeing the result of such negligence, Sarah erupted and let her husband have it. He was high and drunk beyond belief, lucky to have not killed or seriously injured a pedestrian or fellow driver during the fetching of the confection. Jared staggered about, flinging insults and degrading comments toward his wife and even his own son. Despite being completely obliterated and clearly displaying it in front of his own parents, Erik's paternal grandparents joined in to attack Sarah as well. They belittled and mocked her, just as their son did. They insisted the party was "too much" and that her requests were too demanding of Jared. They were enablers. Erik began to cry, adamantly refusing any further birthday parties for the rest of his life. It would be the last time he ever spoke to Grandma and Grandpa Serling face to face. It would not, as we know, be the last time Jared would ever get completely fucked up and ruin something for his beautiful little family. Erik staved off such cruel and painful memories and entered the tainted shelter house with a false confidence, not just as a show for Connie, but perhaps for himself. Several others were already gathered inside. Two skater kids made lackadaisical attempts at their tricks, still succeeding in impressing the girls that had tagged along with them. Maron recognized the two skateboarders as freshmen in his study hall. They always sported band t-shirts and black skinny jeans. The taller of the two boys was quiet and filled the position of sidekick to the shorter boy. The smaller of the pair was more vocal as well as combative at times. The girls were complete strangers, perhaps attendants of another school. A noticeable aroma of reefer hung in the air. Erik confidently approached the quartet.

"Hey guys, you mind if we hang here," the boy politely spoke. The shorter kid slightly scrunched his face at the proposition. The taller kid obliged.

"Yeah, man. That's fine. We were gonna leave soon, anyways," the understudy spoke as he brushed his shaggy hair from his eyes. The girls took note of Connie and Hannah.

"Your guys's dresses are beautiful," one of the female strangers, who was a sophomore from Norhauk, squawked. Hannah smiled out of her innate politeness. Connie pretended to pay attention to the artificial compliment for only a moment. The four punks vacated the area only minutes later. The single motion-activated light flickered from its mount on the ceiling up above. Maron had recently found out that Hannah was an aficionado of classical tunes, not surprisingly, as music was a topic she was more than passionate about. He built a playlist on his phone, just that morning, consisting of Sinatra, Aretha Franklin, and The Five Satins, amongst other big names. Upon hearing the opening tune to "Come Fly with Me", Hannah squealed and charged her boyfriend, wrapping him in a loving embrace and transitioning into a smooth and rhythmic waltz.

Connie felt slightly envious of the gesture and pulled Erik out into the makeshift ballroom. The kids swayed and danced and glided about the concrete slab. Erik was not so mindful of the picnic tables, on which he buckled the back of his knees several times, Connie giggling at each. Much to Maron's shock, Hannah was the first to propose the first lustful idea of the night. She whispered in his reddened ear, and the boy went bug-eyed. Hannah smirked and walked away from her date toward the small, wooded area at the edge of the park. She threw back one challenging glance and roped Maron in. The two scampered across the gravel lot and, together, explored more than just the woods.

"You go, girl!" Connie called out, following up with a shrill laugh. Erik hoped to get lucky as well, but his girl gave no such indication. And so, they slowly swayed together to the sound of artists' voices which were considered new and popular and fresh long before their own time. Within ten minutes, Hannah and Maron returned to the poorly illuminated shelter house, kissing and grinning at one another, as if no other human beings existed. They returned to a shelter house where a little boy's birthday was shattered to pieces less than just a decade before. That cruel chapter of Erik's life may as well have been forgotten in the moment. It was dead and gone, just as all of the bad times. The couples decided to head out, hoping to locate the other half of their group. The wind picked up a bit, chilling not only the girls by this point. The dreams of these two couples, of these star-crossed and unlikely lovebirds, would all come true in only a few short years' time. Reg and Durand never left the bench. Reg pulled his small folding knife from his pants pocket and carved their initials into the weathered and splintered wood. Durand couldn't stop smiling at the act of romantic vandalism. Damien and Sasha were passionately kissing in the dugout of the eastmost baseball diamond. The boy was rounding third base and soon slid into home plate. He couldn't wait to boast to Erik and Maron now that he had claimed his own maidenhead, shedding his own in the process. Shiloh was vomiting into the pond, fending off a swarm of ducks in the process. A more perfectly simplistic teenage night was never had. The group all met at school the following Monday, just as they always had, right in front of Erik's locker.

Chapter 28

The Club lived and loved on. Life resumed, with a notably lesser degree of bad collective luck for all whose tales I've so passionately and explicitly recounted to You. An enduring part of human nature is our nagging need to know all and to be content with and to approve of not just our own affairs and their outcomes, but with those involved in the stories we become so engrossed in as well. I'll do my best as a tired Storyteller to provide some degree of closure, just for You.

Chapter 29

Shiloh would go on to graduate. He even made the honor roll the last half of his sophomore year right up to the point of receiving his diploma. Kurt was released just months before, and he was able to proudly attend his baby boy's biggest life achievement up until that point. Kurt was given a job at Mazetti's, as a "utility" worker, for lack of a better term. He had a hand in all matters concerning the store, from maintenance work to stocking to running a cash register if the time called for it. Kurt Robertson eventually worked his way up to the title of store manager after Sr. decided to let up on the reigns a bit. Kurt didn't touch a drop of alcohol since the day of his sentencing. The next, and final, thirty-eight years of his life would be spent dry as a bone, as well. Aside from purchasing the occasional scratch-off ticket with a few spare dollars he found lying around, he refrained from gambling, too. After a few months at Mrs. Hadley's, the haggard father managed to find himself an apartment across town, which dwarfed all other homes he ever resided in, as all until that point were of the mobile variety. He was immensely proud of this upgrade, especially considering the fact that it was the product of hard, dedicated, and sober work. Shiloh maintained his job at Mazetti's up until he started his electrical apprenticeship at the age of twenty. He got into a local union and was immediately utilized, heavily, upon his hiring. The young apprentice made good on his word in contacting Holly once he was of age. The two shared their first date at Mazetti's, of all places, once they finally closed on a busy Saturday night. Shiloh prepared the deli sandwiches for the sacred occasion all on his own. Holly was just shy of finishing her degree in accounting, of all things, when she fell pregnant. She finished out school and would be the feminine half in a shotgun wedding with none other than Shiloh Robertson. Holly would never have to use her degree in the professional capacity, as Shiloh worked diligently to provide for his new bride and their growing family. The two would have eight children together before Holly reached thirty-five. Kurt was a busy Papa, to say the least. When the grandfather wasn't commandeering a delicatessen, he was busy giving piggy-back rides and reading stories to a beautiful and healthy litter of Shiloh and Holly Jr.'s. Maron would wed Hannah not long after graduation. As promised, he inherited his family's rightful home. Sarah went nowhere, however. Maron gave an oath on his soul that she and Erik would always have a place to call their own. Sarah would also have her hands full once stepping up to her role as biological and honorary grandmother. Maron and Hannah tried desperately for a child but turned up empty-handed for years. It was discovered by an assiduous team of doctors that Hannah had multiple reproductive conditions, which heavily decreased her chances of conceiving a child naturally. The news nearly broke her. However, Maron was no stranger to damning medical reports regarding the women he cherished, and he refused to rest. Through numerous consultations and the strenuous process of in vitro fertilization, Hannah would become the mother she always dreamed she could be. They welcomed a beautiful baby girl and raised and nurtured her in the same walls and under the same roof her father knew and loved so dearly. She was named Gloria, and possessed many of the same attributes her grandmother, whom she would never get to meet, displayed as well. She looked strikingly similar to her predecessor. However, it was the mannerisms and behavior the little girl displayed that would make Maron a profound believer in the concept of reincarnation. The young father would find work as a nurse at the same hospital his own mother was treated at. Before long, Little Gloria had yet to finish grade school, anyway, Maron would become a celebrated oncologist. He would be the guest of honor at many a celebratory dinner. He gave numerous speeches and received a plethora of awards and accolades. Shortly after his official retirement in the field, the hospital wished to dedicate something in his honor. He graciously declined, insisting that if they so chose to do so, that it be in his mother's name instead. The wing of Norhauk Hospital that specialized in cancer care was officially named after Gloria Calhoun, when Maron was sixty and a grandfather himself. Hannah was there for it all and fell more deeply in love with the man with each passing day. Damien and Sasha's relationship did not last relatively long in comparison to their friends'. By spring of junior year, Sasha had found herself a new boyfriend. Damien bitterly passed many months by isolating himself and turning to drinking and the abuse of prescription pills. Shiloh kept silent for as long as he could until his adoptive brother overdosed before work one afternoon. He was thankfully resuscitated, and Shiloh spilled all to Mr. and Mrs. Mazetti. Damien attended a four-month rehabilitation program in Columbus. He returned home as the man he was always meant to be and the type of man his father was proud to have raised. He bought a lavish home on the outskirts of town and officially became the owner of the family's shoppe at the age of twenty-eight. He fathered two boys by his first wife, the eldest of which was aptly named Damien Jr. The younger boy was called Paolo. Damien would divorce and remarry a doctor at the hospital, who Maron was gracious enough to introduce him to. This relationship, from start to finish, barely surpassed the mark of three years. Damien spent the remainder of his life a bachelor. Women came and went, but the store, his boys, and his family's proud name remained for his eternity in this mortal world. Some nights, as he closed up the store with Kurt and his boys, he would think of Sasha. He would dream of her, as well. He dreamt of what was and what could have been. And upon the early morning stirrings of consciousness, The Dreams' bittersweet smoke clouds would dissipate, until the next time. The two would come across one another from time to time, as the occupants of small towns often tend to do. Sasha married a man she met in college, bearing three of his children, all girls. Paolo was in the same grade as Sasha's youngest. Whether at a school choir concert or a football game, or on the rare occasion that Sasha stopped by Mazetti's for last-minute dinner ingredients, the two would always greet one another with a smile, unaccompanied by words. This was the furthest that Damien would ever reach for the rest of his life. He decided, for the sake of his own sanity, that it had to suffice. Durand would take his team to the state championship game his senior year of high school. The Ice Cats would go down in a valiant effort in an overtime quarter. They lost by a field goal. Such heartbreak did not impede Durand's love for the game. The all-star would attend college at Notre Dame, yes, that "Notre Dame", where he swiftly won the starting quarterback spot. Beatrix and the girls watched him on TV every Saturday in the fall. The determined mother would earn a promotion to the title of manager at the health department. She soon moved out of the cramped closet of an apartment, proudly purchasing the home across the street from Steve and Jessica. Durand sustained a gruesome blow during his senior year with the Fighting Irish. Upon an extensive series of tests, he was found to have suffered neurological damage due to CTE (chronic traumatic encephalopathy). The doctors knew this began as early as middle school. At the recommendation of the neurologists, as well as the unbending demand of Beatrix, the young man hung up his jersey for good. His dreams of the draft were dead. This came as disappointing news to both the Detroit Lions as well as the Indianapolis Colts, both of which teams took a profound interest in the boy. Durand went through his own spell of self-medication. This only worsened when Reg officially broke up with him, leaving him for a girl. The relationship had nearly lost all of its spark at that point, anyway. The nature of the boys' relationship was mostly tucked away in the closet after high school graduation, on Reg's part. Reg felt that if either hoped to be taken seriously as a college athlete prospect, the boys had to falsely display the outward appearance of heterosexuality and masculinity. Durand went along with it. Reg enjoyed great success at the University of Kentucky. At the age of twenty-two, he was drafted by the Titans in the third round. Durand, having retired from the physical aspect of the game of football, was still heavily involved in a coaching role. He earned the title of the youngest offensive coordinator in the National Football League, representing the Philadelphia Eagles. The Eagles and the Titans would square off in week three one season. Philadelphia pulled off a crushing upset victory, squashing their opponents forty-nine to seven. At the game's conclusion, Reg shook Durand's hand with a glazed and absent-minded stare. He uttered one solitary word: "Faggot." The two never spoke again. Durand lived his life openly and honestly. His old flame did not. Durand was diagnosed with HIV at the age of twenty-nine. He continued to coach and served as an activist and public speaker. His high school jersey is proudly displayed in Canton. Reg lived his life in denial. After his football days expired, due to frequent injuries, he blew the majority of his savings. Months after a one-night-stand, he was delivered the news that he would be a father. He remained friends with the mother and undoubtedly did a bang-up job as a dad. His daughter, Desiree, would grow into quite the athlete herself, excelling in a multitude of track and field events. She was the only honest and good thing left in Reg's life, so he made the most of it. He had his own moments of self-doubt and regret, not dissimilar to Damien's. These thoughts would only cease upon Reg's death in a horrific car accident. He was but a day older than fifty. Lastly, I will speak on the leader of The Club's fate. He remained with Connie throughout his earthly and eternal heavenly existence. The two were madly in love. Erik rediscovered his passion for the acoustic guitar, often serenading his beautiful girlfriend with his own renditions of their favorite songs. His best was "Romeo and Juliet" by Dire Straits. Connie would shed more than a tear at its conclusion every time. They married before they could legally taste champagne at their own wedding. The womanly half of the storybook couple pursued a career in pharmacology shortly after their sacred vows were spoken. She procured a job at the local CVS as an assistant to some degree when she found out that she was with child. The couple welcomed a bouncing baby boy on an unusually warm April afternoon. A beautiful little girl soon joined the mix as well. She looked like a miniature version of her mother in every sense but grew up to display the level-headed and leaderlike qualities of her father. Erik took an internship at an insurance agency. He was diligent and devoted and learned the ropes of the trade. He became an agent by the age of twenty-three. He would reach managerial status not long after, as Connie elected to take a break from her career as a pharmacist to spend more time at home with the couple's children. There is much more to all of us than what meets the eye. Sometimes we have to do a little digging to uncover the diamond. In some cases, like Erik and Connie's, the effort is justified. In many others, such strenuous labor proves fruitless. I suppose they were some of the lucky ones. Luck both graced and evaded The Club, as you have borne witness to. All of its members managed to carve out a life of their own, though. This is an accolade many of us stumble and grasp for throughout the entirety of our existences. I pray we all achieve such comfort and certainty. Maybe one day. Perhaps it shall come as soon as tomorrow with the junk papers that are stuffed in our mailboxes. Maybe it will arrive through a phone call from a long-lost brother or a father who realized the error in his ways, deeply desiring to make amends before it is too late. Perhaps it will just fall into our laps on a crisp and Magickal October afternoon, as it did for young Mr. Serling.

ABOUT THE AUTHOR

I began laying the groundwork for what would become "Castalia Boys" on January 1st, 2022. This was my first attempt at writing in a "professional" capacity at the age of twenty-seven, nonetheless. I have two children, with one due in June of '23. These bundles of joy have inspired as well as annoyed me since the conception of the book. I wouldn't have it any other way. My fiancée has been a beacon of encouragement and has served as my primary editor throughout this entire process. I am eternally grateful to her. Tomorrow, as well as many tomorrows after, I will be expected to report to my "real" job and reclaim my title as "Electrical Maintenance Technician." It's a fine career path; it's just not as fun as writing. Now, I'll have to rip out this page of my boss's copy of the book, should he choose to buy one. Seriously though, getting back into the swing of writing on a consistent basis has been one of the greatest things I could have done for myself. And I'm far from finished.

Back Page

"The Town often masks Its Own evil and proudly displays
Its good for all to admire. It lets us see what It wants us to
see; It keeps up Its picturesque and charming postcard image
for all outsiders to adore."

Everything happens in Small Towns. Some of the most
revolutionary inventions, notions, and people were conceived
and fostered and reached their full potential in a Small Town,
much like my own. If this little book of mine should reach
hands and eyes in the likes of New York City or Los Angeles,
readers of these metropolises will glance at its pages with all
the shrewdness and comprehension of my own family. The
Small Town is not merely a geographical location in the form
of a generational farming village in northwest Ohio. It is a
collection of Our grandest plans and most fond memories.
It's all of Our greatest fears and shames and secrets of the
Heart. We are The Town, and The Town is Us. We have
more in common than most may realize.

www.ingramcontent.com/pod-product-compliance
Lightning Source LLC
Chambersburg PA
CBHW051335020726
47501CB00007B/2094